PRAISE FOR THE NOVELS OF MAYA BANKS

"Takes readers into the black depths of anguish . . . Her characters are a testament to the strength of the human spirit and to the power love has to heal even the deepest wounds."

—Linda Howard, *New York Times* bestselling author

"Incredibly awesome . . . I love Maya Banks and I love her books."

—Jaci Burton, *New York Times* bestselling author

"Really dragged me through the gamut of emotions. From . . . 'Is it hot in here?' to 'Oh my GOD' . . . I'm ready for the next ride now!"   —*USA Today*

"[A] one-two punch of entertainment that will leave readers eager for the next book."   —*Publishers Weekly*

"Any book by Maya Banks is a book well worth reading."

—Once Upon a Twilight

"For those who like it naughty, dirty and do-me-on-the-desk HAWT!"

—Examiner.com

"Hot enough to make even the coolest reader sweat!"   —Fresh Fiction

"Definitely a recommended read."   —Fallen Angel Reviews

"[For] fans of Sylvia Day's *Bared to You*."   —Under the Covers

"Grabbed me from page one and refused to let go until I read the last word."   —Joyfully Reviewed

"An excellent read that I simply did not put down . . . Covers all the emotional range."   —The Road to Romance

"The sex is crazy hot."   —Scandalicious Book Reviews

DOMINATED

THE ENFORCERS

Maya Banks

BERKLEY BOOKS, NEW YORK

BERKLEY

An imprint of Penguin Random House LLC
375 Hudson Street, New York, New York 10014

This book is an original publication of the Berkley Publishing Group.

Library of Congress Cataloging-in-Publication Data

Names: Banks, Maya, author.
Title: Dominated / Maya Banks.
Description: Berkley trade paperback edition. | New York : Berkley Books,
2016. | Series: The enforcers ; 2
Identifiers: LCCN 2016003596 (print) | LCCN 2016008630 (ebook) | ISBN
9780425280669 (paperback) | ISBN 9780698191822 (epub)
Subjects: LCSH: Man-woman relationships—Fiction. | Sexual dominance and
submission—Fiction. | BISAC: FICTION / Romance / Contemporary. | FICTION
/ Contemporary Women. | GSAFD: Erotic fiction.
Classification: LCC PS3602.A643 D66 2016 (print) | LCC PS3602.A643 (ebook) |
DDC 813/.6—dc23
LC record available at http://lccn.loc.gov/2016003596

PUBLISHING HISTORY
Berkley trade paperback edition / May 2016

PRINTED IN THE UNITED STATES OF AMERICA

10 9 8 7 6 5 4 3 2 1

Cover art: *Steel chain over Vintage black background* by usanee hirata / Shutterstock Images.
Cover design by Rita Frangie.

Penguin
Random
House

DOMINATED

PROLOGUE

He took the express elevator that only ran between his penthouse and the lobby, praying the entire way that Evangeline would even look at him, much less listen to anything he had to say.

God, let her be sweet, generous and forgiving one last time and he'd never give her reason to doubt him again.

As soon as the elevator doors opened, he bolted into the apartment yelling her name. He winced when he saw the mess in the kitchen, the contents of what appeared to be an extensive menu dumped on the floor, skillets and pots strewn across the bar, the stove and the floor along with the contents.

When he hit the living room on the way to the bedroom, his dread only increased when he saw the silver trays with appetizers scattered all over the room, liquor and wine bottles smashed and huge wet stains on his furniture and carpet.

Paying them no heed, he burst into the bedroom, prepared to beg, on his knees, for her to forgive him. He had a hell of a lot of explaining to do, and that explanation would raise questions he wasn't prepared to answer without further fear of driving her away. If he hadn't done so already.

But Evangeline was nowhere to be seen. All the jewelry he'd gifted her with, including the items she'd worn tonight, were scattered on their bed, and the remnants of the dress she'd worn lay in pieces on the floor.

When he checked her closet, it was full except for a couple pairs of jeans and a few casual shirts and one pair of tennis shoes. Most noticeable was that his small travel bag was missing.

He sank to his knees, his chest so tight it felt as though it were being crushed.

His worst nightmare had come to life. She was gone. He'd driven her away. He'd treated her despicably.

Not since his childhood had he felt such desolation and helpless despair. But this, this was *his* doing. He'd done the unthinkable. He wasn't the victim. Evangeline was. His sweet, innocent angel whose only crime was loving him and wanting to take care of him and show him he mattered.

And he'd repaid her by taking her gift and throwing it back in her face in the most despicable way a man could hurt the woman he cared about.

He buried his face in his hands, raw agony clawing at his insides. "I fucked up, Angel. But I'm coming for you. So help me God. I know I failed you. I let you down. But goddamn it, I will *not* let you go. I'll never let you go. I'll fight for you with my last breath. I can't live without you," he whispered. "You're the only thing *good* in my life. The only sunshine I've ever experienced in a life steeped in gray.

"I can't live without you. You're my only reason for living. You have to come home, because without you, I have—I am—nothing."

"Find her," Drake said harshly, the nights without sleep evident in his haggard appearance. "This is your *only* priority, your *only* job. Find her and bring her back to me."

He'd gathered his sentinels. The only men in his inner circle, a tight band of men—brothers—his partners in business and the only men he trusted with his life—and Evangeline's.

The only men he'd allow to see him at his lowest, unguarded. Vulnerable. Nothing mattered to him. Not exposing his weakness. Not allowing his iron control that had maintained him through most of his life to slip. They all knew that Evangeline was . . . special. All important. They liked and respected her. Rare enough to garner one of those traits. Unheard of for a woman to have been awarded both.

Because of this, they were *all* pissed. At him.

"Goddamn it, Drake," Maddox hissed out. "How could you do it? There had to be another way."

"There was no other goddamn way and you know it!" Drake raged, fury and helplessness eating him alive, gutting him until there was nothing left but a soulless shell of a man standing helplessly in front of his brothers begging for their help.

Looks were exchanged. Some of sympathy, some of resignation as they realized Drake was right, and still others of quiet fury that Evangeline had been treated—betrayed—in such a despicable manner.

Goddamn useless woman. Can't even give good head. Your only use is in my bedroom.

His cruel words sliced through his mind, a jagged cut making him bleed all over again, a vicious reminder of the unforgivable things he'd said to her. All in the effort to convince the fucking Luconis she meant nothing to him.

When in fact, she was his goddamn world. And, *he couldn't find her!*

He couldn't blame her. He'd devastated her. Had ripped her to shreds until she was bleeding from the verbal wounds he'd inflicted. And Jesus, his physical treatment of her. No, the only person at fault was himself.

Silas had remained silent, his features carved in stone, but his eyes were a dead giveaway in a man who usually gave away nothing at all.

"She didn't deserve this," Silas said in his quiet voice. But then he never had to raise his voice to make his point. When he spoke, others instinctively ceased talking and listened to him. He was a man who commanded authority and respect.

"No, she didn't," Drake said hoarsely. "Don't you think I *know* that? Do you think a single night goes by that I don't replay the image of her broken, in utter despair, her tears—goddamn it, her *tears*—and worse, her fear. Of me. Of her humiliation. Her absolute belief in every insult, every word I hurled her way in an effort to make sure the goddamn Luconis never suspected what she meant to me. I'll never forget. As long as I live, I'll *never forget that night.*"

His tone grew savage, fury radiating from him like a beacon.

"She could be anywhere out there. Alone. Afraid. Her parents haven't heard from her. And those bitches she called her best friends . . ." He broke off and had to visibly compose himself.

He and Maddox had gone there first only to discover that they hadn't heard from her either. Except, when after making their disgust known, they'd turned to leave when Lana caved, admitting tearfully that Evangeline had called that day, the day she'd planned to visit them. To reconcile. And that she'd told her not to come. Guilt had been reflected in the eyes of all her "friends."

It was then that Drake had understood that she'd never *planned* to execute her surprise to him, hadn't lied to him in order to set up her playing hostess for him. She'd been hurt by her friends' rejection, and so she'd turned to the one true thing in her life, seeking his approval, needing it, because she had no one else.

And Maddox felt as guilty as Drake did because if he'd gone up with Evangeline, as he usually did, he would have known her girls weren't home and he wouldn't have hesitated to take her somewhere else for the evening. He'd never expected her to make her escape and hurry back to Drake's apartment to pull off her surprise for Drake. To let him know he mattered to her. She'd put everything on the line for him and he'd repaid her with a betrayal so cutting, so deep that he'd destroyed something so beautiful and innocent that he couldn't think about it without losing his tenuous grip on his sanity.

Justice cleared his throat and ran a hand through his hair, hesitating almost as if he worried about Drake being even more pissed than he already was at what Justice was about to say.

"This may sound crazy, Drake," Justice began warily. "But hear me out, okay?"

Drake made a sound of impatience. Every moment they stood in his office talking was another moment Evangeline was God only knew where on the streets, alone, devastated, thinking he'd lied to her about *everything.*

"Make it quick," Drake snapped. "While we stand here discussing her, she's out there, cold, alone, hungry, with nothing."

Grief swamped him all over again, and he was forced to sit down in the chair behind his desk or risk collapsing. He covered his face with his hands, missing the shocked looks of his closest men and the uneasy looks they exchanged.

"I think you've gone about this the wrong way," Justice said quietly.

Drake's head came up, his lips twisted in a snarl. His other men stared questioningly at Justice, wondering if the man had lost his mind by crossing Drake or questioning his judgment.

"Hear me out," Justice repeated. "You've protected her at all turns, kept her secret, afraid she would be used against you. Which is why you had to do what you did when things changed and there was no other *way* to protect her."

Silas's brooding expression became one of distaste, letting Drake—and the others—know exactly what he thought of what "had" to be done to ensure her safety—her life.

"Instead of hiding her, keeping her secret, I think you should go public with her. *Very* public," Justice said emphatically.

"Are you insane?" Drake asked hoarsely. "Are you just trying to get her raped, tortured, *killed?*"

Justice held up his hand in the same request for Drake to hear him out. The others also fell silent, suddenly very curious as to where on earth Justice was going with this.

"No, you don't hide her," Justice said quietly. "You make her your fucking *queen.* You let the goddamn world know she is yours and that you'll kill anyone who so much as looks at her wrong, threatens her, tries to use her to get to you. Think about it, Drake. You are the most feared man in the city. Do you honestly think they would be fool enough to go after what you value the most?"

"He has a point," Silas said quietly, surprising the others by speaking up. "We would double, even triple her security, but the thing that will protect her the most is your name. Think about it, Drake. When have you ever publicly laid claim to a woman or made it clear that anyone harming her will die a long, agonizing death?"

Drake growled impatiently. "Having a security detail, even as good as all of you are, won't protect her from a sniper, a bomb or someone simply walking up to her and shooting her."

Maddox swore and sent Drake a look of disgust and agitation. "You've lost all intelligence and rationality when it comes to Evangeline. Killing Evangeline does fuck-all for your enemies except piss you off and have you out for blood. Their blood. Something that no one wants, not even the most powerful of your enemies. They'd be stupid fucks who could kiss their lives and empires good-bye the minute they ordered Evangeline's death. The *only* way Evangeline could be used to 'get' to you is if they take her *alive* and *keep* her alive to extort what they want from you in return for her release. And in order to get to her, they would have to go through her security detail and there's no way in hell that's ever going to happen."

"We," Justice interrupted, thumbing toward the other men gathered in the room, "would never allow someone to get close enough to Evangeline for someone to abduct her, and someone will be on her twenty-four-seven when she's not in your place. And when you and Evangeline are out, a security detail protects you both and monitors your every movement."

"Only in private will you not have the security team. Your apartment's security system is top of the line. Better and more sophisticated than most classified security systems. At the push of a button the entire building goes into lockdown mode and you have a safe room that is impenetrable, even to explosives," Silas interjected. "I know because I installed it myself."

"I don't want her to be a goddamn prisoner," Drake said in an agonized voice.

"It won't be any different than before," Jax said, speaking up for the first time. "When did Evangeline go anywhere without one of us? She never seemed to mind. Hell, she liked us. Or at least she did . . ."

His voice trailed off in what sounded like regret and remorse, as if Drake's actions would alienate her from them all. And judging by the looks on his men's faces, it was something they'd all considered. And didn't like very much at all.

His men adored her. They liked her when they truly liked no women. And now they were faced with losing her trust every bit as much as Drake was. He couldn't find it in himself to be jealous. The only emotion he could conjure was guilt because through his actions, Evangeline would lose people who'd become important to her, people she'd taken under her protective wing, and she'd made them all feel as though they were important, that they mattered.

"I and only I bear the responsibility for what was done to Evangeline," Drake said in a low voice. "And you know as well as I do that Evangeline doesn't have a vengeful bone in her body. She's sweet to the core and has the purest, most honest heart of anyone I've ever known. She won't hate you. Only me. And that's my cross to bear. None of you will suffer for my arrogance and stupidity."

He paused, pondering the conversation, lowering his head in thought, so much rushing through his mind. God, had it been that simple? Had he been so stupid, so wrapped up in keeping Evangeline from the world out of fear? But no, that was only part of it. The selfish part of him hadn't wanted to share her with *anyone*, not even his brothers, though it had been necessary.

"You're right," Drake said tiredly. "Goddamn it, you're all right and it's something I should have thought of."

His tone was full of self-derision. He who was always in control of any situation. Every possibility accounted for. But Evangeline had turned his carefully ordered life upside down and when it came to her, he didn't think clearly, rationally, and if he didn't get his head back in the game, it would get them both killed. His brothers too.

Silas cleared his throat and once again, heads turned in surprise. He'd already broken his characteristic silence once, and now it appeared he had more to say.

"There's more you've done . . . not right," he said, amending what he had been going to say, but the words floated in the room as if they had indeed been spoken.

There's more you've done wrong.

His gaze met Drake's unflinchingly. Silas was not afraid of Drake. Drake considered him an equal in every sense of the word. Every bit as lethal, if not more. No, Silas didn't fear Drake, and Drake respected him for that.

There was a pronounced hush over the room as everyone waited in anticipation of what Silas was daring to do. Suggest that Drake had been wrong about many things. Not even some of his closest dared what Silas dared.

"You never made her secure about her place in your world—your life," Silas said in his quiet tone.

"The hell I didn't," Drake said savagely, but he didn't like the under-tone of defensiveness in his own voice. Guilt. Because Silas had struck a chord.

"You come to her after work and you leave before she awakens. You send one of us to take her where she needs to go, to see to her needs. That's your job, Drake. She's your woman and you've given her no rea-son to believe she matters as more than a body to warm your bed, a sub-missive to your dominance. She exists solely for your convenience."

Rage nearly blinded Drake, and only the fact that Silas had scored a huge point prevented him from launching himself at the man he called his executioner. A man who would likely give Drake the fight of his life, because the two men were closely matched, though Drake strongly sus-pected Silas had an edge.

"If you find her, if she will listen to you, if she will forgive you or at least allow you the chance to make up for the horrible injustice done to her, you're going to have to prove with actions and not just words that she is more to you than a woman who will warm your bed for a few nights and be sent on her way with an expensive gift for her time."

"You know goddamn well she hates taking anything from me," Drake snarled. "Gifts, jewelry, clothes."

"And why do you suppose that is?" Maddox said, interrupting, his stare penetrating.

"Because she only wanted me," Drake whispered.

And suddenly everything Silas said made sense. He closed his eyes because so much more made sense to him now. Evangeline wanted him. Just him. His time. His heart. The one thing he hadn't—couldn't—give her. But it didn't mean he couldn't show her that she did mean something to him. Spend more time with her instead of pawning her off on one of his men every day.

Then he swore and wiped a hand over his face. "There are other ways to hurt her in order to get to me. Her girls, even if they did toss her. No one else will know that. Her family, her mother and father, whom she'd do, hell, *has* done, everything for. They'll have to be protected too because if someone kidnapped her friends or family, Evangeline would be distraught and would beg me to do whatever I had to do to get them back."

He grimaced and closed his eyes. "And I could never deny her anything except when it comes to her safety. Her happiness is first and foremost and if someone did take her loved ones, I would be helpless because I could never look Evangeline in the eyes again if I stood by and did nothing, refusing to give in to extortion and blackmail, something I would have never even considered in the past."

Some of his men looked dumbfounded. They made no effort to hide their shock, though those closest to him didn't look surprised at all. There was respect in their eyes as was their equal determination to keep Evangeline—and those she loved—safe.

Hatcher shifted position, his look one of unease. He opened his mouth more than once only to shut it and press his lips firmly together as if squelching what it was he wanted to say.

"What's on your mind, Hatch?" Drake demanded.

Hatcher sighed. "Christ. Don't take this the wrong way. I like Evangeline. She's sweet. *Too* damn sweet and innocent for her own good, and I don't want her to get caught up in a mess of our making and get hurt or killed any more than any of you do."

"But?" Drake pressed, knowing Hatch had a lot more on his mind than extolling Evangeline's virtues.

Hatcher's unease grew and sweat glistened on his brow. "Just hear me out," he muttered, repeating the same request Justice had made moments earlier. "You're in deep with her already. You've never even considered keeping a woman this long, much less making her your queen and making sure everyone in the world knows it. Maybe . . . maybe it's better that way."

"What way would *that* be?"

Drake's voice was a whip through the room, coiling and snapping with fury because he had a good idea of where his man was going with this, and if he was right, it was going to take Silas, Maddox *and* Justice to keep him from killing Hatcher.

"To make a clean break," Hatcher said, his gaze hardening. "A break that has already been made and is probably best left alone. She makes you vulnerable. Hell, she's already made you vulnerable. You're in too deep, Drake. You don't see it, but the rest of us do, and you're going to get yourself killed and maybe us with you. She's going to end up costing you *everything*."

There were mixed reactions, from looks of *what the fuck* to cold stares that would melt stone and then absolute fury, from Justice, Maddox, Silas, Hartley, Jax and Thane, their faces, eyes, the set of their jaws.

"You're already making, or planning to make, concessions you would have never allowed before. Maybe you should consider letting her go instead of making her your queen. Get rid of her, break it off and make it well known you're finished with her and have no attachment to her whatsoever. It's what you've always done in the past. It's what you've already done, so leave it *alone*. You've never gotten as emotionally involved with a woman and you damn sure haven't turned over the entire goddamn city looking for one who clearly doesn't want to be found. If you want her safe, then that is the best way you can do it because no one, especially after you ripped her apart in front of the Luconis, will even think twice about her. But going public with her? You'd be throwing her to the goddamn wolves and you know it."

Drake stared so coldly at Hatcher that the temperature became frigid in the interior of the office. The others were visibly uncomfortable because they knew that Hatch, as well-meaning as he was attempting to be, had just fucked up. But then he didn't know Evangeline. Had spent only a few moments in her presence while the others had spent a lot of time with her and understood only too well Drake's obsession with her and that he would never simply "let her go."

"Evangeline *is* my life," Drake said, his rage mounting with every breath. "And if I lose her, I'm dead anyway. If you *ever* suggest that I get rid of her again, I'll rip you apart with my bare hands. You are to speak of and to her with absolute respect. You are to treat her with the utmost regard, more so than myself. Evangeline will be your—and our—number one priority. Her happiness, her safety, comfort. Her every need will be met by all of us. And we will extend to her friends and family the same courtesy and protection that we give to Evangeline herself.

"The most important priority in my life is Evangeline and her happiness and well-being, and I expect—no, I *demand*—that every man who allies himself with me swears to protect her and be willing to give his life for her just as he would for me. And if there is ever a choice between me and Evangeline, there will be no question. Evangeline is to be saved at all costs and I am charging you, my brothers, with ensuring her safety and well-being if I am no longer around to do it. She is never to want or lack for anything. Are we understood?"

Hatcher's eyes reflected his shock at Drake's vehemence. After a prolonged moment of silence, he finally managed a hoarse "yes" accompanied by a clipped nod of his head. By the looks on more than one of Drake's men's faces, Drake wasn't the only one contemplating beating the hell out of Hatcher for his "input." Drake made a mental note to never have Hatcher assigned to Evangeline without one of the others with him. Not until he could be sure of Hatcher's absolute loyalty to Evangeline.

Drake had had enough and was thoroughly sick to his soul over the idea that one of his men had actually suggested that he allow Evangeline to think the worst and that he'd washed his hands of her. The mere thought made him physically ill.

He gestured for them to leave but when he looked up, Maddox, Silas and Justice still stood before him, regarding him solemnly.

For a long moment there was silence, and then Maddox said quietly, "She's the one."

Drake didn't pretend to misunderstand what Maddox had stated. He knew damn well what Maddox was inferring. Drake had always avoided commitment and relationships like the plague. He'd never trusted anyone but those gathered in his office now, much less a woman. He'd vowed never to become emotionally involved with any woman, not only because he had yet to meet a woman who stirred him enough to want one but also because of the danger and risk posed to her for no other reason than whose arm she was on.

Now? Yeah, Evangeline was the one.

But instead of answering the question with a simple yes or no, he simply leveled a stare at them, one filled with determination and fire uncharacteristic of his usual cold, aloof features.

"I'm never letting her go. Even if it means tying her to my damn bed every night. If she ever wants out, then she's going to have to *convince* me that I'm not who or what she wants and that the lifestyle I demand isn't what she wants, and she's going to have to tell me she isn't happy. But she'll never want for another thing in her life. I'll make damn sure of that."

"There will never be another like her for you," Silas said as though refuting that Evangeline would ever leave. But there was something else in Silas's piercing gaze. Perhaps he sought to know just how deep Drake's feelings for Evangeline ran. Silas seemed so sure of Evangeline, that she'd forgive him. But maybe Silas worried that Drake would betray her again?

"No," Drake said flatly, in response to Silas's statement. "How could there be? You only taste that kind of perfection once in your life, and if you're too stupid to hang on to something that good and bust your ass to make damn sure you keep it, then you don't deserve it."

He lifted his gaze to Silas, anger and determination surging through his veins. He didn't owe him or any of them a damn thing and yet this . . . Evangeline . . . and what she meant to him was too important to fuck up by being anything but blunt. There could be no doubt or he couldn't be assured of their complete and utter commitment to his search. He swept his eyes over Maddox and Justice, including them in his impassioned, angry statement.

"Get this in your heads. Evangeline is *everything* to me. There is no Drake Donovan without Evangeline. If something ever happens to her, and especially if something happens to her because of me, I won't survive it. I won't want to. She gives me purpose. A reason to live. A reason to get up in the morning and face a new day. You don't get that kind of light only to have it extinguished and hope to ever recover from it."

His men seemed stunned, not over his feelings for Evangeline, because they shared them to a degree, but because he'd just laid bare his soul to them all. Understanding quickly followed their surprise while Silas merely gave a clipped nod as if satisfied that Drake had just passed some test he was unaware had been put to him.

Well good. Drake had gotten through to them and now that he had, he knew they would die for Evangeline. They'd put themselves between her and any threat because they knew if anything happened to Evangeline, they'd lose Drake too.

"We will protect her—and you—with our lives," Silas said.

Maddox and Justice repeated Silas's vow, purpose and determination now blazing in their eyes.

They'd all climbed their way up from nothing. They all had nebulous pasts, nothing given to them. Everything they had, they'd fought for. They were family, all pledged to one another by a bond stronger than any blood bond would ever be.

And now for the first time, they would be widening their intimate circle to include . . . a woman. Drake's woman. None of them had ever involved themselves with any woman long enough for it to be considered a semblance of a relationship. They sated their needs, always ensuring that the woman was cared for, pleasured in return, and they were generous when they cut them loose. But no woman had ever even threatened to crack the hard shells around their hearts.

Until now.

Until Evangeline.

Part of his men felt envy, and part of them felt pity because now Drake had a hell of a lot more at stake than before. Before he had only himself and his brothers to worry about. He was feared and revered. No one dared to strike at him. But now Drake had a weakness and it could well be his ultimate downfall. His being impervious to *any* weakness had been what had made it impossible for his enemies to strike at him. Because Drake had no one or nothing he gave one fuck about. Now? He had a woman who was his entire world. And God help the fool who ever tried to put so much as a scratch on Evangeline because Drake would appear like an avenging angel or the scariest demon from hell and wreak savage vengeance on whoever wronged his Evangeline. And he would do it personally. He wouldn't have Silas go after the bastard. It would be too personal. Drake would be unstoppable and would tear apart anyone who ever hurt his woman.

2

"Mr. Donovan! Mr. Donovan!"

Drake nearly growled in frustration at the unwanted intrusion as he stalked toward the elevator. It was three in the morning and he and his men had spent the day scouring the city, yet another hopeless day of searching for Evangeline that had come to nothing.

He whirled on the doorman and some of what he was feeling must have been reflected in his expression because the doorman recoiled and stopped in his tracks a few feet from where Drake stood at the now-open elevator.

"Whatever it is, it can wait," Drake snapped. "I am not to be disturbed."

For a moment, the doorman seemed to grapple with indecision, and in disgust, Drake turned and walked into the elevator. The doorman lunged forward, holding out his hand to prevent the doors from closing.

"It's about Evangeline, uh, I mean Miss Hawthorn."

At the mention of her name, Drake stepped off the elevator and grasped the older man by the lapels of his coat.

"What about Evangeline?" Drake growled. "Do you know anything?"

The man's face was gray and his eyes flickered downward in guilt. What the fuck?

But then the doorman had seen Drake leave the building just a few minutes after he'd arrived with the Luconis. He sucked in a breath. Oh dear God. How stupid could Drake be? The doorman would have to have seen Evangeline leave as well. And the condition she was in when she'd left.

The doorman liked Evangeline. Had always had a friendly word for her, as Evangeline had for him. There had been genuine affection between the two, but Drake had never paid it any notice because Evangeline inspired that in everyone she met.

But what if . . .

The dread was crawling more insidiously through Drake's body as his grip tightened and then finally relaxed, freeing the man to take a few stumbling steps backward.

It had never occurred to Drake to question the man. He'd been too frantic to find Evangeline, turning the entire goddamn city over like a deranged madman. What if the answer had been here all along and Evangeline had had to be out there somewhere, alone, desperate, hungry and devastated while Drake wasted time chasing all the wrong leads?

"Do you care for her?" the doorman asked in a nearly accusatory tone.

Oh yes, this man knew something and he was mad as hell over what Drake had done to Evangeline. And now Drake had to tread very carefully because if he gave this man any reason to believe he intended to harm Evangeline, he'd never get any information from the doorman Evangeline had taken under her wing. Just as she'd done with everyone else she came into contact with.

"Very much," Drake said in a soft, dangerous voice. "Do you know where she is?"

"I saw her that night," the doorman said in a bitter voice.

His eyes still reflected accusation as though he found Drake solely responsible for Evangeline's departure. Drake was. Absolutely. But how much did this man know? Did he know where Evangeline was now?

"There was a terrible misunderstanding," Drake said, nearly strangled by baring his personal issues to a complete stranger. But for Evangeline, to have her back in his arms, he'd do anything. "None of which was Evangeline's doing. *She wasn't supposed to be here.*"

The agony couldn't be suppressed in his voice and he could swear the doorman's gaze softened just the slightest bit.

"She'd planned a surprise for you," the doorman said quietly. "And after, she was devastated. I wanted to help her. I tried. But she told me that if I did, I'd be out the door just as she now was."

Drake flinched and then the familiar ache of sorrow invaded his chest, depriving him of breath. The doorman had tried to help her and Evangeline had refused aid because she worried Drake would fire him if he found out. For just a moment he'd allowed himself hope that the doorman could provide him answers. Could tell him where to find Evangeline.

The doorman rubbed his hand through his hair, suddenly looking weary and uncertain.

"May God forgive me if I'm wrong. May *she* forgive me if I'm wrong."

Drake surged to attention. "What? What do you know?" he said, switching tactics because he now knew what the man was battling. He was uncertain of Drake's intentions toward Evangeline and so was reluctant to give Drake any information that would help him find her. Now, unless Drake could convince him that he was doing the right thing and that he wouldn't betray Evangeline by giving Drake any information he held, Drake would never pry it from the man, even at the risk of his job.

"It is very important that I get her back," Drake said in a quiet voice. "I'm only half a man without her. I must beg her forgiveness, but I can't do that until I find her and bring her home where she belongs."

Some of the doorman's wariness faded as he studied Drake's face pensively. "You know, Mr. Donovan, I think I believe you."

"I just pray she does," Drake whispered.

The doorman sighed. "I put her into a cab and sent her to a hotel in Brooklyn that my sister manages. Evangeline, Miss Hawthorn I mean."

"It's okay," Drake said, momentarily halting the doorman. "I understand she is special to you, as she is to us all. You do her no disrespect in calling her Evangeline. If I had to guess, she insisted on it."

A smile curved the older man's lips. "That she did, Mr. Donovan. That she did."

"Now, back to the hotel you sent her to?" Drake asked, trying to temper his eagerness.

"She had nowhere to go," the doorman said, a frown once more in place. "No money. She had nothing with her other than a few changes of clothing. I couldn't let her go like that, without somewhere to go where she would be safe."

"You did the right thing, and you have my utmost gratitude for ensuring her safety. You will be rewarded."

At that the older man's face hardened. "My reward will be seeing her here, safe and happy again."

Then Drake frowned. "But that's been five days ago now. Do you know if Evangeline is still there? She's not the kind of person ... that is, she'd never accept charity. She's too proud. She'd never stay somewhere she couldn't pay her own way."

"My sister gave her a job as a cleaner, even though Evangeline was honest and up front and told my sister she didn't plan to stay long. Just until she earned enough money to move on."

Drake's blood froze. Move on. God. How close he'd come to losing her for good. If she was even still there.

"Her shift starts in an hour," the doorman said quietly. Then he lifted his chin, staring Drake down as an equal, fire in his eyes. "Don't make me regret breaking her trust, sir. I would never do anything to hurt that young lady. She's seen far too much hurt as it is."

"On that you and I agree," Drake said, closing his hand over the doorman's shoulder. "Thank you. I'll never be able to repay you for your kindness to Evangeline when she needed it the most and for helping me find Evangeline to make things right, though God knows I don't deserve it."

"Just bring her home, Mr. Donovan," the doorman said in a somber voice. "It's just not the same here without her."

The words hit him where Drake lived. Right in the heart. Because they were absolutely true. Nothing was the same without Evangeline.

He nearly turned and hurried back out of the apartment building after gaining the name and address of the hotel from the doorman, but he needed to shower and change and he needed to call Silas and Maddox. They were the two who liked Evangeline the most, had the most vested interest in the search. Maddox still carried the weight of guilt for allowing Evangeline to escape in the first place, and Silas... Drake wasn't sure what the connection between his enforcer and Evangeline was, only that it was the most unlikely friendship he'd ever encountered.

But one thing was for certain. Silas was fiercely protective of Evangeline, and Evangeline was equally protective of Silas, taking on anyone and everyone who dared malign him in any way. It would only be fitting for Maddox and Silas to accompany him to bring Evangeline home, to ensure her safety—and his.

Silas swore violently under his breath when the car bearing him, Drake and Maddox pulled up to the dilapidated hotel five minutes after Evangeline's shift was to start. Drake sent him a startled look, one eyebrow arched in question.

But Silas offered no explanation. His only response was a dark, brooding scowl, one that was echoed on Maddox's stony features. Neither man was happy that this was where Evangeline had been living and working while they'd been combing the streets of the city looking for her.

But at least the doorman had been caring enough to ensure that Evangeline had a safe place to go. For that, the doorman would have Drake's undying gratitude.

"Wait here for me," Drake said as he opened the door to get out. "And hope like hell that I can convince her to come back with me."

3

Evangeline plopped the mop down into the bucket of soapy water and then settled it into the wringer, using all her strength to wring as much of the water from the mop as she could before beginning the arduous task of cleaning the reception area.

She knew she had to be quick about it and not interfere with the comings and goings of the customers, which was why it was done at four in the morning each day. Her back ached, her feet were swollen and sore and her eyes burned from the storms of tears she cried every night when she lay on her cot unable to sleep.

She knew she looked bad and that her movements were robotic as she performed her task by rote. If it weren't for the fact that her heart ached with pain that never subsided, she would have sworn she'd already died and was merely a zombie stumbling through her daily routine.

A few more days. All she needed was a few more days and she'd have enough money to buy an airline ticket back home to her parents. She was no stranger to hard work. She'd work two, three jobs, whatever it took to support her parents, and it would have the added bonus of giving her no time to think about . . .

A shudder rolled over her and her eyes burned like acid had been poured into them. Damn it, she would not cry here. Only at night, in the dark where no one could see or hear, did she allow her grief to consume her.

Who was she fooling? She wouldn't stop thinking about Drake and his cutting betrayal until her dying day. Putting half the country between them certainly wouldn't help. Not when her heart would forever remain in New York. With a man who had no heart, no soul, no capacity to love.

Oh God, what was she going to do? Why hadn't she listened to her friends? Why had she been so naïve? And now, because of her own stupidity, she'd lost not only Drake but also her best friends.

What she wouldn't give to be at their apartment right now, pouring her heart out and apologizing for betraying *them*. But she never wanted any of the people she loved to see her at her lowest point.

She had a few days yet to build her meager funds to afford the trip home and also to somehow find a way to get over what Drake had done to her so that she could face her family and not have her devastation reflected so clearly in her eyes and in her body language.

Sadness gripped her because once again she was fooling herself. A few *days* to get over Drake? She didn't have a prayer of ever being free of Drake's impact on her life, even as short-lived as their affair had been.

But she could at least promise herself never to love with all her heart and soul again. How could she when Drake would forever possess pieces of them?

Weariness assailed her and she wobbled as she gave another shove of the mop, and then grief consumed her in a giant swell, robbing her of strength. She grasped the handle of the mop in a desperate bid not to crumple onto the floor and give in to the heart-wrenching despair cutting her to ribbons.

Her hand shook. Her entire body trembled and so she stood there, breathing in and out, hanging on to the mop handle for dear life. And then she made the mistake of looking up and all the blood left her face. If her grip hadn't already been so tight around the mop, she would have folded on the spot.

Drake strode into the doorway of the hotel and looked to see no clerk on duty. He heard the soft sound of water and the slap of a mop on the floor and instinctively turned, seeking the source of the sound.

Evangeline.

His heart accelerated as she slumped tiredly, clinging to the mop handle, and Drake drank in the sight like a starved man, devoid of all life. Until now. His knees shook and his hands . . . God, his hands trembled uncontrollably and a knot formed in his throat that prevented him from doing anything but absorbing the only shining thing in his life.

Evangeline. His angel. He'd found her. Finally.

But when she lifted her head and their gazes locked, recognition was swift and he was gutted by the piercing fear that flared in her eyes. The immediate step back she took, her eyes turning wild, like an animal poised to flee from a predator.

His eyelids were on fire, burning, his nostrils flaring with a sudden expulsion of emotion—and from the effort of holding back the tears that threatened to unman him. Because beautiful angel eyes that had once looked at him with love and trust were now filled with terror and apprehension and worst of all . . . shame. It made him want to put a fucking bullet through his head for all he'd done to her.

She was quickly assessing her escape routes and he moved in like the predator he was, but his usual cold aloofness that fit him like a second skin when he closed in for a kill had been replaced by utter panic. He couldn't lose her. Not again. Not ever. The last days had been hell. The kind of hell he'd never experienced and never wanted to repeat.

He was shaking as he held out his hands in a placating manner, as though she were a trapped wild animal desperately seeking escape. Any escape.

"Evangeline," he said hoarsely. "Please, baby, don't run. *Please.* There's so much I have to tell you. To explain. It's taken me days to find you. The worst days of my entire life. Please don't make me go through that again."

Her lips curled contemptuously and a combination of anger and devastation glittered in her eyes, glossy with unshed tears. She looked so utterly fragile, worn to the bone. As though he'd already lost her, no matter that she stood a mere few feet away from him. Almost close enough to touch. Just a few more steps . . .

"What you went through?" she whispered. "What *you* went through?"

Her voice rose to the point of hysteria and now her tears flowed freely down her pale cheeks. He noted her pallor, the weight she'd lost in the days since he'd so callously discarded her, the shadows under her eyes that looked far too close to bruises for his liking. She looked . . . defeated.

He closed his eyes, halting the progress of the hand he'd lifted, hoping beyond hope that she wouldn't flinch away, that she'd reach for him despite the fact that she hated him with the same passion with which she'd once loved him. He wanted that back. God, he was perilously close to begging. No one had ever loved him until Evangeline. His generous, loving angel who didn't give a damn about his money, his power, the expensive gifts he'd showered her with or the entire wardrobe that cost more than she made in five years. She'd simply wanted him and the one thing he couldn't offer her. His love. And his trust.

And now he had no hope of ever regaining either.

"Angel," he whispered, his voice cracking. "You have every reason to hate me, to despise the very sight of me. What I did was unforgivable. But I *had no choice.* Please give me a chance to explain. If after, you still hate me, if you still want me out of your life, I'll let you go. It will fucking *kill* me, but I swear to you I'll let you go and you will never want for anything for the rest of your life whether I'm a part of it or not. You will never have to work in these conditions. You will be financially secure. I've already seen to it even though I know it isn't what you want from me. You've never wanted anything from me but . . . *me*. Give me a chance, Angel. God, give me a chance to make this right. So that you'll want me again. Just me and nothing else. I will never doubt you, I never have. But I will make damn sure you never have reason to doubt *me* again."

"Bitch."

"Whore."

"*Worthless.*"

Her whispered words, so much agony inflected into every single one, words he'd thrown at her, direct arrows that had crippled her self-confidence, nearly destroyed the thin string to which he was clinging desperately. The one that was keeping him from losing all vestiges of his control. Because those words he'd thrown at her were now darts directed back at him, each piercing him like a kill shot.

He had recognized it in the restaurant, that awful evening that seemed a lifetime ago, that what he'd done to her had been far worse than the damage inflicted on her by Eddie, her ex. But knowing and seeing were two different things, and now he was seeing her, seeing just how much he'd ripped her to pieces and destroyed something so utterly beautiful and innocent.

"*That's* what I was to you, Drake," she said, still whispering, her body shuddering violently with each broken breath.

"No!" he shouted, making her flinch and recoil from the raw fury in his voice.

Her eyes were wide with fear, uncertainty, and so much pain, pain he well understood because he'd been living in hell from the night he'd betrayed her. But even knowing the anguish he'd suffered, he knew it in no way compared to her pain and suffering, and that only gutted him even more because never had he wanted to cause her such pain and ugliness. He'd made a sacred vow to himself. Vows. And he'd broken both as surely as he'd broken her.

"*Never*," he said savagely. "They were lies, Angel. Terrible, ugly, *necessary* lies. Oh God, if I could only go back, if I could only have that day back. I would have made certain you were never involved, never exposed like that. In my arrogance I thought I could keep you safe and separated from that aspect of my life. It's a mistake I'll have to live with for the rest of my life. I know you can never forgive, but God, please, I'm begging you. Give me the chance to explain, to try to make you understand the world I live in. A world I should have never allowed you into, but I could no more deny myself your sweetness and light than a starving man could refuse food and water. Angel, you were—are—the only good thing in my life, and God help me but I couldn't do the right thing and let you go. I had to have you. I needed you. I *still* need you."

Her brow furrowed, her expression perplexed. Her eyes were bewildered as she took in the anguished words he'd delivered with so much emotion and self-loathing. She seemed to filter through each and every word he'd said, her expression ever changing as she processed the conflicting statements. He didn't even know if he'd made any goddamn sense. All he knew was that he was desperate and he would do or say anything to get her to come home with him.

"Necessary? *Necessary?*" she repeated, her face creased with pain. "It was necessary for you to humiliate me, to strip me bare in front of those m-men, to debase and degrade me, make me feel like a worthless whore?"

Sweet heaven, but every single word from that night was solidly ingrained in her memory because she recalled them verbatim, had absorbed them and worse of all, *believed* them.

Drake groaned, and he didn't even recognize his own voice, so great was the agony. Like a wounded animal or a beast mourning the loss of his mate. He was both, but not nearly as wounded as the beautiful woman standing so close and yet so very far away.

She shook her head and then covered her face with both hands, her knees giving way as she slid toward the floor. Drake vaulted over the cleaning equipment in an attempt to catch her, but he was too late and so he skidded to a halt and collapsed to his knees in front of her, his arms immediately going around her, ignoring her sudden recoil, her rejection of his touch and body. Ignoring her reaction, he anchored her shaking body to his, holding on in a vow to never again let go.

"My angel," he said, choking on the words. "My beautiful, sweet, innocent angel. Please, baby, please let me take you away from this. Let me explain. I swear to you I won't hurt you. Never again. Give me a chance to make this right. Give me yourself again. I'll never hurt such a precious gift again. I swear it on my life."

She went limp against him, a tortured moan escaping her lips just before ragged sobs shook her entire body. Hot tears spilled onto Drake's neck, his heart breaking with each sorrowful gasp she took. But he read her acquiescence, or perhaps it was simply that she was no longer strong enough to fight, but he knew he had to take swift advantage now when her defenses were down or he might never get another chance. Praying she'd forgive yet one more sin in the never-ending list of his transgressions, he swept her into his arms, standing and carrying her down the hall of the run-down hotel and out to where his car waited.

Maddox and Silas were both standing guard, and when their gazes found Drake carrying a sobbing Evangeline, Maddox's whispered "Thank God" echoed firmly in Drake's mind. Silas looked relieved and for a moment, fire burned in his eyes as he took in the heaving, sobbing slight figure in Drake's arms. He looked at Drake accusingly, but Drake ignored his man. All that mattered was that he had Evangeline back and at least a chance to explain and make right the many wrongs he'd done to her.

Drake eased into the back of the car, holding Evangeline tightly to him as her silent sobs racked her tiny frame. Maddox hurried around to the driver's side while Silas slid into the passenger seat. Maddox looked inquisitively at Drake, silently asking where Drake wanted to take Evangeline.

"The Conquistador," Drake said quietly. "Make sure they have the penthouse suite prepared for my arrival."

There was no way in hell he would bring Evangeline back to his apartment where the abomination against her had been carried out. Not now. Maybe never. Silas nodded his approval, immediately understanding why Drake had chosen as he had.

Drake frowned as he held Evangeline's slight body tightly molded to his. They had been separated mere days and yet he could feel the fragility in her, the weight she'd lost. The hollows in her haunted eyes. Had she eaten? But he knew the answer. There'd been no one to take care of her, no one to see to her needs. No one she could turn to. Not the women she'd called friends for so long. Not her parents, because her pride wouldn't have allowed them to know how desperate her circumstances were.

She was wasting away, as surely as he'd wasted away in the seemingly interminable time of their separation, every minute, hour, day . . . hell. No less than he deserved, but for the first time in so long he felt the stirrings of hope and the feel of sunshine that had shunned him since she'd gone, taking with her his light and his hope. And that wasn't all that had been taken from him. He'd lost all the things he'd taken for granted. Her laughter, her delight in the simplest things. Her selflessness, her innate generosity, her goodness and innocence that affected not only him, but everyone she came into contact with. His men had been as desperate to find her as he'd been, and now that he had his miracle in his arms, he'd do exactly as he and his men had discussed.

No longer would he attempt to keep her a secret, afraid that she would be used—hurt—to cripple him and his empire. He was going to make her his fucking queen, and word would go out far and wide that she was *not* to be fucked with, or those who did so would face the wrath of Drake Donovan and his entire army of loyal brothers.

Drake's name was spoken of only in hushed, respectful and fearful tones. If so much as a hair on Evangeline's head was hurt, Drake's fury would know no bounds. He'd lay to waste anyone who dared touch her. Personally.

Evangeline stirred in his arms and immediately tried to push away from him, her tear-filled eyes fearful and anxious.

"Where are you taking me?" she asked dully. "Was my prior humiliation not enough? Do you want the entire world to see you wash your hands of me?"

Maddox, having overheard the resignation and devastation in Evangeline's voice, swore long and viciously, his hands gripping the steering wheel as he took a turn more quickly than he should have, jostling Evangeline back up against Drake's chest, where he wrapped his arms around her to secure her against him. Silas's big body tensed, fury emanating from him in waves. He turned to look at Evangeline over his shoulder, his eyes oddly tender.

"I would never allow that, Evangeline."

Silas's quiet vow made her go utterly still and she stared frozen at Silas and then looked back at Drake, confusion in her eyes. Drake groaned and pulled her closer into his arms.

He stroked her bedraggled hair, inhaling the sweetness of her scent, a smell he went to bed every night savoring and holding close, cursing when he left their bed the next morning.

"There is a lot I must explain, Angel," he said in a tormented voice. "Much I must make you understand and pray your generous heart can forgive me for. But never will I let you go again. I will never wash my hands of you. You're entrenched into my heart and soul, and losing you cut them both right out of my body and only now have they been returned to me."

"Bitch . . . whore . . . worthless," she whispered as a fresh torrent of tears slid down his neck.

"No!" Drake growled. "Baby, no! Never. My God."

Silas was staring at him in shock, and oddly, pain registered in his gaze. Then his expression became murderous. It took Drake a moment to realize Maddox had stopped the car and both men were staring him down, rage emanating from them both.

"Tell me you didn't say those things to her," Silas said in a low voice.

"Goddamn it," Maddox swore. "Goddamn it, Drake! She believed you! She *still* believes you."

"How could you?" Silas asked accusingly. "I knew it was bad. I knew what you had to do, but Jesus, Drake. You went too goddamn far!"

Drake closed his eyes, holding Evangeline closer as she wept.

"Just drive," Drake said hoarsely. "God, get us to the hotel so I can explain."

Silas shook his head, sorrow creeping into his gaze. "Some wrongs can never be righted. Some words can never be taken back. Especially when they've taken root."

"No!" Drake denied. "I'll make her believe me. If it's the last thing I ever do, I'll make her believe in me again."

Worried looks passed between Silas and Maddox. Doubt. Drake felt some of his euphoria over finding Evangeline slip away only to be replaced by dread. Because having her back was only half the battle. Now he had to convince her to *stay*.

4

Evangeline resigned herself to the fact that she had no choice but to face Drake. He wasn't giving her any alternative. And it pissed her off that she was being a weak crybaby and not someone stronger—a woman who would spit in his face, ram her knee in his balls and then tell him exactly what he could do with his *necessary* destruction of her.

She wanted to laugh at the idea that he thought her desperate enough to swallow that load of bullshit. Necessary her *ass*.

No.

Gullible was the more appropriate word. And she was certainly guilty of being just that.

Gullible. Naïve. Needy. Impulsive—oh yes, certainly impulsive. Too stupid to live. Just to name a few. And to think she'd patted herself on the back for supposedly learning her lesson after Eddie and walking away from *that* disaster all the wiser.

She pried herself from Drake's arms and turned away, unable to look at him and see her own stupidity reflected in his eyes. Instead she fixed her gaze sightlessly through the window and vowed not to shed another tear over Drake Donovan. She couldn't bear his touch because it brought back all the nights those hands had covered every inch of her body and how much pleasure they'd given her.

What she wouldn't give to be able to kick his ass. To be one of those women who could stand up for herself. The kind of woman that men respected because they knew they couldn't get away with fucking her over. She hadn't even been a challenge. She'd given token protests, knowing the entire time that she would concede and give Drake anything he wanted.

She bit into her lip in disgust. She couldn't even summon the courage to tear into him with words, knock him down a rung or two. The simple truth was, all she wanted was . . . She closed her eyes wearily.

To be left alone. To be able to go somewhere private away from public scrutiny so she could lick her wounds and forget Drake Donovan ever happened. And then die a very private death, one she'd already died a dozen times in the few days since the blinders had come off.

She wanted to go home. Her desire to be in her mother's arms was a physical ache. It had been a mistake to come here, for her to think someone as gauche as her could ever exist outside her small-town upbringing, much less fit in.

She snapped her lips shut before hysterical laughter could escape them.

Far more embarrassing than ever believing she could have made a life here in the big city teeming with sophisticated urbanites was the fact that she'd actually allowed herself to think the differences between her and Drake didn't matter. That she could hold her own in his glamorous world. That she could satisfy a man like him, whose demands were all-consuming. That he would possibly ever be happy with mousy, decidedly *unglamorous* Evangeline.

Oh God, if she didn't shift her train of thought, she was going to die of humiliation. What a pitiful, tragic weakling she was. She was going to have bruises from the number of times she'd kicked herself over her presumptuousness.

Her mother had always said that if something seemed too good to be true, chances were it was precisely that.

Where had that little nugget of wisdom been when Evangeline found herself catapulted into Drake's glittery world?

But at the end of the day, she had no one to blame but herself. She'd willingly worn blinders. *Embraced* them. She hadn't *wanted* to know the blunt truth. She was too busy immersing herself in a fairy-tale world of her own making to ask the important questions, to question her own judgment. Because if she did, then her fantasy would shatter and break apart, collapse around her like a devastating landslide and bury her in its suffocating debris.

Eddie, her ex, had been right about one thing. The sudden, bitter thought burned like acid and left an acrid taste in her mouth. She was nothing more than an ostrich going through life, burying her head in the sand at the first hint of adversity. Only, right now, Evangeline didn't feel shame over the comparison. Who the hell *embraced* adversity? Certainly not her. She didn't thrive on pain—whether hers or someone else's.

Although a secret part of her wished she could have that night back all over again. Just five minutes of it. With foreknowledge this time instead of having her feet cruelly pulled from beneath her. She'd love nothing more than to take Drake Donovan down a few notches.

The thought took hold and pleasurable warmth bathed her stomach. Drake being humiliated by a woman. Now that was an image that had staying power. His business cronies holding their sides and laughing as Evangeline bloodied his nose. She'd follow it up with a knee to his balls that would have him singing falsetto for weeks to come.

She leaned her forehead against the window of the car and closed her eyes to the blurred sidewalks. Another warm trail slid silently down her ravaged cheeks. Damn it!

What was the point in this? Why had he come for her? And what was all that crap about *necessary* this and *necessary* that? No one had put a gun to Drake's head and forced him to tear Evangeline to pieces, and yet Drake seemed to expect her to think *he* was the victim here.

She shook her head. Oh hell no. She wasn't playing stupid little mind games, nor was she going to give him absolution, something he apparently wanted or needed, judging by his demeanor and words.

He could damn well make his peace with God in the end. But since he had no soul, it was doubtful he even believed in a higher deity. Her eyes slid to the corners of her lids in his direction in disgust. Who was she kidding? He likely thought he *was* God.

Fear and panic slithered down her spine as the car slowed to a halt in front of a prestigious New York City hotel. She wanted to laugh at the idea of Drake hauling a woman dressed in a service uniform into the swanky interior. He'd likely receive looks of pity. A man with his wealth and social standing being so desperate as to fraternize with the common folk.

"Angel?"

Drake's hesitant address broke into her bitter reverie. She whirled around, careful to keep as much distance as possible between them.

The fury she'd finally worked up the nerve to express came to an abrupt halt when their eyes met. She flinched at how haunted and . . . devastated . . . he looked. She promptly slammed her eyes shut before her resolve could weaken even further than it already had.

What the hell was wrong with her? This was her opportunity to take him apart verbally just as he had done to her. To rip him to shreds and destroy him every bit as much as he had her. To give him a taste of what it felt like to be on the receiving end of . . .

Hatred.

She dropped her face into her hands as a shudder rolled violently through her body. Oh God, oh God. She was sounding—acting—just like *him*.

Tentative hands skimmed up her arms, hesitant as though Drake feared rejection. But hadn't he already rejected her? She hated mind games. Why had he come after her? Why was she in his car? He'd washed his hands of her. He'd made that clear enough. So why the elaborate charade?

Her head ached vilely but not nearly as horrifically as her heart.

"What do you want, Drake?" she asked in a low voice. "What will it take for you to leave me alone—in peace? Surely that isn't too much to ask. I've had to come to terms with how very wrong I was about you, but I didn't think I could possibly be *this* wrong. That you would derive enjoyment from my emotional pain."

She stared through her tear-filled vision to meet his agonized gaze, determined to stand her ground.

"I get that you're done with me. You made that *very* clear. But are you truly going to embarrass and humiliate me just because you can? So you can physically and emotionally abuse me again?"

So wrapped up was she in her impassioned plea that it took her a few seconds to realize that Silas and Maddox had exited the car, leaving her alone with Drake. It shouldn't have felt like yet another betrayal from people she hadn't anticipated it from, but it did. And it shouldn't have hurt. But it did. Drake's men owed her nothing. Their loyalties lay with him. What was she but yet one more woman Drake had amused himself with?

Slowly, as if fearing her rejection—well, that made two of them in the same boat—Drake reached up to gently cup her chin, holding it in place so she was forced to hold his gaze when she would have dropped it, giving in to despair.

"Angel, listen to me. Please."

She went utterly still because this wasn't a side of Drake she'd ever before witnessed. Humble. Upset? And dear God, he sounded precariously close to *begging*.

His thumb stroked across her cheek in a tender pattern, his eyes drenched with the same welling emotion that she felt in her throat.

"What do you want?" she whispered, her voice breaking with the strain of her heartache.

"You. I want you. Only you. Always you."

She flinched and would have reared back, but his other hand went to her shoulder to restrain her and hold her in place. Her breath stuttered out as though she couldn't make her lungs cooperate and breathe for her.

"No, don't. Listen. Just listen."

She bit into her bottom lip, refusing to shed another tear over this whole messed-up situation.

"There is so much I need to say to you. I need to explain. I don't deserve your understanding and I damn sure don't deserve your mercy, but if it were possible, I'd be on my knees in front of you right now begging for one chance to make things right. Come up with me so we can talk. So that I can give you what should have already been yours—what is rightfully yours and already belongs to you. I know I'm not worthy of your consideration. I *know*. But at least let me explain and try to make you understand. I'm not demanding any promises from you, but I can give you *my* promise. If you still hate me, if you still can't stand the sight of me, if you never want to see me again after I've told you everything you need to know, then . . ."

He broke off and drew his hand away from her shoulder to run it raggedly through his hair. It was then she saw a startling revelation in his eyes. If his hand hadn't already been curved around her chin guarding her mouth, her hand would have flown to her lips to stifle her gasp of shock.

He was afraid.

"Then what?" she asked in a low voice, her lips trembling against the firmness of his fingers.

"I'll let you go," he said in a lifeless voice.

He said the words as if he'd just been handed a death sentence. And she didn't understand any of this. The whole thing.

"You already let me go," she said dully.

"No!"

Rage sparked in her blood and rushed through her veins until she was dizzy with it.

"Yes. Oh yes, you did, Drake." She sent him a scornful look that conveyed precisely what she thought of his method of farewell. Then she shook her head. "No, I guess that isn't true either. You didn't let me go. Letting someone go implies an act of kindness. A noble gesture. You threw me out like I was no better than garbage!"

Drake's eyes closed briefly and then settled back on her face. "I owe you an explanation."

"It's a little late to be thinking of that now," she said scornfully.

He shook his head. "Angel, please. Just come inside. Let me explain. Give me five minutes. If you want nothing ever to do with me again after five minutes, I'll have Maddox drive you wherever you want to go, but it will not fucking be back to work at the run-down rat's nest where I found you."

His voice became fierce and his eyes blazed with a savage light. Her breath caught and hung in her throat as his face loomed closer to hers. Raw hunger emanated from the glittering orbs and her pulse accelerated wildly in her veins.

"I swore to provide for your safety and well-being whether I was in the picture or not, and I don't break my word. You will be free to do what you wish, how you wish, without ever having to mop fucking floors or work in places where I can't be assured of your security at all times."

She knew her attempt at a smile was tragic. How could she smile when she was bleeding to death from the inside out? Drake Donovan never broke his word. Oh, but he had. Not only had he broken promises made to her as her dominant, but he'd lied to her. The entire time they were together. It was all one huge lie because nothing had been real.

Except her love for him.

And it was a well-known fact that one-sided love was doomed from the start. She couldn't love him enough to make up for the fact that he didn't and would never love her.

"Angel, you break my heart," he said, his throat clogged with emotion.

"I'd say we're even then," she whispered without malice.

5

Drake knew he was being a coward holding off his conversation with Evangeline for as long as possible, but he hadn't yet figured out exactly what he wanted to say or how to say it. All of his focus and energy over the past few days had been centered on finding his angel. He'd purposely blocked all other thoughts from his mind because he wouldn't entertain for a moment the thought that he wouldn't find her and bring her back where she belonged.

But now that he had what he wanted most . . . No, having her back ran a close second to gaining her forgiveness and understanding. Her trust wouldn't be earned so easily the second time around, and he knew he had to tread carefully. He couldn't afford another mistake like this one or he'd lose Evangeline forever. He was lucky he hadn't lost her this time.

You don't know you haven't already lost her. She was here physically. But she damn sure wasn't with him emotionally. She was reserved, in self-protection mode, determined not to give him the power to ever hurt her again.

He paced the floor outside the bathroom of his hotel suite as he waited for Evangeline to reappear after her shower. He'd laid out clothes for her on the counter so she wouldn't feel vulnerable and at a disadvantage when he cleared the air. Or died trying.

No, she would listen to him. She had to. Evangeline wasn't like the many other women of his acquaintance. She didn't emotionally manipulate men—anyone—with tears, nor did she pout or withhold forgiveness in order to punish people.

But everyone had their limits and he hoped like hell that he hadn't put himself beyond redemption. That he hadn't done permanent damage to her loving, generous heart. He was jaded and cynical enough for both of them. The idea of Evangeline becoming someone like him—hard, distrustful and suspicious—made him sick to his soul.

You don't deserve her.

Maybe Hatcher, as fucked up as his reasoning had been, had been right. For the first time, Drake allowed doubt to creep into his mind. Was he doing the wrong thing by fighting for Evangeline? By doing a complete one-eighty and making her his queen, thus rendering her off-limits to anyone who valued not only their material wealth but also their life?

Because no one who knew Drake, whether personally or by reputation only, would ever doubt that if something or someone Drake valued came to harm, he would turn the fucking world over until every last person who even knew of the plan, regardless of whether they actually participated, paid dearly.

Drake would ruin anyone who put a finger on Evangeline. And then the person would die, and it wouldn't be a quick or merciful death. He would repay ten times over every mark, scratch, hurt, fear or threat Evangeline suffered.

He shook his head, dispelling the cloud of doubt in a pissed-off motion. Hatcher was lucky to still have the use of his limbs after bringing that shit up to Drake's face. And Drake's other men hadn't been any happier about Hatch's "helpful" suggestion.

The sound of the door made Drake turn in his tracks, and he held his breath as Evangeline hesitantly appeared in the doorway of the en suite bathroom, her fingers gripping the door frame so tightly that her fingertips were chalk white. Her hair lay damply against her face and trailed down her shoulders, and when she saw he was looking at her, she shifted and curled her arms protectively around her midsection as if to hide herself from his scrutiny.

She was wearing a simple pair of jeans and a long-sleeved T-shirt, and he noticed that she'd put her socks and shoes back on, as if ensuring that she was prepared to flee at any moment. Unease and indecision flickered through her expressive eyes, and after she'd sought out his position in the room and briefly locked gazes with him, her stare skittered away and she refused to look up at him again.

He sighed and lowered his hand from his bedraggled hair and let it dangle down his side.

"Are you willing to listen to me, Angel?" he asked quietly. "To give me a chance to explain?"

One small shoulder lifted in a half shrug and her bottom lip disappeared between her teeth as she chewed nervously at it.

"I guess I don't understand what there is left to say," she said in a soft voice. "You made yourself abundantly clear where I stand, or rather where I don't stand. How can rehashing it do either of us any good?"

No longer willing or able to maintain the distance yawning between them, he closed in to loom over her before she could even emit her gasp of surprise. He cupped her cheek and caressed her baby-fine skin with his thumb and fingers.

"It was a lie," he said starkly. "It was all a lie. Oh God, Angel. You weren't supposed to be there. I had no idea you were there or I would have never brought those men to our home. I was caught completely off-guard and I had to act fast or you would become a target."

The look she sent him was acid-filled and disbelieving. He couldn't blame her.

Drake sighed and then put both his hands between them to collect hers in his grasp. Then he backed slowly toward the bed and settled down on the edge, pulling Evangeline down with him.

She went utterly rigid, every muscle in her body protesting his nearness. Too bad. He wasn't letting her out of his sight again. No matter what it took, how long it took, he would win her back. Until then he would dream of the day when she came willingly into his arms with love and laughter in her eyes. Just as she'd done so many times before that fucked-up night.

He wasn't the most patient man in the world. He had to cough to cover the choked laughter that threatened to bubble from his throat. His men often said that Drake was the most impatient bastard on the face of the earth and that he had no experience with sitting back and waiting on anything, or the *desire* to do so.

When he wanted something, it was his. End of story. And he'd mow over every single obstacle between him and what he desired. Now, for the first time, he had to exert a modicum of patience. Because if he didn't, he risked losing everything that mattered. And God, he hated it. Hated that he wasn't even now in bed with Evangeline, her naked, his body covering hers as he reasserted his dominance and control over her. But not just his dominance and control. She was the woman he cherished most in his life. Never before had he been with a woman who inspired so great a need and desire to protect and take care of her.

She required exquisite care in his handling of her. He owed her that and so much more. So very much more. She deserved to be treated as something infinitely precious. He knew she was strong, despite her protests to the contrary. She wouldn't break, but that didn't mean he had the right to push her. To take her strength for granted. She might not have broken—yet—but that didn't mean she hadn't come way too fucking close for his peace of mind. Never would he forget seeing her in the hotel she'd found work in and how close to her breaking point she appeared to be. And he'd done that to her. No one else. He only had himself to blame.

There was a fragile air about her that had never existed during their time together. What kind of an asshole would it make him to blithely ignore the delicate state she was in and forcefully go on as though nothing had happened?

Never would he leave her without his rock-solid support, and he damn sure wouldn't assume anything when it came to her state of mind, her sense of self-worth and what was going on in her head, especially when it came to her thoughts regarding him and her place in his life.

"I made a mistake with you," Drake admitted.

She blinked, clearly not expecting him to admit fault. Her features reflected her surprise, and he understood why. Drake wasn't a man to readily admit failure. Normally he was too self-assured and didn't give a damn what others thought of his choices.

"Angel, I have many powerful, ruthless enemies. Men who would use any means available to strike at me. I've long frustrated them because I don't have any weakness to exploit. There's nothing I care about enough to make concessions or to yield to blackmail and extortion."

He took a breath and looked directly into her eyes.

"Until you."

Her eyes widened and then she bit her lip in consternation. He could see the wheels spinning madly in her mind as she tried to process his sincerity.

He wanted to touch her, to yank her into his arms and prove his words, but he didn't have this in the bag, not by a long shot. She didn't believe him and he couldn't blame her. Not when he'd made it a practice to be aloof and hold himself at a distance from everyone.

He dragged a hand through his hair until the short strands stood up on end in complete disarray.

"I handled you all wrong. I hid you, what you meant to me. Tried to keep you a secret and out of the public eye."

She sent him a puzzled look. "Why? I don't understand."

He sighed. "Because if my enemies even got a hint of what you mean to me, how important you are to me and that I'd do anything to keep you safe, they would have gone after you. They would have been relentless and once they got their hands on you, they would have used you to take me down. They would have threatened you, and Angel, these aren't men to make idle threats. If I hadn't complied with their demands, they would have made you suffer horribly and eventually killed you."

"But I'm no one," she said, her voice rising. "That doesn't make any sense. I'm just . . . I'm just your . . ."

"Don't say it," he said in a whiplike tone. "Whatever you're thinking, don't you dare say it. That's bullshit. If you think you aren't important to me, then that's another sin for me to bear because I should have shown you. You should know that you're special. Not just to me but to my men. All of us."

She shook her head, falling silent as she grappled with his heated declaration.

"So I kept you tightly under wraps," he continued, self-loathing creeping into his voice. "I was arrogant. I thought I could have you, keep you to myself and keep you safe. That my enemies would never know of you. It was stupid and I know better. Goddamn it, I know better!"

"So the business meeting you had, the men you brought to your apartment when I was supposed to be somewhere else, those are your enemies?" she asked skeptically.

He nodded and she frowned, perplexity furrowing her brow.

"Why would you bring these men into your home, then?" she asked. "Why would you take such a risk if they hate you? And why didn't you just tell me why you didn't want me there instead of skirting around the issue? If you had told me it would be dangerous, I would have never interfered. I wouldn't have made such an ass of myself, that's for sure."

Pain glittered brightly in her eyes, and her cheeks colored as she ducked her head away, refusing to meet his gaze any longer.

He cupped her chin and gently turned her until she looked him in the eye again.

"You did *nothing* wrong, Angel. That whole night is on me. My fault. You did something very special for me. But I couldn't allow the Luconis to so much as suspect what you meant to me. That you were more than a temporary mistress or someone to warm my bed before I tossed you out."

His expression became bleak as memories of that night, of how badly he'd humiliated Evangeline, repeated over and over in his mind. The look on her face. The devastation and her tears. The despicable things he'd said and *done* to her.

"It was all a lie," he whispered. "I had to put on the act of my life and convince those men that you were nothing to me. And, Evangeline, they had to believe it because if they had any suspicion that I was faking it, they would have gone after you. And if I had allowed you to play hostess, there is no way they could spend more than five minutes in your company and not see the truth."

"What truth?" she whispered.

"Of what you mean to me," he said in a low voice. "I couldn't take the risk. One slip-up, one unguarded moment when I looked upon you with pride or when you smiled at me, how I'd soften. I would have been an open book, Angel. And you would have paid the ultimate price for my lack of control when it comes to you."

"So you struck at me first," she said grimly.

Drake closed his eyes in pain. "I was gutshot. I knew what had to be done, and it sickened me. Having to stand there and pretend to be so callous, pretend you meant nothing to me. God, the things I said and did. You have to know I didn't mean them, Evangeline!"

She studied him quietly, her teeth worrying at her bottom lip. She was quiet and pensive and her struggle was clearly highlighted in her face and eyes.

"I don't know what to believe," she finally said. "There's too much I don't understand. You said you did things wrong with me by keeping me a secret. But if you caring for me put me in danger, then what else could you have done except keep me a secret?"

Then her eyes widened and her mouth rounded.

"Oh," she murmured. "Never mind. I understand."

"What do you understand?" Drake demanded, not liking the resigned look on her face.

"You should have never gotten involved with me," she said quietly. "That's what you're trying to say."

"No!" he said in a near bellow, causing her to flinch and draw in on herself as she regarded him cautiously.

He reached for her hand and sandwiched it between his, feeling her slight tremble as she stared at him with huge, questioning eyes.

"I should have never kept you a *secret*," he said savagely. "Never should have tried to downplay your importance to me."

She cocked her head to the side, her expression growing even more confused.

"But you just said that if anyone had known that, I would have been used to hurt you."

His jaw clamped down hard as he stared fiercely at her.

"What I should have done, and what I will do going forward, is make it known that you're my queen. My woman. The most important person in my life. It will be made clear how I will retaliate if someone so much as touches a hair on your head. Security will be tightened around you, but you know and are comfortable with the men who will be guarding you."

All the color leached from her face, making her eyes seem enormous. She opened her mouth but no response came forth, and for a long moment she simply sat there staring agape at him. Then finally she shook her head as if trying to dispel the confusion and cobwebs surrounding her.

"We aren't together, Drake," she said hesitantly.

"The hell we aren't," he said savagely. "I drove you away, Angel. I got back to my apartment as fast as I could without arousing suspicion because I planned to explain everything that night and then beg your forgiveness. When I found you gone, I went crazy. I've spent the last five days turning this city upside down looking for you. And now I've found you. If you think I'm going to let you walk away from me without one hell of a fight, you're out of your mind. You belong with and to me, just as I belong to you. What happened that night will never happen again. It shouldn't have happened to begin with, but at the time it was the only thing I thought would keep you safe."

"What are you asking for exactly, Drake?" she asked skeptically.

"Whatever you're willing to give," he bit out. "In time, everything. But for now I'll take whatever you're willing to give me, as long as you give me the chance to make this up to you and to prove how important to me you are."

"So you want us to go back to the way things were before? Pretend like that night never happened?"

He flinched. "Of course I don't expect it to be that easy. I have a lot to make up for. You gave me your trust and now I have to earn it back. You gifted me with your submission and I have to make you feel safe and cherished enough to submit once again. But I want you with me, Angel. At all times. Once you are public knowledge, I'll never allow you to go anywhere alone."

Evangeline closed her eyes for a long moment, her fingers twisted together in a bloodless knot on her lap. Her despair and indecision was a tangible presence in the room.

"I don't know what I should do," she finally said, exhaustion creeping into her speech and her posture.

"What do you want, Angel?" he asked softly. "Forget about *should*. What do you *want*?"

She turned her head and her tear-filled gaze met his.

"I want things back the way they were before," she said with trembling lips.

"They can be," he said truthfully.

She made a grimace. "You make it sound so easy."

"Isn't it? I made a terrible mistake, my angel. One I won't forget for a very long time. One that I'll regret for the rest of my life. But I won't make that mistake again. No longer will I attempt to hide your presence in my life or your importance to me. Just give me the chance to show you how it can be. Don't give up on us yet."

He was coming precariously close to pleading. And he'd choke before ever begging for anything. But at the moment, if getting on his knees and making himself utterly vulnerable in front of her would convince her to give him another chance, he'd do it without any hesitation.

What was pride if he lost the one thing that mattered most to him?

A tear slithered down her cheek and she huffed in a shuddering breath as she tried valiantly not to break down into sobs. He gathered her in his arms and held her tightly, rocking back and forth as he pressed kisses to her damp hair.

"Give me—us—another chance, Angel," he whispered. "I'll make it up to you, I swear."

Slowly she lifted her head, pushing back until she was able to look him in the eye. Fear shone brightly in her gaze, and her forehead was furrowed with worry.

"But if you didn't want anyone to know about me before . . ." She shook her head as if trying to clear her confusion. "What's changed?"

she whispered. "If I could be used against you before, won't it be even more probable now? I don't want to be used to destroy you, Drake."

He inhaled sharply and it wasn't until her face began to fade in front of him that he realized he'd been holding his breath. He let it out in a long exhale and gathered her in his arms once more, unable to stand even the slight distance she'd put between them.

"Let's just say that a message will be delivered loud and clear," Drake said grimly. "That if anyone so much as looks at you wrong, they're dead. I have enemies. I told you that. But I am feared greatly. I don't have a reputation for mercy. My men will make it known that only someone with a death wish would try to get to me through you. But at the same time, security will be tightened around you and someone will escort you at all times when you aren't with me."

A peculiar pain settled into his chest and something that resembled panic scuttled around his insides. Maybe she wouldn't like the kind of life he offered. Not many would. She'd be living in a veritable prison.

Oh, she'd have every imaginable luxury and convenience. She'd be spoiled and pampered, her needs put before all others. But the one thing she wouldn't have was . . . freedom. If she remained with him, she would be consigned to a life of high security. No one would have unfettered access to her.

How long would she be able to live in such suffocating circumstances? How long before she'd rebel and lash out over the extreme protective measures Drake put into place? Not many people would willingly consign themselves to a veritable prison no matter how luxurious that prison might be.

"Can you forgive me, Angel?" he asked softly. "Can you forgive me in time? Will you give me the chance to make it up to you? To prove to you that I would never again subject you to what I did that night? I know it's a lot to ask. I wouldn't blame you if you wanted nothing further to do with me, but I don't want to live without you. You are all that's good in my life. The only good. The very best part of me, and I damn near destroyed that in my panic and fear that you would be used to strike at me. I could never live with myself were something to happen to you because of me. And I'm going to do everything in my power to protect you from the bastards who would think nothing of abusing a woman in order to achieve their goal. Every single one of my men is devoted to your safety and protection. They will protect you with their lives. I need you to believe that. And I need you to believe that you are the most important thing to me and I will never let you go without one hell of a fight."

Her expression was dazed, and the internal war she was waging with herself was evident in her stormy eyes. She looked . . . afraid. He wanted to let loose a string of curses that would singe the hide off the most hardened man, but the last thing he needed to do was push her in the opposite direction.

"So we just get back . . . together?" she asked in a choked voice. "Pick up where we left off?"

"No," he said, completely serious. "We, or rather I, start over. New beginning. Better this time. I have a lot to make up to you, and I'm not going to pretend otherwise. You, however, don't need to change a damn thing. You did nothing wrong. You gave me a gift most men can only dream of receiving, and I didn't nurture and protect that gift as I should have. That changes right now and going forward. If you'll say yes and agree to stay with me."

"Oh, Drake, I don't know what to say," she said in a choked voice.

Tears welled in her eyes and he hastily thumbed at the moisture as it began to leak down her cheeks.

"I was so happy. You made me happy. And I wanted to make you happy. Everything was . . . perfect. And then . . ."

"Shhh, my angel," he said, cradling her once more in his arms. "It will be perfect again. I promise. I don't expect you to forgive or forget any time soon. All I ask is the opportunity to prove to you that I can be the man you deserve. Just say yes and we'll take it one day at a time, and I'll promise to try to make each day better than the last. I have no doubt we'll hit a few roadblocks along the way, but I can promise you that what happened that night will never happen again. I'd give everything I own to be able to go back and make it never happen."

She leaned her forehead against his, closing her eyes as she battled the tears streaking silently down her cheeks.

"I want this—you," she whispered in an aching voice that throbbed with emotion. "But I'm scared, Drake. You have so much power over me. You have the power to make me so very happy, but you also have the power to destroy me like no other. I don't think I'll survive so much pain again. I've been dead for the last five days, and I hate how vulnerable you make me feel, that I depend on you for so much happiness. It scares me to death. Can you understand that? I can't imagine you being helpless, at someone else's mercy and dependent on them just to maintain your sanity and keep it together."

"I do understand," he murmured. "I understand far more than you realize because you hold me in the palms of your hands, and you have as much power over me as you say I have over you. And I have to tell you, it sucks. I hate feeling so helpless. I've never been dependent on another person in my life. I'm always in control and yet when I'm with you I feel anything but in control. I feel as though I'm walking through a minefield, and one wrong move and I destroy something very precious and beautiful. I damn near did just that. I certainly inflicted a lot of damage, and that makes me a complete bastard. Believe me, Angel. I will *never* forget. I will never forgive myself for what happened that night. It's something I'll have to live with for the rest of my life. I haven't eaten, I haven't slept, I've been a shell of a man for the last five days, and self-loathing has slowly eaten a hole in my soul until there's barely anything left, if anything at all."

"Drake, no," she cried out. "Stop. Just stop! You can't torture yourself this way. It does neither of us any good. If we're going to make this work, then we have to put it behind us and move forward. If you stay bogged down in the past, it will destroy us *both*. If I can forgive, then you should be able to do the same."

Drake sucked in his breath and his pulse accelerated wildly. He was shaking and desperately trying to hold himself together as her words penetrated his anger and grief. He grasped her shoulders and pushed his face toward hers until they were nose to nose.

"Do you mean that, Evangeline? Are you saying what I think you're saying? Are you giving me another chance?"

His heart felt like it was about to burst out of his chest. It was beating far too fast and for a moment, he feared the strain would be too much and he'd have a heart attack. His entire body shook. Not one part of him was calm or still as his gaze bored into hers, seeking confirmation of the hope that had taken root and snaked insidiously through his veins.

She swallowed and he saw how difficult this was for her. How monumental a decision she'd reached. But then she slowly nodded.

"I need the words," he said hoarsely. "I have to be sure. I need to hear you say it out loud."

"Yes," she said softly. "I'll give you—us—another chance. I won't lie. I'm scared out of my mind. But I'm willing to try."

It was too much for Drake. He crushed her into his arms, holding on to her for dear life. He rocked back and forth, alternating murmuring against her hair and brushing kisses over the silken tresses.

A huge knot in his throat prevented him from articulating his thoughts and emotions, so he simply held her, touching her, caressing her, kissing her over and over as he silently gave thanks for this beautiful, sweet and generous woman in his arms.

He didn't deserve her, no, but no way in hell would he ever willingly give her up. She had become vital to him. As necessary as breathing. He couldn't imagine his life without her now. Never did he want to go back to the stark, barren existence he'd endured before Evangeline had stormed into his life and changed everything.

For several long minutes, he simply held her, unable to form any semblance of words. Reluctantly, he loosened his hold on her and pressed a kiss to her lips before gathering her hands in his.

"I need to know if you no longer want to live in the apartment we lived in before. It's perfectly understandable if you don't. I don't want to do anything that brings back bad memories. But if we choose to live in one of my other residences, I'll need a week or so to properly secure it and get it up to the same standards as my current apartment. We can move each day so we don't spend the same night in one place until all of the work is done and a new main residence is secured."

"I'm okay with going back to your apartment," she said after a brief moment.

He studied her demeanor, her expression and her eyes, looking for any sign of hesitation or fear. But he saw nothing.

"Are you sure?" he asked anyway.

She nodded. "There's no sense in spending all that time and money to outfit another dwelling when the one you have is already suitable."

"Then let's go home," he said gently, holding his hand out to her as he stood.

With only a slight hesitation, she slid her soft palm over his and allowed him to pull her up to stand beside him.

"You won't regret this, Evangeline," he said with utter gravity.

Her gaze searched his for a few seconds and then she offered his hand a gentle squeeze. She hesitated only a brief second as she seemed to overcome her internal struggle and then let out a deep breath. Hope seized his chest when her eyes softened. She licked her lips once and then uttered the sweetest words he'd ever heard.

"I believe you, Drake. I believe you."

6

Evangeline's nerves were a wreck by the time they arrived at Drake's apartment. Though she had agreed to remain here instead of having Drake go to the time and expense of setting up another residence, it didn't mean that the mere thought of walking back into a place that had hosted her utter humiliation didn't have her on the verge of an anxiety attack.

To make matters worse, as soon as they entered the lobby Evangeline saw Edward and cringed at the sympathy and worry in his eyes as he hurried over. Oh God. She just wanted the floor to open up and swallow her whole.

But Drake must have sensed her mortification and warned Edward off with a look, because Edward halted and then turned to busy himself with another task. By the time they made it onto the elevator, she was shaking and on the verge of hyperventilation.

She hugged her arms around her waist and lowered her head to stare at the floor. Her eyes were burning and she'd endured enough humiliation without dissolving into tears in front of Drake. Again.

To Drake's credit, he didn't prod her or call attention to her near meltdown. Instead they rode to the top floor in silence. But Drake did wrap one arm around her, solidly anchoring her against him so that his body heat seeped into her chilled flesh.

Was she an idiot? Was she a naïve fool for agreeing to this lunacy after what he'd done to her?

Her head still bowed, she shuffled off the elevator and into Drake's apartment. To her surprise, Drake stopped her just inside and simply pulled her into his arms, holding her tightly.

"Thank God you're back," he murmured. "Thank God I found you in time."

She rested her forehead against his chest and stood there, absorbing his touch like an addict in withdrawal. He rubbed his hands up and down her back and then reluctantly pulled away, cupping her chin and tilting it upward so she met his gaze.

"Come into the living room and sit down while I fix you something to eat. You haven't been taking care of yourself," he chided. "You've lost weight."

"I had it to spare," she said dryly.

He scowled. "You were fucking perfect the way you were. Now come so I can take care of my angel. You're going to eat and then get some rest, and I plan to ensure you do both."

She frowned up at him. "Don't you have work? You're already late. I can manage on my own."

He gave her a pinched look but didn't respond. Instead he steered her in the direction of the living room and settled her onto the couch, tucking a blanket around her. He fussed for a few moments longer, ensuring her comfort, and then instructed her not to even think about getting up.

"I'll be back in a few minutes and we'll have breakfast together. And then you and I are going to bed and getting some rest. I haven't slept since the night you left," he said, a trace of pain in his voice. "And you don't look as if you've slept any more than I have."

She flushed guiltily but didn't refute his statement.

With one last caress to her cheek, he turned and disappeared into the kitchen, leaving Evangeline to sag against the couch. She closed her eyes as weariness overtook her. He was right about one thing. She hadn't slept. Not at all. She'd lain in her small bed at night praying for oblivion. For a few short hours where she could escape her pain and grief. Instead she'd spent the interminable nights wiping tears from her swollen eyes and asking *why* over and over.

She tugged the blanket more snugly around her, inhaling Drake's scent, absorbing it. His presence was everywhere in the apartment. Even with him in another room she could still feel his overwhelming presence. It shouldn't comfort her, but it did.

The last five days had been miserable. The worst days of her life. She never wanted to repeat them again. Maybe it made her a fool—a desperate fool—for taking him back so easily, but she needed him. Craved him. She only felt safe when he was with her, which was absurd considering he had been the one to destroy her.

Unease gripped her when she went back over his explanation, his justification of his actions. Just what was Drake involved in that would net him so many enemies? Inspire enough hatred that they would use her to cripple him?

She wasn't stupid. She had no illusions that Drake was a model citizen, but she simply couldn't imagine him being involved in anything truly heinous. But then she'd already acknowledged that when it came to him she was an ostrich with her head stuck firmly in the sand.

The simple truth was she didn't want to know. Ignorance truly was bliss, and as long as she didn't know for sure how he made his living she couldn't very well pass judgment on him. She was happier not knowing, and if that made her a bad person, then it was something she would just have to accept.

Or perhaps she just needed time to work up the nerve to confront him about his business practices. At any rate, that time wasn't now. Not when things were already so fragile between them. When the time was right, she'd broach the subject and then decide if she could live with the results of her inquiry.

Oh, Mama and Daddy. What is happening to me? This isn't the way you raised me.

They would be so ashamed if they knew she was at least temporarily turning a blind eye to the right thing. The very last thing she ever wanted was to disappoint them. They were good people. The very best. And they'd always taught her to do the right thing no matter the sacrifice.

"Angel."

Drake's gentle voice roused her from her introspection, and she opened her eyes to see him carrying a tray with two plates.

"Sit up, baby. You need to eat and then you need to get some rest. We both need to rest and I can't think of a better way to do so than with you in my arms."

She sniffed appreciatively and her stomach protested the many days of not eating. Of not having the strength or will to force herself to eat. A hot flush swept over her body, causing her to shake, and sweat broke out on her forehead. Her stomach lurched and rebelled and then squeezed and tightened into a hard knot.

"I'm not sure I can," she said honestly, clutching her belly with one palm. Nausea boiled in her stomach, leaving her weak, clammy and shaking uncontrollably.

Drake cursed and swiftly set the tray on the coffee table before sliding onto the couch next to her, enfolding her in his arms. He urged her to the edge of the cushions supporting her back.

"Lean forward and put your head down," he said gently. "Take in deep breaths. In through your nose and out your mouth. I'll get you some soup. Think you could handle that?"

She nodded miserably, her embarrassment growing with each passing minute. She was acting like a helpless twit who couldn't survive without her man.

Drake sat there a few moments longer rubbing his hand comfortingly up and down her spine, and then he gently massaged her nape.

"Will you be okay while I get the soup?" he asked in a low voice.

"Y-yes."

His lips brushed the top of her head and he disappeared back into the kitchen only to return a few minutes later with a steaming mug. He placed it between her palms and told her to sip.

The warm fluid soothed a path from her throat all the way into her stomach, and some of her tension eased and she relaxed. She managed to consume half of it before she leaned forward to put the cup on the coffee table.

"Enough?" Drake asked gruffly.

She nodded, tension suddenly reinvading her muscles.

"Then let's get you to bed," he said, rising.

She swallowed nervously, then nodded. As she started to rise, Drake simply slid his arms beneath her and picked her up off the couch. She landed with a soft thud against his chest, and he stood there a moment with his lips pressed firmly against her forehead.

She felt a shudder roll through him and realized he was as deeply affected as she was. And nervous.

Her heart tightened at the fleeting vulnerability in his eyes, and she reached up to cup his jaw, forcing him to look down at her.

"I've missed you so much," she said softly.

Fire ignited in his eyes, and relief that was nearly staggering.

"God, I've missed you too, Angel," he said in a husky whisper. "I'm never letting you go again."

As he strode toward the bedroom, she allowed his impassioned words to sink in. Did he mean them? Or was he saying something in the heat of the moment? She didn't want to ruin everything by asking him for clarification. She was afraid of what that might mean. Fantasy was preferable to reality even as she knew that fantasy always eventually gave way to the painful truth. For now, until she could better make sense of her relationship with Drake and where she stood with him, she chose to think he meant every single word and that she was something special to him, that he cherished her and that he wanted . . . *forever.*

The word trailed off in her thoughts. She was unable even to give it voice in her own mind because of the hope it inspired and the knowledge that if it was simply a dream, it would crush her. For once, she wouldn't look ahead with the practicality her parents had instilled in her. She wouldn't attempt to predict the future and prepare herself for the eventuality of her and Drake parting ways. Instead she chose to live in the moment. One day at a time. One precious fantasy and dream at a time. If and when the time came for her to face cold hard facts, she'd hold the cherished memories of her time with Drake close to her heart for the rest of her life.

Because one thing was for certain. As practical as she liked to think herself and knowing that nobody was the one and only in someone's life, she knew without doubt that there would never be another like Drake for her. No one who would even come close. Drake knew her inside and out, perhaps better than she knew herself. He knew what she needed and moved to provide it before she even recognized it. And she was supposed to think there was another man out there who could possibly see into her heart and soul the way Drake did? Not likely.

Drake was a once-in-a-lifetime soul mate, never to be repeated or replicated. And damn it, she didn't want to settle for second best. Ever. If she couldn't have her other half, the one meant and made for her, then she'd choose to live her life alone and hold close the memories of the only man to know her better than she or her family knew herself.

She mentally shook herself, angry that she was allowing her insecurities and fears to put a damper on her reunion with Drake. No one was perfect. Yes, what Drake had done was horrible. She'd been humiliated and devastated, her heart ripped out of her chest. But if he was to be believed, and he'd given her no reason not to believe him, his actions were justified even if extreme.

She'd seen his expression when he'd admitted his fear of her being used to weaken him. As if the idea of her being hurt or abused in order to extort from Drake devastated him every bit as much as he'd devastated her by his actions. She wasn't the only one hurting and reeling from the events of that night. His eyes had been utterly bleak and he'd looked . . . defeated when he'd begged for her understanding and forgiveness.

Her stomach clenched, because she hadn't given him either. Yet. She was still too afraid to trust him. She was still in self-preservation mode, afraid to make herself vulnerable once again and open herself up to pain and betrayal.

Oh, Drake, I'm so sorry. Tears pricked her eyelids, but she refused to ruin the moment by giving way to the tears threatening to fall.

Drake had laid himself bare to her. He'd put himself at her feet, and a man like Drake was not someone to ever humble himself in front of anyone, man or woman. And yet he'd done just that. He'd risked everything. His pride. All to make things right with her. And she hadn't offered him anything except wariness. Certainly not mercy, understanding or forgiveness.

Peace descended as she decided to right the wrongs between them at the very first opportunity. She would wait for just the right opening and give Drake what he'd given her. She'd bare her soul and strip herself as bare as he'd stripped himself so they were on equal terms and footing. If such a proud, powerful man could go to such lengths to humble himself, then she could certainly do the same and give back to him what he'd given her.

If it turned out she was wrong—about Drake, about their relationship, about everything—then she wouldn't have a single regret for doing the right thing. She couldn't control his actions, his decisions, his thoughts or feelings, but she could certainly control her own and use them in a loving manner.

Her heart fluttered with hope, swelled with need and ached for fulfillment only Drake could provide. Five days was such a short time and yet it had seemed an eternity of loneliness and a lifetime to grieve for all she'd thought she'd lost. Now she had a second chance. The opportunity to right previous wrongs. Both of them did. And she planned to make the most of this chance and show Drake how very much he mattered.

"You look miles away from here," Drake murmured as he laid her on the bed.

She flushed, but he didn't chide her or even ask what she'd been thinking. Instead he began divesting her of her clothing, pausing to kiss and caress each new area of flesh exposed. By the time he stood to remove his own clothing, she was panting breathlessly, her body tingling with desperate need unlike any she'd ever experienced.

Her gaze fed hungrily on his muscled physique, his wide shoulders and broad chest. His jaw was lean and chiseled, his eyes fiery with answering hunger and need. Heat rose in her cheeks and spread through her body when his straining erection bobbed into view.

He was rigid, his cock bulging, the veins heavily distended, and his erection lay flat against his lean abdomen pointing aggressively at his navel. Moisture beaded the dark plum-colored head, and she licked her lips without even registering she was doing so.

He groaned and closed his eyes, his chest heaving as if he were trying to maintain control. "You're killing me, Angel. Do you know the last five days have seemed like an eternity without you?"

She smiled at hearing his words that echoed her exact thoughts of just moments before.

"And that I lay here every night, aching, missing you with every breath?" he whispered as he came down next to her on the bed. "That I couldn't sleep for wondering where you were, worrying whether you were safe. God, all I could see was your face after what I did to you. And the fear that kept me awake was that even after I found you, you wouldn't forgive me, that you wouldn't give me—us—another chance. I'm not complete without you, Angel. The last five days have proved that beyond a doubt."

She turned on her side, snuggling close to him, and put a finger to his lips to stop the flow of self-recrimination.

"Shhh, darling. You weren't the only one who couldn't sleep at night. I lay awake aching, wanting, needing and missing you with my every breath. I cried myself to sleep every single night."

He flinched and closed his eyes, sorrow and regret etched deeply into his features.

"I didn't say that to make you feel bad," she whispered. "I only said it to let you know that we both suffered. That we both grieved. But we have another chance now. Let's make it perfect this time."

"You're far too good for me," he said gruffly. "Too sweet, too innocent, too compassionate and too loving. I don't deserve your forgiveness or your love, but God help me, I need them. I need you."

"And I need you," she said just before she pressed her lips to his. "Make love to me, Drake. Take away the loneliness of the last five days. Make me forget. I need you so much."

He rolled over atop her, his eyes blazing. He planted both forearms on either side of her head and straddled her body, staring down into her eyes until she was drowning in his gaze. Then he lowered his mouth to hers and took her lips in the most tender of kisses.

"Are you sure?" he asked in a strained voice.

"Please," she begged softly.

He stopped her plea with his mouth and swept his tongue inside, tasting her, making love to her tongue with his.

"You'll never have to beg me for anything," he said. "All I have is yours for the taking."

Her heart did a peculiar twist that momentarily robbed her of breath. He sounded so serious, as though he were making a vow for all time.

"Then I want you. Now," she said, wrapping her arms around his neck and lifting her head to kiss him back. "Now," she urged. "Hurry."

"You aren't ready for me," he said. "I don't want to hurt you."

She shook her head, shifting her body restlessly beneath his. She was ready. More than ready. She needed his ownership. For him to reclaim her body in the most primitive way a man could claim a woman.

"I'm ready," she insisted. "Please, Drake. You said I'd never have to beg for anything."

She parted her thighs, spreading herself open to him, and then she looped her legs around his waist, feeling his erection bump and prod at her opening.

His face was a wreath of strain and it was evident he was at war with himself over whether to give in to her plea or practice more restraint out of fear of hurting her. Finally his instincts overrode all else and he positioned himself at her entrance, and after only a brief hesitation, wherein he searched her expression intently, he thrust forward in one powerful motion.

She cried out and he lowered his head and then buried his face in her neck as his body heaved, his breaths coming in ragged bursts. Her nails dug tightly into his shoulders, and she closed her eyes as the beauty of his possession surged through her veins.

It was like coming home. After so many days of grief, desperation, sadness and loss, she was back where she most wanted to be with the man she most wanted to be with. She couldn't ask for more than this right here, right now.

"Why are you crying, Angel?"

She blinked and realized that Drake had pulled his head up and was now staring down at her, concern and worry reflected in his eyes. She hadn't realized she was crying but now she registered the warm trails slipping slowly down her cheeks.

She gave him a shaky smile. "I'm happy," she said simply. "You have no idea how horrible the last five days have been. I thought I'd lost you forever."

Guilt darkened his eyes and he briefly looked away as if to compose himself before he once more locked gazes with Evangeline. He slowly withdrew and she moaned as he rippled through her delicate tissues. Then he surged forward again, burying himself as deeply as he could go.

"Never again," he vowed, holding her gaze fiercely. "The entire world will know what you mean to me. Anyone who fucks with you, even tries to fuck with you, will be signing their own death warrant and they'll know it."

She fought off the surge of unease, determined not to give way to anything but the here and now and the beautiful sense of homecoming she felt in Drake's arms.

"Love me," she whispered, arching up against him, demanding more.

There was no hint of the dominant lover Evangeline had come to crave over the course of their relationship. This was a man making love to her with reverence. There was tenderness and apology in every kiss, caress and stroke in and out of her body. It was a side of Drake she hadn't seen. Oh, he'd been gentle and loving during their lovemaking. It wasn't always an exercise in dominance and kink, but there was an emotional side to him that brought tears to her eyes and a deep-seated ache to her soul.

She craved his dominance—needed it—and yet she realized she needed this too. It gave her reassurance that before she wouldn't have thought she needed, but in the aftermath of that horrible night, insecurity had taken root and bloomed. Now? She needed both. She needed the harder edge, but she also needed this softer touch. She needed his . . . love.

Would that be something she could ever hope for from him?

She pushed that discomfiting thought from her mind and gave herself completely to the beauty of their lovemaking, surrendering heart, body and soul to the powerful release that swelled and built until she could bear it no longer.

"Drake!"

"I've got you, baby," he said tenderly. "Come with me. Let go."

He thrust powerfully, rocking his hips against hers until no part of him wasn't buried deeply within her. His face blurred in her vision as euphoria flooded her body and she began to spiral out of control, unraveling faster and faster until she was panting to catch her breath.

Drake growled and then gathered her tightly in his arms. He rocked into her one last time and then buried his face in her neck as they both fell over the edge and into oblivion.

For a long moment he let his weight rest atop her and then he rolled, holding her tightly against him so their positions were reversed and she lay sprawled atop him on the bed. His big, strong hands caressed the length of her spine and she snuggled her face into his chest, nuzzling and offering tiny kisses to his sweat-dampened skin.

"Don't leave me again," she softly whispered.

His grip tightened around her and she felt the betraying tremble of emotion in his body.

"I won't, Angel. I need you too much."

7

Evangeline woke to toasty warmth and the solid comfort of being wrapped in strong arms and anchored to a hard body. It took her a few moments to sort through her foggy thoughts and initial confusion. She wasn't on the small cot in the tiny storage closet at the hotel that had been converted to a sleeping area for her. Nor was she weighed down by the desolation of loneliness and despair.

Slowly the events of the previous day filtered back to her. Drake appearing at the hotel where she worked. Him taking her home. Making love to her. Them napping for a few hours and then spending a quiet evening in his apartment watching movies. They'd eaten takeout and she'd fallen asleep nestled in his arms on the couch and that was the last she remembered.

Obviously he'd carried her to bed without her ever stirring.

She blinked at the bright wash of sunlight that filtered through the blinds over the windows, and then alarm hit her because it was too light. Hastily she shoved herself up on one elbow so she could see over Drake's side to the clock on his nightstand.

Oh crap. He'd overslept. It was nearly nine and he was always up and gone well before now.

Drake's arm snagged her waist and dragged her back down against his deliciously warm body.

"Go back to sleep," he muttered.

She glanced anxiously at his face and still-closed eyes. She touched him on the shoulder to get his attention. He lazily opened his eyes so they were half lidded and he studied her, desire reflected in his dark gaze.

"It's almost nine," she said urgently.

He continued to regard her lazily, not reacting to her statement in any way. Then he smiled.

"I'm well aware of the time."

"But you're late!"

He smiled. "As the boss, it's my prerogative to be late on occasion, and that occasion happens to be this morning when I'd much rather spend the morning in bed with my woman and then take her somewhere good to eat for lunch. As for the rest of the day, we'll take it as it comes, but I'm sure I can find ways to occupy myself."

She shivered at the blatant sexual innuendo in his voice. As he said the last, he tugged at the sheet she was clutching to her breasts so that it fell down to her waist, baring her nipples to his view.

"Now that's a nice way to wake up," he said in a silky voice.

He leaned forward and sealed his lips around one sensitive peak and sucked it between his teeth. She gasped and shivered as a thousand chill bumps danced across her skin. Both nipples puckered instantly and her groin clenched with instant need.

"Get on top of me," he growled. "Now."

Oh, but she loved the command in his voice, and she silently rejoiced that her dominant lover hadn't disappeared for good.

Obediently, she rose on her knees and then threw one leg over his and moved to straddle him. She shimmied upward until his already rigid cock lay against the V of her legs and rested against her belly.

"Are you ready for me?" he asked.

"Yes. Oh yes," she said breathlessly.

"Show me."

A little self-consciously, she slid her hand between them, burrowing between her sensitive folds until she touched her opening. She pressed one finger inside, collecting the moisture before withdrawing and then extending her hand for his inspection.

"The question is, are you ready for me?" she asked daringly, her eyes sparkling.

He cocked one eyebrow at her boldness and then lifted his head and strained forward, sucking the digit into his mouth and licking it clean.

"Delicious," he said, the sound rumbling from his chest like a purr. "I'm more than ready for my woman. Take me, Angel. Take your man and ride him long and hard. Don't show me any mercy."

"Oh, I have no intention of going easy on you," she said breathlessly. "I've missed you so much, Drake. I'm only whole when I'm with you."

In response to her impassioned statement, he dragged her head down and slammed his lips to hers, devouring her mouth in a breathtaking kiss. His hands were possessive as they roamed over her body, stroking and caressing, reacquainting himself with every inch of her skin.

Her arms were shaking as she leaned forward to brace her palms against his shoulders. When she would have released her grip on one of them to reach down to position him at her opening, he stopped her.

"Let me. Hold on to me. I won't let you fall, baby. I'll always take care of you."

She complied, arching upward so he could angle his cock and press the head to her entrance. She stopped breathing when he breached her a mere inch. But he didn't move any farther. Instead, he moved his hand out of the way and laid both arms beside him on the bed and he stared up at her, his eyes glittering with desire and need.

"I'm all yours," he purred. "Take me hard. Take me sweet and slow. Show me how beautiful you are and give me your pleasure."

Unable to wait a moment longer, she slid down in one hard, swift motion, gasping at the sudden, overwhelming sense of fullness as he stretched her impossibly wide.

"Don't let me hurt you," he ground out.

"You would never hurt me," she said softly, leaning down to kiss him as she clutched him like a greedy fist and pulsed around his turgid cock.

She flexed her internal muscles, milking him as she rippled around him. His anguished groan of pleasure and desperate need fueled her confidence. That she had a measure of power over this dominant man thrilled her and left her breathless. Gathering her courage, she began to move sensuously atop him, rising and arching up until he was nearly free of her clasp and then slowly sinking down to engulf him whole.

His fingers flexed and curled into the sheets on either side of his body until his knuckles turned white and he tilted his hips up to meet her downward advances. Then as if unable to control his need to touch her or command her, he moved his hands to her hips and dug his fingers in, yanking her downward in forceful motions.

"You're so damn beautiful," he rasped. "I'm never letting you go, Angel. I hope to God you're with me because I can't let you go. I need you."

Her heart turned over, squeezing with violent emotion. Tears stung her eyelids and she leaned down so her face hovered just over his as she looked at him tenderly.

"I need you too, Drake. I'm not going anywhere. For as long as you want me, I'm yours."

Satisfaction gleamed savagely in his eyes. "Kiss me," he commanded.

She slanted her lips over his and licked at them, coaxing them to part, and then delved inward, tasting him, absorbing his essence. One hand left her hip and tangled roughly in her hair, anchoring her against his mouth so there was no escape.

"You are perfect," he said in a gruff, choked voice. "I don't deserve you.

Not after all I've done, but God help me, I can't let you go. But I'll make it up to you, Angel. If it's the last thing I do. I'll make it up to you."

"You already have," she whispered. "You came for me."

Suddenly he wrapped his arms around her and rolled swiftly, planting her underneath him, his weight pressing her into the mattress. He plunged deeply, spreading her legs even wider. Then he looped them over his shoulders, baring her so she had no defense. She didn't want any defense.

"I won't last much longer," he said through gritted teeth. "How close are you, baby? I want you with me."

She reached up to caress the firm line of his jaw. "I'm with you, Drake. Don't stop."

He closed his eyes and took a breath, pausing for one brief moment buried deeply within her body. Then he began to pump hard and furious, the slap of flesh on flesh loud in the room.

Every muscle in her body tightened in preparation for her release. It built higher and higher until she was a bow at full draw, so tight she felt like she was about to explode. She closed her eyes but his sharp demand for her to open them and look at him had her obeying and she locked onto his intense gaze, watching the intensity of his eyes as he drew closer to his own orgasm.

"Now," he panted. "Come with me. Let go. Now!"

He pounded furiously into her, driving her body up the bed until her head bumped the headboard. Her entire body shook and quaked. A scream hovered on her lips and then it was simply too much. She couldn't hold back any longer and she let out a sharp cry as the world exploded around her and her body went limp, euphoria foaming through her veins, her muscles going lax.

Pleasure, so much pleasure. Sweet, indescribable pleasure carried her on wave after wave. She was flying, floating on the clouds, completely weightless. Tears slipped down her cheeks, not of sadness but of immense joy and contentment.

"Don't cry," Drake whispered as he sipped at the trails of moisture and kissed them away. "Never cry, my love."

"I can't help it," she said in a quivery voice. "It's so beautiful. The most beautiful thing I've ever experienced. I'm so happy right now, Drake. When I thought I would never be happy again."

He looked tortured by her sincere statement, and he lowered his body to hers. He gathered her in his arms, holding her tightly as he continued to kiss away her tears.

"Things will be different from now on, Angel," he said with utmost sincerity. "I swear it on my life. You are my single most important priority. You come first. Your happiness and safety come before all else. I and my men will ensure it. In time you'll trust me again. Just give me a chance."

"Oh, Drake, I do trust you," she said, cupping his cheek with her hand. "Please believe that, if you don't believe anything else. I've already forgiven you. Let's not dwell on the past, and focus on the future."

He looked overcome, dropping his forehead to hers, his breaths coming hard. He closed his eyes and pressed sweet kisses to her lips.

"I don't deserve you," he said bleakly, repeating his earlier statement. "But I'll be damned if I let you go."

"I won't let you let me go," she said. "I need you, Drake. I can't live without you. I don't want to live without you."

He crushed her to him, his body shaking with emotion. His eyes were closed and he simply held her. "Thank God," he whispered. "Thank God."

They lay there a moment longer and then Drake reluctantly lifted his weight from her and rolled them to their sides so they faced one another.

"I'm spending the day with you," he announced, to her surprise.

Though he was admittedly late for work, she'd fully expected him to go in at some point and she couldn't contain her look of surprise.

"I'm taking you to lunch and then I thought we'd go for a carriage ride in Central Park. After, I thought we could go by the market to pick up some groceries. I'd like for you to cook for me tonight and spend the evening in."

Her cheeks warmed with pleasure. "Any special request?"

He kissed her. "Surprise me."

Her mind immediately began to race, thinking of some of her specialties that she hadn't prepared for him yet.

"Tomorrow I have to go back in to work, but I'll arrange for a security detail to take you anywhere you'd like to go."

Her heart immediately sank. She was in no way prepared to face Drake's men yet. Humiliation crawled over her body at the mere idea.

"Maybe another time," she murmured. "I don't have anything in mind for tomorrow. I'd rather stay in the apartment and relax."

He kissed her one last time before moving to the edge of the bed to get up.

"Whatever you want, baby. You only have to ask and it's yours."

Butterflies scuttled around her stomach and into her chest at the tenderness and affection in his voice. And he wasn't blowing smoke up her ass. Drake simply wasn't that kind of man. He was blunt to a fault and didn't spare any feelings when speaking his mind. And every single declaration he'd given her since tracking her down had been utterly sincere.

Drake didn't need to offer platitudes or stroke anyone's ego in order to persuade them to do his bidding. He was a take-it-or-leave-it kind of guy. She admired his honesty even if at times it was painful. But at least she never had to wonder where she stood with him. There was no guessing and no doubting whether he really wanted her to be a part of his life.

She still had a hard time wrapping her head around the fact that out of all the beautiful, sophisticated and far more worldly women in the city, he'd homed in on her. And he'd done so immediately with no subtlety, no playing games, flirting and dancing around the issue. He took what he wanted and refused to accept no for an answer.

Perhaps she wouldn't be named feminist of the year, but she reveled in his dominance, his authority, the fact that he called all the shots and expected her to stand back and allow him to take care of her in every conceivable manner.

If she had a choice between being a cherished, pampered princess or being a ball buster and refusing to allow Drake to control her existence, she didn't even have to agonize over her decision. Drake made her feel like she was the only woman in the world to him, the most beautiful woman he'd ever been involved with; she had no doubt he'd been involved with countless women, and yet they were nowhere in sight and Evangeline belonged heart and soul to him. That had to say something, right?

Even as confidence, something entirely new to her, bolstered her in a way she'd never experienced, she chastised herself for being too confident. Too arrogant. She could very well be a temporary challenge for Drake. An amusement. Other women could have been the same, explaining why they were no longer in the picture: because Drake grew bored and in need of a new challenge, so he tossed them and moved on to his next conquest.

She bit into her lip and nibbled in consternation. *Stop, Evangeline! For God's sake, you're being a hapless coward.* If Drake truly was invested in their relationship, if she kept on with her insecurities and lack of self-confidence, she would be the one to drive him away. Not the other way around.

He chose you. He could have any woman and yet he saw you on a surveillance cam and he chose you. That has to mean something.

Though Evangeline hadn't spent a whole lot of time in Drake's club, she wasn't blind. She'd seen firsthand all the beautiful people. Men and women but especially women. In all shapes, sizes, ethnicities, some small and curvy, others tall with killer legs and a million-dollar smile, not to mention their beautiful hair, skin, clothing and makeup.

And yet for some reason still baffling to her, Drake had locked onto her and claimed her within seconds of them meeting face-to-face for the first time. She shook her head. These things simply didn't happen to a girl like her from a podunk town in Mississippi. She was clumsy, awkward, shy and extremely conservative, which was why she'd only recently lost her virginity to a man who was all wrong for her. And naïve. God, she had to be the most gullible, naïve woman on the planet. So what on earth did Drake see in her?

"Evangeline, what's wrong?" Drake asked sharply.

She flushed guiltily at being caught out lost in her thoughts. No way in hell she was going to tell Drake what she'd been thinking, even if she did have the propensity to blurt out the truth no matter how embarrassing it might be. For the first time she was going to lie to him, and she'd promised never to lie to him. But it would only anger him and ruin what had been a perfect morning. She justified her lie by telling herself it wasn't a damaging lie. She wasn't betraying him or withholding the truth about something that truly mattered. But even acknowledging that didn't make her feel any better. She hated lying. Hated it.

"I was just trying to think of what to cook for dinner tonight," she said lightly.

He studied her for a moment and more heat scorched her cheeks because he didn't swallow her lame excuse in the least. But to her surprise, he didn't call her on it, nor did he push her for answers.

"Let's go take a shower together and then we'll go get lunch. After, I'll take you on that carriage ride."

She sighed in contentment. "That sounds like a perfect day."

8

"Are you ever planning to allow Evangeline out of the apartment?" Maddox asked dryly.

Drake glanced up sharply, and a perusal of his men netted the same question in their eyes that Maddox had voiced. The question came out of nowhere and had nothing to do with the business matters they were discussing. For that matter, his personal affairs weren't open for discussion. Apparently he needed to make that clear.

"What the hell are you talking about?" Drake demanded. "I fail to see how my relationship with Evangeline is any of your business."

His tone was icy and his features glacial as he stared his men down. There was disapproval in their eyes and it pissed him the fuck off. He was tempted to beat the fuck out of each and every one of them. He'd be damned if they were going to pass judgment on his relationship with Evangeline. Fuck that.

"Oh, I don't know. Let's see. She hasn't so much as set foot out of your apartment since you brought her back there. Hell, no one has so much as seen her. You were going to make her your queen and go public with her, but she's more scarce now than she ever was before."

Drake's eyes narrowed at the implied criticism in Maddox's voice. As though Drake were purposely keeping her under wraps.

"She is free to come and go as she likes," Drake said in an icy voice. "She's aware of the necessity of higher security, and she accepts that. I've offered to have some of you accompany her wherever she'd like to go, but so far she's refused, preferring to stay in."

"Hell, she's probably embarrassed," Justice said in disgust. "She has no way of knowing what or how much we know, though she likely suspects we were privy to every single detail of what went down that night. It's understandable why she wouldn't be eager to face judgment from others."

"Who the hell says she would be judged?" Silas demanded in a pissed-off tone.

Justice shot him a look of impatience. "Evangeline has pride. In spades. I'm not saying any of us would judge her. She did *nothing* wrong." He shot a pointed look in Drake's direction that had Drake baring his teeth. "But *she* doesn't know what we think or know or what side of the picture we line up on. It's likely she's avoiding all of us. I don't blame her. I can't say I wouldn't do the exact same thing in her shoes. By her way of thinking, she's been shamed enough."

"Fuck that," Maddox growled. "The hell I'll let her believe that shit."

Silas held up his hand to silence Maddox. "I'll sort Evangeline out."

Drake slashed a look in his man's direction. "Oh, you will?"

Silas met his stare without backing down. "Yeah, I will. I'll let her know that whatever fucked-up shit she has going on in her head is just that. Shit. We had an agreement before for a once-a-week takeout date. So I'll get takeout and bring it over to your place tomorrow and I'll set her straight then. No way in hell is she going to hide away in shame for something she was innocent in."

Drake held on to his temper by a thread. Only because he knew Silas would cut his own throat rather than ever betray someone he considered a brother—his only family—was he able to control his anger at the condemnation in Silas's voice. Hell, it wasn't as if Drake didn't harbor enough self-blame without it being served up to him at every turn by the men loyal to him.

Even as the initial rage threatened to erupt, it abated just as quickly. He was grateful for Silas's fierce defense of and regard for Evangeline. Drake knew of no other recipients of either from Silas save those currently gathered in Drake's office. And going public with Evangeline instilled paralyzing fear in Drake—not an emotion he was accustomed to at all. But with his relationship becoming very public, he needed unconditional loyalty to Evangeline from every single one of his men, because he would be relying on them as well as himself to keep her safe at all times.

And Justice was likely correct in his conclusion. Drake cursed the fact that he hadn't even considered that Evangeline would be mortified to face his men, but now that Justice had suggested it, it certainly seemed highly probable. That night had been degrading and mortifying for Evangeline. Of course she wouldn't want to be around people who knew every single detail.

He was also dead on about Evangeline having fierce pride. It was one of the things Drake admired most about her.

"Silas is right," Drake conceded. "The air needs to be cleared and Evangeline needs to be put at ease. I won't have her uncomfortable with the people I trust her life with."

He paused and leveled a steely look at each of his men in turn.

"However, once Silas has set the matter to rights, under no circumstances is that night ever to be brought up in Evangeline's presence. Unless she brings the subject up, it is to be forgotten, and even should she broach the topic, you will say nothing that upsets or embarrasses her in any way. I damn near destroyed her in my attempt to keep her off the Luconis' radar, and I will not have anything said or done that brings her further pain."

Maddox made a sound of disgust. "What kind of bastards do you take us for? Evangeline is a sweet woman. Far too innocent and sympathetic for her own good. Hurting her would be like kicking a goddamn puppy. Only a complete piece-of-shit dickhead would seek to humiliate or shit on her."

"I just want to make sure we're all on the same page," Drake said calmly. "I'm not letting her go, which means she's going to be a regular part of our daily lives. The sooner Silas smooths things over with her and makes her feel at ease with all of you again, the sooner the memory of that night will fade."

"I'll take care of it tomorrow," Silas reaffirmed.

Drake nodded his consent. "See that you do. Maddox, perhaps you should take Evangeline out the following day. Have her make a grocery list and shop for the items she needs. She enjoys cooking and she likes to feel that she's contributing in some way and that she has value. I won't take that from her. Bring Justice with you. She needs to grow accustomed to being around you all again without any residual awkwardness."

"She can cook for me any time she wants," Justice said, his tone hopeful. "Maybe if I'm a really good boy, I can finagle a dinner invitation from her."

Drake rolled his eyes as the others chimed in with their appreciation of her culinary skills and their desire to be included for dinner. He wasn't a stupid man. His men appreciated more than just her cooking skills. If Drake wasn't careful and he fucked up with Evangeline again, more than one of his men would move in without hesitation and treat her like royalty, spoiling her shamelessly. Then he'd have to beat all their asses.

Drake sat back in his chair and singled Silas out. "I need as many eyes on the street as possible. With the leaks about my relationship with

Evangeline steadily going out, I want everyone's ear to the ground and I want to know of any possible threat to her *before* it has a chance to be carried out."

"I'm already on it," Silas said, unruffled by Drake's intensity. "I have eyes and ears everywhere. If someone is planning a move, I'll know about it. As long as Evangeline isn't left alone and especially not wandering around the city by herself, she'll be safe."

Drake scowled. "She won't be wandering around the city without several men on her. She goes nowhere without protection, and guards will be posted at the apartment when she's there alone during the day."

"You realize the most expedient way to give credence to the rumors of your serious attachment to Evangeline would be to show up to a society function with her on your arm," Hartley mused. "You've never brought a woman to any of the events you've attended. The few times you choose to attend a function, you're always a lone wolf and very unapproachable. I imagine that alone would cause quite a stir. Add in the planted seeds of a serious relationship with Evangeline and you'll have the entire city buzzing."

Drake stiffened, his jaw clenched tight to the point of pain. He didn't like the idea of using Evangeline or of trotting her out like a show pony just to get his point across. *Fuck.* But Hartley also made a solid point. If he wanted it spread far and wide that Evangeline was his pampered, cherished queen and that anyone fucking with her would die a very painful death, then he had to offer concrete evidence and not just talk. Actions had to back up the words.

Which meant an evening in polite company, rubbing elbows with people he despised or who despised him, people who wanted his backing and financial support in their latest schemes or simply people whom he found tedious and fake. None of the scenarios were appealing. And exposing Evangeline to a veritable viper's nest left an acid taste in his mouth. She didn't deserve to be mocked and bullied, and she damn sure didn't deserve to be tormented and persecuted because of her lack of social status.

He liked and *respected* that she was fresh and unspoiled by greed and ambition. She was as genuine as they came, someone a month ago he would have never believed existed, or rather only existed in the realm of too good to be true. He'd become jaded and cynical at a very young age—he'd had no choice. But Evangeline was a breath of fresh air. Nothing like he'd ever encountered before. She made him believe that there was actual goodness in the world, however limited in quantity.

She was as he'd dubbed her, an . . . angel. Good to her bones and incapable of deception and betrayal. Jesus. He was starting to sound like an infatuated, starry-eyed prepubescent kid without a fucking clue about how the real world worked.

It was Evangeline who didn't have a firm grasp on humanity and its devious nature, and it was his duty to shield her from those who would think nothing of tearing her apart and taking advantage of her inherent goodness.

He inwardly grimaced. It sounded like he was criticizing Evangeline. Like she had a flaw and was too stupid to live, when nothing could be further from the truth. It wasn't that she didn't have a grasp on reality. She had firsthand experience courtesy of her first lover and now Drake, the man who'd vowed never to hurt her. She was just extremely sweet and chose to see the good in people and not the bad until she had no other choice. Her heart was too tender, and that was where she needed someone to protect her from those who would take advantage of her generous spirit.

"Some of you will go with us," Drake ordered. "It's not optional. I'm not throwing her to the wolves, and you and I both know they'd take her apart and enjoy doing it. She will be surrounded by me and a group of you the entire time and no one, and I mean no one, will get through you to her and fill her head full of shit or make her feel like she doesn't belong or I'll have your balls."

"It's the bitches you'll have to be on the lookout for. Much more so than any men," Maddox stated in a matter-of-fact tone. "As soon as the women whom you've tossed or outright rejected see her on your arm, when no woman is *ever* on your arm, the claws are going to come out and they'll try to tear her to shreds."

The others nodded solemnly in agreement.

"Which is why you will all form an impenetrable barrier around her and head off anyone who attempts to get to her," Drake said emphatically.

Zander groaned. "Jesus. Does this mean I have to wear a damn monkey suit?"

Thane snickered. "If the rest of us have to suffer, then so do you."

"This is no joking matter," Drake said, his expression stony. "Evangeline is to be protected at all costs. I will not have her abused or humiliated ever again. If anyone gets by you, then you answer to me. Are we clear?"

"Evangeline is ours, boss," Justice spoke up. "She's yours, yeah, but by proxy, that makes her ours too. The only way someone will get to her through me is if I'm dead."

As Drake studied his men's expressions, he realized that Justice spoke the truth. Evangeline did in fact belong to them all. She was one of them, which meant each of them would protect her like they did one another.

Drake nodded his acknowledgment and acceptance of his men's vow to put themselves between Evangeline and harm's way. Some of the tension that had knotted his insides ever since he'd decided to go public with Evangeline eased, and he relaxed for the first time since Evangeline left him.

His men—his brothers—were solid. The best of the best. He trusted them with his life and now he was trusting them with Evangeline's, and he knew Justice wasn't just saying meaningless words. He and all of his men would put themselves in front of Evangeline. They'd die for her just as they'd die for him. That kind of loyalty couldn't be bought. It was earned and in turn reciprocated because he'd go to the wall for any one of them and they damn well knew it.

"I'll go through my invitations," he conceded. "There's always a pile of them on my desk. I'll choose one that garners me and Evangeline the most exposure and then I'll put on a show that can't possibly be mistaken. After that night, there will be no doubt in anyone's mind that Evangeline belongs to me and is under my absolute protection."

Silas stared piercingly at Drake as if peeling back the layers and leaving Drake a wide-open book.

"And is that all it is? A show?" he asked in a somber voice.

Drake's features became icy and he stared coolly back at Silas, matching his enforcer's intensity.

"She is mine and that is all you need to know. What is between me and Evangeline is strictly that. Between us and not open for discussion or analysis."

Silas's lips tightened but he didn't press the issue. Maddox didn't seem any more pleased with Drake's response than Silas had been, but like Silas, he left it alone.

"Now, if that's all we have to discuss, I'm calling it a day," Drake announced. "I'm staying home and not going to the club tonight, so I'll need you, Zander and Hartley to cover, Maddox. If there are any problems, call. Evangeline and I plan to stay in tonight, but I can always bring her with me if something needs my attention."

9

Evangeline paced the living room of Drake's apartment, restless and on edge. She was about to go stark raving mad from her self-imposed seclusion over the past several days. She wanted to get out, get some fresh air, take a walk, *anything*. But to do so would require a security team of Drake's men. Men she was mortified to face.

She knew she had no reason to feel shame. She was not at fault, but she couldn't stand the thought of facing their scrutiny and the knowledge of what had happened in their eyes. Whether she found judgment or sympathy, neither was a desirable option.

With a sigh, she flopped onto the couch and spread her arms out as she lay back. She had to find something, anything to do. No one could sit around and do nothing every single day. It disgusted her that she'd become one of those women who had no life except whatever surrounded her man. She wasn't a helpless twit, but one couldn't tell by looking at her. God knew she wasn't acting like an independent, self-sufficient woman.

Was she insane for taking Drake back so easily? There were still so many unanswered questions swirling around in her mind—questions she wasn't sure she wanted the answer to—but at the same time, a nagging worry assailed her. She couldn't live in ignorance forever, could she?

She couldn't live her life as a coward with her head stuck in the sand. Soon, she had to confront Drake and ask him the questions burning a hole in her brain. Even if it meant losing him.

Pain surged through her veins and grief overwhelmed her. She closed her eyes. No, she wouldn't go there. Surely there was a perfectly reasonable explanation for the secrecy Drake was shrouded in, the extreme security measures he implemented and his overzealousness when it came to her safety.

As her mother often said, it did no good to borrow trouble.

The buzz of the intercom startled her from her troubled thoughts and she jumped, getting to her feet from the couch to hurry over to the com.

She pushed the button. "Yes?"

Her voice was shaky and she breathed in deeply to calm her frayed nerves.

"Miss Hawthorn—Evangeline," Edward said in a friendly voice. "There is someone here to see you. Shall I send him up or should I tell him you aren't receiving visitors?"

Her pulse ratcheted up. Who on earth would be here to see her? Surely Eddie wasn't that stupid. No, it couldn't possibly be him.

"Who is it?" she asked nervously.

"His name is Silas. He works with Mr. Donovan, as I'm sure you're well aware."

Evangeline's heart sank and a knot formed in her stomach. Oh God, she wasn't ready to face any of Drake's men yet. Why was he here? It was on the tip of her tongue to tell Edward she was indisposed, but she refused to be a coward any longer.

Squaring her shoulders, she sucked in a deep breath. "Send him up, Edward, and thank you."

"You're very welcome, Evangeline," he said warmly.

She paced in agitation as she waited for the elevator to arrive and then realized that she was standing just outside the opening as if worried over his unexpected visit. She hurried into the living room and flipped on the television and settled on the couch as if she'd been enjoying a relaxing day in without a care in the world. The last thing she wanted was for Drake's men to see her as a fragile weakling.

She tensed when the elevator doors opened, but she forced herself to relax and then she rose, a welcoming smile plastered on her face. Her features felt stiff and frozen and fake as hell. She only hoped Silas wouldn't see right through her guise.

When she rounded the couch to greet him, she was surprised to see him weighted down by multiple takeout bags. Flustered, she hurried forward to rid him of the ones on top and sent him an inquiring look.

"What's the occasion?" she asked in bewilderment.

He set the bags on the island in the kitchen and then took the sacks she was holding and began taking out the containers and lining them up buffet style.

"We had an agreement to have a once-a-week takeout date," he said calmly. "Or did you forget?"

She flushed, heat scorching her cheeks, and she glanced away, unable to meet his gaze.

"No," she said in a low voice. "I just thought . . ."

"You thought what?" he demanded bluntly.

She licked dry lips and fidgeted, twisting her fingers together in agitation.

"I wasn't sure you would still want to come over and eat with me," she whispered.

Silas let out an uncharacteristic torrent of savage curses that had her flinching. Then he reached and pried one of her hands loose from the other and cradled it in his.

"Look at me, Evangeline."

It was no request. No one with half a brain could possibly interpret his statement as anything more than a command. Reluctantly, she lifted her head to look into his eyes, and the black anger simmering there nearly had her running away as fast as she could. He looked . . . dangerous. And he was extremely pissed.

"Listen to me, Evangeline, and listen good because I'm only going to say this once and you're going to heed my words or so help me, I'll make good on my threat to spank your ass."

She swallowed, her eyes going wide with panic.

"You did *nothing* wrong," he said in a forceful tone. "You are not to blame for anything that happened that night. The fault lies solely with Drake, but he was in an impossible situation and he did the only thing he could to protect you. He had no idea you would be here. If he had, he would have never brought those men within a mile of you. He hates himself for what he did, and I can't say I'm very happy with him myself, but at the same time, given the circumstances and the fact that he was completely unprepared, he did the only thing he could, and no one has punished him more than himself for hurting you."

"He explained," Evangeline whispered. "I don't fully understand, but he said the same thing you did."

"Now perhaps you want to explain to me why the hell you think that I or any of the others would possibly hold you responsible or think badly of you when you were the one hurt and humiliated?"

She bit into her lip, determined not to cry. Damn it, she'd cried enough. No more. It was time to stand up and be stronger. She was made of sterner stuff. How could she possibly prove worthy of a man like Drake when she was forever acting like a weak crybaby?

When she didn't immediately answer, Silas sighed and squeezed her hand in a comforting gesture.

"I and all the others have Drake's back. Unconditionally. Each of us would give our lives for him without hesitation, and he'd do the same for us. That loyalty and protection extends to you as well, and furthermore, our protection of you is not contingent on your relationship with Drake. Not anymore. Should anything ever happen between you and Drake, our loyalty to you doesn't go away. If you ever need anything at all, I expect you to contact us, and if you absolutely can't bring yourself to do that, then you better damn well contact *me*. And I mean for anything at all. You get me?"

She stared at him in shocked disbelief. "But I'm nobody! You don't even know me that well. Your loyalty is and should be to Drake."

"Now you're just pissing me off even more," he growled. "If I allow an innocent woman to suffer for doing nothing more than be a beautiful person inside and out, that doesn't make me much of a man. And if that costs me my relationship with Drake, then so be it. I'm quite used to being a lone wolf and not answering to anyone. Now, enough of this ridiculous conversation. The food is getting cold."

Shaken by his emphatic statement, she went to the cabinet and pulled out several plates and gathered utensils from the drawer. When she returned to the bar, Silas was opening the various takeout containers.

"I wasn't sure what you were in the mood for, so I got a variety. I have all your favorite Thai and Chinese dishes as well as finger foods and appetizers, including chicken wings, cheese sticks, spinach dip, queso and chips, two kinds of chicken strips and a few other things I threw in for you to try."

Her mouth watered and her stomach grumbled appreciatively.

"It looks wonderful," she said softly. Then she met his gaze and stared sincerely at him. "Thank you, Silas. This means the world to me."

His expression softened. "Next week, I'll get something different for us to try. This time I wanted to get food I knew you'd like."

"I'm looking forward to it," she said honestly. "I hate being cooped up in here. I'm going stir-crazy."

He frowned. "Then perhaps it's time you stop hiding in Drake's apartment and get out more. You have no reason to be ashamed with me or any of Drake's men. They know he was an asshole. I know he was an asshole.

And none of it was your fault. Tomorrow morning Maddox will be by to take you shopping along with a few of Drake's other men."

"For what?" she asked, even more flustered than before. "I don't need anything."

He chuckled and she stared at him in astonishment because Silas wasn't a man prone to laughter. It transformed his entire face, making him look younger and extremely handsome.

"Who says shopping is all about need? Shopping is supposed to be fun, or so women tell me."

Her brow furrowed as she became pensive.

"I supposed I could get started on my Christmas shopping," she said awkwardly, thinking of her limited cash and wondering how far she could make it stretch now that she had considerably more people to buy for.

Silas was staring at her, as if he could read her like a book. When his eyes narrowed and he suddenly got up and walked over to the drawer where she'd stashed the credit cards and cash he'd given her, she realized he'd done exactly that. Read her thoughts as if they'd been broadcasted in neon lights.

"Did you forget about the money and credit cards?" Silas asked.

She shook her head miserably.

"Then you know to use them," he said pointedly.

She sighed unhappily. "This isn't easy for me, Silas. I hate the idea of being a kept woman and doing . . . nothing."

His expression softened and he closed the drawer before returning to his seat at the island. "I understand pride when I see it, Evangeline. And I respect it. Drake has more money than he'll ever use in ten lifetimes. He won't even miss what little you spend of it. But if he knows that you refuse to use his money or credit cards, he will not be happy. He already feels guilty enough over what happened to you that night and his part in the whole sordid mess. Will you continue to punish him by refusing the things he wants to give you?"

She stared at Silas with an open mouth, acknowledging the points he'd scored with his statement. She had no desire to punish Drake any more. They'd both suffered enough, and all she truly wanted was to be able to move on and forget that night ever happened.

"It's that important to him?" she asked softly.

"Wouldn't it be to you?" Silas asked. "If someone you cared about refused to accept any of the things you gave them, wouldn't it bother you?"

She bit her lip but slowly nodded.

"I have it on good authority that Drake will be taking you out one night soon. Perhaps you can use tomorrow's shopping trip to buy an appropriate dress and shoes and all the other accessories. Drake is a very important figure in the circles he travels in, and though he would cut off his tongue before ever telling you how to look or dress, I've learned enough about you to know how much pride you have and that you would want to make Drake proud of you."

Her mind began racing a mile a minute. "Taking me out? Where are we going?"

"I'm not certain which invitation he's decided to accept," Silas replied. "But he will be making a statement. One you won't possibly be able to misinterpret. He wants the world to know you are his and that he values what is his. So knock him—and everyone else—dead. Buy a kick-ass dress that will make Drake the envy of every man in attendance, one that will ensure he won't be able to keep his hands off you the entire night."

Evangeline burst into laughter. "You have that much confidence in me?"

Light entered Silas's dark gaze and his eyes twinkled with responding laughter. "Bet your sweet ass I do."

"Well then. I certainly don't want to be an embarrassment to Drake. Can I rely on Maddox and the others accompanying us shopping tomorrow to give me an honest opinion on a dress and shoes?"

"Leave them to me," Silas said. "But, Evangeline, I better not hear of you giving them any problems with whatever they feel you should buy or buying you what they think you need. You get me?"

She sighed. "Yeah, I get you. Now, can we eat before everything gets cold?"

Silas sent her a look that said he well knew she was ducking the issue, and there was warning in his eyes. She wasn't stupid. Yes, Silas had been very sweet and kind to her, but she had no doubt that were she to disobey him or piss him off in some way, she'd find herself across his knee with his hand on her ass in a split second.

10

An hour after Silas left from their takeout date, Evangeline stood in the master bathroom, trying to decide between greeting Drake in a sexy negligee or forgoing clothing altogether and waiting for him in the living room naked.

In the few nights since her return to his apartment, the daily ritual of her waiting for Drake to arrive home for the day had fallen by the wayside, and Drake had said nothing to her about it. He had, in fact, been exceedingly careful about everything when it came to her. Almost as if he feared that saying or doing the least wrong thing would result in him losing her.

Well, enough of that. The only way to fully put that horrible night behind them was for things to return to normal as soon as possible and remain that way. If she could give him the knowledge that she wasn't going anywhere and that the only way he would lose her was if he chose to end their relationship, she would do anything in her power to give him that assurance.

Starting tonight.

She modeled the lacy scrap of silk that called itself nightwear and then decided not to bother. She wanted Drake's eyes on her as soon as he walked off the elevator. Not on what she was wearing.

She wanted to please him, but most of all she wanted her Drake back. Strong, arrogant, completely dominating. And forceful.

She shivered just thinking about his touch, the strike of leather against her skin. His mouth on hers. On her breasts, between her legs.

Eyes closing as she further immersed herself in her fantasy, she let the negligee fall to the floor at her feet and stepped away, toeing the material to the side and out of the walkway. Then she brushed her hair until it sparkled and flowed down her back.

Knowing she only had a few more minutes until Drake arrived, she hurried out to the living room and knelt on the fur rug so that she faced the elevator and would be the very first thing he saw when he stepped off.

Anticipation licked over her skin and flames ignited in her veins. Her pulse accelerated and her breaths puffed erratically over her lips. Then her breath caught in her chest when the elevator doors began sliding open. Her gaze lifted hungrily, seeking him out. She searched his expression for any hint of disapproval or sign that she had made a mistake by choosing to greet him this way.

When she saw the savage fire ignite in his eyes the moment his gaze came to rest on her, the breath that had been trapped in her chest finally escaped. She sagged in relief even as exhilaration hurtled over her.

Drake had waited impatiently for the elevator to arrive on the top floor. Though he had left work far earlier than was usual for him, it still felt like an eternity since he'd left Evangeline in bed that morning.

It was becoming increasingly more difficult to leave the soft warmth of her body each day. He awoke each morning with her wrapped possessively around him, her head nestled in the curve of his arm and her hair spread out all over his chest.

When the elevator doors opened, all the breath left his body in one forceful exhalation that left him off balance.

Evangeline.

She was waiting for him. Naked, the soft glow of the living room lights making her shine like an angel. She was kneeling on the carpet in a position of subservience, her head slightly bowed, but her gaze met his boldly, desire clearly illuminated in her beautiful eyes.

When he saw the faintest flicker of uncertainty shadow her gaze, it instantly propelled him into motion. Over his dead body would she feel fear or uncertainty over offering him such a precious gift.

He strode to where she knelt and then slid to his knees in front of her, both of his hands reaching out to cup her face. He drew her forward and crushed her lips to his.

"Now this is every man's dream to come home to," he murmured, still devouring her lips.

She looked shyly up at him when he released her mouth. "I hoped you didn't mind. I just...I just wanted..." She broke off and looked downward with obvious discomfort.

He nudged her chin upward with his fingers until their gazes met once more.

"What did you want, Angel?" he asked gently.

"I want you," she said earnestly. "I want for things to be the way they were before..."

She flushed and once more averted her gaze.

"You have to know I'd give you anything in the world you want, Angel."

"I just want you," she whispered. "Like before. Your dominance."

Her words shattered the tenuous hold on his control. Control he hadn't even realized he'd been exerting since her return. But now he acknowledged it had been there. Fear of pushing her too hard, too far, too fast. Of losing her. And yet here she was, on her knees, sweetly pleading for the one thing he wanted most to give her.

With an agonized groan, he swept her into his arms, leaving his brief-case on the floor. He carried her into the bedroom and carefully laid her on the bed. For several long seconds, he merely stood over her, staring down at her beautiful body. At the warm welcome in her eyes.

He was home.

The thought humbled him in a way he'd never been humbled before. None of the places he'd lived had ever felt like home. Until now. Because of his angel. It didn't matter where they lived. As long as she was there each day when he got home, it would always feel like a real home.

"What are you thinking?" she asked softly.

"How lucky I am," he said honestly. "How beautiful you are. How much I want to make love to you right now."

Slowly, she rose to her knees on the mattress in front of him.

"Then take me, Drake. Make me yours. Tonight I want to be every-thing you want and need. Only for you. All for you."

His chest tightened with an unidentified emotion. For a moment, he was bereft of words as he stared at what belonged to him.

"What is it you most want tonight, Drake?" she whispered close to his ear.

Her lips brushed against his neck, just below his ear, and then she nuzzled down his jawline until she reached his lips.

He dove his fingers into her thick mass of hair and anchored her against him so that every breath he breathed in was her.

"Make love to me," he murmured. "Tonight I am yours to do with as you wish. As you command."

"Then undress for me," she said in a soft voice.

Captivated by the seductive enchantress before him, he readily com-plied, pulling off his suit coat and then yanking his shirt from his pants. In a matter of seconds, his shoes and socks went sailing across the floor followed by the remainder of his clothing and underwear.

Her gaze was fastened on his straining erection and he damn near came on the spot when she licked her lips in anticipation.

"I'm all yours, Angel. Tell me. Now that you've got me, what are you going to do with your man?"

"Speaking isn't exactly high on my agenda," she said huskily. "I had more in mind to *show* you."

He groaned in tortured satisfaction when her tongue flicked out to swipe at the moisture already beading the head of his penis. She licked teasingly around the head, pausing at the sensitive underside to stroke with her tongue until he was straining forward, trying to push farther into her mouth.

She sucked him deep, eagerly complying with his silent demand for more. Her cheeks puffed and then hollowed as she exerted more pressure and took him to the back of her throat. He let out a guttural-sounding protest when she allowed him to slide free of her mouth, but then she reached for him, pulling him to the bed.

He reclined and she followed him down, throwing her leg over him to straddle his hips. His cock was positioned at the V of her legs and lay against the soft skin of her belly. He rested his hands on either side of her hips, his fingers digging into her flesh as he urged her to ride him.

Like a goddess, she rose, hovering over him while she tucked the head of his erection to her opening. They both gasped when her pulsing wetness contracted around the tip and began sucking him in even deeper.

She closed her eyes and clutched at his shoulders for support and then she eased down, pulling him deeply inside her welcoming warmth.

Her body blanketed him, coming down on top of him so that he felt every inch of her silken skin. Her hair teased his skin and he delved his fingers into the fine strands, pulling her head down to meet his kiss.

Their tongues met and dueled, clashing and rolling, licking, sucking until they were breathing the same air. All he could taste, could feel was her. Never had he experienced anything sweeter than an angel's touch.

She broke away and then threw her head back as she began to undulate wildly over him. His eyes feasted on her, the bob of her breasts just in front of him, her hair flowing wildly around her shoulders, and he felt how tight she was around him as she rode up and down.

"Look at me, Angel," he said sharply.

Her eyes flew open and she met his gaze.

"Look at me when you come. See me. Only me."

Even as he said the words, he took over, gripping her hips and arching up and into her, thrusting even deeper. She planted her hands on his chest, fingers splayed out as she braced herself on him for support.

"Let go," he growled. "Let me have it all. Give it to me."

She contracted violently around him as her entire body shuddered atop his. She let out a cry and then as she no longer had the strength to hold herself up, she collapsed on top of him as he emptied himself into her body.

She snuggled as close to him as she could, melting into his arms. He curled his arms around her, gathering her against his chest as he buried his face in her hair.

"I don't know what I ever did to deserve you, Evangeline, but I'm never letting you go," he murmured.

She rested there a long moment, their bodies still intimately joined before she stirred and lifted her head so their gazes met.

"I made dinner for you," she said shyly. "Would you like it in bed or do you want to eat in the kitchen?"

His heart did a funny little flutter in his chest and for a moment he couldn't form a response.

"It's early yet. Let's get dressed and eat in the kitchen. Afterward, we can watch a movie on the couch."

"That sounds nice," she said with a smile.

He patted her affectionately on the ass and then rolled, holding her with him until they were on their sides facing one another.

"Take a shower with me and then I'll help you put supper on the table."

"Hmm, that's such a hard decision," she teased. "You spoil me so much, Drake."

His expression went serious and he stroked the hair from her cheek with his fingers. "Not nearly enough, Angel. Not nearly enough."

Evangeline sat across the island from Drake, watching as he enjoyed the dinner she'd prepared. Her cheeks had warmed to the point of discomfort when he'd praised her efforts effusively after sampling each of the courses.

When she'd tried to be dismissive by explaining it was a simple meal of baked chicken with herbed rice, scalloped potatoes and vegetables, he'd scolded her and told her there was nothing simple about her cooking such a wonderful dinner for him.

At times like this, Evangeline allowed herself to venture into dangerous territory and fantasize about cooking dinner for Drake every night. Of him coming home to the smells of a home-cooked meal and of her trying out new recipes on him.

Telling herself to live for the moment and not allow herself to be hurt by assuming she had a tomorrow was fruitless. There was little point in chastising herself for her dreams because she lived them, lived in them, every single day. If the day came that Drake no longer wanted her, then all she would have left of him were the memories that she made while still with him, and she was determined to make the most of them.

"Silas said that Maddox was taking me shopping tomorrow," Evangeline said lightly. "He mentioned a function you intended to take me to and that I should pick out something appropriate for the event. But he didn't know which event you had decided on, so he wasn't sure what exactly would be appropriate for me to wear."

Drake's eyes flickered a moment and then he grew pensive. Then he reached for the briefcase he'd discarded earlier when he arrived home. He drew out three cards, all addressed to him, and laid them out on the bar so Evangeline could look at them.

"I've narrowed it down to three possibilities," he said with indifference. "I thought I'd let you select which one you'd prefer to attend."

Evangeline reached for the ornately scripted invitations and carefully read each.

"I'll wear a black tux, no matter which you choose, so feel free to select anything you feel would go well with what I'm wearing."

Evangeline outlined the one that announced it was a kickoff to the holiday season at Carnegie Hall with her finger.

"I love the holidays," she said wistfully. "What exactly is this one for?"

Drake took the invitation from her and then handed it back.

"It's a fund-raiser for the NYPD. Proceeds will go to an organization for widows and children of police officers killed in the line of duty and also to a separate organization to benefit officers wounded in the line of duty and their families as well while they are recovering and aren't back on active duty yet."

She looked up at him in surprise. "Are you a contributor to these two charities?"

Her heart leapt in her throat because he was presenting her with the perfect opportunity to ask him questions she'd been wanting to ask but had been holding off. Now that the chance had landed right in her lap, she was nervous and worried over what his response would be.

He nodded indifferently. "I contribute to a number of local causes. I have an entire staff who oversee what charities I donate to. They ensure that the charities are on the up-and-up and that the funds are distributed in accordance to what is advertised."

"Do you often go to these functions or do you usually just write a check?" she asked.

Drake looked uncomfortable for a brief moment. "I rarely attend them. I let my staff handle all requests for donations and I have an organization set up where the money comes from."

"But I assume everyone knows you own that organization?" Evangeline persisted. "Otherwise how would they know to invite you personally instead of sending an invitation to the organization?"

She had each invitation turned up so that Drake's name and address were visible.

He nodded.

"So why are you—we—going to one now if it's not something you usually like to do?"

"I want the world to see you on my arm," he said, his voice gruff with possession. "It's only fair to warn you in advance, Angel. All eyes will be on you and me. One, I rarely make an appearance at these events, and two, I never appear with a woman on my arm. I imagine you will make quite the stir."

Her eyes widened and her pulse accelerated.

"I don't want you to concern yourself over the matter," he soothed. "My men will attend with us and will encircle us at all times. No one will get through them to you. No one will speak to you unless you invite them to."

It was the perfect opportunity. The question was on the tip of her tongue and yet she bit her lip, not wanting to ruin such a perfect, intimate evening. One in which Drake had just said that he wanted to show his claim on her to the world. Something he said he'd never done with another woman.

Was she really going to ruin something this perfect?

"Angel, what's bothering you?" Drake asked, his gaze resting intently on her features.

She closed her eyes briefly and then licked her lips. "Is what you do so very dangerous?" she whispered. "Security was extremely tight before . . . I mean when we first met. And then now, after that . . . night . . ." She swallowed, and before losing her nerve completely she pushed ahead. "You said you did and said all those horrible things that night to protect me. Because you said it would put me in danger for any-one to know what I meant to you or that I meant anything at all. But then you changed your mind and said you wanted everyone to know about me. That it would be the best way to keep me safe. That if every-one knew how important I was to you, no one would dare try to hurt me. And yet you've tripled security. I can't leave the apartment without an entire contingent of men. What is it that you do, Drake? I know you own a club and that you own an entire building in Manhattan that you selectively lease out to other businesses. You own *this* building, don't you?" she asked hesitantly.

He gave a clipped nod.

"Surely that wouldn't account for the need for the amount of secu-rity you employ. What else do you do exactly?" she asked nervously.

His gaze was full of warning when he looked at her. "Don't ask ques-tions you aren't prepared to hear the answer to, Angel. You don't need to worry about what I do or who I do business with. It will never affect you. Never touch you. All you need to focus on is pleasing me and in return I'll spoil you and lay the world at your feet."

She opened her mouth to respond, but he reached across the island and laid his hand atop hers and squeezed it, lacing his fingers securely through hers.

"Let it go, Angel. For me, let it go. Can you do that for me?"

He looked almost . . . vulnerable. There was a plea in his eyes that connected deep.

"Yeah, Drake. I can do that for you," she murmured.

And in that moment, she realized exactly what the decision she'd just made meant. She should feel guilty. This wasn't the person she'd been taught to become or the person she'd ever thought she would be, and yet she felt nothing but relief when she saw the warmth and approval in Drake's eyes. His own relief over her not pushing him for answers he was uncomfortable giving her.

And then he got up and came around to where she sat across from him and pulled her into his arms. His lips melted over hers in the sweetest of kisses.

"So am I taking my angel to Carnegie Hall?" he asked as he pressed his lips to her brow.

She smiled. "I'd like that, Drake. And it's for a very worthy cause."

He smiled back and then lifted her into his arms and carried her toward the bedroom.

"In that case, I'll make a substantial donation in your name in addition to the one my organization makes. You'll be in great demand, Angel. You'll have everyone vying for your attention."

She snorted indelicately as Drake dropped her onto the bed with a small bounce.

"More like your money," she said. "I won't have anything to do with it."

He covered her lips with his, kissing her long and sweet. "That's where you're wrong, Angel. No one can possibly be in your presence more than a few seconds without falling in love. You already have every one of my men twisted around your little finger."

"And if there's only one man I want twisted around my little finger?" she asked breathlessly.

His eyes gleamed as he undressed her with gentle, loving hands. "It's probably a safe bet to say he's already firmly wrapped around every part of you he can get his hands on."

And then he made long, sweet love to her. Over and over into the first shades of dawn, he brought her to the heavens and she knew without a doubt that no matter what else happened from this day forward, she'd made the right decision in not pushing Drake for answers as to his business practices.

Maybe that sealed her fate and perhaps it would doom her to go down with him, but she couldn't find it within herself to regret a single moment of her time with Drake.

He'd promised her that he would protect her with his life. That his men would protect her with their lives and that no part of his business dealings would touch her or affect her. And she believed him.

Because she loved him.

12

Evangeline came slowly awake and realized she was sprawled atop Drake, stark naked and weak as a kitten from all the times he'd made love to her through the night. She let out a contented sigh and his response was to rub his hand up her spine and then down her arm.

"Is my angel all right?"

She rubbed her face against his chest and thought if it were possible she'd be purring right now. "Mmm-hmm."

His chest vibrated with his chuckle and then he tilted her head back and kissed her warmly.

"I have to get into the shower, baby. I'm late and I have an important meeting. Maddox has already called to say he'll be over in an hour to take you shopping."

"I love waking up to you," she murmured.

"I'm glad, since you're going to be doing it every single day," he said with an affectionate tweak to her nose.

He sat up but urged her to get comfortable again in the blankets that he tucked around her. He stared down at her for a moment and to her surprise he looked uncomfortable. Then she realized he was trying to say something to her.

"What do you think about flying your parents here for Thanksgiving?" he asked in a low voice. "Would you like that? Do you think they would like that?"

She sat straight up in bed, her mouth wide open in shock. Then she launched herself at Drake, squealing with excitement the entire way. She hit him square in the chest and knocked him over. He laughingly hugged her to him as she peppered his entire face with kisses.

"Is that a yes?" he asked between her kisses.

"Oh my God, yes! Yes, yes, yes! Oh, Drake, do you mean it?"

She stared down at him, silently pleading for him to have meant it.

"I would never tease you over something I know is that important to you," he reproached. "You miss them. I see how you light up when they call and also how sad you are when you speak of them. I have the means to bring them to visit you, and I wouldn't be much of a man if I didn't do everything in my power to make my woman happy."

"Oh, Drake. You're so wonderful to me," she said, on the verge of tears. "I can't thank you enough for this. You'll never know how much it means to me to be able to see them again. You've done so much for them already and now this."

She lost the battle to keep the tears at bay and they slid freely down her cheeks. Drake gently thumbed them away and then pulled her into his arms, cradling her against his chest.

"I want to meet the people who mean so much to you that you'd put your entire life on hold in order to support them. They must be pretty special to you. And as you are special to me, then I think your parents and I will have at least one thing in common."

She buried her face in his chest to stifle her sobs, but her shoulders shook, betraying her emotion. She curled her arms around his neck and hugged him tightly.

"You are the most wonderful man in the world, Drake Donovan," she choked out.

"No, I'm not," he said in a hard tone. "Never forget that, Angel. I'm not a good man at all. I'm selfish and possessive and I'll do whatever it takes to keep you happy so that you stay with me. That doesn't make me good. It makes me a self-serving bastard."

She smiled at him through her tears, utterly unfooled by his gruffness.

"Oh, I can't wait to tell them the news! Can we call them tonight after you get home?"

He smiled at her excitement and then kissed her before tucking her back into bed again.

"Enjoy your day shopping. I'll take you out to dinner tonight and we'll call your parents afterward if you like. I'll make arrangements for their transportation to the airport and have my plane fly them to the city. I'll have Silas and Maddox pick them up from the airport and I'll put them up in a hotel in Times Square. Unless you'd prefer they stay here with us?"

He looked questioningly down at her as he said the last, and she realized just what he was doing for her. He had no desire to have his privacy encroached on by two strangers, and yet he was going to great effort to give her and her parents a Thanksgiving holiday to remember.

"I think they'd love to experience Times Square," Evangeline replied casually. "We can always have them over for dinner and I can spend the day with them while you're at work."

There was a flicker of relief in his eyes, replaced quickly by warmth and approval. He kissed her one last time before heading to the shower.

"I'll have the arrangements made. No expense will be spared in ensuring their absolute comfort," he assured Evangeline.

Evangeline lay back on the pillow and closed her eyes, savoring the moment. Everything was so utterly perfect. Tears pricked her eyes again when she thought about seeing her parents for the first time in two long years.

They would absolutely love Drake. How could they not when he went to such great lengths to make their daughter happy?

She hugged herself and dozed, waking only when Drake leaned over to kiss her good-bye and to let her know that Maddox would arrive in half an hour.

She leaned up, the sheet falling to her waist as she hooked her arm around his neck and kissed him back.

"Ah, Angel, how you tempt me to stay home and let business go to hell," he said, sounding aggrieved.

"Thank you so much, Drake. This is the best gift anyone has ever given me," she said earnestly.

"You have until tonight to think of creative ways to express your gratitude," he said in a teasing tone.

Her eyes narrowed and she cracked an evil smile. "Oh, don't think I won't be very, very creative."

"I can't wait," he murmured, kissing her one last time. Then he patted her affectionately on the ass and said, "Better get out of bed so Maddox doesn't see what only I get to see."

"As if you have anything to worry about there," she said, rolling her eyes.

"You don't think every single man who works for me wouldn't give his right nut to see you naked?" he asked incredulously.

She groaned and buried her burning face in the pillow. "Oh God, Drake. Stop! I'll never be able to look them in the face now."

With a chuckle, he walked out of the bedroom, saying he'd see her later in the day.

Evangeline lay there only a few moments longer, savoring her excitement and the acknowledgment that she was in love with Drake. Looking back, she realized she'd fallen in love with him from the very first. It was why she'd been so devastated the night she'd left him.

Refusing to spend another moment reliving the most horrific night of her life, she slipped out of bed and took a quick shower. She dressed casually in jeans and an oversized sweater and quickly brushed out her hair to let it air-dry while she waited for Maddox to arrive.

She realized she was ravenous after spending the entire night making love to Drake. Hopefully Maddox and whoever else he brought with him on shopping duty wouldn't be in a huge hurry. Or maybe she could bribe them with breakfast.

Confident that she could win them over with a home-cooked breakfast, she began pulling out the ingredients and in just a few minutes was manning several skillets.

Fifteen minutes later, Edward buzzed to let her know Maddox was on his way up. A short time after, Maddox stuck his head into the kitchen.

"Oh my God, please tell me there's enough for me," Maddox said with a mock groan.

"Forget him," Justice said, walking by Maddox with a shove. "I love you more, so I should get fed."

Evangeline laughed and shook her head. "Sit down. All of you. Who else is here or is it just the two of you?"

"Jax and Hartley are downstairs keeping an eye on things," Maddox said.

"Do we have time to eat, then?" she asked anxiously.

"Sugar, if you made enough for us, you can take as long as you want to," Justice declared.

She grinned. "Give me five minutes and I'll serve it up."

Both men plopped onto stools at the bar with such eager looks that she had to laugh. She shook her head as she began dishing up the omelettes, hash browns and fried ham and bacon. After plating everything, she opened the oven to check on the homemade biscuits and decided they were just perfectly done.

She pulled them out of the oven and then dished up several biscuits onto plates for Justice and Maddox. She placed a plate in front of each and smiled at their reactions.

"I've died and gone to heaven," Maddox breathed.

Evangeline settled into a stool across from Maddox and picked at the food on her plate. It was the first time she'd seen Maddox since that night and she realized she had no idea if he'd gotten into trouble because she'd given him the slip at her girlfriends' apartment.

Suddenly she wasn't as hungry as she'd been just earlier, and she pushed her food around with her fork while she waited for the two men to finish.

"Evangeline, what's wrong?" Maddox asked quietly.

She jumped, startled by his perceptiveness. Then she glanced quickly at Justice, blushing at the thought of having to air this out in front of him. He surprised her, however, by picking up his empty plate and making his way to the sink. Then he sauntered back toward the living room, saying he'd wait for them there.

She glanced nervously in Maddox's direction, hoping he'd accept her muttered "nothing" as answer enough.

No such luck.

He frowned at her and then to her dismay he walked around to her side of the bar and took her hand.

"What's bothering you?" he asked bluntly.

He frowned again when he realized how hard she was shaking.

"I'm sorry," she blurted out. And then she hung her head, no longer able to hold his gaze.

"What the fuck for?"

She flinched at his explosive outburst and tried to pull away, but he gripped her hand tighter and then gently touched her cheek, forcing her to look once more at him.

"Evangeline? What in the hell do you have to be sorry for?"

There was genuine shock and dismay in both his tone and expression.

Her face was on fire and she could have stabbed herself for even bringing the matter up when apparently there had been no need.

She sucked in a deep breath and focused her stare at the area over his right shoulder.

"I'm sorry for sneaking out on you the way I did that . . . night," she whispered. "I hope you'll forgive me and I hope you didn't get into trouble because of what I did."

His mouth fell open in sheer astonishment, and then his gaze became stormy and black with rage. She shrank back but he pressed more firmly into her space and grasped both her shoulders in his hands.

"Look at me, Evangeline," he ordered fiercely. He waited until her gaze slowly swung back to him and then his eyes softened. "You have *nothing* to apologize for, for fuck's sake. Christ, tell me you haven't been avoiding me all this time because you were worried I was angry with you."

She shrugged. "I wasn't sure. I mean, I didn't know. It was horrible. I wish that night had never happened."

To her further dismay, tears slid down her cheeks, leaving a hot trail over her skin. Maddox moved his hands from her shoulders to cup her cheeks, using his thumbs to gently wipe the moisture away from her face.

"Listen to me, sweetheart. No one and I mean not a single one of us is angry with you. We were pissed as hell at Drake for what he did, even though we understand why he did it. But never once did we think any less of you. In no way did you deserve what happened that night, and no one knows that more than Drake. He was unbearable until he found you again and brought you back home. But, honey, listen to me. If he hadn't gone after you, if he hadn't decided to close ranks around you and make the threat known that if anyone tried to hurt you in any way, they'd be one dead motherfucker, then one of us would have. Do you understand that? We will never let anything happen to you."

She gave him a look of complete shock and bewilderment. "But, Maddox, you barely know me! I'm not worth ruining your relationship with Drake over."

"Bullshit," he said rudely. "You're everything to Drake but apart from that? You're important to us. You're important to me. I've never had a sister and I won't lie to you and say I view you solely as a little sister because I'm pretty sure my thoughts could never be considered brotherly and I doubt they're legal in most states between siblings. But if I ever had a little sister, I'd like to think she'd be just like you."

His face swam in and tears clouded her vision once more. Then she threw herself into his arms and hugged him tightly.

"Thank you," she whispered in a choked voice. "You have no idea how much that means to me. I've never had anyone but my parents and then my girlfriends here, and now . . . well, I don't even have them."

Her mouth turned down and her lips trembled as she said the last.

"You have us, Evangeline," Maddox said gently. "And I'm pretty sure Silas squared away whatever shit you have twisted up in that head of yours yesterday."

He was looking pointedly at her and she flushed again. "You know what he said to me?" she squeaked.

He chuckled. "Well, not in exact words. He didn't give us a play-by-play. That's just not Silas's style. He's not much on words. I believe his exact statement was, 'I'll let her know whatever fucked-up shit she has going on in her head is just that. Shit.'"

Evangeline groaned.

"He's right, babe," Maddox said pointedly. "You were thinking some fucked-up shit and that's not cool. So I want us to come to an agreement that whatever fucked-up shit you've been thinking ends now. You get me?"

She sighed. "Yeah, I get you."

He gave her an approving smile. "That's my girl. Now, you ready to go do some shopping?"

"Oh my God," she said in panic. "I have no idea what I'm supposed to get! Drake is taking me to some policemen's benefit at Carnegie Hall. He said he'd wear a black tuxedo and I could wear whatever, but I don't want to screw this up, Maddox."

She sent him a pleading look.

"He never goes to these things. He told me that himself. But now he not only wants to attend, he wants me to go with him. What if I embarrass him?"

"Whoa, honey," Maddox said. "First of all, you will never embarrass him. Drake doesn't give one fuck about what anyone thinks about him, and trust me, if anyone tried to say anything bad about you in his hearing, he'd take apart the asshole with his bare hands. Provided he could get to them before I did. Secondly, I happen to have excellent taste in women's clothing and know what looks good on a beautiful woman such as yourself. I won't let you buy anything that doesn't make you look like a million dollars. Deal?"

She hugged him again and squeezed him tightly. "You're the best, Maddox. I never had a brother but if I did, I'd want him to be just like you."

He kissed the top of her head and rubbed his hand lightly down her back. "You're killing my ego, babe. Just saying. You're supposed to say that if Drake ever fell out of the picture, you'd be all over me like white on rice."

She laughed and then punched him in the gut.

"Are we going shopping or are we standing around gabbing all morning?" Justice called from the living room.

"Guess that's our cue," Maddox grumbled. "Get a coat, babe, okay? It's chilly out today."

Evangeline hurried to the hall closet just next to the elevator doors and pulled one of the casual coats off the hanger. Justice took it from her and held it up so she could slide her arms into the sleeves when the intercom buzzed. She frowned and glanced at Maddox and Justice.

"Are you two expecting anyone else?" she asked.

"I take it you aren't expecting anyone, then?" Maddox asked, his stance immediately alert.

She shook her head and pushed the button to answer the call.

"Evangeline, you have visitors," Edward said over the intercom.

"Who is it?" Evangeline asked, casting a nervous glance in Maddox's direction.

"Their names are Lana, Nikki and Steph," Edward said, his tone growing uncomfortable. "They said they are friends of yours. Shall I send them up or tell them you aren't available at the moment?"

Her mouth fell open and she stared in shock at Maddox, a clear plea in her expression about what she should do.

Maddox's expression became one of fury. "They the bitches who used to be your friends?" he bit out.

Wordlessly she nodded. What were they doing here? Why had they come? Lana had made it quite evident that Steph wasn't the only one with reason to be unhappy with Evangeline.

"Do you want to see them, Evangeline?" Justice asked gently. "If you don't, say the word and Maddox and I will get rid of them. You won't have to see them. I swear."

She twisted her hands and then wrung them in agitation. "I don't know," she whispered.

"It's your call," Maddox said quietly. "Justice and I will be here the entire time. You won't have to face them alone. And at any time, we can get rid of them. You say the word and we'll make it happen."

Swallowing hard, she punched the button again and hesitated, looking once more at Maddox for reassurance. Then she said, "Send them up, Edward."

Maddox swore and then reached for Evangeline's hand. "I don't like seeing you so pale and afraid of these bitches, babe. You go sit down in the living room and get comfortable. Justice and I will let them in and have a little understanding with them."

"Don't frighten them," she said quietly.

"You mean like they're frightening you?" Justice said bluntly. "You don't owe them a goddamn thing after they shit on you the way they did."

She bit her bottom lip and turned unhappily toward the living room. She let Maddox help her into one of the chairs, and then he grasped her shoulders in his hands and looked her in the eye.

"They say one wrong word to you and their asses are out with instructions not to ever return."

She nodded and then clenched her hands together in her lap as she tried to compose herself for the confrontation ahead.

Maddox walked away and she waited tensely for the sound of the elevator. A few moments later she heard it arrive, and then she heard Justice and Maddox speaking in low tones but she couldn't make out what they were saying. Finally the wait became too much and she bolted out of her chair and turned toward the foyer, where she saw her friends standing looking with openmouthed astonishment at Justice and Maddox, who both wore black expressions.

"Evangeline?" Steph asked as she stepped forward.

The two women stared at one another for a long moment, and then Steph let out a cry and ran toward Evangeline. A second later Evangeline found herself in Steph's embrace as Steph noisily sobbed on Evangeline's shoulder.

"I'm so sorry, Vangie," Steph said over and over. "I was such a bitch to you. Please forgive me."

And then Lana and Nikki both pushed in, pulling Evangeline into a group hug. Evangeline stared at Justice and Maddox over their shoulders, her eyes huge with bewilderment.

She gave them what couldn't possibly be misconstrued as anything but a plea for help as her three friends continued to hug and cry all over her. Finally Maddox waded in and gently took Nikki's and Lana's arms while Justice collected Steph, and the two men herded the women into the living room to seat them.

"Not leaving you, babe, so don't get any ideas," Maddox said in a low voice as he passed Evangeline en route to the kitchen.

Justice stood in the middle of the living room, his arms folded over his broad chest, looking every bit the part of a surly bodyguard while Maddox acted the consummate host and poured drinks for everyone.

Then he sat down right next to Evangeline and directed his gaze to the women in the living room.

"Evangeline?" Lana whispered. "What happened with Drake? Are you still with him? Who are these men?"

"We work for Drake," Justice said. "And she is definitely still with Drake."

"Oh," Nikki said, her eyes wide. "We were just worried. He came looking for you the morning after the night you called and spoke to Lana. He was, um, well, he was pretty pissed at us. But we didn't know what happened. We still don't know and we wanted to come and apologize to you in person. We were horrible to you," she said, her voice hitching as another tear slid down her cheek.

"Can you forgive us, Vangie?" Steph implored. "I was the worst of all and I'm so sorry. You know I love you and I was just so worried that you were being taken advantage of."

"Funny, that's the same thing I'm concerned about," Maddox said in a steely voice.

Lana, Nikki and Steph sent shocked looks in Maddox's direction. Then Steph turned her gaze to Evangeline, her voice turning to a plea.

"You don't think we're trying to take advantage of you, Vangie. Please tell me you don't think that."

Evangeline shook her head in confusion. "I don't know what to think," she said honestly.

Maddox put his arm around her in support and squeezed her shoulder. She looked at him in appreciation, thanking him silently with her eyes.

"Why are you here now?" Evangeline asked in a hushed whisper. "Why not before? When I n-needed you."

Her voice broke and she went silent, refusing to break down into emotion. She could feel Maddox's anger vibrating his body, but she placed her hand on his leg to prevent him from tossing her friends from the apartment.

Lana lurched from her position on the couch and went to her knees in front of Evangeline. She curled her hands around Evangeline's and stared pleadingly into Evangeline's face.

"We love you, Vangie. We made a mistake. We were worried about you and hurt when you wouldn't listen to us, but that didn't give us the right to act as we did. You ask if we're taking advantage of you *now*. And the answer is no, but we did take you for granted *then*. That's our sin, honey. Can you forgive us for that? Can we ever be friends again?"

"Oh, Lana," Evangeline said, reaching to hug her friend. "Of course we can be friends. I still love you all so much and I've missed you terribly."

And then suddenly Nikki and Steph were crowding in as the four women noisily hugged and said their apologies. For the next hour, they chatted and caught up, with the girls filling Evangeline in on the goings-on at the bar where Evangeline had worked with them for so long.

Knowing she'd likely already strained the limits of Maddox's and Justice's patience, Evangeline excused herself by telling her friends that she was running late for an appointment and that they could come over another time.

Justice walked them down to the lobby while Maddox remained behind with Evangeline. As soon as they left, Evangeline sank back into her chair feeling like she'd been hit by a truck.

"You okay, babe?" Maddox asked gently. "That was a lot to throw at you all at once."

"Thank you for being here," she said gratefully. "I'm not sure how well I would have handled that if I'd been alone."

It made her sound pathetic and needy, not to mention helpless, but at the moment she was too grateful that she hadn't been by herself to care how it made her look.

"Promise me that you won't allow them here unless someone is with you," Maddox said in a hard tone.

Evangeline looked at him in question.

Maddox sighed. "You're too damn sweet and trusting, sweetheart. I find the timing of their visit a little suspicious. If they did any checking into Drake, and it's likely they did, then they'd know you landed a man with deep pockets. Hell, he already covered their rent, so who's to say they weren't sniffing around looking for another handout?"

"What?" Evangeline asked, utterly appalled at what he was suggesting. "You think they faked the whole thing?"

She was so aghast that Maddox looked remorseful for having suggested any such thing. But neither did he retract his statement, and that weighed heavily on her. Could he be right?

She covered her face with her hands and let out a soft moan of anguish.

"Hey, babe," Maddox said, his voice heavy with regret. "Don't put too much stock into anything I said. I'm a suspicious bastard. It's my job to be. Especially when it comes to people cozying up to you. They could be legit. All I'm saying is take it slow and be careful. Watch your back and as I said before, don't agree to see them unless one of us is with you, yeah?"

"Okay," she said shakily.

He reached down to take her hand and helped her to her feet. "Come on, let me get your coat for you again so we can be on our way. Drake wants you back in time for dinner tonight."

"You know, you aren't the hardass you make yourself out to be," she said teasingly.

He sent her a mock ferocious look and scowled in response. "You ever tell anyone else that, and I'll be the one spanking that pretty ass. Not Silas."

13

Drake arrived at his apartment shortly after five that afternoon and was met by Maddox when he entered the lobby. Drake homed in on Maddox's mood right away and tensed, searching his man's face for any sign of what was bothering him.

"Evangeline's had a tough day," Maddox said in a low voice.

"What the fuck happened?" Drake demanded, alarm splintering up his spine. "Why the hell am I only now finding out about it?"

"Her girls showed up here right as Justice and I were about to leave with her to go shopping. Justice and I stuck to her side and they came up crying and making a fuss and apologizing for being bitches."

Drake's gaze narrowed. "And you don't buy it."

Maddox shook his head. "No, I don't. I upset Evangeline when I suggested as much, but the point I was trying to make was that I didn't want her entertaining her girls without one of us around."

"How upset is she?" Drake asked.

"She seems to be okay now. Justice and I distracted her and we had a good time. When I left her in the apartment half an hour ago, she was going to go shower and get changed for dinner with you. She seemed to be relaxed and in good spirits, but when it all went down, it hit her like a freight train and it pretty well knocked her on her ass."

"Fuck," Drake swore. "She doesn't deserve this shit."

"On that we agree. Look, I'll keep an eye on her girls and see what they're up to. I called Silas a few minutes ago so he can put his ear to the ground. If they're up to something, Silas will find out. There isn't much that can be hidden from him."

Drake nodded. "I appreciate this, man. She's been hurt enough because of me as it is, and I'll be damned if she's going to be hurt by self-serving bitches who use her to get to me."

"Just make her happy," Maddox said bluntly.

"I'm certainly going to try," Drake returned in an even voice. "Good night and thanks for taking care of Evangeline today."

Maddox crooked a grin. "My pleasure. I got breakfast out of the deal. That was all the thanks I could ask for."

Maddox shot him a salute and then sauntered out of the building, leaving Drake to get the elevator up to his apartment. As he rode up, he swore at the knowledge that Evangeline had been upset by her former roommates. Maddox had warned him about bitches being the ones to cut Evangeline to ribbons, but he hadn't considered it would come from her own friends. He should have seen it a mile away and made damn sure it never became an issue. But he'd let the matter drop when it appeared they were out of the picture. His mistake and one he wouldn't be making again.

He entered the apartment, his gaze immediately searching for Evangeline. His blood immediately surged when he heard her call his name as she entered the living room. She was fastening a pair of the diamond earrings he'd given her and was wearing a sexy, feminine cocktail dress that just clipped the tops of her knees.

She hurried toward him barefooted, a welcoming smile on her face.

"I thought I heard the elevator," she said breathlessly. "I wasn't sure what time to expect you. I'm sorry I wasn't here to greet you properly."

He lifted one eyebrow. "Define *properly*. Because from where I'm standing, the view is pretty damn sweet. Have to tell you, baby. That dress? Is definitely coming off you as soon as we get back home later."

She shivered delicately against him as she wrapped her arms around him in welcome.

"Does it make me a terrible person to say that I'm suddenly very eager for dinner to be over with so we can get back home?" she asked breathlessly.

He smiled and captured her lips with his in a long, tender kiss. "Have I mentioned how much I adore terrible women?"

Her expression became troubled and she nibbled at her bottom lip. His eyes narrowed in question.

"What's wrong, Angel?" he asked sharply.

"I have something to tell you," she said in a low voice. "My friends Steph, Nikki and Lana all came over today. It was a shock. I had no idea they were coming."

He relaxed and hugged her to him and then guided her toward the couch in the living room. "Maddox told me what happened. Are you all right?"

She nodded slowly. "I'm fine. Now. At the time I was caught completely off guard and had no idea how to react."

"What does your gut tell you?" he asked, cupping her chin and looking her in the eyes.

She looked surprised by his question. Then she pondered it for a moment before letting out her breath. "I honestly don't know," she said truthfully. "I think it's too soon yet. I think I need more time before I make up my mind."

He nodded his approval. "Good girl. It doesn't make you a bad person to reserve judgment until you have more evidence. It makes you smart."

Her cheeks went rosy with her flush at his praise and he kissed the tip of her nose. "Give me ten minutes to change and I'll be ready to go if you are."

"I just need to get my shoes," she said in a breathless voice.

"Zander and Hartley will be accompanying us to and from the restaurant," he said as they walked toward the bedroom. "We'll eat alone, but they'll be seated a short distance away."

He said it in a casual tone but watched closely for her reaction. She frowned slightly, her forehead wrinkling with worry.

"Is there really that much of a threat to you?"

He stopped and pulled her to him. "I'm more concerned with there being a threat to *you*. It's why I insist on you being protected at all times and always having an escort when you leave our apartment."

She looked at a loss for words as she stared up at him. "Why would anyone threaten me?"

"Because I care a great deal about you and anyone with eyes can see that. I don't want to frighten you, Angel, and I damn sure don't want to give you any reason to not want to be with me, but I won't lie to you. You are in danger simply by being with me."

He lifted her hand and pressed her soft palm to his lips.

"I won't allow anyone to harm you. I protect what is mine and I treasure and value what is mine. You belong to me now, Angel. You are what is most important to me and what I cherish above all else."

She looked stunned by his declaration. A shimmer of tears reflected in her eyes as she stared at him in shock.

"Oh, Drake," she finally whispered. "I don't know what to say."

"Say that we're worth it. That the disruption to your normal routine and the irritation of always having someone shadowing your every move is worth the price of being with me."

She threw her arms around his neck and went up on tiptoe to try to reach his height. "Oh, Drake, don't you know? You're worth *everything*. There's nothing I wouldn't do to be with you. For as long as you want me. I'm yours."

Her sweetness pierced his soul and spread sunlight wherever she touched. Pieces of him that hadn't felt warmth in so long came to life under her touch and bloomed like a wildflower. He held her tightly to him, simply absorbing the feel of something so very precious in his arms and against his heart.

What would he do without her now? What had his barren existence been like before she'd barged into his life and turned everything on its head? God help him, but he couldn't bear the thought of ever losing her. If she were to ever be hurt because of him, he'd never rest until every last bastard paid for it with their blood.

He eased her down onto the bed until she was perched on the edge, and then he took the shoes she was holding and slipped them over her feet. Then he brushed another kiss over her lips as he straightened back to his full height.

"I'll be right back. Don't go anywhere."

He hurried to the closet and changed into one of his expensive evening suits. After sliding his feet into the Italian loafers arranged at the end of his closet, he returned to collect Evangeline.

"You ready, Angel?"

"Where are we eating? Or rather *what* are we eating tonight?" she asked as he escorted her to the elevator.

"Seafood," he replied. "It's an excellent restaurant in Midtown. One of my favorites. I have a standing reservation there and a table always available so we won't have to wait."

"I love shrimp," she said with a smile.

"That's because you are one," he said, chucking her chin with his knuckles.

When they reached the lobby, Zander and Hartley were waiting to escort them to the car. Both men slid into the front seat, with Hartley driving. Drake helped Evangeline into the backseat and then slid in next to her.

"Good evening, Zander. Hartley," Evangeline acknowledged sweetly.

"Evening, Evangeline," Zander returned. "You have a good day, sweetheart?"

She smiled. "Yeah. You?"

"It would have been better if we'd gotten the invite to breakfast," Hartley said dryly.

Evangeline blushed, but her eyes shone with pleasure. "How about I get y'all next time?"

"Deal." Zander pounced.

"One would think you never feed your men," Evangeline teased Drake as she settled back against his body.

He wrapped his arm around her, anchoring her against him, and settled in for the drive.

"They just know a good thing when they see it," Drake said. "And they're jealous as hell that I saw it first."

"That ain't no lie," Hartley said.

They zipped through traffic in record time and several minutes later, Hartley pulled up to the restaurant and Zander hopped out to open the door for Drake. He got out and then reached back for Evangeline and helped her from the car.

She'd taken all of two steps when the entire world around her exploded in a myriad of flashing lights. Drake let out a savage curse that was echoed by Zander. Evangeline stumbled, but both Zander and Drake were there surrounding her.

"Get the goddamn camera out of her face," Drake ordered. "Or I swear to God you'll be eating it."

There was the sound of a scuffle, but Drake urged Evangeline forward into the restaurant and off the sidewalk where they were exposed. The maître d' looked appalled and immediately escorted Drake and Evangeline back to a waiting table, apologizing profusely the entire way.

"What happened?" Evangeline asked in bewilderment when she finally eased down into her chair.

"Photographers," Drake spat.

"They bother you?" she asked in bewilderment.

He looked pained, but he nodded. "It will be worse now I've been seen with you."

She sent him a stricken look. "I'm so sorry, Drake. I don't want to be a problem for you."

He reached across the table and picked up her hand, lifting it to his mouth. "Hush. You are not a problem. This will be a pain in your ass, Angel. They're bloodsuckers and they're relentless. Once they get their teeth into a bone, they refuse to let go. They'll follow us everywhere."

"I don't care," she hissed. "They'll never make me regret being with you."

Fire smoldered in his eyes and he squeezed her hand, holding it between them on the table.

"They won't bother us here. Our table is private and we aren't seated where photographs can be taken through the windows."

"Then let's enjoy our evening and forget about those leeches," she said. "I can't wait to get home and call Mama and Daddy. Oh, Drake. They're going to be so excited that they get to come to the city for Thanksgiving."

"I'd say you're pretty excited yourself," Drake said indulgently.

"You are so good to me, Drake. I'll never forget all you've done for me."

A waiter appeared and Drake ordered for both of them, choosing a shrimp variety platter for Evangeline. After pouring wine for both of them, the waiter disappeared, once more leaving them to their privacy.

Evangeline shifted in her chair and looked questioningly at Drake.

"Do you think I did the wrong thing by letting my girlfriends up to our apartment? Maddox insisted that I never let them up if I'm alone."

"Evangeline, you don't have to ask my permission to invite someone up to our apartment," he said gently. "It's your home as well as mine. I hope it feels that way to you. I think you did just right by listening and taking what they said with a grain of salt, and I also agree with Maddox that you shouldn't allow anyone up unless I or some of my men are there with you. When it comes to you, I find it better to play it safe."

Evangeline sighed. "They probably think I'm an unforgiving bitch holding a grudge, and I've never been like that before."

"I think they will consider their own part in all of this and realize that you are leery of being hurt again. No one can blame you for not immediately accepting their apologies or their wishes to pick up where the four of you left off. I think you know that isn't possible now. Too much has changed, Angel."

"You're right, of course," she said with a sigh.

"I for one am not sorry," he said in an unrepentant voice. "Their loss is definitely my gain."

"Only you could make me feel like I did the right thing," she said with a grin. "Clearly I need to take more lessons from you. My girlfriends always despaired of me for being too nice and too forgiving. Somehow I don't think that's the case now that they are the recipient of me suddenly being an unforgiving mean girl."

"I like your mean girl," Drake said with a lazy, sexy grin. "Feel free to be as mean as you like later on tonight when I get that dress off you."

She arched one eyebrow at him. "I thought that was your job to keep me in line. You're slacking lately, Mr. Donovan. I'm beginning to think you have secret fantasies about me being a dominatrix and I have to tell you, that image is so not sexy."

He burst into laughter, his eyes gleaming with amusement.

"So I'm not doing my duties, huh. Is that what you're saying, my angel?"

She sat primly in her chair with her hands in her lap as she looked across at him. Then she leaned forward so her whispered words wouldn't carry farther than their table.

"You've been treating me like I'm made of glass. I won't break, Drake. I want your dominance. I need it. I can't even remember the last time you flogged me or spanked me. You've been exquisitely tender and don't think I don't appreciate your regard, but what I want most is for things to go back to the way they were before . . . that night. Or is that not what you want anymore?"

She was completely vulnerable in that moment, having bared her secrets and her desires to him. She caught her bottom lip with her teeth because she was trembling, afraid she'd gone too far and angered him with her criticism.

"My darling angel," Drake said in a tender tone. His eyes were warm with desire and approval. No sign of irritation was present, to her immense relief. "Have you been feeling neglected by me? Have I not been doing what I should to keep my angel happy?"

She flushed and ducked her head, mortified by his words. "Oh, Drake, no! That's not it at all."

"Baby, I was teasing you," Drake said, reaching over the table to touch her cheek. "Look at me, Evangeline."

There was authority in his voice and it sent a delicious shiver chasing down her spine. Chill bumps danced down her arms, prickling the flesh as he caressed her face.

"Never hold back from me your thoughts, your needs, your desires. You are right. I have been discreet with you lately. I'm sorry for that. I couldn't bear the thought of pushing you too hard or doing anything that made you uncomfortable with me. This is new territory for me, Angel. I've never overly concerned myself with what a woman thought of me. I've always been a take-it-or-leave-it kind of guy. But you, I care about. You, I don't want to lose. And I've already fucked up so much with you and I came so very close to losing you. As a result, I fear I've been too cautious with you and for that I apologize."

"You aren't going to lose me, Drake," she said softly.

This time it was she who reached across the table and pulled his hand into hers while his other hand remained at her cheek, caressing her softly.

"I want to be the woman you want and need me to be. I want your authority and your control. I never want to change who and what you are because then it wouldn't be real. I need *you*," she whispered. "However and whenever you want me. However you need me. I want to be the one who makes you happy. It's important to me."

She was pleading with him with her eyes, and his gaze softened as his hand lowered from her face. He gathered her hands in his and laced their fingers together.

"I once told you that you would never have to beg me for anything I can give you, Angel. That still stands true. Whatever you want, whatever you need, it's yours. I am yours," he said in a serious voice. "Do you understand that? Do you get that? Yes, you belong to me and I am a very possessive man, but I am also yours and, Angel, you are also a very possessive woman."

His eyes gleamed wickedly.

"I like it. I have to tell you it's a huge turn-on to have a woman so possessive of me," he said with a grin.

She blushed, her cheeks flooding with warmth, but she didn't look away from him in embarrassment. There was no censure in his voice or words. No admonishment.

"Okay, so I totally admit that I would kick a bitch's ass if she looked at you wrong," Evangeline muttered.

Drake chuckled, a grin flirting with his lips. "Then we're even, because I'll kick a man's ass if he looks at you for a second longer than necessary. Even if I can understand the urge to stare shamelessly at you. I may not blame the man for breathing and for having eyes in his head, but I can and will beat his ass for looking too long."

She snorted. "You are so full of it, Drake. I'll never understand what you see in me, but I'm not complaining."

He scowled at her and shook his head in disapproval. "Now that will get your ass spanked, Angel. You don't talk down about yourself. I'd never let anyone else get away with that shit, so I'm damn sure not allowing you to perpetuate a complete lie."

She looked at him, flustered, with no idea what to say, so she shut up and didn't say anything at all. But she felt a burst of warmth in her chest at the way he was so quick to call her out on talking down about herself.

He leaned over the table so that she would hear his next words. "You are the most beautiful woman I've ever known," he said in a husky voice. "Now if you think I make it a habit of saying that kind of shit to every woman I meet, you couldn't be more wrong."

She fidgeted in her chair. Would dinner ever get here? The sexual tension between them was so thick it could be cut with a knife. She was dying to get out of public view and back to their apartment and to Drake's promises.

His gaze swept over her face and he smiled, as though he knew exactly what she was thinking. The damn man probably did. He knew everything else.

Just then the waiter approached the table and Evangeline nearly wilted in relief. The food looked and smelled delicious, but she couldn't keep her eyes—or thoughts—off Drake.

"Eat, baby," Drake said with a smile. "I'll take care of all my angel's needs later. Promise."

She sighed and glanced down at her plate. It was going to be a long night.

14

The ride back to the apartment was mostly silent. Evangeline was snuggled into Drake's side, her head resting on his shoulder as she took in the twinkling lights of the city. It was a comfortable, companionable silence, not one borne of awkwardness.

She liked that they were so comfortable around one another and so at ease. Who would have thought all those weeks ago when she'd gone to Impulse to rub Eddie's nose in what he was supposedly missing that she would be where she was now.

Her mother had always said that life was full of surprises and that it wasn't meant to be predictable. She'd taught Evangeline from a young age to embrace each day as the gift it was because no one was ever guaranteed tomorrow.

She turned Drake's wrist toward her so she could see the time on his watch.

"Everything okay?" he murmured. "You have another pressing appointment to get to?"

His teasing made her grin saucily up at him.

"As a matter of fact, I have a hot date lined up with some hunk I met at Impulse. I told him I'd sneak out at midnight and meet him."

Drake smacked her on the ass with enough force that fire broke out on her skin and a soft moan escaped her lips.

"Maybe I should tie you to my bed for the night," he drawled.

"Mmm, maybe you should. After all, I can be a very bad girl, remember?"

"I think you're just asking for the crop or my belt."

"Well duh," she said, rolling her eyes. "I mean, what does a girl have to do in order to get punished these days? You're getting soft in your old age, Drake. If you aren't careful, you won't be able to keep up with me anymore and I'll have to put you out to pasture and retire you from stud services."

He choked on his laughter and then coughed, his body heaving against hers.

"Is that some kind of Southern-speak? Because I have no clue what you're talking about. Cheeky wench," he said without heat.

She laughed. "Putting someone out to pasture is a polite way of saying that person can't keep up any longer. In other words, you're getting to be an old man and I'll have to find someone else to satisfy my needs."

"I have a recommendation, should you ever want or need one," Zander drawled from the front seat.

She clapped her hand over her mouth in mortification and practically dove between Drake and the backseat in an effort to hide.

Drake's body shook against her. "Forget we weren't alone in the car, Angel? I'd say Zander just gave you back some of what you were dishing."

"Can I crawl in a hole and die now?" Evangeline said with a groan.

"That's what you get for being such a smartass," he said smugly. "And I'm very much looking forward to spanking that ass when we get home."

"I was checking the time on your watch because I was seeing if it was too late to call my parents when we get back home," she said anxiously. "They're an hour behind us, so they should still be up if you don't mind me calling them tonight."

He squeezed her to his side and pressed a kiss to her brow. "Of course I don't mind you calling them, baby. I know how excited you are to tell them the news. How about I sit in on the call with you, that is if you don't have any objections, and then afterward you can express your gratitude in very creative fashion."

He said the last with a wicked grin and an evil gleam in his eyes.

"I'll see how quickly I can get through the call," she murmured.

"No hurry," Drake said in a casual voice. "No hurry at all. We have all night, Angel. And I plan to make the most of every minute. I think it would be a good idea for you to stay home tomorrow and sleep in. I have the feeling you won't be up to much else after I'm done with you."

She stared at him through narrowed eyes, and there was a firm set to her lips.

"Don't make promises you can't keep, Mr. Badass. So far you're all talk and no action, so I'll expect you to back up all those words."

He lifted one eyebrow in her direction. "That sounds very much like the gauntlet has been thrown down."

She shrugged nonchalantly. "Just make sure you don't trip over it. I wonder what all those tabloid photographers would think of the great Drake Donovan if it got out that he wasn't satisfying his woman."

"I think you've created a monster, Drake," Hartley said in a dry voice.

Evangeline groaned again. "Shut up! Can you at least pretend not to hear what we're talking about? I'm not saying another word."

She glared toward the front seat, where Hartley and Zander were both laughing. When Drake joined in, she elbowed him firmly in the gut, causing him to grunt and gasp for breath.

"My angel is getting sassy on me," he said, his statement laced with approval. "I like it."

She continued to glare between him and the men in front, her lips pressed tightly together in silence.

Luckily for her, they arrived at the apartment a few minutes later, and she refused to meet either Zander's or Hartley's gaze when they opened the door for her and Drake.

"Don't be too rough with him tonight, sugar," Zander called just as Evangeline and Drake entered the building.

She slapped both hands over her ears, but the sounds of the men's laughter still filtered through.

When they got on the elevator, Drake waited a few floors and then punched the stop button, and the elevator stopped its ascent between two floors.

"Drake?" she asked carefully. "What are you doing?"

"We have a few minutes before we have to call your mom and dad," he said, his voice gruff with arousal. "I've been hard as a fucking rock all night. All you have to do is breathe and I get hard. Take your panties off."

Her eyes widened and she stared back at him in stupefaction.

"What were you just told to do?" he asked in a dangerously velvety voice.

She reached underneath the short skirt of her dress and slowly peeled the lacy scrap of underwear down her legs until it hit the floor between her feet.

"Now unzip my pants and pull my dick out of the fly."

Her hands shaking, she slowly unzipped his pants. His cock surged into her waiting hand, utterly rigid and straining.

"Pull your dress up around your waist and hold it there," Drake said, his eyes glittering with a hard edge.

As soon as she complied he reached down and hooked his arms underneath her ass and hoisted her up his body. He walked her back until her shoulders hit the wall of the elevator, and then he positioned his penis at her opening.

"Are you ready for me, Angel? Can you take me this way? We only have about two minutes before security opens the elevator after the alarm went off. Or we can finish and I can hit the button to resume," he said silkily.

Nothing on earth would make her drag this out so long that his security found them naked and in a rather awkward position regardless of whether she was ready. Excitement licked up her spine instead of the mortification she would have expected. The risk of being caught spurred her desire instead of squelching it.

"Yes," she hissed out. "Please. Take me hard, Drake."

In one brutal push, he was balls deep inside her and her gasps echoed through the elevator. God, he was so huge this way. She could feel him in every part of her deepest core, pulsing and throbbing.

"Wrap your legs around me and hold on," he growled.

She curled her legs around his waist and hooked her ankles together and then clutched at both his shoulders with her hands as he began slamming into her. Her head rolled back to rest against the wall and she closed her eyes as he continued to power back and forth into her damp heat.

"So damn beautiful," Drake said through clenched teeth. "Never seen anything so beautiful in my life."

"Then you must not ever look in the mirror," she said between gasps.

"I'm not going to last. How close are you, Angel?"

She was already fluttering wildly around him, clutching at his erection.

"Close," she managed to get out. "So close. Please. I need . . ."

And then he let go of his carefully cultivated control. He pumped into her with forceful, long thrusts, burying himself to the hilt over and over until the world blurred and the walls seemed to spin and rotate around her.

She let out a sharp cry just as the first flood of his release bathed the walls of her vagina. He buried his face in her neck and continued the powerful thrusting motions with his hips until finally he plunged deep and held himself there, unmoving as jet after jet of his come filled her.

Her chest was heaving with exertion and she was noisily sucking in mouthfuls of air as he stood there holding her against the wall, his cock wedged impossibly deep.

He reached out with one hand and hit the button for the elevator to resume and they rode the rest of the way in silence, still intimately connected, her legs tightly wrapped around his hips.

When the elevator door opened, Drake hoisted her up in his arms and slowly walked into the apartment, still holding her closely to him and keeping himself still linked to her.

"Wow," she mumbled.

He chuckled. "Good?"

"Uh-huh."

"Not very much to say right now, huh?"

"Nope."

He laughed again and carried her into the bathroom and set her on the counter next to the sink. He started a shower for them and then stripped them both out of their clothing before carrying her underneath the warm spray, where he proceeded to wash every inch of her hypersensitive body.

When he was finished rinsing them both, he pulled her out of the shower and wrapped a towel around her. He dropped a kiss on the top of her head. "Let's go call your parents and then, my angel, I'm going to reward my very bad girl."

15

Evangeline leaned back into Drake's arms after disconnecting the call to her parents and sighed in contentment.

"They seemed excited," Drake said indulgently.

"Oh, they are," she said. "*I'm* excited, Drake! I still can't believe you're going to so much trouble to bring them here for Thanksgiving. Thank you."

He smiled warmly at her. "It's such a small thing, Angel. How could I not do something that brings you so much happiness? And I admit, I'm looking forward to meeting them."

"They're both dying to meet you," Evangeline admitted. "I'll warn you now. They'll probably ask you a thousand questions. My dad will grill you as to your intentions toward his little girl, and my mother will be watching us both like a hawk."

Drake looked amused at her chagrin. "I think I can handle a little interrogation. Don't worry, Angel. Everything will be just fine."

She snuggled further into his embrace and nuzzled her face into his chest.

"So tell me. Just how bad have I been and what's my reward?" she asked innocently.

"It should be here anytime now."

She pushed herself off him and stared down into his eyes. "What will be here anytime?"

He smiled. "Your punishment. My reward. Your reward as well."

"What is it?" she demanded.

He captured one of her hands and brought it to his mouth, kissing her open palm.

"You remember Manuel?"

A warm buzz flooded her veins and she shivered without realizing it. She nodded, not trusting herself to speak at that exact moment.

"He will be paying us a visit tonight. I expect you to be a *very* good girl tonight and obey my commands without hesitation."

"I would never shame you in front of another man," she said quietly.

"I know that well, Angel. Now, go into the bedroom and prepare yourself. But hurry. He will be here shortly and I want you here, in the living room, on your knees, when he arrives."

She immediately got up and hurried to the bathroom to brush her teeth and her hair and to clean up. Mindful of Drake's instructions, she took only a few minutes and then hurried back to the living room to stand before Drake and await his command.

His eyes were full of approval as his gaze stroked over her naked body.

"Go and kneel on the carpet in the middle of the living room," he said in a husky voice. "Manuel is on his way up now."

Dutifully, she positioned herself where he'd directed and then slowly eased down to her knees so she faced the foyer and she would be the first thing Manuel saw when the doors opened.

She swallowed nervously, trying to recall as much as possible about that night. So much had been a pleasurable blur. She could barely recall Manuel's features. How he looked. She seemed to recall placing him around Drake's age. Perhaps a few years older.

He was a handsome man with midnight-black, short-cut hair with a tinge of salt and pepper. Just enough to give him a distinguished look. He'd been well spoken and very solicitous of Evangeline that night. But her focus had been solely on Drake and his pleasure.

Just what did Drake plan for tonight? Would he want to watch her being dominated by another man as he had before, or would he want to participate more this time?

The doors slid open and Manuel saw her immediately. Desire and approval flickered in his dark eyes as he stepped forward into the apartment. Drake rose from the couch to greet Manuel and the two men shook hands.

"Evangeline, you remember Manuel," Drake said.

"Yes," Evangeline said in a hushed, submissive tone. "I hope you've been doing well, sir."

"Such a sweet and respectful submissive you have, Drake," Manuel said, his gaze unapologetically devouring Evangeline. "I count myself among the most fortunate of men to be given such a gift."

"She is yours tonight," Drake said simply. "I will watch and even participate but you will direct her, not me. As was the case the first night, the only thing you may not do is kiss her lips. Everything else is fair game."

"What are her limits?" Manuel asked bluntly.

"She has none," Drake replied.

Manuel lifted one eyebrow in surprise.

"You will use your judgment and I trust you to know how far is too far and as I trust you, so too then will Evangeline trust you. She knows I would never let her come to harm."

Manuel turned his attention to Evangeline and her pulse accelerated. Her nostrils flared from the expulsion of air trapped in her chest.

"Tell me, Evangeline. How rough do you like it? How rough can you take it? I have no desire to hurt you. I want to make this as pleasurable for you as it is for me and Drake."

"I want whatever you choose to do to me," she said, meeting his gaze without hesitation. "I want it to be real. I don't like fake."

Drake's eyes glowed with pride and that gave her an infusion of confidence.

"You and I will get along quite well then," Manuel said with a smile. "I'm not into games either. But since this is only our second time together and this time I, not Drake, will be in control, I want you to come up with a safe word and use it if you need me to stop."

"I won't need you to stop," she said calmly. "Drake would know long before I ever did if you needed to stop. He won't allow you to go too far. I trust him completely."

"It's a very cherished gift indeed for a dominant for his submissive to have such faith in him. Drake is a very lucky man."

"It is I who is the lucky one," she whispered.

Drake walked forward and rested his palm against her cheek. "On that we will just have to agree to disagree, my angel. I am well aware of who is the fortunate one. But you are right. I will never let anyone take things too far with you and hurt you. But at the same time, if at any time, for any reason, you want Manuel to stop, then you say the words. You got me?"

"Yes," she whispered.

Drake turned back to Manuel. "She is yours," he said, gesturing toward where Evangeline knelt.

Manuel stood for a moment, staring, his hungry gaze roving possessively over Evangeline's nude body. She shivered in response, her nipples puckering into taut buds. Her vagina clenched and her clit throbbed, pulsing. She was excited. More excited than she'd been the first time Drake had invited Manuel over because now she knew the pleasures that awaited her. The first time, she'd been nervous and unsure, apprehensive and worried that Drake would be angry if she responded to another man. But he'd reveled in watching her response to a man he'd handpicked for her and when she'd seen that, recognized it, she'd relaxed and let go, immersing herself in the wickedly decadent ecstasy Manuel—and Drake—had given her.

And judging by the gleam in Manuel's eyes, that had only been the tip of the iceberg. She had a feeling that the first night had been a test of sorts, one that she'd passed, and that tonight there would be no holding back.

She couldn't wait.

Manuel unzipped his slacks and pulled out his huge erection, pumping it to further rigidity with his hand. Then he closed the distance between them until his cock bobbed deliciously before her lips.

"Suck my dick, Evangeline," he said, using coarse language that excited her. "I hope you're prepared because I'm going to deep-throat you. I'm going to fuck your throat until all you can taste, feel and smell is me. But first, I'm going to ask Drake to restrain you because I want you completely at my mercy so I can exert my will on you and there'll be nothing you can do about it except take what I give you."

She moaned softly, her body twitching and tingling as her desire heightened. Unconsciously, she arched forward, thrusting her breasts outward, her nipples so hard that it bordered on pain.

As Manuel stood there, slowly sliding his hand up and down his length, teasing her with what was to come, Drake roughly pulled her arms behind her and tied her wrists tightly together. Then to her shock, Drake thrust his hands into her hair, yanking her head back and then palming the sides with his hands, holding her firmly in place as Manuel planted his feet on either side of her thighs so that he was straddling her while she was in a kneeling position.

"Open," Manuel commanded tersely.

She obeyed instantly and he slowly slid the underside of his erection over her tongue, rubbing back and forth with a grunt of satisfaction.

"Hold her," he directed Drake in a rough voice.

It was all the warning she got before he plunged hard all the way to the back of her throat. Her gasp was cut off by his enormous girth, as was her breath. It took all her discipline not to choke and fight the invasion, but she forced herself to relax and lean into Drake's grasp, trusting him to take care of her.

Manuel paused and glanced down with a tender smile that told her that her nearly imperceptible move hadn't gone unnoticed. He sighed.

"This is one I would steal from you, my friend," he said to Drake. "Never before have I been tempted to take another man's woman, but I would take her away and never suffer an ounce of remorse. She is a priceless treasure."

"You're welcome to try," Drake said in an icy tone. "I would kill the man who ever tried to take her from me."

"As you should," Manuel said approvingly. "As would I." The last was said ruefully and he dropped his hand to caress Evangeline's cheek in a gentle, intimate manner as he thrust more slowly, gaining more depth with every stroke. "You have what every man like us dreams of. I hope to hell you know that and safeguard her appropriately."

Manuel's cock slid from her mouth, the head resting on her lips as he stared down at her, lust and something altogether different glittering in his eyes. Sadness?

Temporarily forgetting herself, and, well, she *was* impulsive by nature, she couldn't halt the question before it formed.

"Did you lose someone important to you, Manuel?" she asked in a soft, gentle tone. "Do you not have a woman to see to your needs?"

As soon as she asked, she flushed with mortification, every part of her body and expression displaying her dismay.

She stared at him utterly stricken. "I'm so sorry," she said, horrified. "Please forgive me, Manuel." She turned to Drake in panic. "Forgive me,

Drake. I overstepped. I shouldn't have said—asked—anything. It isn't my place to question you. It is my duty to see to your needs and to heed your orders, to be what you need. Not to pry into your personal affairs. *Please* forgive me," she repeated, her distress radiating like a beacon.

"Evangeline, look at me," Manuel said in a tender but firm voice. Said gently but an order nonetheless.

She looked up at him in dread, sorrow over failing him but most of all failing *Drake* crushing her chest.

"Don't look like that, my sweet, loving Evangeline," he said with a tender smile. "How could I possibly find fault with a woman who shines with such beauty and compassion. You have a giving heart, one that captures every single person around you. Yes, I lost someone and no, I don't have a permanent woman. I haven't wanted one. Not since . . ."

He trailed off, his expression somber.

"No one has spoken to the heart of me in a long time. Not until you. It is why I teased Drake by telling him that if he weren't such a good friend I'd spirit you away and suffer no guilt or remorse whatsoever. But your heart lies with him. Any fool can see that. You'd never be happy with any other man."

"No," she whispered. "Only Drake."

Drake's hands tightened in her hair, his body trembling against her back. He stroked his fingers through the long strands and then bent to kiss the top of her head.

Evangeline looked intently up at Manuel, never once breaking from his gaze. "I know your heart lies with another as does mine, but I would like it very much if I could be the woman to give you at least one night of peace. And pleasure. Take me, Manuel. It's all right to pretend. Do to me as you will. Do *with* me as you will. I won't break. I can take anything you give me. I want it and you need it. Let me give you solace tonight."

"I would never seek to break you, little one," Manuel said, affection and respect softening his gaze. "I want to give you pleasure, and for a moment I want to touch the sun again."

He slid his cock to the back of her throat as Drake held her head firmly in place, though it wasn't necessary. Even though this night was for her, at Drake's instigation, she sensed Manuel's desperate need of comfort. And she ached to chase the shadows from the big man's eyes.

Dutifully, she remained in place as Manuel stopped, lodged at full depth, and he remained there, head thrown back, harsh lines of pleasure carved into his sensual features.

"What would you say if we both took you, possessed you, over and over this night?" Manuel asked in a sexy, passion-laced voice. "Drake and I."

She shivered delicately, closing her eyes at the sudden, nearly violent wash of desire and edgy need that splintered through her body.

Manuel chuckled. "I'd say we have our answer, Drake."

"Indeed we do," Drake murmured, kissing her neck as his fingers tangled more deeply into her hair. "My angel can take a lot and I want to give her the world. Tonight is merely the icing on the cake."

She moaned softly, absorbing his loving words like an addict in desperate need of a fix.

Manuel withdrew and Evangeline turned ever so slightly so she could stare up at Drake. She knew she was disobeying. That she was to answer to Manuel. That her focus was to be on Manuel. But she simply couldn't deny the words hovering on her lips.

"Don't you know, Drake? You are my world," she said softly.

The fire in his eyes blazed into an inferno and he bent to crush his lips to hers, devouring her mouth, uncaring that another man's cock had just been inside it. Somehow that made it even more sexy and her clit pulsed, her nipples becoming more rigid.

"You have the spanking stool still?" Manuel asked Drake.

Drake gave a clipped nod and then walked away from Evangeline, and she felt the loss of his warmth keenly. Manuel cupped her chin, directing her gaze to him.

"I had thought to flog you tonight," he murmured. "To mark your beautiful skin. To take you beyond the limits of your control. To push you to your breaking point. But I find I haven't the stomach to do it. There are many more uses for a spanking stool, as you'll soon discover."

The gleam in his eyes promised her untold pleasure and chill bumps erupted over her flesh, dancing in waves over her body.

Drake returned a moment later, pushing an apparatus that resembled in some ways a saddle turned sideways on what looked like a sawhorse. But it was plush, not at all like the wooden, splintered sawhorses her father had used in his shop before he'd been injured. This was obviously an apparatus made for comfort. And kink.

The saddle indention meant to cradle a person's stomach was leather, thick and soft. There were metal hoops at the bottoms of the front and back legs of the apparatus, and she puzzled over what they could be used for.

Manuel was extremely solicitous of her as he helped her to her feet and unfastened the bonds around her wrists. He held her a moment until he was certain she was steady, but his arm remained around her, stroking, caressing, only heightening her pleasure. For men as rough and dominant as Manuel and Drake, they were exceedingly gentle with her, treating her like spun glass that would break if handled too harshly. It puzzled her because these were men who took unapologetically, who didn't ask. They simply possessed.

He cupped one full breast with one palm, rubbing his thumb over her nipple until she was nearly gasping at the exquisite sensation. But then he slid his other hand down her abdomen, lower, and plunged his fingers into her sensitive folds, stroking and petting her feminine flesh.

He circled her clit, rolling it between his fingers, careful not to exert too much pressure and hurt her. Then he slid his middle finger downward and plunged inside her opening, caressing the walls of her vagina.

She went up on tiptoe, her face a wreath of tortured pleasure. She was already so close to orgasm and he'd barely touched her! He slid deeper, pressing carefully against her G-spot, and she nearly came right then. Her legs trembled, her knees shook and buckled and if he hadn't caught her, she would have collapsed.

"Easy, little one," he said. "We have the entire night ahead of us. No need to rush, is there?"

He pulled both hands away and she groaned in dismay. He laughed softly and then guided her toward the spanking stool Drake had positioned in the middle of the living room. Where on earth did he keep this anyway? She'd never seen it. What else did he have hidden in his vast apartment that she didn't know about?

Drake's eyes were smoldering as his gaze raked over her naked body and Manuel's hands resting possessively on them. Approval, lust and desire were reflected in those dark orbs and it gave her a heady thrill. She felt confident. Sexy. Desirable even.

Her eyes met his and she smiled a mysterious sultry smile that promised the world, and it was a message he didn't miss.

He nodded to Manuel and then she found herself positioned belly down over the luxurious leather cutout of the bench. Manuel spread her legs while Drake took her arms and spread them. They tied her ankles and wrists to the mysterious loops she'd wondered about. Now she realized their purpose and her pulse accelerated with excitement because she was utterly helpless to take whatever they chose to do to her.

She couldn't wait.

Manuel rubbed lightly over her ass, petting and caressing, spreading the cheeks, allowing cooler air to blow over the now-exposed intimate areas.

"I want that pussy first," he purred. "Then I'm going to fuck that sweet ass. And while I'm fucking you—and, Evangeline? I'm going to fuck you hard—you're going to suck Drake's dick. You don't get to come until you get us both off. If you disobey my command, I'll forget all about my decision not to mark your beautiful skin and I'll make it so you can't sit for a week."

She sagged, her muscles turning to jelly. She closed her eyes at the provocative image and swallowed hard. She didn't want mercy. She wanted it all. Hard. Rough. She wanted the edgy pain that transformed to the most exquisite pleasure.

She stirred restlessly, soft sighs escaping her lips, impatient for them to begin.

A hand delved into her hair and at first she wasn't sure if it was Drake's or Manuel's but no, it was Manuel, pulling almost painfully so that she faced an enormous, very erect penis jutting toward her lips.

Drake.

She moaned softly and licked her lips in anticipation.

Drake's answering groan drowned hers out. "You're killing me, Angel."

"Open," Manuel ordered, his voice cracking like a whip.

All signs of the gentle, tender lover had disappeared, leaving in its place a fierce, dominant male, bristling with authority.

Obediently she parted her lips and Drake surged inside, filling her with his familiar taste. She licked, swirling her tongue around the head, along the length as he pushed deeper. Her cheeks puffed out to accommodate him and the hand in her hair tightened.

"That's it," Manuel rumbled. "Take it. Swallow him whole. Just as you're about to do me."

Again, there was no warning, no preamble or workup. He entered her in one brutal thrust and she emitted a cry around Drake's girth. God, it hurt. The delicious, decadent kind that no woman alive minded. She was impossibly stretched, not yet fully prepared for his entry, which made it all the more tight.

He withdrew and slammed back into her, causing her to whimper.

"Does it hurt, little one?" Manuel asked silkily.

"Mmmm."

Laughter rumbled from his chest, vibrating him against her ass as he stood pressed against her, wedged as far as he could go inside her.

"This is only the beginning," Manuel whispered close to her shoulder. "I'm going to hurt you a lot more, but I guarantee you'll love every minute."

Oh yes. She would. There was no doubt there. Pain mixed with the forbidden was a heady, euphoric sensation unlike anything she'd experienced in her life. Never would she have imagined enjoying the fine line between too much and not enough.

When he hammered into her again, she tensed, every muscle in her body coiling as her orgasm rushed her, threatening to explode before she even realized it.

Manuel ripped himself from her aching body and Drake plunged to the depths of her throat. Manuel brought his hand down over her ass in a sharp, stinging blow that yanked her from the hazy euphoria surrounding her.

"Do *not* come," he said harshly. "Or you'll be getting a hell of a lot more than my hand."

Desperately she sucked air in through her nose, battling to get breath around Drake's cock, which hadn't so much as budged. She began to struggle but Manuel rendered another stinging blow to her other cheek.

"Take it. You are not in control here. You are ours to do with as we want. Anything we want, Evangeline. Do you understand that?"

She nodded, or at least she tried. She closed her eyes and forced herself to relax. Forced herself to come down from her impending release, though her body tingled as though it had received an electric shock.

Then Drake began to fuck her mouth in long, ruthless strokes, using her mouth as he would her pussy. Deep, hard, Manuel's hand twisting in her hair and yanking back so she was powerless to escape Drake's punishing thrusts.

Then Manuel rubbed cool gel to the seam of her ass, pressing his thumb inward to lubricate the opening.

"Not too much," Manuel said, a smile in his voice. "I want you to feel it when I take that ass."

As if she wouldn't.

And as before, he gave her no time to prepare or adjust. He was on her, still holding tightly to her hair and spreading her with his other hand before jabbing into the tight, tender opening.

Her eyes flew open, wide with shock, knowing he'd barely gained entrance and yet it felt as though he'd shoved a baseball bat up her ass. Oh God. She'd never survive this.

"Take me," he said harshly. "All of me, Evangeline. Take me *now*."

He surged forward, ruthlessly opening her in one brutal thrust, lodging himself so deeply that his hips flattened the globes of her ass.

She was utterly filled. Drake in her mouth, her throat, and Manuel deep inside her ass. Trapped between two dominant, alpha males.

Heaven.

Remembering Manuel's directive that she didn't get to come until she'd gotten both men off, she went to work on Drake, lavishing him with her tongue, tightening the suction of her mouth until his hands gripped her head, holding her tightly as he fucked her in long, hard thrusts.

"That's a good girl," Manuel purred. "Your woman wants to come, Drake."

"Yes, she does indeed. And she's been a very, very good girl, so I say we give her what she wants," Drake said in a husky, silky tone that sent shivers cascading over her back.

Without further words, the men set a relentless pace, one that had

Evangeline gasping for breath, her senses reeling, the entire room blurring around her. Her orgasm bloomed, unfurling like the softest petals of a rose in summer, but she staved it off, focusing all her attention on giving Drake as much pleasure as he would soon give her.

Manuel swelled impossibly larger, his thrusts hard, frenzied, his hips slapping loudly against her behind. His hands gripped her hips, holding her so tightly she knew she'd wear the marks for days. And then with a shout, he ripped himself out of her, causing her to whimper at the sudden loss of the overwhelming fullness.

Drake also yanked from her mouth and then she felt the hot splatter of semen from two directions spurting onto her lower and upper back. It was the most sinfully naughty sensation she'd ever experienced. Who would have thought that she, who'd until recently had no sexual experience at all, would be having a decadent ménage à trois with two of the hottest men she'd ever met in her life?

And one of them belonged to her.

Her breath caught in her throat when she felt the blunt tip of . . . something . . . nudge her vaginal opening and then Manuel's fingers gently caressing and stroking her throbbing clitoris. Her eyes went wide with shock when the object slid inside her, thick and hard, and she realized it must be a vibrator or dildo or whatever the sexual toy was called.

"How do you want it, Evangeline? Soft and slow or fast and rough?" Manuel asked, stilling his motions.

It was hard to form a coherent thought much less put it into words.

"Soft and slow with your hand. Hard and rough with the . . ." she choked, unsure of what he was using exactly.

Manuel chuckled. "Dildo, Evangeline. You have a dildo stuffed into your sweet pussy. And your wish is my command."

He began stroking her softly and slowly as she'd requested but then he began thrusting fast and hard with the dildo, making her cry out as her body strained against the bonds securing her.

Drake knelt in front of her, his hands tangling in her hair, tilting her chin up to meet his kiss. His tongue swept in, tasting and ravaging her mouth. He swallowed her cries, inhaled her breaths and gave her his own. And when she came, she came screaming into his mouth, the sound muffled by his tongue and lips.

She was jittering and shaking like a live electrical wire when Manuel carefully pulled the dildo from her still-spasming vagina. The walls clutched greedily at it, not wanting to let go of the delicious sensation of being stuffed so full. But it was nothing compared to the real thing and she wanted Manuel's and Drake's cocks. Deep inside her. Coming inside her. Branding her, possessing her, owning her.

With Drake still kissing her and stroking his hands through her hair and caressing her face with gentle fingers, Manuel loosened the ropes and freed her. She sagged over the bench, too boneless to move. Lucky for her, she didn't have to.

Drake swept her into his arms and sat on the couch holding her on his lap while Manuel appeared with a drink, pressing it to Evangeline's lips.

"Drink," Manuel said gently. "You must be thirsty. We must take care of our lady tonight. Can't have her wearing out on us."

She smiled, peeking at him from underneath her lashes. "No chance of that happening."

She drank thirstily and Drake watched in fascination, in awe that the act of her drinking was sexy as fuck. Everything about her just did it for him. He knew he was in some deep shit, but for the first time in his life, he didn't give one damn.

Sometimes a man didn't mind being well and truly captured and trussed like a Thanksgiving turkey. What man had a woman like his angel? She sensed Manuel's desperation and his loneliness and she responded just as he would have expected her to. With compassion and such sweetness that one could get a toothache from it. The very best kind.

The night was young and he had in no way exhausted his own need of Evangeline. Some might say he was one fucked-up man to not only allow but to actively seek out another man to command and fuck his woman. He gave a mental shrug. He'd long since stopped making excuses or trying to come up with explanations for the dark needs and desires that drove him. Some things just were, and this was one of them.

His allowing another man to touch his woman, under his close watch, in no way diminished his fierce possessiveness when it came to Evangeline. If anything it made him more so because he knew how very lucky he was to find a woman who understood him. One who willingly gave in to his sexual kinks. Hell, reveled in them just as much as he did.

And he knew Manuel was in no way sated either. Nor would he be when the night was over, but that was all his friend would have. A night. Never a regular arrangement. Only at Drake's discretion and whim.

Both men had in common the desire to please and pleasure Evangeline. To bring her to orgasm over and over, to hear her soft moans of ecstasy, her cries of pleasure and the warm glow of contentment in her beautiful blue eyes, hazy with passion.

Drake exchanged glances with Manuel, and Manuel simply nodded. It was time. Manuel extended his hand to Evangeline and she slid her fingers over his palm to allow him to assist her up. His hands roamed over her body, cupping and caressing every curve and swell, paying special attention to her plump breasts, her ass, and then delving between her legs.

Evangeline's eyes went cloudy, her pupils dilating as passion flared in the dreamy orbs.

"Turn around," Manuel directed, freeing her from his hold.

Obediently, she did as she was told and then Manuel drew her back against his chest and began walking them backward to the couch. He sat but put a firm hand to her back, silently telling her to remain where she was. Drake tossed him the lubricant and Manuel applied a generous amount to his dick, pumping up and down until he was as erect as Drake already was.

But Evangeline did that to him. His own cock was straining upward, lying flat against his abdomen, pointing at his navel. He was about to burst from wanting to be inside her, and the knowledge that her ass would be stuffed full of Manuel's dick, thus making her impossibly tight, had pre-cum leaking from the tip of Drake's erection.

"Sit down on me," Manuel said, strain evident in his voice. "Back slowly down. I'll guide you. Reach behind you and spread your ass for me."

Her cheeks went pink, a flush working its way up her neck until her entire face was rosy. But again, she did as instructed, instilling fierce pride in Drake at how magnificent this woman was.

His woman. She belonged to him and only him, and the knowledge that he was making an overt claim, was openly acknowledging that fact, nearly brought him to his knees. He who'd never called anyone his. He who'd never had anyone, save his brothers. No one he cared about. No one who cared about *him*.

It was humbling and yet it sent adrenaline spiking through his veins. A stunning revelation and one he'd never imagined admitting to anyone. But his men knew he'd staked his claim—there was no doubt about that. Anyone with eyes and a modicum of common sense could see that Drake was firmly snared, and the hell of it was he didn't give a flying fuck who knew it.

When his brothers had broached the subject of him going public, of making a very public statement that this woman was his, cherished and protected and not to be fucked with, he'd been reluctant. Hesitant. And yes ... afraid. He who feared nothing and no one. Yet one fragile female scared the fuck out of him. Two months ago, he would have laughed in the face of anyone suggesting he'd be brought to his knees by a blond-haired, blue-eyed temptress. On the surface, he was the dominant, the one in control, but he knew the truth. He was anything but in control of his relationship with Evangeline, because he would move heaven and earth to make her happy, would do anything at all to keep her. He was, in effect, at her mercy.

He watched as Evangeline slowly followed Manuel's dictate and allowed him to grip her hips and pull her down to his lap. Her hands hesitantly slid over her luscious ass and then parted the globes, her breaths speeding up, the color still high in her cheeks as she battled her uncertainty.

Even though she was self-conscious and unsure of herself, she obeyed every command given. And she did it for him. Even as she went willingly with Manuel's firm pull, her eyes locked with his, never once looking away, as if she were telling him, *This is all for you. Only for you. Always for you.*

His chest tightened to the point of a physical ache and he almost betrayed his emotions by rubbing it to alleviate the slight discomfort. Then her eyes closed as Manuel began penetrating her, strain evident in the crease of her brow, her breath puffing in quiet, audible sounds.

"Open your eyes, Angel. Look at me. See only me."

She readily complied, and he lost himself in the smoky haze swirling in her eyes, the blue more brilliant, beckoning him to lose himself further.

He was already hopelessly lost with no possibility of ever finding his way out. He had no desire to.

She emitted a startled whimper when Manuel abruptly pulled her all the way down, seating himself to his fullest depth in her ass. Manuel leaned against the couch, throwing his head back, his fingers digging fiercely into Evangeline's hips. He stretched out his legs, spreading them, effectively spreading her wide as well so her pussy was open and exposed to Drake's view.

Manuel angled himself further down into the soft couch, sliding forward so Evangeline was perched on the very edge in perfect position for Drake. He remained still, Evangeline's opening stretched impossibly wide around his cock. It didn't look possible that she could even accommodate him. The position made her pussy entrance so much smaller, so small that Drake would have to work at getting inside her.

Just the thought of her silky tissues trying to ward off his invasion and how exquisitely snug she would be around him had him sweating and already on edge, moisture seeping from the crown of his dick. It wasn't possible that there could be a more incredible feeling in the world than her velvety walls wrapped around his cock, clutching and resisting as he persistently pushed his way in.

Hell, if he managed to get balls deep in her, he'd come in two seconds. He'd never last and he was known for his rigid control and discipline. But with Evangeline he had none. She made him frantic, irrational, with no control over his release whatsoever.

But damn if he wouldn't enjoy every single minute—or rather second—of being balls deep inside her with her milking every drop of his come. And this time, he wasn't pulling out. Neither was Manuel. They were going to fill her with their semen until it ran down her thighs, a visible stamp of their ownership and possession.

Evangeline didn't say a word. She was too disciplined and too determined to ever disappoint Drake by subverting his authority. But it was in her eyes as clearly as if she *had* made the request aloud.

Please.

As if he could deny her anything.

"Spread her wider," Drake directed Manuel.

Evangeline's eyes went wide and she automatically glanced down at her already splayed legs as if wondering how Manuel could spread her further.

Drake's eyes were riveted to her now wide-open pussy; the soft, puffy pink lips beckoned his touch. He wanted to touch her everywhere, taste her, but there was plenty of time for that later. Right now his dick was about to burst at the seams at the thought of that deliciously tight clasp just waiting for him to push in.

The silky flesh glistened with moisture, making it shiny and so very inviting. She was wet. Very wet. But even so, it was going to be a difficult task to get inside her. He was going to have to take it slow or risk tearing her, and the last thing he wanted to do was cause her pain.

There was pain that was pleasure and then there was pain. Never would he cause harm to her while satisfying his own selfish desires.

He moved in between her spread legs, grasping his thick erection with one hand. He rubbed the weeping head up and down her satiny opening to her clit and then back down again to tease her entrance.

She moaned desperately as her hips, though firmly in Manuel's grasp, bucked upward as if trying to sheathe him herself. Finally he lodged the tip of his dick in her tiny hole and pressed forward with steady pressure. Her eyes flew open, wide with shock, hazy with desire. She found his gaze and he felt it like a jolt to his senses.

Her eyes said it all. *Take me. I'm yours.*

Hell yes, she was his.

With a groan he pushed all the way in, sweating and swearing as her body resisted his advance, tightening around him as if to push him out. The war of wills was fierce. Him against her natural defenses. He would win. Of course he would win. He'd have it no other way.

His jaw clenched tight, he withdrew the barest of inches and then slammed into her, seating himself to the balls. There was a chorus of moans and sighs, a mixture of reactions from Evangeline, Manuel and himself as the three struggled against the wicked edge of heady pain mixed with the sweetest of pleasures.

As soon as he was all the way in, the walls of her vagina fluttered around him, clenching, going even wetter with her impending orgasm.

"Come, Angel," he murmured. "Come as many times as you want."

With a startled cry, her body erupted around him, spasming, going slick and clutching desperately at his dick. He had to grit his teeth to keep from coming himself. Manuel groaned and cursed, his hands moving restlessly at Evangeline's hips as he too fought for control.

Drake began fucking her hard. He moved with ruthless, powerful strokes, fucking her through one orgasm until he felt her stir and her body tighten as she began the fast climb to another.

"Jesus," Manuel muttered.

She was wild between them, bucking, moving mindlessly, her head twisting back and forth as ecstasy overtook her. She no longer had any control over her body. It was Drake's to command. Drake's to take care of. And take care of her he would.

He drove her through another orgasm and then Manuel could no longer hold up under the enormous strain and he began bucking his hips up, powering into her from behind while Drake slammed into her from the front. Manuel collapsed onto the couch, still holding Evangeline up to Drake like a pagan sacrifice. He nuzzled his lips against her neck, pulling her damp hair away from the tender flesh so he could lavish more attention on it.

But Drake wasn't finished.

"One more. Give me one more," he commanded. "Come for me, Angel."

"I can't," she gasped.

"Yes, you can."

Despite her denial, he felt the ripple of her tissues and he knew he wasn't going to last much longer. But he was determined to give her ultimate pleasure first. So he slowed, forgoing the brutal pace he'd set, and began sliding into her with long, leisurely thrusts. Fuck, she felt good. Sweat beaded his brow and his features were a mask of strain, delicious torment licking from his balls to the tip of his dick.

"Drake!" she cried out, her hands fluttering in a helpless gesture as though she didn't know what to do.

"Hold on to me, baby," he said huskily. "Let's go together. You and me. Come with me now."

Her fingers dug into his shoulders, holding on frantically as he pushed himself inside her until his balls pressed against her ass. Once. Twice. On the third thrust, he was bathed in the hot surge of her sweet release and it triggered his own. He began pumping harder, filling her with his seed until it spilled from her cunt.

He thrust one last time and then locked them together, holding himself still as his cock twitched and pulsed, expelling what seemed like a gallon of semen into her pussy. She sagged, utterly spent, against Manuel's chest, her eyelashes fluttering closed.

Transfixed by the sight, he kissed both her eyelids and then her nose and finally her mouth, resting against her as she lay sandwiched between the two of them. His chest rose and heaved, pressing her farther into Manuel, and no one spoke, unwilling to break the sensual fog that surrounded them.

"Wow," she mumbled, her words slurring, her eyes only able to open partway. "I think y'all killed me but I can't think of a better way to go. That was . . . amazing."

Manuel nipped at her neck and Drake kissed her delectable mouth.

"Glad you enjoyed it, Angel, but I assure you, the honor was all ours. You gave us something very precious tonight and don't think we don't know it, or that we'll forget it."

"Never," Manuel vowed in a somber voice. "You are a very special woman, Evangeline, and Drake is one lucky son of a bitch who better be glad he saw you and claimed you first or you'd be in my bed right now."

Evangeline smiled crookedly, looking intoxicated, drunk on passion. She never reacted to Manuel's statement, one that Drake knew to be absolutely sincere—Manuel wasn't a man who said shit he didn't mean—but instead she focused on Drake, her eyes warm and bright with love and affection. She reached out to cup his jaw, caressing his much rougher skin with baby-soft fingertips.

"Do I get a shower before we start all over again? I seem to recall a promise of having all night and by my math, we still have several hours left."

16

Evangeline paced the living room floor in agitation. Tonight was the benefit at Carnegie Hall and, other than knowing what she was going to wear, she had no idea how to pull off hair and makeup. Drake had warned her about the media and that photographers would be everywhere, and the last thing she wanted was to embarrass Drake by looking like the gauche girl-just-off-the-farm that she was.

She picked up her cell phone and plucked up the courage to punch Silas's contact. She nearly hung up the minute the call connected but she forced herself to put the phone to her ear and wait for him to answer.

"Evangeline?" he said on the second ring. "Everything okay?"

"Yes. No. I mean nothing's wrong. It's just . . ." She broke off with a sigh and sank onto the couch.

"Are you at the apartment?" he asked.

"Yeah," she said lamely.

"I'm only five minutes away. I'll be right there."

The call ended and the line went silent. Alrighty then. And that was the law according to Silas. He was going to think she was a flaming moron when he realized why she'd called him. She let out a groan of dismay and flopped back on the couch.

And that was where Silas found her exactly four minutes later when he strode into the apartment.

"What's wrong?" he asked sharply, plopping down on the couch beside her.

"You're going to think I'm an idiot," she mumbled.

He stared expectantly at her, obviously waiting for her to expound.

She sighed again and sat up. "Tonight is the benefit Drake's taking me to at Carnegie Hall."

"Yeah, and?"

"I have a dress and shoes. But I need help with hair and makeup. I don't want to embarrass Drake and make a fool out of myself," she said, growing more distressed by the minute. "He said there would be photographers and cameras everywhere. Oh God, Silas. What am I supposed to do? I don't belong at things like that. I should have never agreed to go."

Silas's lips grew thin. "Bullshit. You'll be the most beautiful woman there. I guarantee it."

"I don't suppose you're my fairy godmother and have a magic wand hidden on you somewhere," she said glumly.

His lips twitched and then curved upward into an honest-to-goodness smile. She was so startled that all she could do was stare in utter fascination. Silas was always so serious and somber. He so *rarely* smiled that she was completely transfixed each time he did.

"I may not have a magic wand, but I'm not without my resources," he said with an arrogant twist to his lips that unseated his smile. "How quickly can you be ready to go?"

At that she blinked. "Ready to go where?"

"I'm taking you to get your hair and makeup done. Then I'll run you back by here so you can get dressed and be ready when Drake gets home from work."

"You know someone who'll do my hair and makeup?" she asked suspiciously.

160

"What can I say, I'm a jack-of-all-trades. Now get your ass up and get dressed so we can get out of here. I'll call ahead so they can get you right in."

Four hours later, she and Silas arrived back at the apartment. Evangeline was completely glammed out and unrecognizable, thanks to an amazing makeup artist who owned an exclusive salon where appointments had to be booked weeks in advance. Silas, however, obviously had some serious pull, because the artist who'd done her hair and makeup had canceled all her afternoon appointments in order to accommodate Silas's request to fit Evangeline in.

She stopped to study her reflection in the mirror in the foyer as they got off the elevator and she frowned.

"This isn't me," she fretted. "I look like some high-class call girl."

Silas frowned and pinned her with his steely stare. "Swear to God, Evangeline. You get one more pass from me and then I will turn you over my knee and spank your ass. You look beautiful. Now go change into your dress and shoes and come out and let me see the finished product. You've got five minutes, so get moving."

She launched herself into his arms and hugged him tightly. He staggered back, bewilderment shining in his eyes.

"Thank you," she whispered. "You're the best, Silas. I don't know what I'd do without you. You're the absolute best friend I've ever had."

His arms tentatively went around her and he squeezed her back, though he was obviously discomfited by her spontaneous outburst of affection.

"You're very welcome, Evangeline," he said warmly. "Now go get changed so I can check you out."

She ran for the bedroom and pulled the dress from the closet, carefully unzipping it from the garment bag. Being careful not to mess up her hair or get makeup all over the dress, she pulled it on and then realized she wasn't going to be able to zip it herself.

Holding the bodice over her chest, she toed out the shoes and slipped them over her feet, admiring the sparkle from heel to toe. She examined herself in the mirror and realized that when it all came together, she didn't look half bad. The makeup artist had asked her what color her dress and shoes were and had then used bronze hues and tones so her skin had a golden glow.

The dress was a darker, shimmery gold that picked up the blond highlights in her upswept hair. Small ringlets dangled down her neck and framed her face. Remembering the huge pair of diamond earrings Drake had bought for her, she dug them out of her jewelry box and then scrounged for the diamond teardrop necklace that was bigger than her thumb.

She fastened the earrings and then looped the necklace over her head so it dangled down her bodice. She glanced at her bare wrist and then shrugged. Why not? It wasn't as though she had a lot of opportunity to wear the expensive jewelry Drake showered her with. If tonight wasn't such a night, she didn't know what was.

She was a reflection on Drake and she wanted to make him proud. If it was true that he'd never attended any public function with a woman on his arm, well, that made tonight that much more epic in her book. She fastened the diamond bracelet around her wrist, satisfied with the end result.

Heels tapping on the marble floor, she hurried into the living room, still holding her dress up with one hand.

"I need help," she said breathlessly. "Can you zip me up?"

"This has got to qualify me for sainthood," Silas muttered. "A man can only take so much, for fuck's sake."

She looked at him in puzzlement. He rolled his eyes and turned her so he could zip her dress.

"Are you really so clueless as to your effect on the male population?"

She blushed to the roots of her hair. "I'm sorry," she mumbled. "I didn't think."

"I'm just teasing you, Evangeline," he said gently. "I'm glad you feel comfortable enough with me to A, call me because you had no one to do your hair and makeup, and B, ask me to zip up your dress. Having been around you long enough to know that you're pretty picky about the people you trust, I'm honored that I can be one of them."

He turned her back around and then took several steps back so he could survey her from head to toe.

"Turn around slowly and give me the full view," he encouraged.

She twirled slowly and laughed when the dress sparkled and glittered in the light.

"I really do feel like Cinderella now," she said with a wide grin.

"What you are is special, Evangeline," he said sincerely. "And very beautiful. I'm glad I'll be going with you and Drake tonight. I'm going to be a smug bastard muttering 'I told you so' the entire night watching grown men make asses of themselves in front of you."

"Oh, that's right!" Evangeline exclaimed. "I had forgotten you're going. I'm so glad. That makes me feel so much better now that you'll be there."

She hugged him again and he carefully held her away from him by her shoulders so she didn't mess up her hair and makeup. Then to her surprise, he lowered his head and kissed her on the cheek.

"I've got to go now so I can change and get back in time to accompany you and Drake to the benefit. Do not allow anyone up unless it's Drake or one of us. Got me?"

"Yes, oh lord and master," Evangeline drawled.

His dark gaze smoldered. "If you were in my bed, you'd know I was exactly that and you wouldn't joke about who was your master."

Butterflies scuttled around in her belly, but she refused to let him shake her.

"Out," she ordered. "You're just trying to rattle me. I have quite enough lord and master to deal with already, thank you very much."

Silas winked and then sauntered to the elevator. "See you in a few, doll. Don't mess up my work of art."

Evangeline went in search of her phone, hoping Drake had texted to let her know when he'd be home. When she didn't find a notification, she nibbled at her lip and briefly pondered whether to text him or not.

They'd never had an actual discussion about her texting or calling him when he was at work. She just took it on herself never to do so because she didn't want to be a distraction or bother. But couples texted one another all the time. In the beginning she had reason to doubt her place in Drake's life, but he'd made it clear ever since their reconciliation that he had no intention of her going anywhere.

"Quit being a chicken," she muttered.

She could have asked Silas whether it was a good idea for her to text Drake at work, but she hadn't thought of it until after he'd left. Shaking her head at her cowardice, she typed in a quick text and hit send before she could change her mind.

Hi. Hope you had a good day at work. Just wondering what time you'll be home. I'll be ready and waiting. xoxo –Evangeline

Her face grew hot. She felt like a complete idiot. What was with the *xoxo*? Jesus, what was she, in high school?

Her phone pinged and she hurriedly punched in her code so she could read the return message.

Will be home in fifteen minutes. Day was good. Will be better when I get home to my angel. xoxo back at you. –D

A million tiny flutters assaulted her chest and she felt her lips split wide open as a huge smile attacked her face. Who knew a text message could be so sweet? She read it twice more, savoring each word. Lord, but she was in so deep she had no hope of ever finding her way out. For that matter she had no desire to.

She squeezed herself and then danced across the living room floor in her sparkly princess heels. It was going to be a perfect night. She loved Christmas and the holidays. Loved Christmas music and decorations and lights. A night at Carnegie Hall with a kickoff to the holiday season was about as awesome as it could get. But being there on Drake's arm? To boldly go where no woman had ever gone before?

A giggle escaped her at the insane direction of her thoughts. Then she let out a dreamy sigh. Drake in a tux, her on his arm for the world to see.

Absolute perfection.

17

Drake squeezed Evangeline's hand as the car came to a stop behind several others waiting to drop off passengers on the red-carpet entrance to Carnegie Hall.

"You look stunning, baby," he said in a warm voice.

Her gaze was riveted to the mass of people at the entrance and at all the news cameras and photographers. Flashbulbs were cascading in waves as people got out of their vehicles. Oh God. Drake had warned her, yes, but she hadn't expected this. Like they were freaking celebrities or something.

"Breathe, Angel," Drake whispered. "Maddox, Silas and I are all with you. We won't let anything happen. I promise."

She swallowed the knot in her throat but it promptly got lodged when their car moved ahead and was next to disembark. The door swung open and Drake got out, shielding the inside of the car with his big body. Immediately, Maddox and Silas both pressed in on either side of him as he reached inside for Evangeline's hand.

He pulled her to stand next to him in the chilly night air and she shivered, dazzled and dazed by the flood of bright lights and the flash of cameras going off in forty different directions.

She flinched when people began shouting questions at Drake. Maddox caught Evangeline's other hand in his and squeezed reassuringly as he pinned her securely between himself and Drake with Silas directly in front of her. They formed an impenetrable barrier to anyone seeking access, thank God.

"Smile," Maddox said next to her ear. "You look terrified. Flash them a gorgeous smile and show them those beautiful baby-blue eyes."

She felt like a robot programmed to carry out voice commands. She smiled so big, it felt as though her cheeks were cracking. She forced herself to relax and look as though she were having the time of her life and hadn't a care in the world. She even made herself look directly into some of the cameras and flash a toothy smile.

After they'd run the gauntlet and Drake had waved off requests for interviews, he pulled her inside the building and she promptly sagged.

"That's insane!" she whispered.

"Come, let's go find our seats. The sooner we're seated, the faster we're out of the line of fire," Drake said.

"You all right, doll?" Silas asked quietly when they took their seats in a private box above the stage. "You need to go freshen up before the show starts? Maddox and I can walk you to the ladies' room."

Grateful for a chance to compose herself and check her makeup to ensure it wasn't smeared everywhere, she nodded and rose. Drake caught her hand and lifted it to his mouth, pressing a gentle kiss to her palm.

"Hurry back, Angel."

She gifted him with a radiant smile and then took Silas's proffered arm and let him guide her out of the box and down the hall to the powder room.

"We'll wait out here," Maddox said. "Don't take too long. No one will come in after you, but there could be someone already inside. Do your thing, quick in and out, okay?"

"Got it," she said, flashing him a grateful smile.

She pushed inside the bathroom and went to the mirror to check her makeup. She used a tissue to dab at the corners of her eyes and then reapplied her lip gloss. She heard a toilet flush and, heeding Maddox's advice to be in and out quickly, she turned and started for the door, when a tall, elegantly dressed brunette stepped in front of her on her way to the mirror.

"Excuse me," Evangeline murmured as she stepped around the other woman.

"Oh, you must be Drake's latest fling," the woman said, humor laced in her words.

Evangeline reared back at the woman's rudeness. "Pardon me?"

The brunette smiled. "Do enjoy it while it lasts, sweetie. And believe me, it won't last long. Drake never keeps the same woman more than a few weeks. But the perks are amazing. And between you and me. If he ever invites Manuel over? Be prepared for a *very* good time," she purred.

Her words fell on Evangeline like well-aimed daggers. Nausea swirled in her stomach until she was afraid of losing its contents, but pride was too ingrained in Evangeline to go down like that. She gathered herself together and managed to calmly stare the other woman down. "I have no idea what you're talking about. Who is Manuel?"

The other woman's tinkly laughter was abrasive and annoying. "Oh, he's a friend of Drake's. They share the same kinks, if you will. And as luck would have it, they share their women on occasion as well."

Evangeline fought against the cold sweat that was fast breaking out on her forehead. Oh hell no, she wasn't letting this woman take her down like this. She fixed the woman with a contemptuous and pitying look.

"You don't know Drake very well at all, do you?" Evangeline said scornfully.

"Well enough," the woman defended with a laugh.

"No," Evangeline snapped. "You don't. Because if you did, then you'd know that Drake is an extremely possessive man and he never shares what he considers his. So if he shared you, then I guess that speaks to what he didn't consider you. And if you do know Drake as well as you say, then you'd also know the significance of my being on his arm tonight when you should know perfectly well that he never takes a woman out with him anywhere. Now if you'll excuse me, Drake's men are outside waiting for me. But I doubt you ever met them either, did you?"

The woman's pale, shocked face was the last thing Evangeline saw on her way out the door. She should be doing a fist pump for scoring a strike against the catty bitch trying to take her down a few notches. But all she wanted to do was weep.

Silas and Maddox immediately zeroed in on Evangeline's distress and demanded to know what was wrong.

"Nothing," she said sharply. "Let's just get back, please."

She stalked ahead, leaving them to fall in behind her or be left behind. They escorted her back into the box and she slid into the seat next to Drake, her heart pounding. She saw Drake look curiously at her from her periphery and then glance sharply at Maddox and Silas.

Thankfully the lights dimmed and applause rang out as the concert began. Once the music started, Evangeline was able to put the unpleasant bathroom encounter behind her. At least temporarily. The symphony was pure magic and she adored every note.

Drake sat watching Evangeline absorb the music with a look of enchantment on her beautiful face. He glanced back at Silas and Maddox, who sat just behind him and Evangeline, and arched an eyebrow in question. Something had upset Evangeline and he wanted to know who the fuck was responsible.

Silas picked up his phone and motioned that he was texting Drake. A few seconds later, his phone on silent, Drake glanced at his phone and had to bite his lip to keep from uttering savage curses. Son of a bitch.

Remember the crazy bitch you hooked up with about a year
ago? Tall brunette named Lisa? She was in the bathroom with
Evangeline and when Evangeline came out she was pale and
shaken. I'm sure Lisa filled her head full of all kinds of shit.

Drake's jaw was clenched so tight with fury that his teeth ached.
Jesus Christ. He tried to think back on just how much time he'd spent
with Lisa. It hadn't been much. Hell, he couldn't even remember what
they'd done together. But that didn't mean she hadn't filled Evangeline
full of poison and ruined her entire night in the process.

Goddamn it.

When the lights came back up as the music ended, the chairman of
the board for the two charities money was being raised for tonight came
out on stage to give his prepared speech engineered to solicit as many
donations as possible. But Drake had had enough and he wasn't going to
torture Evangeline a moment longer than necessary.

"Get the car," he said back to Maddox. "We're leaving now."

Evangeline turned, having heard Drake's command. "Is it over?" she
whispered.

"The good part is," he said. "The rest is just speeches and soliciting
donations. As I've already given one in your name as well as my founda-
tion, it isn't necessary for us to remain."

She nodded stiffly and then turned her attention back to the stage. A
few moments later, Silas tapped Drake on the shoulder to indicate that
Maddox was waiting out front. Drake reached for Evangeline's arm and
then slid his fingers down to tangle with hers. He pulled her up next to
him and then wrapped his arm tightly around her waist and guided her
out of the box.

Silas's expression was black but most notably, worry was evident in
his eyes as he studied Evangeline's somber countenance. As soon as they

stepped outside, Silas immediately stepped directly in front of Evangeline, blocking her from the photographers and news cameras. Someone shouted at her, calling her Drake's latest skirt, and she flinched, mortification brimming in her expressive eyes.

Silas snarled and decked the guy who'd shouted the insult and bodies went flying. Drake picked Evangeline up and dove into the car, sending both their bodies sprawling across the backseat. As soon as Silas jumped into the front, Maddox roared off.

"What the fuck happened back there?" Maddox demanded.

"Dick mouthing off to Evangeline," Silas growled. "Better give your lawyer a call in the morning, Drake. Son of a bitch had it coming to him, but it doesn't mean he won't scream like a little bitch and try to sue."

"If he does, me and the boys will pay him a little visit," Maddox said grimly.

"That's enough," Drake ordered.

Evangeline was already freaked out enough. The last thing she needed was to be privy to the seedier side of Drake's world.

He picked her up and cradled her in his arms, holding her against his chest as he stroked one hand up and down her arm soothingly. He kissed her hair and left his lips there a long moment.

"You okay, Angel?" he murmured.

She nodded stiffly, and he cursed under his breath. Whatever the crazy bitch said to her in the bathroom must have really done a number on her.

"Take us home and drop us off," Drake said tersely.

Silas turned slightly in his seat and focused his gaze on Evangeline. "You all right, doll?" he asked gently.

It was like a fist to Drake's gut when tears filled Evangeline's eyes. She turned quickly away but not before he and Silas both saw her distress. Drake pulled her more firmly into his arms and tucked her head beneath his chin as they rode the rest of the way in silence.

When they arrived at his apartment building, Silas got out and opened the door to help Evangeline. Drake emerged behind her and slipped his arm around her shoulders.

"Thank you for everything, Silas," she said in a quiet voice. "At least I looked the part tonight, thanks to you."

Silas reached out and cupped her chin in his palm. "You are every bit the part, Evangeline. You have more class in your little finger than that skank in the bathroom will ever dream of having."

She flushed red and moved her head away from Silas's grasp. "Good night, Maddox," she called back as she started toward the entrance.

Drake quickly caught up to her and once more took her hand as they got on the elevator. Once inside, Drake pulled her into a hug and rested his chin atop her head.

"What happened tonight, Angel?"

She tensed against him and burrowed her face into his chest. He allowed her to dodge the question for the elevator ride. They would talk about it once they were inside the apartment, and hopefully he would be able to undo whatever damage had been done.

When the elevator opened, Evangeline tried to break away from Drake's hold and walk into the apartment, but Drake held tight to her hand and led her into the living room, where he gently pushed her down to sit on the couch before taking the seat next to her, angling so they faced each other.

"What did the bitch in the bathroom say to you, Evangeline?"

He knew he sounded harsh, but he wasn't about to let Evangeline worm her way out of telling him what the conniving little bitch had done.

Evangeline looked mortified and refused to meet his gaze. He was having none of that either. He put a finger to the side of her cheek and directed her gaze forward until finally she was looking at him.

He sighed. "Angel, you know there were women before you," he said gently. "I've never claimed to be a saint, but I can tell you that there have been no other women since I met you. I haven't even looked at another woman. How could I? You're the only woman I want."

And astonishingly it was true. From the moment Evangeline had barreled into his life, other women had simply ceased to exist for him.

Evangeline averted her eyes, looking down where she was twisting her fingers together in agitation. "It wasn't that," she said softly.

"Then what was it?"

"It was what she said," Evangeline choked out. "She said . . ." She closed her eyes and he was alarmed to see a hint of tears just before she'd slammed her eyelids shut.

In that moment Drake wanted to track down the damn woman and verbally cut her to ribbons just as she'd apparently done to Evangeline. Whatever she'd said had gotten into his angel's head. Had made her doubt herself and had dealt a blow to her self-confidence. Fuck that.

"She told me to enjoy it while it lasted. That you never kept a woman for long."

When Drake would have spoken, she cut him off with a wave of her hand.

"It wasn't that. I mean I may be sweet, naïve and too trusting, as I'm reminded at every turn, but I know a jealous, catty woman when I see— and hear—one."

Bitterness tinged her words and Drake was reminded of the Evangeline he'd met that first night in the club. The Evangeline unsure of her place in the world. Unsure of her own self-worth. He wanted to put his fist through the wall.

"She knew about Manuel," Evangeline said painfully. "She asked me if you'd invited Manuel over and went on about what a good time it was and how the two of you knew how to treat a woman. And for once I had a cutting remark. For once I stood up for myself and I put her in her place."

Drake's brows drew together in confusion. "Then what . . . ?"

Tears shimmered in Evangeline's eyes, brighter now, threatening to spill over.

"I'm not proud of what I said, but I won't lie and say that at the time it didn't feel a little bit good because for once I wasn't a doormat and a victim. But . . ."

"But what?" he prompted gently.

"Oh God," she whispered. "It was a lie. All of it was a lie and it hurts."

Drake was becoming more frustrated by the moment. "What was a lie?"

"I told her that evidently she didn't know you as well as she thought she did because you would never share anything you considered yours, and the fact that you *had* shared her should tell her what you didn't consider her. Then I told her that knowing what she knows about you, she should also realize that you never appear in public with a woman on your arm and that I was on your arm at a very public event so what does that tell her?"

"Good for you, baby," Drake said softly, proud of her for standing up for herself.

If anything she looked more miserable. And . . . sad. What the fuck?

She lifted glossy eyes to his. Lifeless, dull eyes that stole the air from his lungs because she looked so unhappy and resigned.

"But you did share me with Manuel," she whispered. "Just, apparently, as you've shared your other women with him. What I thought was special was nothing more than something you've done dozens of times in the past. I thought that I was doing something solely for you. I *wanted* to do something that was just for you. For your pleasure. That wasn't about me. How you must have laughed over the idea that I was doing something special for you. It was humiliating to see that knowing look on that woman's horrid face. How smug and confident she was that I'd soon be replaced and was nothing more than another woman in a long line of women you have sex with."

Drake damn near exploded on the spot. It took every measure of control he possessed not to completely flip out, but that would only scare the shit out of her and the last thing he wanted was for her to fear him. Ever. God. Not Evangeline. He cultivated a healthy dose of fear in everyone else, even the women he involved himself with. He had no problem with them knowing if they ever crossed him they'd pay dearly. But Evangeline was the one person on the planet that it would kill him if she feared him. He wanted her trust. Her absolute faith in him that he would never hurt her.

His hands were shaking with fury. Not at Evangeline. Never at Evangeline. He could well understand the source of her upset now that the story had come out. How to explain the difference between her and all the other women he'd fucked? He wasn't even sure he could explain it to himself, much less anyone else.

He reached for her hands, carefully prying them apart and twining them with his so he held them in her lap.

"Angel, look at me."

Though he said it in a tender voice, it was a command nonetheless.

With seeming reluctance and a good degree of embarrassment, she lifted her chin until her sad eyes connected with his.

"If you don't think what I have—what I feel—with you and for you is very different than what I've had or felt for any other woman, then you're wrong. Yes, Manuel has participated on occasion when I've had sex with another woman, though not often. But the difference is, no other woman has ever wanted to do something so selfless as to ask me what I want and express her desire to do something solely for me. It's always been about them. Their wants, their needs. They could give a damn about mine. Manuel's involvement was to a degree for me because it's something I enjoy, but mostly it was at the women's behest and, trust me, their attention was focused entirely on Manuel. They didn't give me one thought, never looked at me. My name wasn't on their lips. They never looked to me for approval or permission. They never set aside their own pleasure for mine and they certainly didn't torment themselves worrying that by experiencing pleasure, by orgasming with another man that they somehow were betraying me."

He took a breath, allowing his words to sink in. She looked startled and cocked her head to the side as she rapidly processed all he was saying.

"Only you, Angel. Only you did and thought those things. Only you did it as a gift to me without one thought of yourself. If you don't think that means anything to me, that you aren't special to me and you're just another woman I've fucked, then I'm doing things all wrong with you and obviously we need to have a very long, serious talk."

She looked shocked, color high in her cheeks, her eyes wide as she studied every nuance of his expression as if discerning his sincerity.

"And you know what else, Angel? You were spot on when you said I'd never share anything I really considered mine, and no, I never considered those women mine. You, however, are mine in every possible way. You belong to me. I own you. And I'm never fucking letting you go.

"I realize that sounds contradictory since Manuel has been over—twice—and you did have sex with him at my behest, but Angel, that wasn't me sharing you," he said softly, loosening his hold on one hand so he could lift his to cup and caress her cheek. "That was you sharing something infinitely precious *with* me. *For* me. And believe me when I say, that makes you more special to me than any other woman has been or ever will be."

"Oh," she said, her mouth rounding in astonished understanding. "I never considered it that way."

"It's a fact," Drake said firmly. "I'm sorry she hurt you. I'm even sorrier that for even one second she made you doubt your place in my life and that your self-confidence took a hit. But baby, if it were any other woman except you sitting here questioning her worth to me, I would have already shown her to the door, because no other woman matters."

Her face crumbled, apology and regret shadowing her eyes. "I'm so sorry, Drake."

He put a finger to her lips before she could say anything further. "You will not apologize for being human and having feelings. Not to me. Never to me. But from now on, if you hear shit that upsets you, then you come to me so I can straighten it out before it gets in your head and takes root. Got it?"

She nodded, though worry was still a ghost in her eyes.

"Now come here and kiss me," he said quietly.

She leaned in immediately, and he loved that she obeyed without hesitation or question. So sweetly submissive. So fucking perfect. And all his.

He ravaged her mouth, thrusting his tongue deep inside like he was dying to shove his dick inside her sweet little pussy. A groan emerged, rumbling from his chest, sounding like a growl in his throat.

"Bed. Now."

They were the only two words he was capable of speaking, but they got his point across perfectly. Not waiting for her to rise, he simply swept her into his arms and strode to the bedroom so he could back up his words with actions. After tonight, he wanted there to be no doubt as to her place in his life.

In his heart.

In his fucking soul.

18

Evangeline stood with Drake on the tarmac waiting impatiently for the inbound plane to taxi to the terminal. She simply couldn't believe that she was about to see her parents face-to-face for the first time since she'd moved to the city, which seemed a lifetime ago.

She squeezed Drake's hand until she was sure it was probably bloodless, but he merely smiled indulgently at her and squeezed back.

"There it is," he said, pointing to the small plane approaching them.

"Oh God, Drake. It's them!" she cried.

The weather wasn't great. A cold front had pushed through in brutal fashion, dumping a mixture of sleet and snow over the city for the past two days. Today's offering was an icy drizzle that the umbrella Drake held over her head did little to shield. She was shivering to her toes but didn't even register the discomfort of the wind and moisture. She was too focused on seeing her mom and dad.

The plane halted several feet away and she waited breathlessly for the door to open. When her mother appeared at the top of the steps, it was too much for Evangeline to bear any longer. She broke from Drake's hold and ran to the bottom, waiting as the two attendants helped her mother down the steps.

And then she was in her mother's arms.

"Mama!"

Tears flowed freely down Evangeline's cheeks, mixing with the rain and icy sleet.

"My baby," her mother said over and over. "Let me look at you."

She pulled Evangeline away and inspected her from head to toe.

"Oh, darling, you look absolutely beautiful," her mother said in a choked voice.

"Where's Daddy?" Evangeline asked anxiously.

"They're getting his wheelchair and carrying him down the steps. Look, there he is now."

Evangeline rocked up on her tiptoes, straining to see as two men provided a chair with their arms for her father and carefully brought him down the steps. At the bottom, he was met with his wheelchair and he was eased down so he was comfortable.

"Come give your dad a big hug, girl," her father said gruffly.

Evangeline threw her arms around her dad and held on for all she was worth. Tears obscured her vision but it didn't matter. Nothing mattered except they were here and she could hold them and tell them she loved them in person.

"Angel, honey. I hate to interrupt, but your parents are getting soaked and you've been standing here in the rain waiting for them for the past half hour. You're going to get sick. Let's get everyone to the van."

Evangeline pulled away from her dad, mortified that she'd been so rude to Drake. She'd practically forgotten he was even here and she hadn't even introduced him to her parents.

"Mama, Daddy, there is someone very special I want y'all to meet."

She reached for Drake's hand and pulled him into their circle.

"This is Drake Donovan. Drake, this is my mother and father."

Drake leaned down to kiss her mother on the cheek. "Mrs. Hawthorn, it's a pleasure to finally meet you in person. I now know exactly where

Evangeline gets not only her wit and intelligence but her beauty as well. If looking at you right now is showing me what I'm in for in thirty or so years, then I'm one very lucky man."

Her mother blushed fiery red. "Oh, nonsense," she said, momentarily too flustered to even respond. "And please do call me Brenda. You're family after all, and Mrs. Hawthorn sounds far too stuffy."

"My pleasure, Brenda." Then he turned and extended his hand to Evangeline's father. "I'm honored to meet you, sir. I've heard so much about the both of you that I feel like I already know you."

"Grant," her father said in his gruff voice. "And I'm pleased to meet you as well, Drake. I'm very grateful to you for looking out for my little girl. Her mother and I have stayed awake countless nights worrying over her living so far away and in such a big city. She's a small-town girl at heart and she's too trusting and softhearted for her own good."

"On that we agree," Drake said. "But it's those qualities that make her so special and I wouldn't change a single thing about her."

"He'll do, Brenda," her father said with an approving nod. "I'd say our girl is in very good hands."

"Come. The van is parked just over here. Let's get you folks out of the weather. We'll get you checked into your hotel and let you settle in and rest, and then Evangeline and I will come get you for dinner."

They hurried to the wheelchair-accessible van that Drake had rented for her parents' use while in the city, complete with hired driver and assistant to help with the wheelchair. Drake ushered the women into the van while the attendants got her father in, and then they piled the luggage into the back with the chair. Drake climbed in next to Evangeline and they headed to Times Square, where Drake had reserved a suite at the Marriott.

"Everything is so big here, Evangeline," her mother exclaimed. "And my word, all the lights. Everyone is in a hurry and busy, busy, busy."

Evangeline smiled. "Wait until you see Times Square, Mama. It's insane there."

Her parents oohed and ahhed the entire way to the hotel, but when her mother got her first glimpse of Times Square, her mouth fell open.

"Well, my word! How does anyone sleep at night with so much racket going on?"

Drake chuckled. "The rooms are equipped with room-darkening blinds so the lights won't keep you awake. If you need anything at all during your stay, just contact the concierge and they'll provide whatever you need. Evangeline supplied you with both our cell numbers. Don't hesitate to call me for anything at all, day or night."

"You're a fine young man, Drake," her mother said, giving him an affectionate pat on the arm. "Your parents must be so proud."

Drake stiffened slightly and his eyes grew cold for a fleeting instant. His smile didn't reach his eyes. "I lost my parents a long time ago."

"Oh, I'm so sorry to hear that," her mother fretted. "My apologies for bringing it up like that."

"No offense whatsoever taken, Brenda," Drake said, warmth returning to his voice. "It was a long time ago. I was only a child. I barely remember them."

But Evangeline knew that was a lie. Whatever memories he did have weren't good ones. In the beginning her relationship with her parents had baffled Drake. Initially he'd been angry over what he perceived as them taking advantage of her because she worked tirelessly to provide for them. It was only later that he'd begun to understand the depths of her devotion to them. And theirs to her.

It was obvious that he'd never had that kind of relationship with the people who'd given him life, and her heart ached for that young boy forced to make his own way in the world. Just as the rest of Drake's men had done. It was the one thing that they all had in common and that tied them together. Troubled, difficult pasts with only themselves to rely on and no one else.

"So what are we doing for Thanksgiving, Evangeline?" her mother asked when they stepped out of the van in front of the hotel.

Evangeline smiled. "I'm cooking for all of us at Drake's apartment. I'd love for you to help me so we can have a big feast like old times."

"Oh, that does sound lovely, darling. Of course I'll help. I'd love to. It will be so much fun for us both to be in the kitchen again. She's such a wonderful cook, Drake, don't you agree?"

"That I do, ma'am," he said. "She spoils me with regular home-cooked meals. If I'm not careful, I'll have to buy an entire new wardrobe."

Evangeline snorted. As if. The man was built like a brick house. He didn't have a single inch of spare flesh anywhere on his body. And she ought to know, considering how well acquainted with his body she was.

After getting her parents checked in and all the luggage brought up to the room, Evangeline hugged her parents after urging them to rest before dinner, and then after setting a time to meet, she and Drake took their leave.

It took all of Evangeline's restraint not to stay with her parents in the hotel room, but they did need to rest. They both looked tired and she was concerned about her father. He wasn't used to traveling and exerting himself as much as he had during the trip. If she stayed, neither her father nor her mother would rest. They would all stay up talking and catching up.

Drake must have sensed her reluctance to leave because he took her hand and pulled her against his side as they walked to the elevator. He kissed her temple.

"You'll get to visit with them plenty before they return home," he said comfortingly.

"I know. It's just hard to let them go even for a few hours when I haven't seen them in so very long," she said wistfully.

"They seem like wonderful people. Just like their daughter."

"*You* are a wonderful person, Drake. Thank you again so much for making this happen. This is the best present anyone has ever given me."

She threw her arms around his neck as the elevator doors closed and they zoomed toward the bottom floor, and then she drew his head down to hers and pressed her lips to his.

They were still locked together when the elevator slowed its descent. Reluctantly Evangeline pulled away, her eyes half lidded and heavy. They got off the elevator and walked to the side street where Jax waited with Thane in a car to take them back to Drake's apartment.

"Do you suppose Maddox would mind going shopping with my mother and me in the morning?" Evangeline asked as they slid in. "I need to go to the grocer and get all the stuff for Thanksgiving. I thought she could go with me, and Dad could hang out at your apartment until we got back."

"I thought I'd take off work tomorrow, so I'll keep your dad company. That will give me the rest of the week off with the holiday."

"You don't mind?" Evangeline asked.

"Of course I don't mind spending time with your father, Angel. You go and spend time with your mom. I'll call Maddox and ask him to be there in the morning to take you."

With a contented sigh, she settled into Drake's arms for the ride back to the apartment. For the next five days, she had the three most important people in the world all to herself. Life was, she thought with hazy mellowness, absolutely . . . perfect.

19

True to Drake's word, Maddox arrived the next morning along with Silas to take her and her mother shopping. Evangeline was delighted that her mother would get to meet the two men she felt the closest bond with. She had a feeling that neither man would quite know what to do with her mom.

And she had a surprise up her sleeve that she hoped went well. She'd approached Drake with her request that morning and when she'd revealed that she'd very much like to invite Maddox and Silas to eat Thanksgiving dinner with them, he'd been surprised but had told her that he had no problem with her inviting them.

He'd looked . . . pleased . . . that she'd thought to include them.

Maddox and Silas were currently in the living room with Drake and her father while Evangeline was whipping up a quick breakfast and her mother was in the bathroom.

"Maddox? Silas?" she called.

They appeared in the kitchen a moment later and she flashed them a welcoming smile.

"Want to help me set the table? I made enough breakfast for everyone. It won't take too long and then we can hop over to the market with my grocery list."

Maddox sniffed the air appreciatively. Then he clutched his chest dramatically.

"Will you marry me, Evangeline? Let me take you away from all of this. Oh wait. This is exactly what I want you to do at my place. But it's the only thing I'll ever ask of you. Well, and sex of course. If you cook for me every day, I'll make sure you never want for anything for the rest of your life."

Silas rolled his eyes and began taking plates down from the cabinets. Evangeline laughed and blew Maddox a kiss.

"As a matter of fact, the real reason I called the two of you in here is because I have a special request."

Both men came to attention and Silas probed her with his stare.

"Everything okay, doll?" Silas asked in concern.

"Oh yes, everything is fine. I wanted to ask the two of you if y'all would do me the honor of having Thanksgiving dinner with me, Drake and my parents?"

Maddox looked poleaxed and Silas's expression froze on his face.

"Thanksgiving is a time to be with family," she continued softly. "And I consider the both of you family. It would mean a lot to me. That is if you don't have other plans already."

"I would be very honored to accept your invitation," Maddox said in a solemn tone.

Silas leaned in and brushed his lips across her cheek. "I'll be here, doll. And thank you for the invite. It means a lot to me."

She smiled, relieved that they seemed to be happy to be included in her plans.

"Have a seat. Let me go get Dad and Drake and we'll eat."

Breakfast was lively and fun, but when Evangeline's mother realized that she and Evangeline were going to have the escort of both Silas and Maddox to the market, her reaction was hysterical.

"Well, I never, Evangeline! Is it so dangerous in the big city that we have to be escorted around by these two extremely good-looking young men?"

Evangeline choked on her drink when she saw Maddox's neck turn red and Silas fidget in his seat.

"They are extremely good looking, Mama, don't you think?" Evangeline said, her eyes twinkling. "Just think. Everyone will be wondering who on earth you are or what celebrity you are, being guarded by Maddox and Silas. Maybe I should have asked Zander or Jax to come along too," she mused.

"You, my darling angel, are a wicked tease," Drake said in a low voice only she could hear. Laughter shone brightly in his eyes and he covered his smile by taking a long drink from his glass.

"Oh my. You're right!" her mother exclaimed. "Oh, isn't this exciting, Grant? Wait until I tell everyone back home. They won't believe me, of course, so you'll take pictures, won't you, Evangeline?"

There was such a look and sound of hope in her mother's face and voice that Evangeline nearly lost the battle and burst into laughter on the spot.

"Absolutely, Mama. I'll take as many pictures as you want. I'm sure Maddox and Silas won't mind at all, will you?" she said sweetly, staring innocently at the two men in question.

Silas coughed and then looked at her mother, sincerity etched in his features.

"It would be my privilege to escort Evangeline's mother around the city. Evangeline is an amazing, beautiful woman and is also one of the most compassionate and loving people I've ever met. I can only draw the conclusion that she gets it from her mother."

To Evangeline's delight, her mother blushed to the roots of her hair and then fanned herself with her hand in rapid fashion.

"Oh my Jesus," she breathed. "Evangeline, what do you do with all these wonderful young men?"

Evangeline choked and Drake squeezed her hand beneath the table, his features working up and down as he tried to suppress his laughter over

Evangeline's mortification. Maddox smirked while Silas's lips turned up into a slow grin.

"Not nearly enough," Maddox said morosely. "I could eat her cooking every day."

"You'll get plenty of my and my mother's cooking tomorrow," Evangeline said pointedly. "You'll be in a food coma for days."

"I can't wait," Maddox said, a wistful note to his voice.

"Are you ready to go to the market, Mama?" Evangeline asked. "I have my grocery list all written up. Maddox, do you and Silas have any special requests for tomorrow's meal?"

"Trust me. We'll eat whatever you put on the table, doll," Silas vowed.

"That ain't no lie," Maddox said emphatically.

"Well, let's be off then, shall we?" her mother said brightly. "I don't know when the last time a trip to the grocery store was this exciting. I plan to enjoy every minute of it."

Drake caught Evangeline's hand as she rose from the table and gently pulled her back to his seat. "Forgetting something, Angel?" he murmured.

She was flustered at first, wondering what he was talking about. But then she saw the devilish gleam in his eye.

"My good-bye kiss, perhaps?" he prompted.

She flushed but was secretly thrilled that he didn't mind kissing her in front of her parents or his men. She leaned down and kissed him long and sweet, running her tongue over the contours of his mouth until he parted his lips and let her delve inside.

He tasted so good. She wanted to melt into his lap and spend the next hour doing nothing more than kissing him.

"Go easy on my men, okay, Angel?" he said in amusement.

"You act like I'm a troublemaker," she said with a sniff.

"Only the very best kind," he murmured.

She kissed him one last time and then went to collect her purse.

"Everyone ready?" she asked once she returned.

. . .

Thanksgiving Day was the most wonderful holiday Evangeline could ever remember experiencing. She and her mother had begun cooking in the morning and they'd eaten shortly after two that afternoon.

At first, her mother had been appalled when Drake had instructed her and Evangeline not to worry about the dishes, but when he'd reassured her that his cleaning service would be in, her mother had a swift change of heart and readily stayed away from the pile of pots, pans, skillets, roasting pans, glasses, plates and eating utensils.

It was that evening that her mother had made an innocent comment that sparked an idea in Evangeline. Her mother had asked if Evangeline planned to put up the tree the following morning—as was their family tradition ever since Evangeline could remember.

Not at all knowing what Drake's feelings on the subject were—he didn't seem the type who went crazy decorating for any occasion—the longer she thought about it, the more her idea took root.

And so before going to bed Thanksgiving night, she made a discreet call to Maddox and made her request.

When Evangeline's parents arrived at Drake's apartment Friday morning, they were accompanied by every single one of Drake's men. When they began walking off the elevator carrying boxes and shopping bags and the pièce de résistance, the ten-foot live Christmas tree, Drake's eyebrows went up and he immediately searched Evangeline out in the crowd now assembled in his apartment.

She smiled but her stomach was a mass of nerves. She really hoped this didn't go badly.

Walking over to him, she slid her arms around his waist and smiled again. "Surprise," she said softly. "And Merry Christmas. It's tradition in my family that the tree always goes up the day after Thanksgiving and remains up through New Year's. I hope you don't mind but I wanted to do something special for you while they were still here to help decorate and enjoy the tree as well."

"You did this for me?" he asked in an odd tone.

She nodded. "Do you like it?" she asked hesitantly.

He hugged her to him and then kissed her lingeringly. "I love it. Thank you."

"Evangeline, dear, you and Drake come and help decorate your tree!" her mother called from across the room. "Your young men outdid themselves. We must have fifteen hundred lights that go on this tree!"

Evangeline looked to Drake and when he nodded, she took his hand and pulled him to where her mother was pulling ornaments from their boxes.

"Your father and I brought you something," her mother said, reaching for a tattered box Evangeline hadn't noticed until now.

She lovingly smoothed her hands over the worn packaging before opening it to reveal its contents. Evangeline sucked in her breath and the sting of tears burned her eyelids.

"Oh, Mama," she said.

"I brought ornaments from our family tree that I thought you'd like to have for your own tree," her mother said, a sheen of moisture in her own eyes. "Some of them you made yourself in school as a child. And there is one for every single Christmas you've celebrated, dating back to your very first Christmas. I also brought you several of the handmade ornaments your grammie made over the years. I know how much you loved and cherished them."

Evangeline sat on the couch next to her mother and hugged her. Then the two women began examining each of the ornaments.

"Thank you," Evangeline said in a hushed whisper. "I love them, Mama."

"You're very welcome, darling. I just can't believe that you're all grown up now with a life of your own. I know we don't say it nearly enough, but your father and I are so proud of you. No one could be more proud of their child than we are. Before we came to visit, I used to fret and worry and I had so much regret that you had to put off school and move to the city in order to help support me and your father."

"No, Mama!"

"Shh," her mother said, laying a hand gently atop Evangeline's. "Let me finish."

Evangeline noticed that Drake, Silas and Maddox were all listening to what her mother was saying, though they weren't being obvious about it.

"As I said, I had so much regret and I worried endlessly about you here on your own. Only having a few friends and being swallowed up by a city full of strangers. But once I got here and saw you, I realized that it's wrong of me to wish all of this away. Because if you hadn't moved here, you wouldn't have met Drake and you wouldn't be as happy as you look right now and I'd never want to take that away from you."

"You're very right about one thing, Brenda," Drake interjected somberly. "As much as I hate the circumstances that brought Evangeline to New York, I, like you, can't bring myself to regret them because were it not for those circumstances, she wouldn't be standing here today in my apartment. I wouldn't have her. And now that I do, how I came to have her isn't nearly as important as her continuing to belong to me."

Evangeline felt like someone had just punched her in the stomach. She felt flattened by his words and the ring of sincerity and truth in them. She stared at him in utter astonishment.

Her mom and dad exchanged pleased, happy smiles as they watched Evangeline grapple with the enormity of Drake's impassioned statement.

"We've got the lights hung, Mrs. Hawthorn," Jax said from his post at the tree. "If you'll tell us what needs to go where, we'll knock out the rest of the decorations."

Evangeline stood, her knees shaky, but she couldn't contain her broad smile. Maybe she'd never smiled this big.

"I'll make everyone a deal," she called so everyone could hear. "If y'all will hang the decorations as my mom instructs, I'll start on a late lunch and feed everyone."

A chorus of whoops went up and then it was a race to see who could hang the ornaments the fastest. Drake went back to sit next to her father, and the two of them quickly became immersed in conversation while Evangeline stood in the doorway of the kitchen surveying her packed apartment and the brilliant glitter of fifteen hundred lights draped from the top to the bottom of the tree.

Her heart swelled with contentment. This was her family now. She watched as the men taunted and ribbed one another, though they were all extremely respectful in front of her mother. She could hug and kiss every single one of them for being so wonderfully solicitous of her during her visit.

She dabbed at the corner of her eye to prevent any tears from falling down her cheeks.

"Evangeline? You okay?" Silas asked beside her.

She turned to see him standing next to her, a concerned expression marring his handsome features. She gave him her second-biggest smile of the day.

"I'm more than okay," she breathed. "Look around, Silas. This is our family. What could possibly be better than family gathered to decorate the Christmas tree and eat dinner together?"

Silas smiled, something he seemed to do with increasing frequency around her lately.

"It's you, doll. You've made us family."

20

It was late when Drake and Evangeline returned to their apartment after seeing her parents back to the hotel. She was already dreading the following day, when her parents would fly back home.

As they walked off the elevator, Drake reached out and shackled her wrist with his fingers and pulled her to a stop.

"Go into the bedroom, get undressed and wait for me on the bed. Lie on your back, arms over your head, legs spread so I see what is mine the minute I walk through the bedroom door."

Her mouth went dry and she swallowed at the knot seemingly lodged there. His voice was so sexy. Low pitched and husky. The mere sound had the same effect as if he'd stroked her with his hands. Each word was its own individual caress over her ears.

"I'll give you five minutes," he warned.

She'd be ready for him in three.

Turning, she hurried to the bedroom, already stripping her clothing off as she entered. She tossed her dress and shoes in the far corner and then crawled on top of the covers and eased down on her back. Then she lifted her arms up over her so they rested on the pillow above her head.

She lay there in a dreamy state of heightened arousal, every sense on alert. Waiting. Her pulse raced to life the moment she sensed his presence. Before he ever made a betraying sound, she knew he was there.

Her eyelids fluttered lazily as she moved her gaze to where he stood by the bed. He was staring down at her, his expression gentle, affection glowing from his dark eyes. She felt a decadent little thrill. It was times like this, times like the previous several days when his every action, word, look and touch whispered to her that he could love her.

She just had to be patient. Drake wasn't a man to make himself vulnerable to anyone, especially another woman. All she could do in the meantime was show him that she wasn't going anywhere. That she loved him unconditionally. The wait would be well worth it. She had no doubt there.

No longer did insidious thoughts latch on and take hold, undermining her self-confidence, making her fear the future and how long Drake would remain in their relationship. He'd done nothing to make her think he was growing tired of her. Just the opposite. It seemed that with every passing day, he openly accepted the bigger role in his life she played.

"What are you thinking, Angel?" Drake murmured as he stroked his hand over her naked curves.

Her entire body was painfully aware. She trembled and shuddered with nearly violent need. There was such a look of intensity in Drake's eyes tonight. As though he'd come to some momentous decision or realization.

She wanted to question him about it, but what was she supposed to say? That she sensed a change in him? In his priorities, and that he'd placed her ahead of all else? It was a very good way of opening herself up to abject humiliation if she was wrong. No, she couldn't try to rush commitment from him. That would be the biggest mistake of all.

"I'm thinking about how lucky I am," she whispered around the knot in her throat. "This Thanksgiving has been the best Thanksgiving I've ever had. I loved every minute of it, Drake. We were like one big family. My parents. Your men. And us . . ."

His smile was spreading warmth through parts of her body that hadn't felt this warm in a very long time. His eyes were like liquid sunshine, his gaze fiery over her skin. More often than not, his eyes and his expression were so very dark. Shadowed. Past hurts and painful memories lurking just beneath the surface. But tonight, his eyes looked almost golden brown and not black.

She was fascinated by that golden gaze. Mesmerized as the light caught the bronze flecks in his eyes.

He tossed his clothing to the side and slowly got up on the bed, hovering above her as he rested on his elbows so his weight didn't crush her. She let out a small moan as his body pressed down on hers. Automatically her body moved to accommodate his. Soft to his hard. She cushioned him on the bed even though his full weight wasn't on her.

He stared down at her, those brilliant eyes still full of such heat and mystery.

"Do you know what I was thinking?" he asked huskily as he brushed his thumbs over her cheeks, tucking tiny strands of her hair behind her ears.

"What?" she whispered.

"That I need, that I *want* to thank you for the best Thanskgiving anyone has ever given me."

Tears swam in her eyes as she soaked in his reverence and the absolute sincerity in his voice and expression.

"I'm glad," she choked out. "I'm so glad, Drake. I want you to be happy. Even if it's not with me."

She could have bitten her tongue for allowing even a second of her insecurities to surface. Especially when Drake was already baring his soul, or at least part of it, to her.

"I didn't mean that like I said," she said hastily. "I swear to you I'm not fishing for anything, Drake. I truly mean that. I want you to be happy. No matter what that takes. I hope I'm the one who can do it. I pray that I am.

But if I'm not, I just want you to know that you have people who love you and care about you. I'm not the only one."

Drake shook his head, his gaze genuinely puzzled. "Surely you don't think I have any plans to end what we share, Angel."

She smiled. "No. I was just trying to say what was in my heart and, well, sometimes that doesn't go over too well," she said ruefully.

He smiled back down at her and swept her lips into a long, sweet kiss that made her feel the sting of tears all over again.

"No one has ever cooked a holiday meal for me," he said absently. He looked uncomfortable with the confession and the ramifications of it as well. "No one has ever asked my brothers to eat a meal with them like you did. And yet you cooked not only for me, but for them as well. Hell, you had them decorating a fucking Christmas tree in my living room."

He looked down at her with an awed expression.

"Swear to God, Angel. You're a fucking miracle. I should have known the day you had everyone eating *cupcakes* in my office that we were all goners. I've never seen my men react to a woman in my life like they have to you. I've never had a woman in my life as long as I've had you," he amended.

Once more, he looked unsettled, as though the realizations he was having unhinged him and he had no idea what to do with each one as it was unveiled.

"They adore you, Angel. And they're loyal to you. Every bit as much as they are to me. You've changed all of us. At times they have no better idea of what to do with you than I do. You surprise them with your unconditional acceptance at every corner. As you surprise me . . ."

"Drake, you have to stop," she said helplessly. "You're going to make me cry!"

He smiled and kissed her cheeks, her eyelids, the corners of her eyes as though he were removing invisible tears.

"I find I don't mind you crying so much as long as you're happy. But if you were ever unhappy about anything, you have to know I'd move heaven and earth to make you happy again."

She squeezed her arms around his waist and lifted her cheek to press to his chest. "I do know that, Drake. And you do, you know. You make me so very happy."

Relief flared in his eyes. "I'm glad. I don't know what I'd ever do without you. I don't want to even contemplate it."

"How about we don't, then?" she whispered.

"That's the best idea I've heard in a long time," he whispered back as he kissed her again.

He licked over her bottom lip and then flicked his tongue to the corner of her mouth before lapping delicately at her upper lip. With a sigh, she relaxed and opened her mouth for him, her lips parting as his tongue slid inward, spreading his taste over her tongue.

When he drew away, his eyes were blazing with intensity and conviction.

"Thank you, my angel. For giving me . . . hope. For showing me what a real holiday with . . . family . . . feels like. I'll never forget this Thanksgiving. Ever. It—and you—mean the world to me."

"Make love to me," she urged, suddenly impatient to feel him on her, inside her, warming her from the inside out.

"Oh I am," he said in a hushed, reverent tone. He kissed her once, twice and then a third time. "I understand that our relationship—and sexual relationship—is built on your submission and my dominance and that a certain amount of kink factors in. But tonight I'm going to make love to you. Tonight, kink has no place in our bedroom. Just you and me, and me loving you. Showing you my love."

She sucked in her breath so sharply she nearly passed out. Oh God, did he even realize what he was saying? Drake wasn't the kind of man to say things he didn't mean in the heat of the moment.

He'd come so close to saying everything she could ever hope for or dream of. For now it was more than enough. He wanted to show her his love. His love was all she ever wanted. Nothing else. Just him and his heart. His love. For all time.

He took his time. Never had he displayed such a remarkable amount of patience or exacting determination to withhold both of their pleasure until they were both senseless with it. He kissed and licked every inch of her body, spending an extra amount of time at her breasts and then between her legs.

She was frantic with need, gasping, arching, crying out as her body throbbed and she climbed higher and higher up the peak. For nearly an hour, he stroked and caressed, kissed and licked, murmured sweet, beautiful words to her that she memorized and sealed into her heart, never to be forgotten.

Each time she urged him to slide inside her and give them both what they wanted, he'd smile and simply ignore her plea, opting instead to bring her to even greater heights of pleasure and blinding need.

She was nearly sobbing, out of her head with mind-numbing ecstasy when finally he parted her legs and gently positioned himself between them.

"Look at me, Angel," he said in a tender voice.

Her eyes locked with his and satisfaction burned brightly in his gaze.

"Take me," he whispered. "All of me."

He surged deep, taking her breath with the swiftness and power of his possession. He was deep. So much deeper than ever before. He seemed as determined as she was for him to take every inch. She could deny him nothing. She lifted her legs and hooked them around his back and lifted her hips so the angle of his entry was even better.

He hesitated the barest of seconds and then powered forward again, burying himself to the hilt.

Her vision blurred and she knew she couldn't possibly hold on a minute longer. She was too close. Too aroused. She needed him too much.

"Drake!" she cried out. "Please. Don't stop. Not now!"

"No, Angel. Never," he vowed.

He drove himself forward, melting into her body as she wrapped arms and legs tightly around him. She melted into his arms, her body soft and pliable, so accepting of him.

The first blast of her orgasm rocked her to her very core. She had no awareness in those few moments as pleasure, sharp, edgy like a knife, sliced its wicked way through her body, all the way to her very soul.

Her eyes blanked, the pupils constricting. She tried to focus on Drake's fierce expression, the possession she saw so clearly outlined on his face, but it was simply too much.

Every muscle and nerve ending in her body tensed to the point of pain. She drew herself up in agony, trying to clutch more fiercely at Drake. She was sobbing. She dimly registered the fact that she was sobbing and begging and pleading.

And then his mouth found hers and he swallowed up her loud cry as she let it out into the night.

The entire world around her burst, exploded into a cacophony of color and sensation. So much pleasure. It winged its way through her body, foaming thickly through her veins, bathing every inch of her skin.

She couldn't breathe, so Drake breathed for her. He swallowed up her air and then offered her his. Nothing had ever felt so intimate and sweet. Never had she felt this kind of love for any other man. She never would.

What would she have ever done if she'd never met Drake? How hollow would her life be even now if he weren't a part of it? She closed her eyes tightly, felt the hot tears slide down her cheek, and she gulped back her sob as she clung tightly to him in the explosive aftermath.

He lowered his heaving body to hers, panting as he struggled to catch his breath. He buried his face in her hair and gathered her so close in his arms that there wasn't an inch of her skin not covered by him.

"Never had anything so sweet in my life," he barely managed to get out. "Never will again. You're the most beautiful thing I've ever had, Angel. Don't ever leave me. Please don't leave me."

She was shocked by the vulnerability she heard in his voice. Shocked that he'd allowed her to witness it. Or perhaps he had no idea what he was saying. But his words, his impassioned plea, rocked her all the way to her heart and soul.

"I won't," she said tenderly. "Never, Drake, darling. I'll always be here. As long as you want me, I am yours."

He crushed her to him, holding her so tightly she couldn't breathe. "I need you, Angel. I need you so damn much."

His words were so hushed that she thought she'd imagined them at first. A euphoric thrill washed through her blood, and peace settled over her. Maybe . . . just maybe fairy tales did come true.

21

Evangeline lay in Drake's arms, so contented that she was utterly bone-less with it. She was draped completely over his body, lying atop him, their legs tangled with the sheets and blankets.

She'd attempted to move once, but Drake's hold had tightened on her and he'd simply murmured, "I like you right where you are, Angel."

Evangeline idly caressed him, running her fingers lightly over the muscled contours of his body and through the smattering of hair at the top of his chest and the slightly thicker and darker line that whorled in the very center before drifting in a straight line to his navel.

The man was a god. A magnificent sexy beast of a man that no other man she'd ever seen could even come close to. And he was all hers.

She smiled her smug satisfaction and lay there a long moment savoring the intimacy of their hold.

And then thoughts from the holiday drifted through her mind and she remembered Drake's stiff response to her mother saying how proud his parents must be of him. And his awed thank-you for the best holiday anyone had ever given him. He'd said that no one had ever cooked a holiday meal for him. For that matter, that very first time she'd cooked for him, he'd said, somewhat bewilderingly, that no one had ever cooked anything for him.

Surely he meant as an adult. Wouldn't his mother have cooked for him when he was a child?

Icy fingers of dread clutched at her heart because somehow she sensed that Drake's childhood had not been a happy one. For that matter, the common tie that seemed to bind all of his men together as brothers was less-than-ideal pasts. None of them had actually spoken of their pasts, but then neither had they ever once mentioned having families. No references to their childhoods. Nothing.

She levered herself off his chest enough that she could look into his eyes, and she did so earnestly, searching his gaze for any sign that perhaps she should let this go or at least bring it up some other time.

When she saw nothing but warmth and tenderness, she nibbled at her lower lip and then hesitantly broached the subject on her mind.

"Drake? Can I ask you something?" she asked tentatively.

His eyes narrowed but he didn't look angry. Just . . . worried. "Of course. What is it, Angel?"

"I wanted to ask you about . . . well . . . you. Your past," she said nervously.

His lips flattened into a thin line and his eyes became glacial. She wasn't sure he even realized the change in his features because it appeared he was making an effort not to become angry or irritated at her inquiry.

"What about it?" he asked in a flat tone.

She sighed and sat up, positioning her body to the side of him so she could look at him and monitor his reactions.

"You never talk about it. Your childhood. Your parents. You were obviously not comfortable when my mother brought up your parents. And I realize this may not be something you want to discuss, Drake. If it isn't, then I'll drop it. But I feel like it still has power over you in some way.

That it . . . hurts you still. And I would do anything to stop you from hurting," she whispered.

"Nothing good can come from rehashing the past," he said grimly. "It's just that. The past. It happened a long time ago and doesn't affect *us*."

She shook her head in denial. "You're wrong," she said softly. She leaned down and hugged him fiercely to her. "It does affect you still, and anything that affects you affects me. And us."

He sighed and she felt the tension whipping and coiling in his body. He was tense beneath her touch, but then he relaxed and wrapped his arms around her as he sat up in bed, pulling her to his chest.

"What do you want to know?" he asked with obvious discomfort.

"Only what you're willing to share," she replied honestly. "I will never demand more than what you're willing to give."

He sighed again and was silent for a long second. "My parents weren't exactly poster people for parent-of-the-year awards. Nothing like yours," he said, and she wondered if he even heard the wistful note in his voice. It made her want to hug him all over again.

"They were scammers. Into drugs. Easy money. Whatever they had to do so that they didn't have to work. A child was the very last thing either of them wanted, and in fact my mother wanted to abort me, but my father realized that I would be a meal ticket of sorts for them. Food stamps. A check from the state every month. And all they had to do was keep me and ensure I remained alive. My happiness and comfort weren't on their list of priorities."

Bleakness entered his faraway expression, but he quickly schooled his features as if determined to give them no more power over him than they'd already once had.

"Oh, Drake," she said, her lips turning down into a sad smile.

He smiled at her then and pulled her down so he could kiss her temple. "You're far too softhearted, my angel. I survived."

"But what did you survive?" she asked pointedly. "No one should have to *survive* their childhood."

"No, but many do," he said gently.

"How bad was it, Drake?" she asked in an anxious voice.

He swallowed. "It was bad," he admitted. "I was just a child who didn't understand why my parents hated me or why they tolerated me, for that matter. I used to pray that the state would come on an unscheduled visit and remove me from their home. I tried running away more than once. Each time, my father found me, beat me into a bloody pulp, dragged me back home and locked me in a closet for days at a time."

She emitted a shocked gasp, her eyes round with horror. Her hand flew to her mouth to stifle her agonized cry.

Drake shrugged. "It wasn't so bad. I preferred being in the closet over being in their way. If they were running low on drugs or food, it got really bad. Withdrawal would hit and they'd lash out at the source of their unhappiness. Me. So I learned to blend in, to be very quiet and to stay in the shadows. Ironically it was probably my father who kept me alive. My mother, as I said, would have preferred to abort me, and she developed quite a nasty narcotic pain pill habit as a result of her emergency C-section when she had me. My father reminded her at every turn that if they got rid of the 'little beast,' as she liked to call me, she'd have to find a job to support her addiction."

Evangeline was too overwhelmed to give voice to any of the million thoughts screaming in her head. She was too horrified and appalled by how pathetic humanity was. He'd been just a child. Someone who hadn't asked to be born. Her hands were shaking and she lowered them to hide them at Drake's side, clenching her fingers together so her trembling didn't give her away.

"There's little point in rehashing my entire childhood," he said in a gentle voice. As though he were protecting *her* from the awfulness of his past. For that alone, she wanted to weep. Because when had he ever had anyone to protect him?

"What happened to them? How did you finally escape?"

He grimaced. "My old man was shot by a drug dealer he owed a shit-ton of money to. Again, he wasn't parent or husband of the year, but he did at least try to look out for me. When he wasn't beating the hell out of me," he added dryly. "And he tried to look out for my mother the only way he knew how. By keeping her supplied with her candy of choice. The result was him running up a tab he had no hope of repaying, and they came to collect one night when I was locked in the closet. Again, the closet likely saved my life because if they'd known I was there, they would have either killed me to make their point or taken me, not knowing my parents didn't give a shit about me and wouldn't have done a damn thing to get me back."

"What about your mother?" she whispered.

It made her vaguely ill, but in this moment, she hoped the woman died a long, painful death.

"They quickly figured out the best way to make her suffer was by not killing her and ending her pathetic excuse of a life. With my old man out of the way, she had no help, no support, and she was in agony with withdrawal. They laughed at her and told her to enjoy cold turkey."

Drake reached for one of her hands and pried it away from the other before lacing his fingers in hers.

"Two days later, she killed herself, and I remember standing over her grave and vowing that her life wouldn't be mine. Would never be mine. I wanted better. I was eleven years old and small for my age because of malnourishment and abuse. But I was already planning my future. One doesn't grow up with drug dealers and gangs without being somewhat street smart and knowing what it takes to survive."

"No one took you in after your mother died?" Evangeline asked in bewilderment.

Drake shrugged. "Someone probably would have. At the very least I would have been placed in the system and shuffled from home to home until I turned eighteen. But that wasn't an option for me. At eleven years old, all I could think was that if my own parents couldn't love me, then how could anyone else?"

She could no longer prevent the tears from leaking down her cheeks. She stared at him, her vision blurry with moisture, and then she launched herself at him, throwing her arms around him, pulling him close to her and the erratic beat of her heart.

"I love you, Drake Donovan," she whispered fiercely. "I'll *always* love you. You never have to be alone again and you'll never be without someone who loves you."

He looked shocked, like it was the very last thing he'd expected her to say. She hadn't meant to say it like that. Not now. Not yet. But there was never a better time and she could not allow him to go any longer without knowing she loved him and would do anything for him. No sacrifice was too great.

"Angel," he whispered, his voice breaking. "I—I don't even know what to say. You have no idea how precious a gift this is. I don't deserve it," he said in a shaken tone.

She put her finger to his lips, her expression fierce. "Do not," she commanded. "Do not ever tell me you don't deserve it. As for not knowing what to say, you don't have to say anything at all. You only have to listen. I love you, Drake. Completely, unconditionally, without measure."

He crushed her to him, burying his face in her hair. His entire body shook with the force of his emotion and she simply held him, stroking his back and shoulders, all the while whispering her love for him in his ear.

22

For once, Evangeline was looking forward to a shopping trip. She'd been a little disappointed that Maddox or Silas wasn't free to take her. She'd grown to rely on the two men and their steady companionship. She was admittedly closer to them than any of Drake's other men, but all of them were warm and friendly with her at all times.

But even knowing Maddox and Silas were busy, her enthusiasm couldn't be dimmed. She was going shopping for Drake's Christmas present. She'd pulled out the cash and the credit cards Silas had delivered to her seemingly a lifetime ago, and she grinned, not feeling any remorse for using Drake's money to buy his gift with.

Today was going to be . . . *fun.*

"Yo, Evangeline, you here?" Zander called from the foyer.

She stuffed the money and credit cards in her purse and hurried out to greet him, a welcoming smile on her face. Her eyes widened when she saw two of Drake's other men accompanying Zander. Thane and . . . Damn it. She couldn't remember the other guy's name and it would seem so rude if she couldn't figure out a way around him knowing that little fact.

She remembered him, of course. He was quieter than the others but very sweet and considerate toward her. It reminded her of Hartley's name. Damn it!

"Hey, love," Zander boomed out, hugging her and smacking her noisily on the cheek.

"Hey, Zander," she said warmly. Then she turned. "Hello, Thane." Then she looked at the third man and, thank God, his name popped into her head at the right time. "Hatcher. How are you?"

The other man seemed surprised by her address, but then perhaps he'd assumed she wouldn't remember him since they hadn't spent that much time together. He looked delighted, however, and smiled broadly back at her.

"Hello, Evangeline. You ready to go shopping today?" Hatcher said, offering her his arm as they headed toward the elevator.

"Yes, I am, and I desperately need y'all's help."

Thane chuckled, causing Evangeline to swing her gaze in his direction. "What's so funny?" she asked.

"Nothing, darlin'. I just get tickled when I hear your adorable Southern accent and how you say 'y'all,'" he said with a grin.

Her mouth popped open. "Like you have room to talk! Aren't we supposed to be on each other's sides as Southern folk trapped together in the big bad city?"

Hatcher and Zander joined in the laughter while Thane held up his arm in a signal of peace.

"Now, darlin', you know I don't mean anything by it. I have to admit, you make me homesick every time I listen to you talk."

His voice dropped an octave and for a moment she truly believed he did get homesick. There was a look in his eyes that made her feel sad.

"That Thanksgiving dinner you cooked reminded me of my mama's cooking," Thane went on to explain. "Best damn meal I've had since I left home all those years ago."

"Then clearly I need to invite you over to dinner more often," Evangeline said firmly. "Southern food is a must and can't be forgotten once tasted. That's a sin in anyone's Bible, I'm sure."

Zander shot Thane a black look and then shook his head in Hatcher's direction. "Can you believe Mr. Slick here and how he just managed to finagle regular dinner invitations without so much as breaking a sweat?"

Evangeline notched her chin up in the air and then slid her arm underneath Thane's. "Y'all would do well to take pointers from a true Southern gentleman," she said with a sniff. "They know what's important to a woman's heart."

"And a Southern lady knows what's important to a Southern man's stomach," Thane said, his eyes twinkling. "It's why all the best Southern ladies know how to cook. They do know how to take care of their man," he said wistfully.

Hatcher and Zander both rolled their eyes in disgust, but Thane eyed them slyly.

"Roll your eyes now. Just wait until I'm having dinner with Evangeline and eating her amazing cooking and you two are out eating tacos or that other takeout shit y'all consume on a regular basis."

"Tell me, Thane. Where are you from exactly?" Evangeline asked as he handed her into the waiting car.

"M-I-crooked-letter-crooked-letter-I-crooked-letter-crooked-letter-I . . ."

"Humpback-humpback-I," she finished breathlessly, her eyes sparkling with fun.

"What the hell kind of foreign language are you two spouting now?" Zander grumbled.

"He's from Mississippi," Evangeline replied, still grinning. "Just like I am!"

"And you were able to tell that from him chanting about eyes and crooked letters?"

Zander's expression was baffled, and he looked at them as though they'd both lost their minds. She and Thane both burst into laughter.

"What part of the state are you from, Thane?" Evangeline asked. "I'm from the south. A very small town about thirty miles north of the coast."

"Jackson area," Thane said vaguely.

Evangeline got the impression that Thane didn't talk much about his past, but then none of Drake's men ever did. They treated their past as though it hadn't happened, was off-limits or it was simply distasteful. Maybe all three.

"What do you say we grab lunch before our shopping ordeal begins?" Hatcher asked with an indulgent smile in Evangeline's direction.

"Ooohh, do I get to pick?" she asked.

"That depends," Zander said, glowering at her.

"Wagyu steak?" she wheedled.

"I'm in," Thane emphatically announced.

"Hell yeah, I'm in," Hatcher said immediately.

"You're outvoted," Evangeline told Zander smugly.

He snorted. "As if I'm going to turn down Wagyu steak."

And so it was half an hour later that Evangeline found herself seated at a table in the corner of the restaurant where Justice had first taken her to eat the sumptuous steak.

"Does it make me a horrible person to say I could eat this every single day for the rest of my life and die happy?" she asked, once their orders had been taken.

"Nope," Zander replied. "It's good stuff. Why eat shit if you can eat the best?"

She rolled her eyes. "Not all of us are in the position of affording to eat like this once a month, much less every day."

"I don't think you have to worry about that anymore," Thane said. "If it made you happy, Drake would hire the chef away from this restaurant and he'd have him to the apartment every day cooking it for you."

"Oh good Lord," she said in disgust. "Not a single one of you better even jokingly suggest such a thing to him. I would die of mortification."

Zander shook his head and chuckled. "There are worse things a man could do for his woman."

"I'm going to the ladies' room to freshen up before our food gets here," Evangeline announced, rising from her chair.

The men immediately frowned and when Thane would have risen to go with her, Hatcher, who was at the end of the table, slid from his chair.

"I'll walk her back," he said easily.

She refrained from rolling her eyes again. Barely. But to be fair, Drake had warned her of the way things would be from now on. It wasn't his fault she'd momentarily forgotten. The day seemed so . . . normal. As if none of them had a care in the world. Just a group of friends out for lunch and shopping. Only, if Drake and, well, Maddox and Silas too were to be believed, there was significant danger to her anytime she was by herself.

That thought was enough to quell any protest she might have made that she could go to the bathroom by herself. Drake didn't ask her for much, and he'd been so generous with her that no way would she throw a fit and act like a recalcitrant child.

"Thank you, Hatcher," she said, smiling at him.

Hatcher walked her toward the dark foyer and gestured toward the end. "The ladies' room is at the very back. I'll stand here and make sure no one gets by me who I remotely think could be a threat."

She shivered at the gravity in his tone but didn't respond, nor did she ask him the question she was dying to ask—if he really thought danger lurked around every corner or if this was just Drake being overprotective of her.

Instead, she hurried into the bathroom, not wanting to take any longer than necessary. Her last trip to a public restroom had been nothing short of disastrous when that tall brunette had ripped her to shreds with those ridiculously long claws of her. Figuratively speaking, of course. She'd certainly scored a few direct hits, but then so had Evangeline.

Given time and distance from the event, Evangeline could actually be proud of herself for not allowing the woman to see how upset she had been. She'd made cutting remarks of her own that had definitely found their target, judging by the way the woman's face had paled and then the flash of feminine rage had sparked in her eyes.

But she'd had no comeback to Evangeline's remarks about Drake not sharing anything he considered his or that Evangeline was on his arm when it was a well-known fact, according to Drake's men, that he never had a "bitch" on his arm in public.

She cringed, flinching from his men's use of the word to describe women. It wasn't flattering in the least, and if she didn't know for sure that they didn't put all women into the bitch category she'd tear each of them a new asshole for referring to the female species in such a derogatory manner.

She finished her business and then washed her hands and did a quick once-over of her makeup. She blinked as she saw the woman staring back at her from the mirror. She stopped in her tracks, staring even harder when she realized the woman she was studying so hard was herself.

How much she'd changed in the short time she'd known Drake and been drawn into his world. Gone were the grubby, secondhand clothes, her hair perpetually pulled up into a messy bun or worse, a ponytail holder, and the plain, unsophisticated features of her face.

She looked . . . Her eyes widened and she gasped as she realized where her thoughts were headed. She looked like she . . . *belonged. Here.* In Drake's world. She looked like someone Drake would be likely to be seen with. When had it happened, this transformation from small-town, hopelessly gauche and naïve girl to someone more worldly and sophisticated? She looked almost . . . *pretty.*

She touched her mouth and then ran her finger over the expensive eye shadow. She wasn't made up heavily. Her makeup was subtle and elegant looking. It made her look naturally beautiful instead of like someone who had to wear several layers of cosmetics to achieve that fresh, effervescent look.

Her lip gloss was sheer with a shine and sparkle she was still enough of a girl to appreciate. What woman didn't love sparkly things? Even if she wouldn't admit it. She had no problem admitting her feminine pre-dilections because Drake enjoyed each and every one of them. He'd con-fided in her several times that he loved how much of a "girl" she was and that it took a strong, self-assured woman to allow herself to be utterly feminine and not concern herself with being taken seriously by the rest of the world.

She smiled. Drake might love that about her, but it was himself he needed to thank for that metamorphosis. Because it was he who'd given her that confidence in herself.

Realizing if she didn't hurry, her food would arrive and begin to grow cold, she finished drying her hands and then walked out the door into the darkened hallway. Almost immediately, she bumped into another person, and she murmured her pardon. But when the person didn't move and she realized that it was a man, when the men's bathroom was all the way at the front of the hall with the women's in the very back, she became alarmed and started to step around the figure so she could call for Hatcher if needed.

But once more, he effectively blocked her path by moving to inter-cept her, and as he did so, he opened his coat to reveal a badge affixed to the waist of his pants. And she also saw the really big pistol in the shoul-der holster he wore. Fear spiked through her blood until she was dizzy from it.

"What do you want?" she croaked out.

"Ms. Hawthorn," the man said in a low voice. "May I have a moment of your time, please? I won't take long. I promise. But it's about a very important matter. A police matter."

23

"What do you want from me?" Evangeline managed to squeak out.

He gave her an impatient look that suggested he didn't buy her dim-witted act. Only it wasn't an act! What could the police possibly want with her?

"Your boyfriend is Drake Donovan, correct?"

An icy chill slithered down her spine, and then her back went rigid and she notched her chin up defiantly.

"I fail to see how my personal life is any of your business, and it hardly constitutes a *police matter*."

"Do you know just what all he's into?" the cop asked, his expression darkening.

"He's a businessman," Evangeline snapped. "He owns several busi-nesses, as a matter of fact. One of them is the club Impulse. Perhaps you've heard of it."

The cop shook his head. "You're too naïve and trusting for your own good, Ms. Hawthorn. He's been linked to organized crime, as well as heading an organized-crime syndicate. The men escorting you around? All soldiers in his organization. He's got his fingers in a lot of dirty pies all over the city. He'll take you down with him. You know that, right? If I were to guarantee you police protection, would you be willing to be an informant? Pass along any information pertinent to our investigation?"

Her mouth fell open in horror. "Are you out of your mind?" she exploded. "No, I won't spy on him for you, the cops or anyone else for that matter. He's a good man. Why don't you focus your efforts on taking down the *real* criminals in this city?" she added acidly.

He shook his head regretfully and then reached into his pocket and pulled out his card. "If you ever change your mind or if you get into a situation where you need help or you come across something you feel we should know, don't hesitate to contact me. I'll make sure you don't come to harm."

She snatched the card from his hands, not because she had any intention of ever using it, but because Drake needed to know who was asking questions about him.

"Drake does a perfectly good job of keeping me safe. Now, if you'll excuse me, my lunch is getting cold."

She pushed by him and this time he let her go and she stalked down the hallway and back into the restaurant, her gaze scanning the area for Hatcher. He was only a short distance away on his phone, but when he saw her, he came to alert and shoved his phone in his pocket.

"Everything okay?" he asked sharply, staring intently at her expression.

"I'm fine," Evangeline said stiffly. "Let's get back before our food gets cold."

Not waiting for him to agree or disagree, she walked rigidly back to their table but made a concerted effort to mask the tension and upset in her features. Fortunately for her, the food hadn't arrived yet and both Thane and Zander were staring inquisitively at her but the waiter interrupted, bearing a tray loaded with their plates before they could question her.

It was just as well, because she needed time to compose herself and figure out her best course of action before she went off and did something half-cocked. But the further into the meal they got, the more furious and sick with worry she became. She couldn't just go shopping like nothing had happened. Drake needed to know immediately that he was evidently being investigated by the police. For what, though?

Her thoughts drifted back to the time she'd asked him exactly what he did and his soft request for her to let it go. For him. And she'd agreed. In that moment, she was wholeheartedly glad he hadn't confided in her because her conscience was clear. She couldn't very well tell the police anything if she didn't know.

After they finished eating, she pondered her options, but this time she suffered no remorse whatsoever for deceiving Drake's men. She flashed pleading eyes on Zander. He might well be gruffer and more of a Neanderthal than the rest, but she knew he'd do what she asked of him with no hesitation. Especially if she hinted that she needed to warn Drake.

"I'm afraid I don't feel very much like shopping after all," she said, pushing back her half-eaten steak. "My stomach is pretty upset and my head is starting to hurt. It's probably nothing, but I'd rather go home and lie down. Perhaps we can go shopping another day this week?"

"Do you need a doctor?" Thane demanded.

She smiled, ignoring Hatcher's piercing stare and the fact that he was all but peeling back the layers of her skin. "No, of course not. I just need to lie down. Maybe take a short nap."

"Let's go. Call the car around, Thane," Zander said after pulling off several bills and tossing them onto the table.

Thane and Hatcher went ahead while Zander put his arm around Evangeline's shoulders and herded her toward the entrance as well. A few minutes later, they were in the car and whizzing back to Drake's apartment.

The men studied her during the ride home, but she ignored their scrutiny, instead focusing her attention on the passing scenery through her window. When they arrived at the apartment, she touched Zander on the arm.

"Will you walk me up? There's no need for everyone to come. After all, I'm just going up to bed."

Zander's brow furrowed as if that were the last thing he was expecting her to ask. "Of course. You two go on ahead. I'll call for a car when I'm ready to leave," he said to Thane and Hatcher.

He helped Evangeline from the car and escorted her inside the building. She looked back to make sure the car drove away and as soon as they were inside, she turned to face Zander, her expression one of urgency.

"Zander, I need you to take me to wherever Drake is. Now."

His eyes widened with shock. "What the fuck? What's going on, Evangeline? And swear to God, if you tell me *nothing*, I'll throttle you."

"I'm not going to say *nothing*," she said in a quiet voice. "What I am going to say is that it is very important I see Drake immediately. And you can't tell him I'm coming. I don't care how busy he is, what he's doing, who he's meeting with. You take me straight to him so I can talk to him immediately."

The urgency in her voice registered because grim worry set like stone into his features. He picked up his cell and made a phone call to his driver or Drake's, presumably. His directive was short and to the point. Come pick him up at Drake's apartment and be here as fast as possible.

Drake disconnected the call from Hatcher, his features rigid. Some cop had approached Evangeline at the restaurant where his men had taken her to lunch. They'd spoken in the hall for a period of time before she'd gone back to the others.

Ice invaded his veins at the idea of Evangeline betraying him. Could he have been so wrong about her?

He paced the interior of his office and then stared out over the Manhattan skyline, his thoughts dark and brooding. Should he plant false information and then see what happened? Feed her just enough evidence that he'd know if the cops came sniffing around that she was the only person who could have given it to them?

Nausea swirled in his gut. She'd said she loved him and he'd been too gobsmacked, too ... humbled by her fervent and tender words and the love he'd seen plainly etched in her eyes to do anything more than hold her tightly to him, so afraid that if he let go, even for a moment, it would have all been a dream. The most wonderful dream of his life, but a dream nonetheless.

He let loose a savage torrent of curses that would blister the hide of anyone in earshot. *Fuck me.* What the hell was he supposed to do with the knowledge that Evangeline, his angel, had spoken to a cop?

She'd probed him for answers that night, seemingly a lifetime ago, when she'd asked him what it was he really did and he'd asked her to let it go, that it would never affect her, never touch her. He'd thought and had been relieved that she had let it go, but had she? Had he only heightened her suspicions, enough for her to go to the police?

He turned and threw his phone across the room. It shattered on impact and he left it there in unrecoverable pieces.

He should be pissed. He should even now be plotting his revenge. But the only thing he could process was ... pain. Endless, unending, overwhelming ... pain.

Closing his eyes, he cupped his nape and rubbed up and down as weariness assailed him. God help him, but he couldn't bring himself to punish her, to throw her out. Could he blame her for what she might think when he'd never offered to trust her? To tell her anything of his life apart from her? He knew enough about women to know there weren't many who'd be as accepting as Evangeline had appeared to be.

His thoughts turned bleak, because he didn't know what to do. But he couldn't be with a woman who intended to sell him and his brothers out to the fucking cops.

He went to the phone on his desk after making a mental note to send his assistant out to purchase another cell phone. He was about to pick up the phone to call Evangeline when the door to his office opened.

His head went up, a reprimand for disturbing him when he'd left clear orders for the opposite poised to fly off his tongue, when he saw who was standing in the doorway of his office.

Evangeline?

He dropped the phone and strode around the front of his desk and over to where she stood, visibly shaken and pale.

"Evangeline, what's wrong?" he asked sharply.

Despite the fact that he was looking at a suspected betrayer, his concern for her temporarily edged out all other thoughts and emotions. She looked frightened. Hell, she looked terrified. And she was shaking from head to toe.

She'd never even been to any of his offices other than the one he kept at the club. Though he'd never forbidden her access, it was an unspoken agreement that she was kept separate from work.

What would cause her to break that tacit agreement now? Then his eyes narrowed sharply and a black frown took over his face.

"Where the hell are the men who are supposed to be protecting you?" he asked in a dangerously low tone.

"Z-Zander came with me," she stammered out. "I'm so sorry, Drake. I don't mean to disturb you, but I had to come right away, so I asked Zander if he would bring me. Please don't be angry with him. I didn't give him a choice. I'm sorry for just barging in on you like this, but I had to talk to you."

Puzzled by her panic, Drake guided her toward the couch in front of his desk. "It's all right, Evangeline," he said in a soothing voice. "Sit down."

He took her hands, shocked by how cold they were and how hard they were shaking. Once settled beside her, he studied her features even more closely than before. Anger and a keen sense of protectiveness surged within him when he took in just how pale, scared and shaken she was. Despite his initial anger over her meeting with the cop, he pushed those black thoughts aside for the moment.

"Did someone try to hurt you?" he demanded. "Did someone threaten you in any way?"

"No," she whispered, the sound nearly a sob. "But someone intends to hurt *you*."

He reared back in surprise because that was the very last thing he'd expected her to say. Certain he'd heard wrong, he put both of his hands on her shoulders and forced her to look directly into his eyes.

"What are you talking about? Tell me everything that has happened and especially tell me why you think someone is trying to hurt me."

She took in a deep, steadying breath and when she lifted her gaze to his, tears sparkled on her lashes. "Zander, Thane and Hatcher were going to take me shopping today, but first, we went to eat lunch. While we were waiting for our food, I went to the bathroom and when I came out, there was a man blocking the hallway. When I tried to step around him, he wouldn't let me pass. He showed me . . . He showed me his badge and he was wearing a gun too. Then he called me by name and told me he needed to speak to me about police business.

"I was confused. I mean, why would the police need to speak to me about anything?" she asked in a bewildered voice.

Oh, Drake could well imagine, and the picture was finally starting to form. Fucking bastards using an innocent woman to try to get to him. It shouldn't surprise him. Little did.

"When I said as much, he said—not asked—that you were my *boy-friend*. And I told him that I didn't see how my personal life could possibly be any sort of police business."

Good girl. He mentally applauded her.

"Then he said, and again it wasn't in the form of a question, did I know what all you were into." She shook her head, anger sparking in her eyes, removing the trace of tears from moments earlier. "I told him you had several businesses, one of which was the club. He called me naïve and told me that you would take me down with him. Then . . ."

Her voice cracked and she shuddered, lifting her hands to rub up and down her arms as though she were freezing to death.

"What then, Angel?" he asked gently.

"He gave me this."

She dug into her purse and drew out a business card, holding it out to him with a look of utter distaste as if she couldn't bear to touch it.

"He asked if I'd be willing to pass them information about you. If I would spy on you," she said in a horrified voice. "I told him no. Never. He told me that he would make sure I had police protection and that you would never be able to harm me."

There was a note of derision and scorn in her voice.

"As if you'd ever hurt me," she seethed. "I told him that you do a good enough job on your own of protecting me. And then I told him to get out of my way and to leave me alone. I knew I had to come here and warn you. So after lunch, I pleaded illness and told the others I wasn't feeling up to shopping, and then I asked Zander to walk me up to the apartment, but as soon as the others left, I asked Zander to bring me here. To you."

She looked anxiously at him as if worried he would denounce her, call her a liar or worse. But all he could do was sit there, absolutely flabbergasted by everything she'd told him. An alien warmth filled his chest. He didn't at all know what to make of her declaration. And he had to know why she'd done it. Why had she warned him?

Shame filled him as he remembered his anger, rage and sense of betrayal just minutes before her arrival. Here he'd been doubting her and her loyalty to him when the entire time she'd been tying herself in knots because she was worried about *him*.

"Why did you warn me, Angel?" he asked in a choked whisper. "I know you have your suspicions. And no, I'm not a good man. So why would you warn me instead of helping them put me away?"

He knew he'd made a serious error in his judgment of her when he saw her reaction to his question. Shock and hurt entered her eyes, and her mouth fell open as she continued to stare wordlessly at him. As though she couldn't believe he would even ask such a question. And God, how he wished he hadn't now.

"I would *never* betray you, Drake," she said, her words nearly inaudible as she worked to get each one out. "*Ever*. I am yours. I belong to you. And that means you have everything that is me and mine. My loyalty. My trust. My love."

She abruptly stood and turned away from him and a sense of panic crawled over his skin like a hundred spiders. At the moment, he'd take the actual spiders over the feeling of panic. Would he lose her because of his lack of faith in her?

Then she whirled around, anger and determination in her eyes. "You're wrong, Drake. You *are* a good man. I don't care what you or anyone else says or thinks. They don't know you. I *do*. And you are very much a good man."

She threw up one hand, her fingers delicately fluttering through the air.

"Can you be ruthless, arrogant and demanding? Absolutely. You're driven and relentless. But those aren't *bad* traits. Those traits are what made you into the man you are today and I very much love the man you are. I still wake up every morning wondering if it's all just been a dream because this beautiful man who could have any woman in the world he wanted chose *me*."

Tears glittered harshly in her eyes once more, and it was all he could do to continue sitting there while she flayed her heart open to bare it—to give it—to him. He'd never felt so humbled in his life than by this sweet, generous and loving woman who stood there fiercely defending him when he'd jumped to nasty conclusions without even asking her about the meeting first.

"And you've been so patient with me," she continued, her voice choked with emotion and the mounting tears she was trying so hard not to shed. "You always take the time to teach me what pleases you, and you please me ten times more in return. I just hope . . ."

She turned away in a valiant effort to compose herself before finally turning back to face him.

"I just hope that you never wake up one day and look at me and say to yourself, *What in the world was I thinking?*"

She closed the distance between them and slipped to her knees between his, reaching for his hands, gripping them tightly between hers.

"I have only one thing to ask, Drake," she whispered. "If that ever does happen, if you ever get tired of me and no longer want me, all I ask is for you not to regret the time we spent together. Because I won't. I'll cherish every single memory I made with you, every single minute, and I'll never regret a single second. All I ask is that you do the same and remember me fondly."

Drake felt as though he'd just been flattened. Like a tank had run over him. He was in absolute awe over the woman kneeling before him. His throat contracted painfully as he realized it was he who should be on his knees in front of her.

Instead he yanked her into his arms, holding her so tightly, it was likely neither of them could breathe very well. Who cared? He'd never get enough of this, of her, soft and sweet in his arms.

"Jesus," he breathed. "You don't get it, do you? There isn't going to be another woman, Angel. There won't come a morning that I wake with you nestled against me or tied to me, so sweet and good and innocent, that I wonder what I was thinking. The only thing I'll ever think when I wake up next to you is that I'll never let you go."

She went utterly still in his arms. So still he wasn't sure she was breathing. He loosened his hold and she drew away, staring at him with features seemingly frozen in place. There was a dim light of hope in her eyes that cut him to the bone. Almost as if she were afraid to question him. Or confirm what he'd said.

She licked her lips and finally whispered in a thready breath, "Never?"

"Never," he said firmly.

She sagged so that her behind came to rest on her heels and her shoulders drooped. Then her hands flew to cover her face, but he saw the evidence of her tears leak from underneath.

"Don't cry, Angel," he soothed, carefully pulling her into his arms again. "Never cry. I want you to be happy. Always."

"Oh, Drake, don't you know? You've just made me the happiest person in the entire world," she sobbed. "I was so scared for you today. I'm still scared," she amended. "What are you going to do?"

Fear replaced all other emotion in her vivid blue eyes. He leaned forward and pressed his lips to her forehead.

"Don't worry, Angel. Can you do that for me? This is nothing new, I assure you. The cops are always poking around my affairs. Talking to people I work or associate with. They've never been able to get anything on me. They never will."

She bit into her lip so hard that he gently thumbed it, rubbing soothingly over the abused flesh.

"Are you sure?" she asked nervously. "Maybe you should call your lawyer. Surely it can't be legal for them to go around harassing people who know you and asking them to spy on you."

He had to suppress his smile over her innocence. "Unfortunately, my angel, it's very legal for them to question anyone they want. You did very well. I'm proud of the way you handled yourself. That couldn't have been easy. I'm sorry it happened. You can be sure that in the future it won't."

"I don't care about me," she said impatiently. "I'm more worried about the fact that this cop seemed awfully determined to get something—anything—on you. Somehow I don't think it would matter to him whether it was actually true."

Her scathing tone did make him smile then.

"Who needs a lawyer when I have you to defend and protect me?" he asked in amusement. "Apparently you are all I need, my darling angel."

"I hope that's true," she said, her expression growing serious. "Because you are all I will ever need, Drake."

24

The weeks leading to Christmas were a magical time for Evangeline. Though Drake had always been loving and tender with her, there was a marked difference in his entire demeanor than there had been in the beginning. He was openly demonstrative with her and had no problem showering her with affection whether in private or public.

His men ribbed him about it, but he took it in stride and blithely told them when they found a woman like Evangeline to come back and they'd talk then. There hadn't been much in response his men could say to that, so they quickly shut up.

Then he'd surprised her by flying them both down to visit her parents just before Christmas, though he'd insisted they return to the city so they could spend Christmas Eve and Christmas Day together at the apartment.

They'd spent three wonderful days with her family, but it was Drake's Christmas gift to them that had blown Evangeline—and her mother and father—completely away.

The day before he and Evangeline were to return to New York, Drake had taken Evangeline and her parents to a beautiful house in the same town they lived in and told them it was theirs.

It had been completely renovated to make it wheelchair accessible, and the kitchen had been gutted and a chef's dream kitchen had been constructed with top-of-the-line appliances and countertops. Her mother had cried tears of joy. Even her father had been overwhelmed and emotional.

But Drake hadn't stopped there. He'd done one better. The new house not only came with a housekeeper who came in three days a week to clean, but he also presented her mother with the keys to a brand-new van so her dad wasn't housebound so much.

Her mother had hugged Drake at least a hundred times and thanked him profusely not only for his generosity but also for making her baby so happy. And one had only to look at Evangeline to see that she radiated happiness. She glowed from head to toe with contentment only someone deeply in love could feel.

And to properly and creatively express her gratitude for all he'd done for her family, Evangeline had wickedly made love to him aboard his jet the entire flight back to New York City. He'd jokingly told her as they'd gotten into the car at the airport that she'd worn him out and that he wouldn't be able to get out of bed to celebrate Christmas with her.

She had very seriously told him that if he couldn't get out of bed, then she would have no choice but to join him there, and since she'd be bored out of her mind she would have to come up with ways to keep herself entertained. He'd informed her that what she was saying wasn't exactly a threat and he could certainly think of worse ways to spend the holiday.

Christmas Eve dawned clear and cold, a brisk wind whistling through the streets, but the skies were completely clear and cloudless, the sun bright overhead, much to Evangeline's disappointment. After all, what was Christmas without snow?

Drake laughed and told her that snow was indeed in the forecast starting early in the evening.

Evangeline hustled around the kitchen the entire morning in preparation for Drake's men to arrive for an early Christmas Eve dinner that afternoon. She'd bought every single one of them a gift and they all lay wrapped underneath the tree. Along with the dozen she'd bought for Drake.

He'd been highly secretive about what he was getting for her, even going so far as not to put a single one under the tree that had her name on it. She pouted every time she looked at the tree, and he merely laughed.

Drake found her tending one of the many skillets at the stove and slid his arms around her, pulling her back against his chest. His lips feathered over the side of her neck and he nibbled at the sensitive flesh just beneath her ears.

"There you are," he murmured. "Planning to spend the entire day in here? I'm starting to feel neglected."

"You poor baby, you," she said without real sympathy. "You won't be complaining later when you taste what I'm making."

He sniffed appreciatively. "It smells delicious. What is it? It doesn't look traditional. Aren't those fish fillets and shrimp over there?"

She smiled. "Yep. I'm cooking you down-home Southern food for Christmas Eve. Tomorrow I'm forgoing turkey and ham, and instead I'm cooking a rib roast with several delicious sides and we'll have lobster bisque as a starter."

He groaned. "God, woman. I'm seriously going to have to hire a personal trainer. I swear I've gained twenty pounds since I met you and you started feeding me."

She lifted an eyebrow and turned her head so she could look up at him. "Where are these twenty pounds you've gained? Because they aren't anywhere I can see them."

He pretended to give the matter serious consideration. "Well, I suppose the fact that you ravish me on a daily basis balances out all the calories I'm consuming. Satisfying you is very strenuous activity."

"I can always curb *my* appetite," she said sweetly. "I'd hate for you to suffer needlessly."

"Try it," he growled. "If I die, I'll go a happy man. Well fed and sexually sated by the most gorgeous, sexy, desirable woman on the planet."

"Wow," she murmured. "Biased much?"

He smacked her playfully on the ass but it carried a bite, causing her pulse to surge to life.

"I'm not biased. I'm a man of discerning tastes. I refuse to settle for anything less than the best. Which is why I waited for you."

She was speechless and precariously close to tears, and she wasn't about to ruin the light and playful mood by sobbing all over him.

He sighed and gave a mock groan of exasperation. "When will we ever get to the point that I can compliment you without you crying all over me?" he chided.

"Never," she mumbled. "Get used to it."

"It appears I have no choice," he said dryly.

The door buzzer sounded and Drake made a disgruntled noise. "So much for being alone anymore."

"Don't be rude and antisocial toward our guests," she reproached.

He laughed at that. "Darling, I'm always rude and antisocial. They'd likely have me committed if I ever wasn't. Or at least they'd think I'd been abducted by aliens."

She elbowed him in the gut as he moved away from her to answer the summons. A few moments later, Drake's men were crowding into the apartment, all carrying brightly wrapped packages that were immediately stuck under the tree.

Then, predictably, they all sauntered into the kitchen with the same question. What were they having for dinner?

Evangeline had set the formal dining table and made certain there were enough chairs for every single person. Two hours after Drake's men arrived, she made the call for dinner and then watched in satisfaction as they all gathered around the table. Drake sat at the head while Evangeline sat to his right and Silas sat to his left. The others took their places down either side with Maddox taking the other end across from Drake.

"Before we all dig in, I just want to thank Evangeline for going to such trouble to prepare such a wonderful meal for us all," Drake said, pride clearly reflected in his eyes as he gazed affectionately in her direction.

"I propose a toast," Silas said, lifting his glass of wine. "To Evangeline. One of the sweetest, kindest and most generous people I've ever had the pleasure of knowing and who also, irrefutably, has the biggest heart of anyone I've ever met."

"I'll drink to that," Maddox said, raising his glass in salute.

"I, as well," Drake said, tipping his glass in her direction. "And don't you dare cry."

She laughed, because if she didn't, well, she would indeed cry. She raised her glass and swept her gaze over all of the gathered men.

"Thank you all for coming and for making this holiday so special."

They were a bit noisy as they all chimed in, but then they drank down part of their wine and Evangeline started the dishes flowing around the table, serving up blackened catfish fillets, grilled and fried shrimp, crawfish étouffée to accompany the fillets and then the vegetables, after which the best came last. Her homemade rolls.

As soon as the first man bit into a fresh, piping hot roll, a groan went up.

"Oh Jesus," Hartley said, his expression one of supreme bliss. "That is the best thing I've ever tasted in my life."

Curious over his reaction, everyone began grabbing for their rolls at the same time and then the table erupted in moans, sighs and exclamations of sheer bliss.

"Goddamn, Drake," Justice complained. "Why did you have to get to her first? I would be her slave for life for nothing more than her rolls."

"I'll have to remember that," Evangeline said mischievously. "Now I know what to do when I want a favor. Just dangle a homemade roll in front of your nose."

"Honey, you won't have to dangle for me," Jax said with his best puppy-dog eyes. "Just say the word *roll* and I'll be at your beck and call."

"You bunch of jackasses," Drake said. "Leave my woman alone. For that matter, leave my rolls alone. There better be some left for me or I'll kick all your asses."

Silas, who'd been silent as he chewed on his roll, glanced over at Drake and in a perfectly straight voice said, "You'll have to go through me first. These rolls are totally worth doing jail time for murder."

Evangeline burst into laughter at Drake's surprised expression. Then the rest of his men started laughing at Silas's still-somber, perfectly straight face.

"Y'all are too much," she said, shaking her head.

They ate, enjoying one another's company. Teasing, bickering and bantering continued throughout the entire meal, and Evangeline decided this must be what it was like to have a large family with several siblings.

She'd love to have a large family of her own one day. As many children as she could safely deliver. She had no idea how Drake felt about children or if he even wanted them, but she hoped with all her heart he did. He would be such a good father. And he'd protect her and their children with his life.

Drake reached underneath the table to catch her hand in a squeeze. His smile was full of warmth and something that looked so very much like ... love. It made her so wistful. She knew he cared deeply about her. Perhaps he even loved her but just hadn't admitted it to himself much less her. She could wait, though. She wasn't going anywhere. She'd wait forever if that was what it took. He—and his love—were worth waiting for.

When they were finished eating, they left the dishes out on the table for the cleaning service to get later that night, and all filed into the living room where a fight broke out over who got to be "Santa."

Evangeline was astonished by so many burly, badass-looking alpha males actually arguing over who got to give out the presents under the tree. Finally Silas silenced them all by announcing that he would pass out presents, and Evangeline thought the others were going to suffer apoplexy, in shock over Silas voluntarily doing any such thing. Justice looked as though he might suffer a stroke or an aneurysm as he stared at Drake's most senior man like he'd just grown a second head.

But Silas merely smiled and asked Evangeline to sit on the couch so he could pass her gifts out to her.

"Wait, what?" she asked in bewilderment. "I don't have anything to unwrap. You're supposed to pass out the gifts I got for all of you."

Silas shook his head as did the others. Maddox scowled at her.

"So you think it's appropriate for you to have gotten all of us something but it's not okay for us to have gotten you a gift?" Silas asked pointedly.

She flushed. "You weren't supposed to know—until now—that I had even gotten you anything."

"We didn't," Silas said dryly. "We were in here to give you our gifts."

"We got presents?" Zander asked in a hopeful voice.

She chuckled because he sounded like an excited little boy at Christmas. In fact, looking around at all of them, they were all smiling and looked eager to see what she had gotten. She was glad now that she had gone completely overboard with her shopping and had gotten each of them multiple gifts.

"I just hope y'all like them," she murmured self-consciously.

"We'll love whatever you got us," Maddox said, shooting the others a warning stare.

Silas began handing everyone's gifts out, and the guys promptly tore into theirs with all the gusto and excitement of a bunch of teenagers. She watched, too transfixed by the smiles and reactions to her gifts to pay any attention to hers. This was a Christmas she'd never forget no matter how long she lived. She slid a glance at Drake to get his reaction. This was their first Christmas together and they'd shared it first with her family and now with his. Later? They'd have their own Christmas celebration in private. But for now she was taking it all in and savoring every single memory made.

Drake smiled at her and mouthed, *Thank you.* She smiled broadly in return, letting him know that he was more than welcome. The silly man. It was he who had done far more for her than she would ever do for him.

Every single man came over to offer Evangeline a hug and a kiss on the cheek, and each sincerely thanked her for the gifts she'd gotten them. Then, of course, they urged her to open hers and she eagerly dove in, ripping the paper to shreds in her haste to see what was inside.

The guys teased her and poked fun, but there was open warmth and affection for her in each of their expressions.

At the end of the evening, Evangeline hated to see them go, although she was looking forward to whatever Drake had planned. He hadn't said much other than he wanted them to open their gifts to one another on Christmas Eve instead of waiting until Christmas morning. And since she hadn't seen the first present from him with her name on it, she had no clue what he could have gotten her.

And, well, after all he'd done for her parents, surely he had to know that there wasn't a single other thing she needed. All she could have ever asked for, he'd already provided. If she hadn't already acknowledged her love for him, then it would have been sealed when he'd gifted her parents with the house renovated especially for her father's needs.

After hugging and kissing everyone good-bye, Evangeline plopped onto the couch and curled her feet underneath her as she watched the flames in the electric fireplace in Drake's living room. Then, remembering the forecast, she got up and hurried to the window, hoping to get a glimpse of snow flurries. But what she saw had her exclaiming her delight.

"Drake, look! It's snowing! Big fat fluffy snowflakes too!"

Drake returned from seeing his men to the elevator and curled his arms around her waist, pulling her into his embrace. He smiled and kissed her temple.

"I see that, Angel. Does that complete your Christmas, then?"

She turned in his arms and looped her arms up and around his neck. "You complete my Christmas, Drake. I can live without snow. I can't live without you."

He kissed her slow and sweet, his tongue stroking the depths of her mouth.

"Come sit on the sofa and let me go get my gifts for you."

Excitement raced through her veins and she was nearly jittering as she returned to the couch. Flashing a knowing smile in her direction, he disappeared into the bedroom only to return a short time later with several wrapped packages. He laid them under the tree and then went back for more. But when he walked back in the direction of the bedroom a third time, her mouth fell open.

"Drake! How many presents did you buy me?" she asked, appalled at the mound of presents piled under the tree.

He grinned as he dumped the third load under the tree and then set off again for the bedroom. She was going to kill him. She didn't need all this stuff! But, remembering his reaction before when she'd resisted the gifts he'd bought for her, she silenced her objections, refusing to ruin the holiday for him. If he enjoyed buying her things, she wouldn't deprive him of that pleasure.

Finally, after the fourth trip, he returned to the sofa and held out his hand to her. She let him pull her up from the couch and lead her toward the tree, where they both sat on the floor. Oh, this was going to be so much fun.

They took turns opening gifts, each expressing the sentiment behind each one. Drake looked honestly pleased by what she'd chosen for him, and she hadn't realized just how nervous she'd been over his reaction until she saw that he truly loved everything she'd picked out.

The whole unwrapping-gifts thing seemed to bemuse and befuddle him in turns. Her heart clenched thinking about the fact that no one had ever likely given him a Christmas present, a birthday present or any kind of present for that matter. If she had her way, she'd give him happiness and joy for the rest of her days.

They'd opened the last of the gifts, or so she'd thought. As she started to get up to start picking up the wrapping paper that lay in shreds all around them, he caught her hand and tugged her back down, only this time, he positioned her in his lap with one arm curled securely around her.

"I have one more present for you," he said in a husky voice.

"Oh, Drake, you shouldn't have," she said helplessly. "I think you bought the contents of one entire department store already!"

He handed her a medium-sized perfectly square and artfully wrapped gift with a huge bow made from satin ribbon. It was almost too beautiful to open.

"Go ahead," he urged. "Open it."

With shaking hands, she reverently removed the ribbon and bow and then tore off the paper. When she opened the box, yet another box lay inside. She pulled it out and then proceeded to open it. When she saw the small jeweler's box inside the second box, her breath caught, refusing to expel from her contracted lungs.

Her fingers glanced clumsily off the top of the box as she tried to get it open. Finally, Drake helped her by flipping the top up to reveal a gorgeous, huge diamond solitaire ring. She glanced hastily at him, her eyes wide with question. She wasn't jumping to any conclusions and potentially humiliating herself, but oh God, she couldn't breathe!

He took the ring from the box and then proceeded to slide it on the ring finger of her left hand. Her vision blurred with tears and her nostrils flared as she fought to maintain control of her raging emotions.

Then he cupped her chin with his hand and looked intently into her eyes.

"Will you marry me, Angel?" he asked solemnly. "Will you be mine, legally, for the rest of our lives?"

"Oh, Drake," she said on a shaky breath. "Are you sure? You really want to marry me?"

"I've never been more sure of anything in my life," he vowed. "You are the only woman I've ever wanted—or will ever want—to marry me. To have my children. To grow old with me. Say yes, Angel. I don't want to wait. I want you to be mine in every way possible so the world knows you're mine."

She flung her arms around his neck and hugged him fiercely, her heart beating insanely fast, so fast she was lightheaded.

"Yes! Oh my God, yes! I love you so much, Drake. I'll never love anyone but you. There is nothing more that I'd love than to be your wife and to have your children. I want an entire houseful," she said wistfully. "How many do you want?"

He smiled, his eyes filling with absolute satisfaction. He looked . . . happy.

"I'll give you as many children as you want, Angel. With you as their mother, I'll never have to worry about our children having the kind of childhood I did." He hesitated, his eyes dimming for a brief second. Then he looked back at her, his expression so fierce and . . . loving . . . that it took her breath away. "Before you, I would have said that I'd never marry. Never have children. The risk was too great. I never wanted any child of mine to have the same kind of mother I had. One who would have aborted me if it weren't for the benefits she would receive for having me.

But then I met you and everything changed. I didn't know women like you existed," he said with awe and reverence. "But thank God they do. And thank God I found you."

"Oh, Drake," she repeated for the third time that evening. It seemed like they were the only two words she was capable of saying. "You've made me so very happy. You are a living reminder that dreams really do come true. You've made all mine come true. How could I not love you? How could I not marry you? How could I want any man but you to father my children?"

"How about we go to bed and practice making one of those babies," he said, a wicked gleam in his eyes. "I wanted to exchange gifts tonight because I wanted to spend our first Christmas together in bed, making love with the knowledge that as soon as I can arrange it, you'll be mine in every possible way in the eyes of God and man."

"I don't think you need any practice in that area whatsoever," she said with a sultry smile. "But I'm completely on board with a trial run. You know, just to make sure that when we do decide to make a child, we do it right."

25

"So let's see the ring," Maddox said when he entered the apartment with Silas accompanying him. "Swear to God, Drake has kept you under tight wraps ever since he popped the question at Christmas. I was beginning to wonder if we'd ever see you again until he finally told us you were coming to the club to celebrate New Year's Eve with us."

Evangeline blushed, but her smile was from ear to ear as she extended her hand so the other men could see the enormous diamond glittering on her finger. The stone was so huge and likely so exorbitantly expensive that she lived in fear of losing it. So she never took it off. Ever.

Maddox whistled in appreciation. "Drake knows how to do it up right when he finally takes the plunge. Never thought I'd see the day, but damn, here you are. The future Mrs. Drake Donovan."

"Congratulations, doll," Silas said in his quiet tone.

"Thank you both," she said, offering each an affectionate hug. "Are y'all ready to go? I admit, after being holed up for the last week here with Drake, I'm getting a little stir-crazy. I'm ready to get out and actually see people!"

Maddox chuckled. "Your ride awaits, my lady. And may I say how amazing you look tonight. I'm tempted to go make you change now because once Drake takes one look at you, he's likely going to make me turn around and bring you right back home."

Silas's lips compressed to prevent his laughter from escaping, but he ruefully acknowledged that Maddox was quite likely right.

"He bought the damn thing, so he can just suck it up while I wear it," she grumbled.

"I can see why he bought it," Silas observed. "But somehow I think he had himself in mind when he bought it for you. And not half a dozen other men who certainly appreciate a beautiful woman when they see one."

"Let's go before one of you does decide to make me go change," she said in exasperation.

Dusk had fallen by the time the car carrying Evangeline, Maddox and Silas arrived at the club. They passed by the front entrance, where despite the cold and the flurries swirling in the air, a long line extended down the block to wrap around the building going down the next street.

"Wow, it looks crazy busy," she exclaimed.

"It's the club's biggest night of the year," Maddox replied. "And it does get pretty crazy. Drake always hires extra muscle and eyes for New Year's Eve."

She made a face. "Reminds me of the first night I came here."

Silas reached over to squeeze her hand. "Don't even think about that tonight. Tonight is your night to shine and have fun."

She smiled at him. "Oh, don't worry. I don't have a single regret about that night other than I wasn't the one who punched Eddie in the face. That would have been the only thing that made it better. It's the night I met Drake."

Maddox grinned. "Very true. And I have to say, sweetheart, that night ranks pretty high on my list as well."

They parked in the back next to Drake's sleek car, and Silas helped her out before positioning her solidly between the two men as they entered the building. They were greeted by several of Drake's employees as they passed on their way to Drake's office. Knowing that Drake had likely already zeroed in on her presence, she smiled broadly and blew a kiss in the general direction of his office.

Beside her, Maddox chuckled. "You're such a little tease."

"*Moi?*" she asked innocently.

"You're good for him," Silas said in a serious tone.

Her eyebrows went up but she said nothing as they rode the elevator up. When the doors opened, she was assailed by a sense of déjà vu. She was brought back to the very first time she'd ridden this elevator, terrified and embarrassed beyond words only to be confronted by the force of nature that was Drake Donovan.

She sighed happily. So much had changed since then. Who would have ever guessed that the woman who'd walked so hesitantly into Impulse that first time would be coming back as Drake's future wife?

Before they'd taken three steps, Drake materialized at her side, his expression comical as he took in her dress.

"Jesus. I didn't exactly intend for you to wear the dress here," he choked out.

She turned in a slow circle, her hands out, palms up. "You don't like it?" she asked.

"You know damn well I like it," he growled. "What I don't like is all of my men seeing you in the damn thing."

"We'll suffer through it somehow," Justice drawled from behind him.

"Oh, I'm sure you will," Drake muttered.

Then he dropped a kiss on Evangeline's lips. "I missed you," he said where only she could hear.

Delight fizzed in her veins like a shaken-up soda.

"I missed you too," she said huskily.

Then she turned to the others. "Where's the champagne? Surely you can't have a New Year's Eve party without champagne?"

"Allow me," Jax said, stepping up with a fluted glass of bubbly champagne.

Drake guided her back to his desk, where he sat in his chair and then promptly pulled her down to sit in his lap. She relaxed against him and sipped at the delicious drink.

"So who's going to dance with me tonight?" she asked mischievously.

Drake's hand tightened at her waist. "I'll be the only damn man you dance with."

"Oh, come on, Drake," she pouted. "Surely you'll let them all have a dance with me at our wedding."

His gaze softened even as fire ignited in his eyes. "They get one minute apiece at the reception."

"You're so generous, man," Zander drawled. "You're taking the prettiest and sweetest woman in the entire damn city off the market and you give us one minute to dance with her. Nice."

"Shut up or you lose her cooking as well," Drake said with a scowl.

"Consider me shutting up right now," Zander said, holding his hands up in surrender.

For the next few hours, the office held a festive air as they refilled Evangeline's champagne glass until she had a full-out buzz going. She laughed, smiled and made jokes over the stupidest stuff, but the men didn't seem to mind at all. Drake grinned the entire time, even going as far as to tell her what a cute drunk she was.

"I am not drunk!" she gasped.

Maddox snickered. "Don't bet on that, sweetheart. You're buzzing pretty good right now, I'd say."

Her eyes narrowed but the problem was, when she did so, Maddox sprouted into three of him. Deciding not to share that particular piece of information with him, she instead ignored him.

"Hey, countdown is on," Hartley announced. "Thirty seconds to midnight."

Evangeline seized Drake's hand and sent him a dazzling smile. "This is going to be the best year ever," she whispered.

His eyes glittered and he cupped her face, drawing her down into a long, deep kiss.

Behind them, the guys started counting. "Eight, seven, six, five . . ."

They got all the way down to one and the dance floor below them erupted at the precise moment the doors to Drake's office exploded inward and men carrying assault rifles, yelling for everyone to get down, poured through the entrance.

Drake surged up from his chair, pushing Evangeline behind him just as two guns were pointed at his head.

"Get down!" one of the men barked. "NYPD! We have a warrant to search the premises."

"What the fuck?" Drake snarled.

Evangeline had to clamp a hand over her mouth to keep from screaming, but when two of the men went for Drake, who hadn't obeyed their command to get down, she launched herself at them, spitting fury.

"You stay away from him!" she shrieked. "What are you doing to him? You can't barge onto his private property, point guns at him and then manhandle him like this!"

Silas and Maddox were both being subdued but not easily. And when one of the cops went for Evangeline, Drake erupted in fury, but it was another cop, the apparent leader, who halted everyone in their tracks.

"Leave her alone," the cop barked. "She's with us. She's legit. Leave her and take care of the rest."

The cop let go of Evangeline's arm, causing her to stumble back, her alcohol-fuzzed brain trying to make sense of what the cop had just said. Dear God, he made it sound like . . . Oh God, he'd actually *implied* . . . No. She would not allow this to happen. She would not let Drake ever think she had any part in this.

She watched in horror as each of his men was cuffed and made to lie facedown on the floor while she just stood there, untouched or bothered by any of the officers. What the hell did they think they were doing? Was this her payback for refusing to help them bring Drake down? They implicated her anyway? Why? What purpose could they possibly have for fucking her over so horribly? Did they hate Drake that much? That they'd seek to take everything he cared about away from him?

No, Drake would never believe them. He wouldn't. He believed in her. But one pleading look in his direction found his gaze on her, smoldering with rage and betrayal. He looked right through her, like she was nothing. Like she was the worst sort of person in the world.

In her fury, she launched herself at the nearest officer. "Stop this!" she screamed. "Get out! I'm calling his lawyer right now. Swear to God we'll sue your asses. Every single goddamn one of you!"

"Back off," one of the cops told her in an icy voice. "We have a legal warrant to search the Impulse offices of one Drake Donovan and to confiscate anything we feel may aid us in our investigation."

"Bullshit!" she yelled. "I'll have your fucking badge!"

She was so furious that she was screaming words that would have her mother washing her mouth out with soap for a year. But she didn't care. She was fighting for her life here. Oh God, Drake hated her. It was there for everyone to see in his eyes as he coldly stared her down.

For an excruciating hour, they tossed the entire contents of Drake's office while Evangeline stood there sobbing. She'd never felt so helpless in her life as she stood there watching her life slowly drain away.

Evidently frustrated with their efforts to find whatever it was they were looking for, the lead officer called a halt to the search. They uncuffed Drake and all his men and then advised Drake not to leave the city any time in the next several days and that they would be contacting him for further questioning once they'd analyzed all the evidence against him.

That was the most ridiculous, trumped-up thing Evangeline had ever heard of. She might not have a law degree, but this wasn't the way the police conducted an investigation. They didn't barge in with a search warrant and then tip their hand when they found nothing and basically tell Drake exactly what their plans were. Did they think he was stupid? Unless . . . it was all a plan to get Drake to do something stupid. Like panic and make a mistake and lead them right to whatever it was they were searching for.

If that was the best plan they could come up with to take Drake down, they were incompetent idiots. He would never fall for something this absurd. It was like freaking amateur hour. And she was supposed to feel safe with guys like these protecting the city she lived in?

As the police filed out the door, leaving the shattered remnants of it behind, Evangeline launched herself across the room and against Drake's chest, horrified at the humiliating treatment he'd been subjected to at their hands.

Tears streamed down her face as she stared up into Drake's cold one. "Oh my God, Drake, what did they want?"

"You tell me," he said in a frigid tone.

He roughly shoved her away from him, causing her to trip and stumble in the heels she wore. She would have gone down, but Silas caught her. He steadied her on her feet, a look of grave concern on his face.

"Are you all right, Evangeline?" he asked, worry evident in his tone.

Silas's actions served to only piss Drake off even further.

"Get out," Drake said flatly. "Get the hell out. So help me God, if I ever see your face again, I'll have you thrown out and I'll serve a restraining order against you so that you can't come within a hundred yards of me. *Ever.*"

"Drake!" she cried, numbness invading her. Coldness overtaking her skin, her blood, her heart. "Oh God, Drake, don't do this. Please. You have to listen to me. I know you're upset right now, but you have to see this whole thing was a ridiculous setup. Can't you see that?"

"Setup? Yes, I suppose you could say that's exactly what it was," he said bitterly. "You played the part very well, Evangeline. You're to be congratulated. Did it give you an extra sense of victory to know you'd gotten further than any woman ever had before?"

"That's enough, goddamn it, Drake," Maddox swore violently.

Drake turned on his man. "You stay the fuck out of this. All of you." Then he turned back to Evangeline, so much hatred shining in his eyes that she realized the futility of her ever thinking he could love her. "The price of betrayal is everything," he said, his voice growing colder with every single word. "I want you out and I don't ever want you near my apartment, the club, any of my businesses, and Evangeline, you don't want to know what happens to people who don't heed my instructions."

His voice had dropped to a dangerously low level, but she was beyond caring, beyond pride. If she lost him, she lost everything anyway. What did it matter if she had nothing else?

She went to her knees in front of him, her eyes begging him to listen to her. To believe in her.

"Drake, please, you have to listen to me. I have never betrayed you," she said softly, painfully. "Not once. I have always had faith in you. I've always believed in you. I've never questioned you. And now I'm asking for the same from you. I'm begging you to trust me. To believe in me until I have a chance to prove I had nothing to do with this."

Drake flinched. Silas and Maddox winced, their eyes brimming with sympathy—and anger, fully directed at Drake.

"I'm on my knees, Drake, and I swore to never allow myself the humiliation I felt the night you degraded me in our apartment, but right now, I have no pride. I have nothing if you don't believe in me. Please say you'll believe in me. Just this once, Drake. I swear you'll never have cause to question me again."

For a moment, she thought she might have gotten through to him. She couldn't bear to look at all his other men. They'd just been harassed and embarrassed and inconvenienced for over an hour and if they, like Drake, blamed her, then she'd find no safe harbor in their eyes.

So far, she'd only borne witness to Silas's and Maddox's reactions, and at least they seemed inclined to give her the benefit of the doubt.

"Listen to her, Drake. Don't be stupid," Silas said with a curse. "Look at her, for God's sake. She's on her knees begging you. Is that what you really want from the woman you're going to marry?"

His words had a whiplike effect on Drake. His eyes grew ruthless and ice encompassed him to the point where she no longer recognized the man standing above her, looking down at her like she was nothing but trash.

"No," Drake bit out, a lethal edge to his voice. "You're right. She isn't at all what I want in the woman I marry. I expect my wife to have utmost loyalty to me and to my men. Not seduce me with lies in order to give information to undercover cops."

All the blood left Evangeline's face. All the life left her body and she sagged downward, her knees no longer able to support her. She listened dully as Drake, seemingly miles away, barked an order to someone—Who?—to get her the hell away from him. To throw her out. Anywhere but here, but get her out of his face and his life forever.

"See her out, Hatcher, Jax," he said in a harsh tone. "Since Silas and Maddox seem to have difficulty heeding my orders."

"You touch her and you die." Silas's voice hissed into the silence, his voice sounding like the harbinger of death. "Get away from her. Now," he barked.

Then, as if he hadn't just threatened to kill one of his own brothers, Silas very gently helped her to her feet, another savage curse spewing from his lips when she stumbled and couldn't get her legs underneath her.

He half picked her up, tucking her underneath his shoulder, and walked toward the elevator, her silent sobs racking her entire body, her head hung in defeat, her shoulders as bowed as her head.

He turned at the elevator and directed his cold, unforgiving stare at Drake. "See what you've done, Drake. Take a long, hard look at what you've destroyed. I'd tell you to have a nice life, but you've fucked up any chance you ever had of that."

Maddox strode to the elevator, holding his hand to prevent the doors from shutting. "Make sure she's safe and cared for," Maddox said to Silas in a low voice. "I'm going to stay here until I find out what the fuck is going on and who betrayed us. This whole thing stinks to high heaven."

Evangeline lifted her head and stared blankly at Maddox. He flinched when he met her gaze, and blind fury welled in his eyes.

"You heard Drake," she said in a vacant tone. "I betrayed you. Him."

"That's fucking bullshit and you and I both know it," Maddox exploded.

"But he doesn't," she said, tears running down her cheeks, her voice cracking under the weight of her grief. "And now he never will."

"Look at me, Evangeline," Maddox said, in a tone he'd never before used with her. It was like a thread of steel, unbending, dominant, forceful. She was helpless to do anything but obey. "He *will* know it wasn't you. But I'm afraid it's too late for him now. He didn't believe you when it mattered. When I bring him irrefutable evidence that proves your innocence, he'll know he made the biggest fucking mistake of his life. And then he'll have to live with the consequences for the rest of it."

"Take care of him, Maddox. Please. For me. Someone is out to hurt him. To destroy his life—and yours. Don't let them get away with it. They lied about me to him. They aren't honorable or noble police. They won't use the law to get to Drake. They'll go around it. So please keep him safe."

"Son of a bitch," Silas said, fury emanating from him in waves. "I can't stomach this another goddamn minute. Let us go, Maddox. Before I go in there and take Drake down myself so the cops have one less thing to worry about. That son of a bitch just cut her down as cruelly and as viciously as a man could ever cut down another woman, much less one he'd asked to marry him. And yet here she stands begging us to take care of him and keep him safe? I'd like to kill the bastard with my own hands."

"He's your brother, Silas. Please. Just let me go. You're needed here. Just . . ."

She broke down into another torrent of tears. Maddox reached out to touch her hair and for the briefest of seconds, she could have sworn she saw moisture welling in Maddox's eyes. But no, that was merely her own tears.

"Be well, Evangeline. Until we meet again. And we *will* meet again. You have my number. If there is anything you need, anything at all, I expect you to call me. If I find out you were in need and you didn't call me, I'm going to be one seriously pissed-off son of a bitch. You get me?"

She nodded, her misery making her increasingly numb to anything else but the overwhelming pain and despair welling from the deepest part of her soul.

"Take care of her, Silas," Maddox ordered softly.

"You know I will. Watch your six," Silas said, his tone growing more rigid and furious with every passing second. "Until we know where the leak is, watch your six."

"Watch yours—and hers," Maddox said pointedly. "She's a vulnerable target, at least until it gets out that Drake is flying solo, and it would be a good idea if we sped up that particular bit of news leaking, if it protects her."

Evangeline flinched and went utterly still against Silas. How much longer could she simply stand there and hold it together when her entire life had just fallen apart around her, and now Silas and Maddox, no matter how well-meaning, stood blithely talking about leaking the news of her and Drake's breakup as if it were nothing more than a weather bulletin.

Maddox cast her one last sorrowful look of apology and then leaned in to kiss her gently on the cheek.

"I'll see you soon, sweetheart. Bet on that. I'll come check on you as soon as I can."

She didn't respond, neither confirming nor denying his statement. He acted on the assumption that she had somewhere to go. That it was as simple as getting a hotel somewhere or finding another apartment on the spot to rent. Kind of hard to do either when she had no money, no job and no hope of either.

The elevator doors opened and she realized that she hadn't even registered them closing or the downward slide to the bottom floor. The club was empty, cleared, no doubt, by the police raid. Confetti and an assortment of litter, drink cups, noisemakers, party hats and other random paraphernalia lay scattered over the floor. It looked as though a bomb had gone off. Appropriate, since the dance floor looked just like she felt.

Devastated.

Silas was on the phone with someone giving instructions, but she tuned out everything as the yawning, gaping hole in her heart opened wider, inch by inch, forming an abyss that would soon suck her straight down. How she longed for the welcoming veil of blackness, of unawareness to overtake her. Somewhere she couldn't think, couldn't feel and didn't have to see Drake denouncing her in front of all his men, over and over and over again until she wanted to scream for it all to stop.

Silas escorted her into the back lot that was now mostly empty except for Drake's car and one or two that belonged to some of his men. A car pulled up, the headlights bouncing over Evangeline, whose gaze was still focused on some distant point as a result of the shock and overwhelming numbness that had slowly invaded her body.

Surely it wouldn't be too much longer before it finally overtook her and she could escape to oblivion for at least a while. It didn't matter if it was cold and she had no place to go, no place to stay and no money to obtain one. Things like that only mattered to people who had . . . hope. A future or at least hope for one. As she'd had with Drake. For the span of a few precious months, she'd known what it was like to touch the sun. For that period of time, she'd looked forward to a future filled with everything she'd ever dreamed of. She should have known that at some point in time it would all be cruelly snatched away from her. But she'd refused to believe anything but Drake's promise to her. A promise he'd broken not once, but twice, in the cruelest way possible.

"Evangeline," Silas said, gently pulling her from the yawning hole in her mind that threatened to envelop her at any moment.

She slowly moved her unfocused stare to him and blinked at the very real worry in his eyes. And the savage fury swirling like a hurricane.

"I'm having my driver take you away from here. Where would you like to go?"

A hoarse sob broke free from her throat and it was a horrible, animalistic sound. Tears ran in never-ending rivulets down her cheeks. She wanted to laugh but she knew if she gave in, she'd never stop. She'd be in complete hysterics with no hope of ever pulling herself together.

Silas cupped her cheek, his eyes dripping with sadness. And pity. God, that was the worst. The one or two of his men who didn't think she'd betrayed them, who weren't pissed at her and didn't hate her, pitied her instead. She didn't know which was worse.

"Evangeline, listen to me, honey. Drake was wrong. *Very* wrong. I, along with the rest of Drake's men, don't believe for one minute that you betrayed us. And when he's had time to calm down and think about it, he'll know it too."

"It's too late," she said, utterly broken. Utterly defeated, so much despair in her voice that even she couldn't detect any sign of life in it. "He made it very obvious he has no caring, no feelings for me. That I'm merely an object, his toy to take out and play with when he's bored. He doesn't trust me even when I came to him and told him about the cop talking to me in the restaurant and even after I told him I would never betray him."

She closed her eyes for a moment against the now-physical pain as the headache that had been brewing ever since the police had burst inside Drake's office blazed through her head like wildfire. She put her hand to her forehead with a soft moan, her eyes still closed as she continued to vent everything she wanted to scream at Drake right now.

"I can't live with a man who not only doesn't trust me but has such a lack of regard and respect for me. Someone who would embarrass and humiliate me in front of all his men and reduce me to begging on my knees and refuse to listen to anything I had to say. I'd rather die than ever be back with him. He's reduced me to nothing and I was a fool for allowing it to happen. A fool for loving him and thinking that my love was enough for us both or that he would one day love me.

"He has no heart. No capacity for love. His callous disregard for me and the fact that he wouldn't even listen to what I had to say, wouldn't allow me to defend myself, proved beyond a shadow of doubt that he does not and will not ever love me."

She stared into Silas's eyes for the first time, her anger yanking her from the numbness for a brief moment. His jaw was clenched tight as he absorbed every single part of her impassioned outcry.

"Any woman could fill the role I have in his life," she said bitterly. "Because no woman will ever have the only thing that truly matters. His heart. His love. His trust. Maybe his wealth and power will be enough for other women. But not for me," she whispered. "Never for me."

The pain in her head was making her sick. And Silas was still standing there as she poured out her broken heart, waiting for her to tell him where she wanted to go. To hell. She was already there.

"I hate his money. I hate his power. And I hate that he's always believed himself to be such a monster, and before today, I would not have believed it or allowed anyone else to believe it either. But what he just did . . ."

She took a long, steadying breath as more tears flooded her aching eyes.

"What he just did not only proved that he has no faith or trust or love in me. He proved that I was wrong about him. That I can't trust him. That I never should have trusted him with the only things I have to give. My heart. My love. My trust. And my loyalty. I gave that all to him when I've never given it to another man. And it meant *nothing* to him."

She broke down into horrific sobs, her hands flying up to cover her face. The pain sent nausea roiling through her stomach, and she gagged, desperately trying to keep the now-sour champagne from coming up.

"Evangeline, is there some place you want to go for the night?" Silas asked. "Your girlfriends' place perhaps?"

"Oh God no," she said in a horrified voice. "So they'll know just how right they were and how stupid I was? *Again*?" Her eye twitched and she put her hand to her forehead again and swallowed back the convulsive retch. "I have nowhere to go, Silas," she said with quiet despair. "You should know that. I depended solely on Drake. It will be a lesson learned the hard way to never, ever rely on any man ever again."

Pain and sorrow reflected like a mirror in his eyes. Then he saw her wince again as the headlights from the car approaching stabbed through her gaze. His eyes narrowed as he homed in on the source of her discomfort.

"Evangeline, what's wrong?" he asked sharply. "Should I take you to the hospital? Are you sick?"

Sick? Oh God, she wanted to laugh again. She was sick to her soul. She would never be able to think of this night without getting sick, and there was no way she would ever be able to forget this night any time soon. Or even in two decades.

"Headache," she croaked. "Making me sick. Don't worry about me, Silas. Thank you for the ride. I'll decide where I want to be dropped off, but just let me ride for a while if you don't mind, please. Just until I figure out what I want to do and where I want to go."

And maybe if the driver would let her, she'd just ride all night and then let the city swallow her up whole.

Silas cursed long and hard, his expression so murderous that it was hard to look at him without reacting in fear. Silas had always been nothing but kind and compassionate with her, but tonight, she saw what she'd never been able to see in Drake before tonight.

A monster.

"I'll take you to my apartment building, Evangeline. Don't worry, doll. If you aren't comfortable staying with me, you can stay in one of the two vacant apartments I keep on either side of mine for privacy."

Her brow furrowed, causing another burst of pain to shriek through her head. "You own an entire apartment building?"

He nodded. "I keep the top floor to myself. In time, I'll renovate the entire upper floor and make one big apartment out of it. I just haven't had time to get to it yet. I lease out the units on the lower four floors. You can stay with me or in one of the units next to me. Whichever one you're more comfortable with."

She lowered her head in shame.

"Evangeline, do *not* bow your head because you feel shame with me." Fury laced his words, and his teeth were tightly clenched together.

"How am I supposed to feel, Silas? You tell me. I have nothing left. Not even my pride. I gave that up for him as well. And he threw me away like I was yesterday's garbage, so now my only option is to go home with one of the men who work for him like I'm some pathetic charity case? That may very well be what I am. God knows the pathetic part fits. But it doesn't mean I have to like or accept it. If I'm worthless, it's because he made me who I am," she whispered.

Silas was seething from head to toe. Well over six feet of bristling, snarling, pissed-off, dominant alpha male.

"Swear to God, I'm going to fucking kill him for what he's done," Silas said through clenched teeth.

"I'm not worth it, Silas. Just let it go," she said wearily.

"Bullshit! You're worth a hell of a lot fucking more than what you've gotten. You deserve far better than what you've been given. And if you think I'm going to sit by and just let it happen? No fucking way. You get me, Evangeline? It's not going to happen!"

His voice was at a roar and a lesser person would be pissing herself out of fear. But she knew he wasn't angry with her, and it made her want to cry all over again from the start.

"I'm taking you to my place," he said, ushering her to the waiting car. "Tonight you're staying at my place. Tomorrow I'll give you the keys to one of the neighboring apartments. It's already furnished. I'll call Maddox and have him go by Drake's apartment and pack you some clothes."

She went pale, all the blood leaching from her face. "No! You heard him, Silas. And even if he hadn't informed me that the cost of betrayal is everything, I'd never take a single thing he paid for."

"Then I'll go out and buy you something to wear in the morning," he said in a voice that dared her to argue.

"Only if you'll allow me to pay you back, and with that in mind, I would greatly appreciate it if you kept it cheap and just got a few pairs of jeans, some T-shirts and maybe a coat," she said quietly.

"I'll buy what I deem appropriate and we will discuss your repayment options at another time," he said, slamming her door. When he walked around and got in on the other side, he pierced her with his stare. "It won't be discussed tonight when you're completely wasted, you've just had your fucking heart ripped out and goddamn tears are still sliding down your face."

With that, he gave the driver the order to drive them to Silas's apartment, and the car drove off through the blustery cold January first streets of New York City.

Hell of a way to ring in the new year.

26

Evangeline woke with a still-throbbing headache, her vision so blurred she could barely make out her surroundings. Her mouth was dry and her throat swollen and so scratchy that it hurt to swallow.

She had insisted that she take Silas's couch in the living room, refusing to allow him to give up his bed and for that matter his personal space and privacy, which she knew he guarded fiercely. There had been a stubborn set to his jaw that told her he was going to dig in his heels, but she'd flatly refused and perhaps in the end, sensing how perilously close she was to losing her tenuous grasp on her control, he'd conceded, though he wasn't at all happy about it.

She could hear him in the kitchen of the small apartment and she smelled coffee brewing, but the scent immediately made her stomach rebel and perspiration beaded her forehead and her flesh became clammy and sticky.

Pain was ever present. Every blink of her eyes was like a shard of glass being plunged into her skull. She wasn't aware of making any sound, but suddenly Silas loomed over her, concern etched into his features.

"Evangeline? Are you okay?"

She didn't even try to lie to him. She shook her head and promptly regretted even that small action. Her hand flew to her mouth as her stomach rebelled and Silas simply scooped her up into his arms and rushed for the bathroom, setting her down in front of the toilet.

"Deep breaths," he said in a hushed tone. "Is it your head still hurting you?"

She nodded much slower this time. "It's awful, Silas," she whispered.

"I'll get something for you to take as soon as I'm sure you can keep it down," he said grimly. "And then you'll need to lie down on the couch and rest. The medicine will likely knock you on your ass."

"What is it?" she asked fearfully.

"Nothing harmful," he soothed. "It's prescription pain medication. I get migraines and they're debilitating. I have to take it in order to ease the pain. Trust me. You'll feel quite nice in half an hour or so. And then, if you're feeling up to it, I'll take you next door and let you in the apartment."

It took all she had not to hang her head again, but after Silas's warning last night, she didn't have the mental strength to take on his anger at what she simply couldn't help but feel shame for.

"Thank you," she whispered. "I won't stay long. Just a day or two until I decide what I'm going to do."

He scowled at that, but then she hadn't expected anything less. "You'll stay for as goddamn long as you need to. Get me?"

"Yeah," she said tiredly. "Whatever. I don't have the strength to argue with you at the moment."

His expression softened. "I have no desire to argue with you, doll. Have your nausea under control now? Think you can take lying down on the couch again? I'll get you some medicine and fix you something to eat."

She let him lead her back into the living room and sank onto the couch while he went for the medication. A moment later, he returned with a glass of milk and a pill for her to take.

After she'd downed it, he took the glass back from her. "Lie back. I'll go fix you something to eat. Don't worry. It won't be too heavy. I know you're still queasy."

"Thank you," she whispered without opening her eyes.

"Anytime, doll. Anytime."

She dozed off and on until Silas came back into the living room with two plates. He sat down on the couch next to her and helped her to a sitting position before handing her one of the plates.

"Feeling any better yet?" he asked.

"Swimmy," she muttered.

"Swimmy? Is that a word?"

"It's how I feel. Swimmy. Like the entire world around me is swimming."

He chuckled. "Ah, I gotcha. Yep, I'd say the medicine is kicking in. Try to eat something. If you're feeling better after breakfast, I'll take you over before I head into work."

She tensed and closed her eyes at the mention of work. Drake. He would be there, no doubt. Just another day like any other. He wouldn't have been up all night last night like she was, devastated by loss.

"Tell Maddox thanks when you see him," she said. "For everything. I owe both of you my thanks. For being my friend. One can never have too many of those, and apparently I have fewer than most."

"When it comes to friendship, I prefer quality over quantity," Silas said matter-of-factly.

"Good point," she conceded.

She stared down at her barely consumed breakfast and to her dismay, tears splattered onto her plate, dripping from her face. She hadn't even realized she'd started crying again.

"Ah hell, doll," Silas said, his face a wreath of torture. "You have to stop crying or you're never going to get rid of that headache."

"I kn-know," she choked out. "I d-don't want to c-cry but I can't s-stop. Oh, Silas, what am I going to do?" she asked miserably. "What am I going to do?"

He pulled her into his arms and she buried her face in his neck as sobs erupted, shaking her entire body. For seemingly an eternity, she sat there, huddled in his arms, sobbing her heart out. When finally some of the horrible sound coming from her abated, she lay limply against Silas, so much misery in her heart and soul that she wanted to die from it.

"You won't die from it, honey," Silas said, his voice rich with sympathy, making her realize she'd said her last thought aloud. "It may feel like it right now, but in time, this too shall pass."

"I used to love that quote," she said softly.

"And not now?"

She shook her head. "This won't ever pass, Silas. You don't just recover from something like this. Nothing will ever be the same again."

"Drake will pull his head out of his ass and realize what a terrible mistake he made," Silas said, though he sounded pissed that Drake had ever believed such a horrible thing about her anyway.

"As you said, even if that happens, it will be too late," she said softly. "He didn't believe me when it mattered. He didn't have faith in me at all. If he doesn't believe in me, how can I be with him? I don't want others to convince him that I'm innocent. He should know that, Silas. He should *know*. I've never given him any reason to distrust me. I've been nothing but honest and open with him and yet he never believed in me the way I believed in him."

She shook her head sadly and closed her eyes, wondering how she could have been so wrong about the man she had loved. Still loved no matter how much she wished differently. But love wasn't something that could be turned off as simply as a light switch. She should hate him. Despise and loathe him with every part of her. And yet she ached. She bled. She grieved.

"I understand, doll. It's a hell of a mess and I hate to see you hurting so badly. You of all people don't deserve this."

Silence fell and he held her for another long moment until finally the medication took full effect and her eyelids grew heavy. When he registered how limp she was, he carefully pulled away and eased her head down onto the cushion of the sofa.

"Rest for a little while," he whispered. "I'll take you to the apartment when you wake."

Drake stood at the window overlooking the busy street that the entrance to Impulse faced and stared broodingly over the dull, gray winter morning. The weather fit his mood to a T. It had been tailor-made just for him. The bleakness spreading like a stain on his soul after Evangeline's deception and betrayal was insidious and hopeless. Like he'd never feel the sun on his skin again, forever doomed to a life of cold drabness.

"Why did you do it, Angel?" he whispered. His eyes closed against the wash of pain. "I gave you everything. But it wasn't enough. Why?"

It always circled back to what he already knew and, as he'd confided in Evangeline, stupidly thinking she was different. If his own parents couldn't love him, how could he expect anyone else to ever love him?

The answer was, he couldn't.

And he'd never make the mistake of trying to make someone love him again.

A sound at his door had him spinning around, a black expression on his face, a warning to whoever was trespassing that they were not welcome. But as his men filed in, expressions of worry, concern, anger … fury … all were reflected. But the single thing every expression had in common was judgment.

It fired his temper and sent his mood even blacker, and he hadn't thought that was possible.

"What the fuck do you want?" Drake snapped in an icy, rigid tone.

None of them tried to disguise the disgust in their expression as they stared Drake down.

"Do you honest-to-God think that Evangeline ratted us out to the goddamn cops?" Jax demanded. "Can you look me in the eye and tell me you believe that shit?"

"You were there. You saw what I saw. What you don't know is that she was approached by the cops when she was out to lunch with Zander, Thane and Hatcher. And yes, I do have proof of that conversation, since she's the one who told me. After Hatcher had already called me, of course."

"But she didn't know Hatcher had called you," Thane bit out, seemingly pissed that his lunch with Evangeline was helping build the evidence against her.

"Says you," Drake said mockingly.

"You have singlehandedly fucked up the most precious gift a man could ever be given, one that you will never find again," Zander boomed out. "And you know what? I don't feel sorry for your stupid ass. You deserve to die a cynical, lonely old man who believes no one is loyal to you. Jesus. I never thought I'd see a brother of mine treat any woman this way, but especially not a woman as special as Evangeline."

"You've lost all respect in my eyes," Hartley snapped. "I would have never thought you were capable of treating an innocent, guileless, beautiful and loyal woman who is everything good in this fucked-up world and certainly the *only* good thing in *your* fucked-up, miserable world so horrifically. You make me goddamn sick."

"Give it a rest," Drake roared. "She's got you all by the balls and you don't even see it. Jesus Christ. Get the hell out of my office and don't come back until you've decided who you're loyal to. Your brother? Or the woman who sold out not only your brother but you and the rest of our brothers as well."

"You destroyed her," Maddox said quietly, speaking up for the first time since everyone had entered the room. He'd stood back, his animosity and rage a tangible presence in the room. "She was on her knees *begging* you, for fuck's sake, and you ripped her to shreds, leaving her no dignity, no pride, and she didn't care because all she wanted was for you to listen to her. To give her a chance. To have the same faith in her that she had in you."

Flashes of discomfort mingled with his men's pissed-off, brooding stares. Stares that all judged and found him guilty. Him. When he wasn't the one who sold them all out to the fucking cops. And yet here they stood, visibly bothered by the image of Evangeline on her knees begging him for a chance.

God. The entire thing was a blur to him. His entire world had shattered and come to a grinding halt the moment he realized that his angel had betrayed him. What had he said to her? He didn't know. He didn't care. He'd only known he had to get away from her before he completely broke down and made more of a fool of himself than she had already made of him.

A vague image of her on her knees, reaching for him as he steadily backed away, raw anguish etched on her face, tears streaming in endless rivers.

Please.

It was all he could remember her saying. The roar was too loud in his head, the pain in his heart too overwhelming. From others he expected nothing less. But not from his angel. And he was pissed that he'd allowed the one person past all his carefully constructed barriers to the very heart and soul of him to do what no one had ever been capable of doing before.

Destroying him.

"You're wrong this time, Drake," Justice said flatly, anger pouring off him in waves, his entire body tense, almost as if it were taking all his restraint not to launch himself at Drake and beat the hell out of him. "I've never questioned you. Never once doubted you. I've followed your lead without question. But you just orchestrated the biggest fuckup of your entire life, not to mention committed an unpardonable sin against a woman who loves you more than she cares for her pride or anything else in this goddamn world. You completely demolished a good woman whose only sin was loving and accepting you with no strings or questions. Just . . . unwavering acceptance. Who else can you say that about? Who else can you say has ever loved you unconditionally? Who's accepted the good and the bad and never left your side, always defended you, fought for you and refused to allow her fear of your world and the life you lead to ever let her leave you? She would have stood by your side and loved you forever, but you just ruined the most beautiful thing that has ever happened to you. All because you're an unfeeling asshole who wouldn't even allow her to defend herself. You never once *asked* her if she betrayed you. You assumed and you judged her, condemned her and found her guilty, and never once did you give her a chance to explain."

His eyes were raging and his hands were balled into tight fists at his sides. The others looked to be in wholehearted agreement with every word that blew explosively from Justice's mouth.

"And then you just threw her out on the fucking streets with *nothing*. Without the job or the place to live that you forced her to give up. She worked herself to the bone to selflessly support her family, and she never once complained. How the fuck do you think she's going to make it on her own now that you made her completely dependent on you? You've broken every promise, the very creed of our lifestyle, by shitting all over the gift of her submission and leaving her to fend for herself."

Justice shot him another disgusted stare and then he shook his head and licked his lips as if trying to rid himself of a bad taste in his mouth.

"You know what? Fuck this and fuck *you*. And fuck throwing her out on the streets after you took so many pieces out of her she'll never be whole again. I'm out of here. I can't stomach you a goddamn minute longer."

Justice turned and stalked out of his office and never once looked back.

The rest of his men symbolically turned around, and like Justice, they walked out.

Drake staggered into his chair and then let his head fall into his hands. Had everyone but him lost their goddamn minds? They were defending the woman who'd tried to take them all down? Were they willing to go to jail because they liked her and she was a great cook who was nice to them?

Doubt and a sense of foreboding crept up his spine. Never before had he questioned his instincts, his gut. They never steered him wrong.

But . . . what if . . .

What if they were right? And he'd made a terrible, unforgivable mistake?

But if they were wrong, then they'd all lose everything they'd worked so hard to achieve.

What about Evangeline?

The question whispered insidiously inside his mind.

Hadn't she already lost everything? Hadn't he, for that matter? He stared around at the evidence of the empire he'd built from the ground up. Did any of it mean a goddamn thing if he no longer had Evangeline to share it with? To share his life with?

No, he was better off without lies, deceit, betrayal . . .

But again that nagging voice, the one that whispered to him incessantly, the one filling him with self-doubt, struck again.

What if she hadn't lied, deceived or betrayed?

What if . . . What if she *was* innocent and he'd made the worst mistake of his life?

27

Evangeline hurriedly let herself inside the apartment Silas was letting her use and set the small plastic bag on the bar of the tiny kitchen. For now, she ignored it, not yet able to face the possible consequences the package would reveal.

Silas had bought groceries when he'd gone out to get clothing for Evangeline, but the thought of food made her stomach twist into knots and promptly rebel. So maybe ignoring the possibility wasn't the best idea, though that's precisely what she *had* done for the last two days. She had to know—needed to know. It was far better to get it over with so she'd know exactly what she was up against.

With icy fingers of dread clutching at her heart, she picked up the bag like it was an offending object that would bite her and walked slowly to the bathroom. She took out the home pregnancy test from its package and scanned the instructions. It seemed simple enough. Pee on the stick and then wait a few minutes for the results.

After complying with the instructions, she washed her hands and laid the stick on the counter and then stared at her reflection in the mirror. She didn't look pregnant, but then did anyone so early in the game? For that matter, she didn't know how far along she was, if she was even pregnant at all. Obviously she couldn't be more than three months along because she hadn't been with Drake for longer than that.

But her periods had never been regular, so she never really knew when to expect her next one. And if that was the case, why was she standing in here like an idiot taking a home pregnancy test when she would likely start within the next week? Wishful thinking? Was that what she was experiencing? After the devastating loss of Drake, was she clinging to any sort of hope of having some part of him? A baby? Their child?

The very last thing she needed was to be pregnant, but at the same time, hope was so keen, so desperate inside her that she realized now that if she wasn't pregnant, she would grieve not only the loss of Drake but of a child who never existed either. Talk about signing up for self-torture.

She closed her eyes and reached for the stick and took in a long, steadying breath through her nose. Finally she worked up enough courage to open her eyes and look at the results.

It took a few moments to blink away the tears and the fuzziness in her vision but then she saw it. Staring her right in the face was a vibrant pink plus sign.

Her legs wobbled and she staggered, almost collapsing in a heap on the floor of the bathroom. Her heart exploded with joy even as an overwhelming surge of grief nearly flattened her.

She eased down on the floor, no longer trusting her legs to hold her, and she drew her knees in to her chest, wrapping her arms around them tightly as she hugged herself fiercely, rocking back and forth. Tears, this time a mixture of grief and unfettered joy, spilled down her cheeks and she actually smiled.

A baby.

Drake's son or daughter.

A small piece of him who would live on through her. His legacy.

Almost as soon as the calming, joyful thoughts took over her battered mind, reality crept in and with it, heartbreak and desperation. She no longer had any reason to be here in the city. The one good thing Drake had done was to deposit a large sum of money into her parents' account as well as buy them a mortgage-free house and a new vehicle, effectively rendering them debt free with plenty of money on reserve to live comfortably for the rest of their lives.

Which meant that she no longer needed to worry about working to support her beloved mother and father. She could go to school, like she'd always wanted. Get an education. Earn a degree and be able to support herself and her child.

She could go home and have the support of the two people who loved her the most in this world. They would help her and after the baby was born, Evangeline could enroll in school and enlist the aid of her parents in caring for the baby while she was in class.

They would never be ashamed of her, especially if they knew the truth, but she would never tell them what caused her and Drake to break up. If she told them, then there would be inevitable questions that would lead them to arrive at suspicious conclusions. No matter what Drake had done, that he hadn't loved or trusted her, she wouldn't brand him a criminal in her parents' eyes. For that matter, she had no idea what he dealt in, so she couldn't be sure if he had illegal dealings or not. And now it no longer mattered because she was no longer in the picture.

Guilt and shame surged to life inside her even as she chastised herself for feeling either. Under any other circumstances she would never dream of keeping her child's presence from his or her father. But Drake scared her. His power and his wealth and his connections frightened her in a way nothing else did. Because she knew, because of his own upbringing, just how adamant he would be that he be in their child's life. If that was all he demanded, she'd go face him down tomorrow and tell him the news of his impending fatherhood.

But the fear that because he hated her so much, he would simply take her child from her, prevented her from ever going to him with her secret.

She had decisions to make and they had to be made soon. Closing her eyes, she pressed her forehead to her drawn-up knees and savored a quiet, private moment with her child, whispering promises to always keep the baby safe. Telling her child how very much he or she was already loved.

She rocked in silence with no idea of the passing time. The realization of what she was doing, what she was *allowing*, was sharp and unforgiving. Once again, she was being kept by a man. The only difference now was that she wasn't in a relationship with Silas. In some ways that made it worse, because she was taking advantage of his generosity without giving him anything in return.

She reached for her phone lying on the counter next to the sink and pulled it down to her. She opened a browser and typed in the URL for an airline she knew that flew into the medium-sized city just thirty miles from her small town.

The ticket was expensive, given it was a short-notice departure, but oh well. She would use one of the credit cards Drake had given her. The least he could do was get her home. It would be the best five hundred dollars he'd ever spent because it would also get her forever out of his life.

She checked the time and then calculated how long she needed to get to the airport—again, she could use the credit card for the cab fare—in time to check in and board and realized that if she booked the flight and left within the next half hour, she could get out tonight on one of the evening nonstop flights.

She dug around in her purse for the credit card and punched in the number before finishing the transaction. After checking her e-mail for the confirmation and flight number and arrival time, she called her mother next.

There was little point in trying to hide anything from her mother. It wasn't as if she'd be clued in when Evangeline told her she would be arriving that night. She just hadn't planned on sobbing all over her mother over the phone. As a result, it took the better part of twenty minutes for Evangeline to explain the situation. By the time she hung up, she had only ten minutes to get on the road. Then she laughed. It wasn't as though she had anything to pack. She'd take the jeans and shirts Silas had bought for her. Those could be packed in a carry-on bag.

After dropping the pregnancy test into the trash by the toilet, she hastily stuffed what clothing she could into a gym bag she found in the closet. Then because Silas—and Maddox—had been so sweet and kind to her, she wrote a note addressed to them both, thanking them profusely for their friendship and their caring. She explained that it was best if she moved on and left New York, and she closed the note by saying that they were her two best memories of the city.

Sad that after living here for as long as she had, the best she could come up with for the entirety of her life here was Silas's and Maddox's friendship.

With a long sigh, she went to the door and then stood on the other side, glancing back as though ensuring she wasn't forgetting anything. She almost laughed, and would have if her heart hadn't been in little pieces all over the floor.

That was the only thing she'd leave behind in this city.

Her heart.

It would always be wherever Drake Donovan was, and she didn't try to fool herself into thinking otherwise.

28

For three days, Drake had barely left the solitude of his office at the club, choosing even to sleep there at night. It wasn't as though he was sleeping anyway. He lay awake, long after the club had shut down, into the early hours of the morning, thinking . . . dreaming . . . about an angel. His angel.

Everyone steered clear of him, for varying reasons. His club employees avoided him like the plague because he bit the head off anyone daring to venture into his lair. And it did resemble somewhat of a lair with the lights dimmed to nearly nothing, the couch rumpled from him tossing and turning on it in an attempt to sleep.

He just couldn't make himself go back home. He couldn't even think about sleeping in the bed he'd shared with Evangeline. The idea of being without her, in the place she'd lovingly called home and made into a home, was repugnant and offensive.

Even as he reminded himself over and over that she deserved none of the respect he was affording her, or rather the memory of her, he couldn't do anything other than what he was currently doing. Living. Breathing. Existing. Minute to minute. Hour to hour. Day to day. One day at a time.

It was a miserable existence he wouldn't wish on his worst enemy, and yet that damn voice that mocked him and whispered to him until he was dangerously close to losing his mind constantly reminded him that it had been his choice. That he had driven Evangeline away. He could have listened. Could have given her a chance to explain.

But he'd done none of those things, and it was a miserable price to pay.

His door opened and he turned, a torrent of blood-scorching expletives poised to let fly, when he saw it was Silas, whom he hadn't so much as seen, much less heard from since the night he'd taken Evangeline from the club—at Drake's orders.

His lips burned with the need to ask Silas how she was doing. What she was doing. *Where* she was. Was she all right?

Silas's jaw was locked, a sure sign he was pissed, but his eyes were glacial, submerged in ice, fixed on Drake so that he could almost feel the chill from Silas's stare over his skin.

"Silas," he acknowledged in a clipped voice.

Silas sent him a look of disgust. "Still holed up in here clinging to that lame-ass story you've talked yourself into believing, I see."

"Don't start with me," Drake warned. "I am not in the mood for anyone to start shit with me. Especially not something you can't finish."

"Only because I know that when the truth comes out, you're going to be crawling on your fucking belly begging everyone's forgiveness, will I allow you to slide. But my patience is wearing very, very thin. Don't push me, Drake. Swear to God, I could kill you for what you did to Evangeline New Year's Eve alone."

Drake snarled, his lips curling so his teeth were bared like an angry predator. "You're so sure she didn't sell us out. I wonder why? Maybe because then the rest of you will have to admit what I've already admitted? That I got my ass handed to me by an innocent-looking, beautiful woman with big blue eyes that make her appear every bit the angel she was?"

Silas shook his head in disgust. "You make me sick to my stomach. And you're talking out of your ass, so just shut the fuck up. I'm telling you, Drake. You will regret your actions and your words. If you had any sense, you'd be on your fucking knees begging her for forgiveness *before* the truth comes out, because then she won't give a fuck because you didn't trust her when it mattered."

Alarm splintered up Drake's spine. Silas's words were laced with conviction, and he was one of the most suspicious bastards Drake had ever met in his life. And he wasn't the only one. If Silas were the only one charging to Evangeline's defense, he could blow it off. But every single one of his men?

He was gutted and racked with indecision, something he wasn't accustomed to feeling. He was decisive in all matters, never questioning his actions, and yet everything about this whole thing felt wrong. He sank down into his chair, grief consuming him for all he'd had, and lost, just three short days—a lifetime—ago.

Even if Evangeline had betrayed him, could he really blame her? The cops had filled her head with God only knew what kind of shit, and he was sure they'd spared no detail, even embellishing his sins—while he'd been closed-mouthed, refusing to give her anything, to trust her, instead asking her to ignore it and look the other way. She would have imagined all manner of horrific crimes, aided by his own secrecy and the fact that he dodged the issue at every turn.

Being someone who stood in the light, standing for what was right, Evangeline might not have been able, in good conscience, to allow Drake to go unpunished for his deeds. And wasn't her innate goodness, her sweetness, what he adored most about her? What had drawn her to him in the first place? And now he was punishing her for those very qualities.

Silas swore viciously. "Jesus Christ, Drake. You're fucking miserable. She's fucking miserable. Why the hell are you doing this to both of you? Is it pride? Because if so, I'm calling bullshit right now. Evangeline sure as hell didn't let pride stop her when she was on her knees begging you to believe in her."

Every word was like a poisoned dart aimed with precision and accuracy. His lips parted, the question hovering on his lips, begging to be asked, to be set free. He could feel his will crumbling, his pride preparing to take a beating.

"Do you really think she had nothing to do with it?" Drake asked, for the first time allowing doubt to creep into his voice.

Before Silas could respond, his doors burst open and his men swarmed in, their expressions thunderous. Fury coiled, whipping and snapping like an electrical charge surging through the air.

"Not now, goddamn it!" Drake roared, unleashing his pent-up rage and sense of helplessness at them. "Get the fuck out of my office and don't return until I've damn well called for you."

Not now. Not when he needed answers from Silas. Cold logic, unimpeded by emotion. He looked to Silas for understanding and backup, but he got neither from his enforcer.

A man—Hatcher?—was shoved forward, causing him to stumble and fall to his knees. He had a bruise already forming around one eye, his lips were split and bloody and his nose looked like it had been pulverized.

"*Here* is your traitor," Maddox said icily, his voice filled with loathing, his eyes flashing with anger. "Not Evangeline. It was never Evangeline. We all knew it," he said, jabbing his thumb in the direction of the others. "Never doubted her, even for a second. Why can't you, her dominant, the man she trusted without reservation and loved in spite of your sins, the man she was going to *marry*, say the same?"

Drake's eyes narrowed and a loud roar began in his ears. His heart was hammering in his chest with enough force to make him light-headed.

"Someone mind telling me what the fuck is going on here? Why is Hatcher on the floor of my office being called a traitor?"

Justice looked at Drake in disgust, a look that was shared by Thane, Maddox, Hartley, Zander, Jax and Silas. "You question whether he's guilty, one of your men, someone you employ, and yet you played judge and jury and hung the woman who loves you out to dry, refusing to hear any explanation or defense whatsoever. What the fuck is *wrong* with you, man?"

"Quit fucking around and just tell me what the hell is going on!" Drake exploded.

"Hatcher was the informant," Thane said coldly. "He was with us the day we took Evangeline to lunch, remember? Consequently, he was also the one to call and tell you that Evangeline was talking to a cop in a hush-hush manner. Interesting coincidence, don't you think? He set the entire thing up. He fed Evangeline to the wolves, and when she basically spit in the cop's face and refused to give him shit on you, then they went with plan B."

Drake's stomach was churning violently. Sweat broke out on his forehead and he wiped his palms on his pants repeatedly. Oh dear God. What had he done, what had he *done*?

"Plan B," Zander drawled, "was for Hatcher to continue feeding the cops intel while setting up a sting operation so they could implicate Evangeline in order for Hatcher to be able to continue feeding them information without suspicion. Tell me, Drake. Assholes or not, dirty or clean, how many cops would have fingered an informant like that in a fucking raid? And leave her to certain death with the people she betrayed? Jesus Christ, man, use your goddamn brain. That whole night stunk to high heaven and you were the *only* one who didn't see it."

Drake shot to his feet, standing over the desk, his gaze boring into Hatcher, who was still on his knees in front of Drake's desk.

"*You* set Evangeline up, you worthless piece of shit?"

Hatcher remained stonily silent, his gaze averted and focused on some distant object, his jaw clenched, his features brooding.

The blood drained out of Drake's face as he remembered someone else on her knees just four nights ago. Evangeline. Her sobs. Her begging. Her pleading with him to listen. To give her a chance. To please believe in her. That she'd always believed in him so could he now do the same for her?

Oh God, he'd failed her at the very first opportunity that presented itself after she'd forgiven him for the unspeakable things he'd done to her that horrific night in their apartment.

His knees buckled as grief consumed him. Regret, so much regret filled him, until he was drowning in it. He collapsed back into his chair and then buried his face in his hands.

"What have I done? Oh God, *what have I done?*" he asked in a raw, tortured voice filled with aching emotion. His throat throbbed with it. His heart was ravaged by it.

All he could see was Evangeline on her knees in this same room, begging him over and over.

Please listen to me.

"She'll never forgive me, and it's no less than I deserve," he said in a voice ravaged by grief and . . . guilt.

"What do you want done with this piece of shit?" Maddox asked quietly.

Drake focused on the traitor. But worse than betraying his own brothers, the men he worked with and had pledged loyalty to, the bastard had betrayed Drake's woman. Evangeline, who was completely innocent, the *only* innocent one of all of them. And Hatcher had ruthlessly used her to further his own greed and ambition. Drake didn't really give a shit what his motives were. Not now. Not ever.

"Get rid of him," he directed at Silas. "Make sure he gets the message loud and clear about what we do with traitors."

For the first time, Hatcher looked scared shitless, and Drake couldn't really blame him. Silas was one scary, badass motherfucker on his best day. But he and Evangeline were tight. Silas held a very soft place in his heart for her, and he wouldn't have much mercy in the message he'd send to Hatcher—and to anyone else thinking to turn on his brother.

"Get him out of here," Drake said, motioning for Maddox to take care of the matter. "I need to speak with Silas first."

"What about Evangeline?" Justice asked, his arms crossed over his chest. "Swear to God, Drake, you fuck this up with her and I'm moving in. You left her with nothing, but I'll step in and treat her with the respect she deserves and she'll never have to worry about a goddamn thing for the rest of her life."

Drake sighed wearily. "I understand, Justice. All too well. Believe me, I get it. I fucked up. I was already well on my way to figuring that out before you came through my door with that piece of shit Hatcher. Another five minutes and you wouldn't have found me here because I would have been gone to find her. I know I was an asshole and I know you all had her back when I didn't. I'm sorrier than you'll ever know. This is something I'll pay for for the rest of my fucking life."

"Save it, man," Maddox said stiffly. "You're apologizing to the wrong people. None of us are Evangeline, and she's the one you need to be on your knees in front of begging her for forgiveness."

Drake swallowed. "If that's what it takes to get her back, then I'll stay on my fucking knees forever."

"Now that I'd pay money to see," Zander drawled. "Come on, Maddox. Let's take the trash out while the boss man talks to Silas, although I'd pay money to see this heart-to-heart too. Imagine, our man Silas acting as a relationship therapist."

If looks could have killed, Zander would have died on the spot under the heat of Silas's intimidating scowl. Grown men had been known to piss their pants when Silas was in their faces.

"I suggest you get the fuck out before I change my mind about who the recipient of my message is," Silas said in a frigid tone designed to freeze a man's balls. Judging by the discomfort on the faces of his men, Drake thought that look had more than hit its mark.

As soon as the others departed, Drake turned desperately to Silas, his eyes as vacant as his heart, surely.

"I have to find her, Silas. You and I both know I don't deserve a third chance with her. Not after fucking things up with her twice now, but I have to try. I won't just walk away or let *her* walk away, even though I threw her out."

Acid was burning a trail down his throat and into his stomach, searing a trail through his vital organs all the way down to his blackened, lost soul.

"I can't live without her," Drake said bleakly. "The last three days have been hell. This morning I told myself I didn't even give a shit if she had betrayed me or not. I was willing to do anything to have her back and promise her anything to make that happen. Even if it meant going straight."

Silas seemed to wrestle with himself for several long moments. A lifetime for Drake, who stood there, barely able to breathe for the pain choking him.

Finally, Silas leveled a stare at him that Drake couldn't possibly mistake. It was Silas's most grave, most serious expression, the one that said he meant business and would fuck you up if you didn't heed his words.

"You mess up again, Drake, and it won't be you or Justice who steps in to take care of Evangeline. Get me? I'll be there for her in whatever capacity she needs for as long as she needs me, and I'll give her the fucking moon. I shouldn't tell you shit. I sure as hell shouldn't help you. And if it weren't for the fact that Evangeline is hurting every bit as much as you are, I'd say fuck you and leave you to rot in your self-made misery."

His words scored a direct hit, making Drake wince with each and every one.

"She's in the apartment next to mine," Silas finally said. "The one on the right. Don't fuck this up again, Drake. That's the only warning you're going to get."

"I appreciate it. I appreciate you being there for Evangeline and for taking care of her after I ripped her apart. She needs people like you in her life. To save her from people like me," he said bleakly.

"Here's the extra key," Silas said, tossing it over the desk to Drake. "I'll expect to be your best man, provided she agrees to marry you still."

"I wouldn't have it any other way," Drake said softly. "Neither would she."

Silas offered a faint smile as he headed toward the elevator. "Be good to her."

"I will," Drake murmured, closing his eyes.

God, just give me one more chance to make her happy and I swear I'll never let her down again.

29

Drake walked into Silas's quiet apartment building, perspiration dampening his shirt, despite the frigid temperatures outside. There wasn't much in his life that he could ever say truly scared him. There wasn't anything he feared, not even death. Death was merely the means to an end. The end of a beautiful, long ride or...a shortcut through unplanned scenery resulting in taking the wrong turn.

But the prospect of losing Evangeline for good?

Fucking *terrified* him.

His hands were shaking when he got off the elevator on the top floor, and every step toward her door at the end of the hall seemed like a mile. He thought about knocking—it made him a complete asshole not to knock—but then if he calmly announced his arrival, she likely wouldn't let him in the door.

Did it make him any less of an asshole to knock first and then if she didn't respond, use the key Silas had given him? He couldn't remember if the apartments in his buildings had dead bolts. Surely they did. Silas wasn't an asshole of a landlord who didn't take care of his tenants. But he was also in the first stages of renovation on the top floor, so the dead bolts might or might not be present.

At any rate, he'd knock and not just barge in and terrify and over-whelm her. After that? Well, he'd take it one step at a time.

He stopped in front of the door and simply placed his palm flat against the wooden surface and then leaned to press his forehead against it as well.

"Please talk to me, Evangeline," he whispered. "Please be the gorgeous, generous, loving woman you've always been and give me the chance I refused to give you. I don't deserve it but I'm begging you, like you begged me."

He had to stop because he damned himself more with every word that came out of his mouth. Straightening to his full height, he knocked sharply on the door and then waited, holding his breath, each passing second an eternity.

His heart sank when he knocked again and heard no reply. Could she be sleeping? Silas had said she was distraught. Upset. He'd even called when Drake had been on his way over to tell him that he'd had to give her pain medication for a horrific headache she'd suffered. Yet one more sin to tarnish his already blackened soul.

Worried that she could very well be ill, he hesitated only a fraction of a second before pulling out the key and inserting it into the lock. A rush of air blew over his lips when the door opened, unbarred by a dead bolt. He stepped inside and softly called, "Evangeline? Angel, baby, it's me, Drake. Are you here?"

Silence was all that greeted him. He walked farther in, only to see the pristine condition that all of Silas's apartments were typically kept in. There wasn't a single thing to denote that she'd even ever been here. Then another rush of self-condemnation blew over him. Of course it would look as though no one had been here. He'd stripped her of everything. All her clothing, her possessions. He'd thrown her out with nothing.

He hurriedly went through the small apartment, a sick feeling entering his stomach when his search turned up nothing. It was as if she'd never set foot in the place. How unlikely was that?

In the kitchen he finally saw the note affixed to the refrigerator. He rushed over and ripped it down and read her neatly scrawled handwriting. It was addressed to Silas and Maddox.

Thank you so much for everything, both of you. I've decided not to stay here in the city any longer. It would be too painful for me to be here, always remembering. You were my absolute best memory of New York City.

Love always,
Evangeline

Drake crumpled the note and then went back through the apartment, searching for what, he wasn't sure. Some clue as to where she might have gone? In the bathroom, he found the first sign that someone had been here recently. Just a tissue, crumpled and soggy looking, though it was dry. Had she cried here, using the tissue to wipe away her tears?

He closed his eyes and inhaled sharply to prevent his own tears from sliding free. He jumped when his cell phone rang and he automatically reached for it, intending to shut it off, when he saw who the caller was. His pulse immediately began to race when he saw Evangeline's mom's name listed as the incoming caller.

"Brenda, how are you?" he greeted her. As if there were nothing wrong. As if his entire world hadn't vanished.

She sniffed and there was the sound of a faint sob as she spoke. "Drake? Is Evangeline with you?"

Drake froze, his blood turning to ice in his veins. "No," he said slowly. "She isn't. I was hoping you could tell me where to find her."

"She was flying home!" Brenda cried. "She called me this morning to say she was catching a late-afternoon flight and would arrive here thirty minutes ago! She wasn't on the plane. She didn't get on the plane. What has happened to my daughter?"

"I'm going to find out, Brenda. I swear to you, I'll find her. Can you tell me anything that might be helpful?"

"You promised me," Brenda raged. "You swore to me that you would protect and look out for my baby, but when she called me, you should have heard how upset she was. She was heartbroken! She said that the two of you had broken up and that she was moving home. I had hoped that since she didn't get on the plane, perhaps the two of you had reconciled."

"Brenda, listen to me," Drake said, utter gravity in his tone. "I did a terrible thing to your daughter. I didn't trust her as I should have. As a result, we had an argument, and yes, we broke up. But I was on my way to where she was staying to apologize and to beg her for forgiveness. She did nothing wrong, except have absolute faith and trust in me when I didn't give her the same back."

Emotion knotted his throat, making his speech so thick it was a wonder she could even understand him. He sounded garbled even to his own self.

"Do you love her?" Brenda asked accusingly. "Because if you don't, then let her go, Drake. No matter how much she's hurting now, she'll only hurt more if she becomes more deeply involved with you, or even married to you, and you don't love her."

"I love her with everything that I am, everything that I will be and everything that I have. It all belongs to her. My heart, my soul, my life. If she'll have me, I'll spend the rest of my life proving myself to her."

There was a prolonged silence and then Brenda finally spoke again, sounding a little more appeased than she had initially.

"Find my daughter, Drake. And when you do, I want to talk to her. I'm sick with worry and so is her father. Please find her and let us know she's safe."

"I will," he vowed, and then eased the phone down to shove it back into his pocket.

"Oh God. Where are you, Angel?" he said in an anguished tone.

He reached into his pocket for his phone, turning away from the sink to call Silas to see if he knew her whereabouts, when from the corner of his eye he saw something distinctive in the trash can.

He froze in place, all the breath leaving his body in one wicked expulsion. He began to shake violently as he stared, unable to move for the fear paralyzing him. It couldn't be. Could it?

Shaking off the paralysis gripping his entire body, he lunged for the trash can and picked up the home pregnancy test, examining the results window. His knees locked and then buckled almost simultaneously, throwing him off balance. It was faint, but there was still a fading pink plus sign.

Evangeline was pregnant?

Another fear hit him, so hard and so viciously that he flailed his arm out to catch himself on the counter. He'd been horrible to her. He'd said horrible things. Had done terrible things. She was alone, desperate, without money or a place to live. That didn't leave a single mother very many options. Surely she wouldn't . . .

He shook his head, pissed at himself for making assumptions when time after time she'd proved nothing but trustworthy and loyal. There was no fucking way she would ever abort their child. He'd seen her look of horror when he'd told her that his mother had wanted to abort him and would have if she hadn't seen the benefits of having a baby.

But she was still missing when according to her mother she should have already landed and been on her way safely to her parents' home.

He had to call in the troops. Fast. He had to get everyone on the street, explore every option, call in every favor ever owed to him. And he needed to make it clear that if Evangeline was harmed, Drake would seek out and destroy anyone who caused it to happen or even allowed it by not intervening. He would also give a big cash reward to anyone who returned her safely.

He grabbed his phone and began making calls even as he went out the apartment door, hurrying down to Silas's. He had a key to get in. Maybe Evangeline had come here. Silas had said she'd stayed with him the first night.

He let himself in, frustrated that he'd been unable to reach Silas with his first call. He shouted Evangeline's name and went from room to room but came up with nothing.

It would be more logical for him to remain here, presumably the last place Evangeline had been before departing for the airport earlier in the day. He would get the word out to all his men for everyone to get over to Silas's. He typed in his demand for them to meet here and then the last words of his message with a sickness that went soul deep.

Hurry. Evangeline may not have much time.

30

"Evangeline is missing," Drake announced when all his men had gathered in Silas's apartment.

There was a resounding chorus of "what the fucks" and demands to know what the hell had happened. Drake held up his hand for silence, his expression black, determination fiery in his eyes.

"As far as anyone knows, this is the last place she had contact with anyone. She called her mother from Silas's apartment this morning to tell her she would be on a flight arriving just after six Central Time this evening. She never made it on that flight," Drake said grimly.

Another round of curses rent the air and Silas and Maddox exchanged helpless, furious glances.

"I shouldn't have left her," Silas said painfully.

Drake waved off his man's guilt. "There's another thing you need to know." He held up the pregnancy test, watching as his men's faces turned to shock. "She's pregnant. With my child," he added unnecessarily. "She must have taken the test this morning. Before she called her mother. It must have been what prompted her to leave."

"Then what the hell happened to her?" Maddox demanded, his fists clenched. "If she called her mother and told her that she would be on a certain flight, then she obviously intended to *be* on that flight. She wouldn't worry her parents like that."

"I know," Drake said quietly. "Which means there's a damn good reason she didn't make that flight."

Fear and uncertainty flickered on his men's faces as they all exchanged glances.

"I'll pull up the security surveillance footage starting from this morning when I saw her last," Silas said grimly. "It's a long shot, but if something happened to her here, then we should get it on camera. If not . . ."

Drake wouldn't consider any alternative. Without a firm starting place, there was no way to know where Evangeline could be. His enemies were many and any one could have sought to strike at Drake where he was most vulnerable. No one had had time to figure out that he and Evangeline had broken up or that she didn't mean anything to him at all. Or that it appeared she meant nothing to him. When she was everything . . .

"Do it," Drake ordered. "We don't have much time. Every minute that goes without us finding her . . ."

He trailed off, refusing to give voice to the possibilities.

"It does no one any good to kill her," Justice said, an edge of uncertainty to his voice as though he were trying to convince himself. "No one with half a brain would kill her. If she's been taken, she will be used to extort something from you, Drake. Money. Power. Protection."

But one fact lay heavy over the group, one that Drake knew was front and center in their minds. Money was the only possibility because Drake would never protect or form a partnership with anyone who'd frightened Evangeline or put their hands on her. Taking her would be a suicide mission.

Silas was on his computer across the living room, punching in a series of commands. After a few moments, he called for Drake. He was pointing to the screen, which was split between six camera views.

"Here is when I left this morning and Evangeline was still in her apartment," he said.

"If we catch anything, we can zoom in on whichever camera got her and follow her progress to the end of the block. I have cameras around the entire perimeter of the building as well as going both directions down the street."

Drake watched in silence as Silas got into his car, and then they watched through an hour of no activity. No sign of Evangeline.

"There she is," Silas said, zooming in on the camera outside her apartment in the hallway.

She was carrying only one small bag. Her hair was pulled into a ponytail and she was pale, her face outlined in clear distress. They picked her up when she got off the elevator and strode briskly out of the building, where the street camera picked her up outside.

At the entrance of the building, she hesitated, looking in both directions down the street. Then she started right, walking toward the corner. Had she hailed a cab? If Silas could pick up any identifying information on the vehicle that picked her up, they could hunt the driver down and find out where he'd taken her.

Silas began cursing and Drake zeroed in on the footage.

She was almost to the end of the street when a dark sedan pulled up beside her and rocked to a halt, as if it had been going at a faster speed. Evangeline warily stepped back and began to circle around the vehicle when a man jumped out of the backseat and immediately went for her.

She fought wildly and Drake's blood froze when the man hit her over the head with the butt of a pistol. She went limp and the man all but threw her in the backseat of the car before the vehicle roared away.

It all lasted a total of a few seconds, and yet each frame was playing in slow motion in Drake's head. Every damn minute of Evangeline's fright, her struggle and the man striking her before abducting her.

"Son of a bitch," Maddox seethed. "Come on, Silas. Work your magic. I want that son of a bitch and I want him now."

Drake lowered his head over Silas's shoulder and in a cold voice said, "I don't care what it takes, who you have to blow, what you have to hack into. Find out who the fuck took her. It's been fucking hours and she's still in his hands."

"Give me five minutes," Silas said, his gaze never leaving the monitor, his hands working quickly over the keyboard as he zoomed in on the car.

Drake closed his eyes, his stomach lurching. Fingers of dread curled around his insides, squeezing relentlessly. The icy coldness of the predator settled around him. He itched for the kill. Clawed at Drake's insides, begging to be set free so he could spill the blood of the bastard who'd hurt Evangeline.

And his child.

God, let his child be okay. Let them both be okay. And then he did something he'd never thought he was capable of doing.

He prayed.

If only one can be saved, let it be Evangeline. I want them both, but God, there will be other children. There will never be another Evangeline.

"I've got him," Silas said furiously. "Punk-ass motherfucking little bitch! It's Charlie McDuff."

The others let loose a torrent of vicious curses.

"McDuff?" Drake asked incredulously. "That fucking pansy-ass wannabe?" Then his eyes narrowed. "You think his father has a hand in this? I find it hard to believe he had the balls to pull this off by himself. He's either extremely stupid or extremely desperate."

Silas shook his head. "No way, man. His old man actually has a brain. He cut Charlie out of the family business a long time ago. He was too unstable and too short tempered. Not to mention dumb as a fucking brick. My money says he's making a move to prove to Daddy and the rest of the world he's the man. He's desperate. He'll probably want money and a position in your organization. When Brian cut him off, I mean he cut him off. Told him to get a fucking job because he wasn't supporting his lazy ass anymore. Worse, Mommy didn't intervene as she normally did. And he's a complete mama's boy. Usually when the old man got pissed, Mommy stepped in, soothed tempers and talked the old man into giving the 'baby' one more chance. Word is even she was pissed over his last fuckup and cut him loose same as Daddy did. So I'd say this was desperation. Well, stupid too, but he's acting out of desperation."

"Jesus," Drake muttered.

He took a moment to organize his thoughts, though terror knotted his insides. Desperate men did desperate things and were highly unpredictable. Then he lifted his gaze to Silas and his men.

"Get the old man on the phone. He needs to know that I'll have mercy if he has nothing to do with his son's latest fuckup. If he can help me find the little bastard, I'll be even more lenient. All that matters is that I get Evangeline back. But if he's involved, if he doesn't cooperate fully, then the entire family will have culpability in Evangeline's abduction."

Silas nodded.

"You know Charlie worked for the Luconis for a while," Maddox spoke up. "About a year back. Another of his attempts to prove he's the man and has what it takes to get the job done."

"What's your point?" Drake asked impatiently.

"He spent quite a bit of time with them is what I'm saying," Maddox said, every bit as impatient as Drake. "The Luconis know quite a bit about his habits, or at least they should. They've been after you to back their takeover of the Vanuccis. They'd probably do anything you wanted in order to secure that backing. Make it a produce-or-you-don't-get-shit deal. If they can help you find Evangeline, they get your backing. Otherwise, they're on their own."

Drake stared back at his man for a long moment, absorbing the implications of what Maddox was saying. If the Luconis could help him find

Evangeline, it would be worth anything. Even backing their takeover of the Vanuccis when he'd planned to pit the two organizations together and stand back while they both crumbled and fell.

Christ, but this was huge. It upped the threat, not only to himself and Evangeline, but to every single one of his men as well. They'd become targets of the Vanuccis as well as anyone who supported them.

"Do you know what you're saying?" Drake asked Maddox. "Do all of you know what he's saying?"

"Yeah," Zander said. "Do you? You willing to take that risk?"

"How can I not if it gets me Evangeline back?" Drake asked hoarsely.

"Then I'd say you have your answer," Jax said.

One by one his other men stated their agreement. And acceptance of the risk posed to them.

Drake focused his gaze back on Maddox. "You make the call. I have to talk to McDuff. Make sure they know no deal unless they can produce Evangeline. *Alive.*"

31

"How sure are you that we can trust the Luconis?" Drake asked grimly as he and his men positioned themselves outside one of the butcher shops the McDuffs owned.

How appropriate that the McDuffs had several family-owned butcheries as their "family business," since they were little more than butchers themselves.

Maddox shrugged beside Drake. Maddox and Silas had insisted on taking position with Drake, more likely to sit on him and keep him from losing his shit than for any real need for their help. The other men had paired up, and surprisingly, the eldest Luconi and appointed leader of the family had sent several of his men to assist Drake in the takedown of Charlie McDuff.

"They're very keen to see Charlie go down," Maddox said as they waited for go time. "The timing is pretty good, not that I'd say there was ever a good time for Evangeline to be abducted."

Maddox's face contorted into a black scowl, his eyes flickering with fury before he continued.

"Turns out, the Vanuccis struck at the Luconis a week ago and the Luconis want blood. Rightfully so."

Drake and Silas turned to Maddox in question.

Maddox sighed. "It's pretty horrifying and, well, after hearing of it, I'm not sad that we're backing the Luconis to take the Vanuccis down for good. The Luconis may not be Boy Scouts, but I've never known them to do this kind of shit. They have a code of sorts, one that excludes women and children. The world won't miss the fucking Vanuccis. They're all a bunch of pond scum."

"Tell me," Drake barked.

"Jacques Vanucci targeted the elder Luconi's granddaughter. She was only twenty fucking years old. Young, innocent and very beautiful. The Luconis aren't complete assholes. They shield their women completely. No knowledge of their business practices. The women in that family are cherished and absolutely protected by every single male member of the family."

Fuck. Maddox had referred to the Luconi granddaughter in the past tense. Drake didn't have a good feeling about this at all.

Maddox sighed and continued on. "It wasn't pretty. He wooed and courted the girl for months. Made it all out to be a modern-day telling of *Romeo and Juliet*. Two people, forbidden from one another by rival families. Told her all kinds of shit, about how he was in love with her, wanted to marry her and how he'd take her away from both families so they could live a happy life. He has money of his own. Told her she'd never want for anything he could give her and their children.

"She resisted at first. Wanted to finish school and get her degree, but the bastard was persistent. She finally agreed, left her parents a note outlining the entire sordid tale and went to meet her boyfriend."

Maddox shook his head. "I'm sure you can guess the rest. He raped her. Let his men take turns. Recorded the entire disgusting thing, and in the end, he killed her then sent the video to the elder Luconi with a message saying no Luconi was safe, man, woman *or* child. Luconi has declared war, and he was extremely eager to count you as an ally. It surprised him at first that you were trying to get Evangeline back, since he believed your show that she meant nothing to you, but when I told him they kidnapped a pregnant woman, it actually pissed him off. It's a well-known fact that the old man has a soft spot a mile wide for pregnant women. He hates Charlie McDuff. Said he was a bad seed. Had too much liking for violence and he hates women. Given the Luconi sentiment toward their women, I can well imagine why he didn't last long working for them. The old man told me he was already on the chopping block, but then he tried to corner the old man's sixteen-year-old granddaughter. I'm surprised Charlie isn't six feet under, to be honest. I think only because the Luconis didn't want to risk outright war with the McDuffs, given their imminent war with the Vanuccis, did Charlie live. But the way I hear it, he wasn't seen in public for months after the beatdown he got when they pulled him off the granddaughter."

Drake's mouth twisted in disgust. "Jesus," he whispered. "And Evangeline is right in the middle of this giant clusterfuck. An innocent pulled between warring factions, and she's in McDuff's hands even as we speak!"

He pounded the dashboard with his hand, a sense of wretched helplessness tearing him apart.

"What are we waiting for?" he seethed. "Every minute we sit on our goddamn hands is another minute she's in *his*."

"Keep a cool head," Silas murmured. "You know this has to be done by the book, man. One mistake and Evangeline pays with her life. McDuff is batshit crazy and highly unstable. If he even *thinks* things aren't going the way he planned, he'll kill her. At this point he has nothing to lose."

Drake's phone rang and he tensed. They'd been expecting Charlie to call. Drake had expected to hear from him hours ago with his demands. Every minute that had ticked by that Drake hadn't heard made his heart die a little more. Why had he waited? Had he taken his time, abusing Evangeline before he called Drake with his demands?

Drake didn't recognize the number, and typically he let such calls go to voice mail and either called back later or not at all. But he answered it on the second ring with a terse "Donovan."

"Drake Donovan," Charlie McDuff drawled smugly. "I believe I have something that belongs to you."

"Yes, you do at that," Drake said softly. Dangerously soft.

Charlie obviously picked up on that note in Drake's voice because he didn't sound nearly as smug or confident when he spoke next. There was a distinct edge to his voice and he sounded rattled. And unstable, and that worried Drake. It scared the fuck out of him and he knew he had to tread very carefully and give the man no reason to hurt or kill Evangeline.

"If you ever want to see her alive again, you'll do exactly as I say. You have two hours to complete the transaction and not a minute longer."

"What do you want?" Drake snapped.

"Twenty million should be nothing for a man of your means," Charlie said, some of the nervousness gone at the mention of the amount. "I'm being very generous. I know you could afford more without even noticing it was gone. But I can be reasonable. I'm going to text you the wiring instructions and the account numbers. As I said, if the funds aren't in my account and verified in the next two hours? Your lady is dead. But not before I enjoy a taste of her. She is rather beautiful, but then I'd expect nothing less from you, Donovan."

"Let me be clear on something, Charlie," Drake said, making no effort to disguise his loathing for the little worm. "You know my reputation. You know I don't fuck around. You know that if I make a vow, I'll die before breaking it. So know this. If you touch Evangeline, if you hurt her, if you frighten her, if there is so much as a bruise or scratch on her when she is returned to me? You're a dead man. Take *that* to the bank."

There was a long pause. "Just make sure the money is wired and you won't have to worry about the condition of your woman."

Then the line went silent. Mere seconds after the call ended, a beep alerted Drake to the incoming text with the account number.

He wanted McDuff's blood. The man was going to die, even though Drake had made it sound as if McDuff would walk away if Evangeline was returned safely. The minute he touched what belonged to Drake, he'd signed his own death warrant.

"We now have two hours, but I don't trust that little bastard," Drake said behind clenched teeth. "I refuse to leave her there a minute longer. He doesn't know we're here. He thinks I'm chasing my tail in the city and nowhere near Brooklyn or his fucking butchery. I'm not waiting one goddamn second longer. With or without you, I'm going in."

"And get Evangeline killed?" Silas's slashing gaze pierced through Drake. His enforcer was smoldering with rage, every muscle in his body coiled like a deadly snake ready to strike.

"We're almost in position," Maddox said, holding his hand over his earpiece to hear more clearly. "Let's go. We need to find the best way in from this side. The others are taking their spots now. Jax did recon so we'd know what we're up against."

"Did he get a bead on Evangeline?" Drake demanded. "Did he see her? Is she all right?"

"McDuff has her tied to a chair in the room where the beef is hung in the back. He said she looked okay, just scared to death and freezing her ass off. Motherfucker has her in the cooler and keeps telling her he brought her there because with the bone grinders no one will ever find any sign of her body. That he'll chop her into tiny pieces and feed her to the buzzards."

"He dies," Drake said in a voice almost too quiet to be heard.

"Oh yeah," Maddox vowed.

The men scrambled out of the car. Drake was thankful for the cover of night as they darted into the shadows cast by the building. There was a window that, if their scan of the building specs was correct, was closed off from the cooler where sides of beef hung. And where Evangeline was being kept.

Silas took a step back and then ran up the wall, hooking his fingers on the ledge of the window before expertly swinging himself up so he clung to the window frame. He worked with the window a few moments before it slid upward with a noisy creak.

He froze, as did Maddox and Drake, and waited several long seconds to see if their cover was blown. When no one appeared, they breathed a collective sigh of relief. Maddox spoke softly into the mic, telling the others they were going in and for them to do the same.

The idea was to surround the cooler and plan the best method of attack, one that ensured that *no* harm came to Evangeline and that she wouldn't be caught in the crossfire.

Silas eased inside the building, took a few moments to ensure that they were undetected and then leaned out the window and motioned Drake and Maddox up.

"Here," Maddox said, making a step for Drake with his hands. "I'll give you a boost up."

Drake put his foot into Maddox's hand and on the count of three he jumped, along with Maddox's forceful push, and it propelled him up the brick wall to grasp the ledge with his fingers.

He swung himself up and then he and Silas leaned as far as they could out the window, hands extended to grab on to Maddox's. Seconds later, they pulled him through the window and shut it firmly behind them.

Now that they were in the same building where Evangeline was being held, it was all Drake could do not to charge into the other room and take out every single one of the bastards. Every nerve in his body was firing. At the moment, he could take on thirty men and rip every single one of them apart with his bare hands.

They crept into the hallway, on alert for any movement, anything that would betray their presence. Drake had confidence in all his men. He trusted them with his life. But the stakes had never been this high before. They were all fighting, not just for Drake's safety and his life. They were fighting for his entire *world*.

Evangeline.

At the end of the hall where Silas had crept on stealthy feet, there was a muffled sound and then a body hit the floor without a shot being fired. Silas motioned to Maddox, and Maddox dragged the body into the room where they had entered through the window.

"Let's go," Maddox said grimly. "Justice said things are getting heated inside the cooler. McDuff is pissed."

Drake's heart lurched, and they turned and ran.

There were four possible entrances to the cooler, and after taking down the guards circling those entrances, Drake and his men crouched at the doors, surveying the number of heavily armed men.

Drake cursed to himself when he saw that every single gun was trained on Evangeline. McDuff stood in front of Evangeline, taunting her. She wouldn't even meet his gaze. She was pale. Too pale. Her hair was tangled and he saw the red streaks on the side of her head, bold against the golden blond color.

Her head was bowed, her hair falling over her cheeks, and she sagged in the chair. Her chin rested against her chest and it felt as though someone had just driven a knife through Drake's heart when he saw the damp trails of tears down her pale flesh.

"I've got Drake by the balls now," McDuff crowed. "He's a stupid man for believing I'd let him off for twenty mil."

For the first time that he'd seen, Evangeline lifted her head, though her stare was unfocused and bleary looking as she looked in McDuff's general direction.

"You're the stupid one," she said in a monotone, without a trace of emotion. She spoke to McDuff like he was a complete simpleton. And then Drake's heart nearly stopped when she said the rest. "He cares nothing about me," she said in a dull voice. "He won't do anything to rescue me. He won't give you what you want. He won't give in to blackmail. When has he ever given in to blackmail? You're dumber than I thought if you think you're going to bring him to his knees over one of his whores he already tossed out and made clear he wanted nothing more to do with. Or didn't you get that memo?" Sarcasm laced the last of her statement, and she stared defiantly at McDuff as if daring him to do his worst because the worst had already been done.

Drake wanted to weep for the hopelessness he heard—*felt*—in her every word and action.

Uncertainty flashed over McDuff's face, followed closely by rage. He lashed out, slapping Evangeline's unprotected face, whipping her head back. Her hair was in disarray all over her head, but Drake saw the blood at her nose and mouth and he surged forward.

Silas and Maddox both jumped on him and held him to the floor. "Stop!" Silas hissed in his ear. "The rest of us want to kill the little bastard for touching her as well, but we have to play this just right and stick to the plan or the asshole will kill Evangeline on the spot. Get it together, man. Think, for God's sake. *Think!*"

Drake slowly shook them off, but he was bristling with fury like he'd never known. Waiting the final few minutes for his men to carefully circle and cut off all escape routes and ensure Evangeline's safety was hell. If that bastard inflicted a single injury, Drake would kill him. Fuck that. Evangeline had been injured. Physically and emotionally. The bastard had hit her, *drawn blood*, not once, but *twice* now. And God only knew what she'd been subjected to *before* he and his men arrived. Drake had to turn it off and stop torturing himself with all that his angel had endured or he'd go insane.

Maddox held up his hand, listened to the receiver a moment and then turned to look at Drake, his eyes flashing, his entire body tense and radiating fearsome rage.

"It's go time."

32

Evangeline slouched uncomfortably in the chair, ropes digging into her wrists and ankles. Her face was buzzing with pain and heat from when the man had lashed out and struck her, but her head was what ached the most. She'd taken a brutal hit that rendered her unconscious when she'd struggled and fought back against the man trying to get her into his car.

She was going to die. Grief overwhelmed her because it wasn't just her who would die. Her precious unborn baby would die with her. Drake would never come for her, would never give a hundred dollars for her, much less twenty million or however much the creep had mentioned.

And since she knew she was going to die, she had no desire to prolong her grief and agony. At first she'd thought only to do whatever it took to stay alive. To fight for her child if for no one else. But realization had sunk in when the man had brought her here, to a place that smelled of blood and death, and smugly informed her that he was going to chop her into tiny pieces so that no one had any hope of ever finding her body, much less identifying it, if Drake didn't come through with the first wire transfer.

"He threw me out, or didn't you know that?" she mocked through swollen, throbbing lips. "He thinks I betrayed him and his men by giving the cops information. Now, you tell me. What do you think Drake would do in that situation? Do you honestly think he'd hand over twenty million dollars to someone demanding it in order to spare my life? You'll probably get a thank-you card from him after I'm dead."

"Shut up!" he raged, turning to backhand her again.

But something caught his hand. And then the entire room erupted in violence. Gunfire. Cries of pain. Savage curses. She closed her eyes, praying her death would be quick and merciful. *Oh, Drake, I loved you so much. I would have never betrayed you. Why couldn't you believe in me? You'll never even know of your child.*

Sorrow was thick and suffocating, tears burning her swollen, throbbing eye. She closed her eyes and lowered her head in defeat as the world went mad around her.

She flinched and stiffened when hands glanced over her bonds. Then a man's voice sounded in her ear.

"Don't fight me, Evangeline. I need you to cooperate fully and do exactly as I tell you. Got me?"

Adrenaline surged in her veins. Her eyes flew open and to her astonishment, she saw *Drake's* men. Everywhere. She looked in absolute bewilderment to see them fighting savagely, murderous expressions on their faces. To her further shock, she saw . . . Drake. He was ruthlessly working his way through two gunmen who posed no obstacle to him and his fury.

What was he doing here? And why? Maybe she had finally lost the remaining vestiges of sanity she'd clung to the entire day. Or maybe she'd died and this was some sort of dying fantasy. But she felt no pain even as she made no move to struggle against Silas's gentle touch as he cut through the ropes binding her.

"Get Evangeline out of here!" Drake barked without looking in her direction. "Make sure she's safe and get her to help. This bastard is mine."

His words sent a chill down Evangeline's spine as she stared dispassionately as Drake circled the man who'd abducted her. Then she was swung into familiar arms and closed her eyes, blocking the horrific reality that Drake could *die*, and she drifted off, retreating to a place where she no longer felt pain, or grief. Nothing. She welcomed oblivion and surrendered to the dark void enfolding her in its soothing embrace.

Silas swiftly carried Evangeline from the room, flanked by Maddox and Justice, who stared down at her, worry in their eyes.

"Stay with Drake," Silas commanded. "Cover him. Have his back. Make damn sure he's safe at all times."

"I'm staying with you," Maddox said stubbornly. "With the help of Luconi's men, we've already taken down any threat. All that's left is McDuff, and the others are keeping close watch. But Drake made it clear that McDuff is his."

Silas carried Evangeline to the waiting car and slid into the backseat; she now had her eyes closed, whether out of self-protection or true unconsciousness, he wasn't sure.

He examined her carefully, looking for injury, but all he saw was the drying blood on the side of her head, the vivid handprint on her face and the blood at her nose and mouth from where the little fucker had struck her. He was gripped by rage and fury to the point that he nearly defied Drake and went after McDuff himself, and damn Drake's orders.

It should be Silas. Not Drake. *He* was Drake's cleanup man. His enforcer. His sole duty was to protect Drake and ensure that nothing threatened Drake's business interests, a vast empire Drake shared with his brothers. He was always the one to take out any threat. It was who he was. What he did. And now, more than ever, this was personal to him when so many other times it was cold and impersonal. Just a job. Nothing more. A necessary evil to protect Drake's empire and the men he called brothers.

But . . . Evangeline needed him more right now. And if she were his woman, he too would want to be the one to take out the man responsible for terrorizing her, threatening her and putting his hands to her.

"Get me to Drake's clinic," Silas instructed the driver.

Drake stared at the pathetic piece of shit he held up by the collar of his shirt. McDuff's face was swollen and bloodied, and the knowledge of his imminent death was in his eyes. He didn't deserve a quick, merciful death. What he deserved was to suffer, knowing his fate. But Drake didn't have the time or the desire. His only priority was in avenging Evangeline and then getting to her as quickly as possible.

He'd been so overwhelmed by rage and his desire to make her tormentor pay with his blood that everything else had been forced from his mind, but now he felt regret because he should have been the one to take Evangeline from this place. To offer her comfort, see to her needs, instead of one of his men. Would she see that as yet another rejection? More evidence in her eyes that she didn't matter to him?

"Please," McDuff said, slurring his words. "I'll do *anything*. Just don't kill me."

"Is that what my woman said to you? Did she beg you not to kill her and my child?"

Horror reflected in McDuff's eyes, and the sniffling coward began to cry. The acrid smell of ammonia rose, and Drake and his men looked at McDuff in disgust. He was pissing himself.

"I didn't know she was pregnant!" McDuff shrieked. "I swear to you. I didn't know! I didn't hurt her."

"Oh?" Drake asked in a deadly voice. "You didn't hit her in the head with the butt of your gun when you yanked her off the street? I didn't just see you slap her in the face?"

McDuff was crying and babbling in earnest now, and as much as Drake wanted to prolong the little bastard's agony, Drake only wanted to get to Evangeline so he could reassure himself that she—and their child—were all right.

With a twist of his hands, it was finished. McDuff sagged and Drake dropped him to the floor, turning away immediately to bark orders at his men.

He found Justice and lifted his eyebrows in silent question.

"Silas and Maddox took her to the clinic. Go to her, Drake. The rest of us will make sure the scene is secure and everything is wiped down."

Zander was waiting to drive him when he strode out of the building, but Drake held his hands out for the keys. "You stay here and help Justice oversee cleanup. I'll drive."

Zander cocked his head and studied Drake for a long moment. "You going to be okay to drive, man? You've been dealt some pretty heavy shit today."

"Not nearly as much as she has," he snapped. "Give me the fucking keys."

Zander handed them over with no further comment.

But when he was about to get in the car, Zander's question stopped him in his tracks.

"Are you happy about it? No one asked. But are you happy about the baby?"

There was an underlying warning in Zander's question. One that said if Drake so much as hinted he wasn't happy about Evangeline's pregnancy, any number of his men would step up to take care of both Evangeline and his child.

Over his dead body.

"I'm happier than you could possibly imagine," Drake said in an even tone. "But my first priority is Evangeline and making sure she isn't hurt. And hope that she'll forgive the unforgivable."

Zander winced and nodded. "She's a good woman, Drake. The best."

"Yeah, I know," he returned softly.

When Drake arrived at the clinic, he found Maddox and Silas pacing outside the exam room. When they saw him, they both stopped and waited for him to approach.

"How is she?" Drake demanded, his pulse racing with fear and worry.

Silas shrugged. "Don't know yet. She was out of it the entire way. She opened her eyes when the doctor came in, but it was like . . . I dunno, man. She was here but she wasn't here. She wasn't aware of anything or anyone. If she knew who we were, she didn't acknowledge us. She hasn't said a single word since we left the butchery to bring her here."

"Christ," Drake said, ramming his fist into the wall. "Any idea if the baby is okay?"

"No, sorry," Maddox said quietly. "We told the doc and he said he'd do some blood work, check her HCG levels and confirm that there is a pregnancy, since all we have to go on is a fading store-bought pregnancy test."

Drake went still. It hadn't occurred to him that she might not be pregnant. As soon as he'd seen the test, their child had become all too real to him. The idea of losing their baby or Evangeline was more than he could bear. If she lost their baby, she'd never forgive him. She might not forgive him regardless of whether there was a child, and who could blame her?

"How long has she been back?" Drake croaked out. "I need to see her."

"Don't know why you couldn't go in," Silas offered. "Maddox and I were just trying to give her as much privacy as possible."

Not waiting for more, Drake opened the door and strode in, pulling up short when he saw Evangeline's pale face. She was lying on a hospital bed, rails up, covered lightly with a thin sheet. She wore a hospital gown and her eyelashes rested on her cheeks.

His gaze quickly found the doctor, who was standing to the side looking at lab results. He glanced up when he saw Drake.

"How is she?" Drake asked anxiously.

"She'll be just fine," the doctor soothed. "Got a little banged up. She's going to have one hell of a headache for a couple of days, but otherwise she appears to be unharmed."

"The baby?" Drake asked fearfully.

The doctor smiled. "Everything appears to be normal in the lab results. Her HCG levels are appropriate for someone six to eight weeks pregnant. She hasn't been awake for me to question her regarding her last menstrual cycle, but my guess is she's not very far along."

Some of the awful tension coiling through his muscles eased and he sagged, weak with relief at knowing that Evangeline and their baby were going to be okay.

"Can I take her home soon?"

The doctor frowned. "Her prolonged state of altered consciousness is worrisome, but given the circumstances, not surprising. She's suffered a traumatic experience, and sometimes our minds act in a way to protect us. I'm not opposed to letting you take her home, since you'll simply be moving her to the top floor of this building; however, I'd like to come check in on her at least once a day, and call me if you have any questions or concerns regarding her condition. I want to know the minute her condition changes. Patty will give you a list of things to be on the lookout for, and if she exhibits any of the symptoms listed, you're to get her back here or to the closest hospital immediately."

"Thank you," Drake said sincerely. "I'll take excellent care of her and make sure she takes it easy until she's completely recovered."

The doctor smiled. "I have no doubt you will. And, Drake? Congratulations, son. You'll make a fine father."

To Drake's surprise, when he turned back to Evangeline, her eyes were open and fixed on the ceiling above her. He rushed to the bed and slid his fingers through hers.

"Angel? Baby, I'm here. You're safe now. You're both safe. Nothing can hurt you now. The doctor says you can come home with me. Would you like that?"

But she didn't so much as acknowledge a single word. It was as though she hadn't even heard him. Her unblinking gaze was distant and so very far away that a chill of foreboding gripped him.

He looked at the doctor helplessly and the doctor grimaced even as he checked Evangeline's vitals again.

Oh dear God, had he done this to her? Was this what he'd done? She was a hollow shell of herself. So very fragile, on the verge of shattering completely. Or perhaps, finally, she already had and he was looking at the remaining pieces.

He gathered her in his arms, closing his eyes as he pressed his lips to her hair.

"Come back to me, Angel," he begged. "Come home. It's safe now. Don't leave me. I love you. I'm so sorry I've never given you the words, but I was afraid. So very afraid. But you make me fearless. You make me strong. You give me the strength to face the absolute worst with the knowledge that with you I can overcome anything. As long as you're with me, my love. As long as we're together."

"I want to go home," Evangeline said in a small, lifeless voice. "To my parents."

Drake went utterly still, torn between jubilation that she was awake and speaking and despair at *what* she'd said.

Dread gripping him by the throat, he slowly pulled away so he could see for himself that she was aware. Her eyes were dull, lacking the sparkle that was quintessentially Evangeline. Her face was bland and expressionless. She might as well be discussing the weather for the emotion she displayed. There was no anger, no passion, no color to her cheeks.

"Angel, please," he said huskily. "Give me a chance to explain. There's so much I must beg forgiveness for, so much I have to make right with you. Please, just come home with me. Let me take care of you and let me explain—apologize. I know I don't deserve your sweetness, your light, your *love*, but, Angel, I'm begging you. Give me one last chance. I swear you won't regret it this time."

Agitation and fear—God, *fear*—registered in her eyes, replacing the flatness with panic. She began to struggle against him until he finally loosened his hold on her and leaned back far enough that she wasn't pressed against his body.

"I want to go home," she repeated, her tone and inflection never changing. Lifeless and dull. Like her eyes. Her body language. Her expression.

Her eyes chased to the doctor, a plea for an ally. Help. One would have to be made of stone not to react to the desperation in Evangeline's eyes. But the doctor remained silent, studying Evangeline with a slight frown.

Drake closed his eyes, trying in vain to swallow the knot threatening to rob him of breath. Tears burned like acid in his eyes and he blinked furiously, refusing to break down. If he let go, if he ever let go of his tenuous grip on his composure, then he would completely fall apart and shatter into tiny, deadly shards.

"Angel," he whispered. "Come home with me. To *our* home. Give me this much this one time and I'll never ask for more. Please let me make this up to you. I can't live without you. I don't want to live without you. Without you . . ."

He trailed off, refusing to give voice to the reality of all he was, or rather wasn't, without her. He couldn't envision his life, his existence, without Evangeline. What had he ever done without her? What had his life been before she stormed in and turned his entire world upside down? He adored every single thing about her. Loved the chaos she'd brought to his well-ordered routine. Loving her was so fucking *easy*. It was impossible *not* to love her. Everyone she met, influenced in some way, fell under her spell, and it took only one of her genuine, innocent smiles and a few sweet words. If only he'd realized his love for her sooner. If only he'd given her his trust as easily.

Oh, it wasn't as though he'd only just fallen in love with her. He'd merely been a blind fool refusing to acknowledge the truth. That he'd fallen and fallen hard from the moment an enchanting blond-haired angel with big blue eyes had nervously walked into his club. The first time he'd kissed her, it had sealed his fate. A possessive, symbolic gesture of his claim.

And he'd proceeded to fuck up the very best part of his life time and time again.

"Without you I'm not whole," he said painfully.

"I want to go home. Mama is expecting me," she said desperately, stirring for the first time, panic and desperation briefly flaring in her eyes.

Her fingers twisted in the thin sheet covering her legs, her agitation radiating from her in nearly tangible waves. He could feel her distress, her entire body quivering, dark shadows coupled with the vivid bruises on her face making her appear so very vulnerable, afraid and . . . defeated.

That alone enraged him. His angel defeated? She was a fucking tigress, but right now she resembled an abused kitten, huddled on the bed, drawing herself into the smallest, tightest ball possible and keeping herself carefully away from his touch as if he were the one responsible for her abuse.

But wasn't he?

He wanted to goddamn puke. He wanted to put his fist through the fucking wall. He wanted to cry for all he'd done—and all that was fast slipping through his fingertips.

The doctor shot him a warning glance, dipped his head in Evangeline's direction and then shook his head, his message clear. *Back off. She's fragile. Don't push her. Give her time to heal.*

Let her go.

"I'll send my preliminary report with her. She needs to see a doctor there as soon as possible," the doctor said in a low tone.

Just as evident was the doctor's firm opinion that forcing Evangeline could prove to be the last straw. Could break her last hold on the control she was so desperately clinging to like a lifeline. He didn't need to voice that opinion. Drake could see it written all over the doctor's face.

Panic clutched and clawed at his insides until he was sweating and shaking. Let her go? It was equivalent to cutting his own throat, but then he deserved no less. He had driven her to this. He had driven her away. She wasn't running from him. He'd violently shoved her away with no remorse or hesitation—at the time. There was plenty of regret now. When it was too fucking late. He'd been given one of life's most precious gifts— certainly the most precious gift he'd ever been given—and he'd cruelly rejected it. Had rejected her and everything she'd so freely given him, never asking for a single thing in return.

Except . . . the one thing he hadn't been willing to give. His trust. His absolute belief in her. The same unwavering, unconditional belief she had in him. He was the worst sort of monster. Just like his mother and father. He hadn't risen above his past. He'd become his past.

Evangeline looked wildly around the room, tears welling in her eyes, with a look of such hopelessness that it was like a knife to Drake's gut.

He gently stroked a hand through her tangled hair. Then he leaned in, unable to resist pressing his lips to her golden crown. It was a benediction. It was a gesture of regret. Sorrow. Grief. Apology. And love. So much love, and it had come far too late. He hadn't given her what she needed most. His belief, his trust, his *love*. But he could at least give her this.

"I'll get you home, Angel. Don't worry. I'll take care of everything. Just rest and focus only on getting better and putting this behind you."

Oh God, please don't let her put me behind her as well.

He couldn't think about that. Couldn't imagine a life without her shining light banishing long-held shadows in the black depths of his soul. Somehow, some way, she had to come back to him. He wouldn't consider any other option. If he did, he'd completely break down.

She relaxed slightly, though there was still a troubled, guarded look shadowing her eyes. As though she didn't trust him to tell her the truth. But then who could blame her when he'd been such a ruthless bastard?

Feeling himself coming undone one piece at a time, he pulled her into his arms, cradling her ever so tenderly against his heart—*her* heart. She owned it. He buried his face in her hair, the strands dampening as tears slithered over the tormented lines in his features as he wept silently, hiding his heartbreak and devastation in her silken tresses.

Ah, Angel, my precious, precious love. Letting you go is the hardest damn thing I've ever had to do or will ever have to do in my life. Wherever you go, you take my heart. My soul. Everything within me. I'll always be with you. I'll dream of you every night, every hour of the day, and pray with every breath that one day you'll come back where you belong. To me. Until then, I'll never be whole. You're my other half. The very best part of me. The only good thing I've ever touched, loved, held close to my heart. Without you I am lost.

Could someone live with half a heart and a broken soul so tarnished by a lifetime of sins? She deserved so much better than what he'd given her. She deserved better than the man he was. And yet she'd chosen him and he'd cruelly betrayed her. He stared bleakly down at Evangeline, who lay limply in his arms. It wasn't true. You didn't need a heart to live, because his had been walking around outside his body ever since Evangeline had entered his world and effortlessly stolen it. And he'd never have it back, he'd never feel truly alive or live, until—unless—she came back to him.

His heart had lived inside her, a part of her, for the last months and he *never* wanted it back. Not unless it came as part of her.

33

Evangeline stared through unseeing eyes as the plane touched down in the small municipal airport just half an hour from her hometown. In the seat across the aisle sat Maddox and across from him Silas sat, staring at her in brooding silence.

Such had been the case ever since they'd taken off from New York City, but she'd refused to meet his gaze. She didn't make eye contact with either Silas or Maddox the entire trip, opting instead to either pretend to sleep or aim her focus out the window. But she could see both men in her periphery and neither was happy. No, they were downright pissed.

That might have set her off; after all, what did they have to be pissed off about? But more predominant than the anger betrayed by their tight, clenched jaws was the very real worry in their eyes.

They took turns studying her, probing as though they were doing a thorough physical exam, and it made her want to squirm right out of her seat. By sheer will alone, she'd forced herself to remain stoic and seemingly unaware of their scrutiny.

She knew they were furious with Drake, and it should have heartened her that their belief in her was so resolute, but all she felt was overwhelming sadness that his men had absolute, unwavering trust in her and hadn't doubted her for a minute, while Drake, the man she loved, the man she thought had loved her even though he hadn't given her the words, the man she'd planned to spend the rest of her life with and have his children, had been so quick to denounce her and throw her out. Coldly furious, his eyes icy and impenetrable, looking through her, not at her, not seeing her, not hearing her. No, he'd shut her completely out without a second thought. No hesitation.

She glanced down at her flat abdomen where her—their—child was nestled, no outward sign of its presence as of yet, and she closed her eyes. Well, at least one part of her dream would endure. She would have his child, but only one, and she wouldn't have any other part of him. Not his love. But then she'd never had his love. Only the foolish notion that he loved her but was too alpha, too stoic, too reserved to say the words. She'd thought he'd shown his love in every way that mattered, and because she believed that he loved her, the words hadn't been important to her. Only that he did love her. It was enough. Had been enough. But it had all been nothing more than fantasy, and she had only herself to blame for immersing herself in a dream world, ignoring the harsh reality, and for not seeing the truth until it was too late to protect herself from utter devastation.

She breathed a sigh of relief when the plane taxied to the small FBO building where her parents would be waiting to drive her home. Oh, please let her keep it together, at least until Silas and Maddox said goodbye and climbed on the plane to return to New York. Then and only then would she allow herself to cry in her mother's arms. She wouldn't humiliate herself more than she already had by losing it in front of Drake's men. Her pride had already suffered irreparable damage when she'd begged Drake on her knees, in front of his men, *begged* him to believe her, to listen to her. Oh, how she'd begged, only for her pleas to fall on deaf ears. She might as well have been talking to stone because that was what Drake had become the moment the asshole cop had wrongly named her their informant.

Tears burned like acid and she clenched her teeth, refusing to break down, refusing to fall apart in front of Silas and Maddox.

"Evangeline," Maddox said in a quiet, somber tone.

She turned her head, her gaze briefly skittering over his face before she focused on a point beyond his right shoulder.

"We're here, sweetheart. Your parents are waiting just outside for you."

When she would have risen, Silas was there, his hand curling underneath her elbow to help her up. He and Maddox assisted her down the stairway that had been pushed to the plane door.

Her parents stood a few feet away, but Maddox motioned them to give him, Evangeline and Silas just a moment. Her father nodded from his wheelchair, his lips pressed tightly together as he critically surveyed his daughter's appearance.

She knew she looked a wreck, but why lie by disguising all signs of her devastation? She'd just ruin her makeup and hairdo the minute she cried all over her mother.

Maddox took one of her hands, holding it loosely between his own, and expelled a deep sigh that was surprisingly sad sounding.

"Evangeline, look at me," he said gently.

She closed her eyes, tears pricking the corners. Oh God. She couldn't do this.

"Babe, look at me, please? Can you not even look at me? Are you so angry with us too?"

The words sounded raw with pain and regret, apology in his voice. Her eyes flew open and immediately found his.

"No!" she denied forcefully.

She glanced at Silas to see if he also assumed she was angry with him. His expression was unreadable. Except . . . his eyes. They looked pained. Raw. Exposed. It shocked her because he was always so inscrutable.

"This is hard," Evangeline choked out, momentarily squeezing Maddox's hand.

"I know," Maddox murmured. "Come, give me a hug. Your parents are anxious to greet you and your mother wants to fuss over you."

She threw herself into Maddox's arms and despite her vow not to cry, hot tears trailed down her cheeks as she absorbed the solid strength of Maddox's embrace.

"You and Silas are the dearest friends I've ever had," she whispered. "I'll never forget you or your kindness. And your support. It means the world to me."

Maddox pressed a tender kiss to her hair as he pulled away. Then he trailed his finger down her wet cheek, pushing a damp strand of her hair behind her ear.

"You are a remarkable woman, Evangeline. I'm grateful to have known you."

She gave him a shaky smile before he nudged her in Silas's direction.

"There's someone else who would like to say good-bye," Maddox murmured.

Evangeline took one hesitant step and then another. And then Silas simply opened his arms and she threw herself forward into his crushing embrace. His arms were like steel bands around her, and he shook as he hugged her fiercely.

"I'll miss you so much," she choked out.

"I'll miss you, doll," he said in a voice thick with emotion. "Take care of yourself and the little one."

Then he drew away and tipped her chin up with his fingers until she looked directly into his eyes.

"If you ever need anything. If you just want to hear a friendly voice or just need to talk, you have my number. You get me?"

She nodded, tears sliding unchecked down her face. She glanced down and the flash of the diamond ring Drake had given her caught her eye and then blurred when more tears flooded her eyes.

Her engagement ring. Her very last material tie to Drake. She'd forgotten all about it. Slowly she slid it from her finger. She didn't need it. She had her baby and it was all the reminder of Drake she'd ever need.

She held the ring out to Silas, her voice cracking when she spoke. "Give this back to Drake, please."

"Any message?" Silas asked softly.

She shook her head. "There's nothing to say," she said sadly.

"Take care, doll. Maddox and I are only a phone call away. Remember that."

She tried to smile, but it was hard when she was dying on the inside, her heart breaking into a million jagged pieces.

"You and Maddox better take care of yourselves," she admonished. "And Drake. Take care of him too."

It hurt to say his name. It was like a physical blow that unsteadied her. Maddox curled his hand underneath her arm and then slipped her beneath his shoulder.

"Come on, sweetheart. Your parents are waiting."

Despite her vow not to fall apart until she was well away from Maddox and Silas and in her mother's loving arms, she wept the moment her mother reached for her.

34

Evangeline surveyed her mother's kitchen in disgust. It looked as if a tornado had struck. Pots and pans were scattered everywhere along with mixing bowls, opened packages, empty boxes and bags. Flour dusted one entire countertop and the cooktop needed a thorough scrubbing. She actually looked forward to that job. It was a good way to work off pent-up frustration by attacking layers of grease and dried food.

Her father had said in a somewhat bemused tone that she was cooking enough food to stockpile for the zombie apocalypse. And, well, he wasn't wrong. She'd cooked, stored and frozen enough dinners to last them well through the spring and into early summer.

With a sigh, she mentally declared enough. There were only so many things she could cook before she ran through the stockpile of groceries she'd purchased mere days ago. She sat on the stool at the island to rest a moment and automatically ran her hand over her still-flat stomach where her child rested.

As expected, in sync with the surge of love and joy that always accompanied thoughts of her baby came a wave of agony and grief so strong that if she hadn't already been sitting, it would have forced her to sink into the nearest chair.

It had been a month. A month! And yet in many ways it was only yesterday. She wasn't sleeping. And despite the fact that she had been cooking like a fiend for the last four weeks, she couldn't stomach the thought of consuming any of her dishes.

And every single day, she was tormented by her conscience. She had to tell Drake about her pregnancy. Everything had happened so fast. One moment she'd been convinced she would die. The next, Drake and his men had swept in like avenging angels and then . . . ? The rest had been a blur. There had been a doctor. Drake talking to her, his eyes dark with . . . what exactly? She strained to remember, but it was all so fuzzy.

He'd spoken to her in serious, impassioned tones, but even looking at him had sent shards of agony through her heart and all she'd been able to focus on, the only words she'd been able to form, was that she wanted to go home. Where it was safe. To escape the pain.

So stupid. As if she'd ever escape the pain of losing Drake. But she had to tell him he was going to be a father. No matter what he thought of her, that he didn't love her, he deserved to know, and she wasn't so vindictive that she'd ever try to keep him from his child. What he did with that knowledge was up to him, but she would tell him.

Would he even care? Would he believe the child was his? He believed in her so little that it wasn't a stretch to think he'd deny he'd fathered her child. There were paternity tests, of course, but she wouldn't force him to accept his baby. If he wanted nothing to do with either of them, there was no way she'd shove an unwanted child down his throat. Never would she allow her child to grow up as he had. Unloved. Unwanted.

Maybe after her doctor's appointment. Her pulse leapt at the thought of going to see the obstetrician her mother had found. What if she'd imagined the positive pregnancy test? What if she'd wanted to be pregnant so badly that she'd blocked out a negative result? But no. When she'd arrived home, she'd had a cursory exam by her old family doctor, who had confirmed her pregnancy but advised her to make an appointment with an OB-GYN. Tomorrow was the earliest appointment she'd been able to get.

After tomorrow, she'd make some firm decisions about her future instead of existing in limbo as she now was. She made a face because this entire situation wasn't fair to either of her parents.

Her mother watched and worried. She hovered anxiously, taking turns with Evangeline's father keeping careful watch over her, but they didn't press, didn't push her, and most importantly, her mother didn't speak or act condescendingly to Evangeline. She didn't pat her on the head and tell her everything would be okay or that time healed all things, nor did she offer her any other trite clichés about recovering from a broken heart.

She very honestly told Evangeline that of course she hurt and of course she was devastated. She loved Drake and that didn't go away in an hour, a day, a week or even a month. That it would be a slow process and all she could do was take it one day at a time and never look beyond the next day or push herself to "get over" losing someone she loved with all her heart and soul.

She adored her mother and her infinite wisdom. Wisdom that only a mother had, gleaned from years of experience and honed by loving and protecting the child she'd carried for nine months and then nurtured through the formative years. It didn't matter that Evangeline was grown. No one ever outgrew their need for a mother.

Her mom had quietly told Evangeline that she needed time to grieve. That in a lot of ways, it was the same as a loved one dying, only in some ways worse because that person was still alive, out there, but Evangeline could ever only look but not touch. In a figurative manner of speaking. With death came finality. The knowledge that you had lost that person forever. In a situation such as Evangeline's, no matter that Evangeline was hurt and devastated and didn't want Drake back, she still loved him, missed him, and in the most hidden, secret parts of her heart was a flicker of hope that somehow things would work out and they could be together again. And so every day they remained apart was its own sort of hell.

Evangeline was in awe of how well her mother knew her, how intuitive she was, because wow, she had Evangeline dead to rights. Yes, she did secretly harbor hope, stupid, naïve hope, that by some miracle of fate, she and Drake would live happily ever after and her child would have his or her father. And every single day that she awoke, alone, in an empty bed missing Drake with every breath in her body, she buried her face in her pillow and wept.

Irritated at how much Drake occupied her thoughts, despite her effort to banish him and distract herself with marathon cooking sessions—as if that did any good—she got up, tossing down the towel she'd wiped her hands on, and attacked cleanup, squeezing the last of the prepared meals into the already overloaded freezer.

She cleaned, scrubbed, polished and then mopped until the kitchen sparkled. When she was done, she leaned briefly on the mop handle and blew a stray piece of hair from her eyes as she surveyed her handiwork. Her parents, as usual, avoided her when she went into a cooking frenzy, recognizing it as her way of working through her grief.

If only it did any good.

"Is it safe to come in?" her mother called from the door.

Evangeline whirled, a smile she didn't have to fake curving her lips.

"Oh my, you've been quite busy," her mother said, shaking her head as she ventured farther in.

Evangeline hastily dumped the mop water into the sink and then put the mop on the back porch to dry. When she returned, she went straight to her mother and enfolded her in a fierce hug. Her mom hugged her back, but when she drew away, she had a bewildered look on her face.

"Evangeline, what's wrong, darling?"

Evangeline smiled, though a sheen of tears already coated her eyes.

"Nothing. I just wanted you to know how much I love you and how grateful I am to have you and Daddy. I don't know what I would have done without y'all."

Her mother's eyes softened and her face shone with love and tenderness.

"Oh, my darling, I love you too. I hate to see you hurting so badly. There is nothing more frustrating as a parent than to see your child in pain and be helpless to fix it."

"You are fixing it, Mama. Just by being here. You and Daddy have been so terrific." She sighed and glanced around the now-spotless kitchen. "I suppose I really should let you have your kitchen back."

Her mother laughed. "I don't know. It's kind of nice to know that I won't have to cook for the next six months."

Evangeline issued a rueful grin. "I guess it's better than the more clichéd ways of dealing with a broken heart. By eating a pound of chocolate a day and watching sad movies."

Her mom rolled her eyes. "I've let you be to do your thing in the kitchen because it isn't hurting anyone, but I'll turn you over my knee if you start with bad habits. No man is worth that level of self-destruction. Besides, you have a child to think of now," she said gently, reaching for Evangeline's hand and squeezing in a comforting gesture.

Pain robbed her of breath for a moment as she imagined her child. A little boy who looked just like Drake. A little girl with her blond hair and her father's dark eyes. Or a dark-haired, dark-eyed daughter. She would be so beautiful.

"And speaking of which," her mother said, continuing on as if not noticing Evangeline's sudden quietness—her mother never missed anything—"do you remember you have a doctor's appointment at one tomorrow?"

As if she could forget. The appointment had been all that she'd thought about for the last week.

She nodded. "Are you still going to come with me?"

An anxious note crept into her voice despite her trying to make it sound like a casual inquiry.

Her mother hugged her fiercely. "I wouldn't miss it, darling. Of course I'm coming. You're carrying my grandchild! I'm very much looking forward to knowing an approximate due date so we can make plans. And I've already started sewing for the little one. Neutral colors, of course, until we know what you're having."

Evangeline smiled, feeling a rush of excitement, the first *good* feeling she'd had in so very long that it was intoxicating. She wanted to hug it to her and hold on to it forever.

"Oh, I can't wait! I can't decide if I want a boy or a girl. I honestly don't care! I already love him or her so much," she said fiercely. "I can't wait to meet my baby and hold her."

Her mother grinned, her eyes sparkling mischievously. "You just called it *her*. Could it be you're secretly hoping for a daughter?"

Evangeline laughed. "No. Honestly, I don't care. I alternate saying *him* and *her* because I hate calling the baby *it* and well, I don't want to give preference to either sex so I just switch back and forth."

"Brenda! Where in Sam Hill are y'all?" her father called from the living room.

Her mother clapped a hand over her mouth. "Whoops! I got so caught up I completely forgot why I came in here. Your father sent me to kidnap you. He's starting a movie and wanted us to watch it together."

Evangeline linked her arm through her mother's and squeezed affectionately. "Then let's go sit down with Daddy and keep him company for a while."

35

Evangeline was quiet on the drive home from the doctor's appointment. Though she'd been euphoric when the obstetrician had ordered a vaginal ultrasound to determine her due date, and she'd seen the heartbeat—had heard it!—when she and her mom had left the clinic, sadness had settled over her.

How different things would be if she and Drake were still together. About to be married. Having a baby. *He* would have gone to her appointment with her and they would have shared in the joy of seeing their child for the first time. Instead, she was a single mom. One of many enduring their pregnancies without a supportive spouse or partner.

She stared blindly out the window as they drew closer to her parents' home, blinking to prevent the tears that threatened to fall. It was time to stop crying and pull herself together. Face reality. Drake—being with Drake—was a fantasy. An impossible dream because he could never trust her, never believe in her, and she could never be with a man who had so little faith in her. She owed herself and her baby more than that.

She rubbed her stomach, still awed by the images on the ultrasound monitor. This was a time for joy and excitement, and she refused to allow Drake Donovan to take that away from her. A child was a cause for celebration no matter how it came to be, and she never, for one moment, wanted there to be any doubt that her child wasn't dearly loved and wanted with every single part of her heart.

Her mom pulled into the drive and cast an almost nervous glance in Evangeline's direction. Evangeline looked at her mom in question, wondering at the odd look on her mother's face. But it was gone as soon as it registered, leaving Evangeline to wonder if she'd imagined it as her mother smiled brightly at her.

"Let's go in and show your father the sonogram pictures!"

Evangeline's heart squeezed and she clutched the pictures to her chest, a surge of love making her heart flutter. She smiled back at her mom and the two women got out and walked to the door.

Her mom went in first and to her surprise headed for her bedroom, leaving Evangeline standing in the foyer in confusion. With a shake of her head at her mother's odd behavior, she headed into the living room to find her dad and share the news from her doctor's appointment.

But when she walked into the living room, she halted in her tracks, her shocked gaze settling on the man standing on the far side, hands shoved into the pockets of his slacks, staring broodingly out the window overlooking the backyard. Then he turned and their eyes locked and her stomach bottomed out.

Drake.

What was he doing here? She sucked in her breath at the raw vulnerability reflected in usually nonexpressive eyes, eyes that never gave anything away. He looked . . . tormented. His expression held utter bleakness and he looked as if he hadn't slept or eaten in *weeks*. He looked as bad as she felt.

What was he doing here?

She tried to open her mouth to ask but found herself incapable of speech. The result was her looking at him completely dumbfounded, her heart in shreds, bleeding.

"I wanted to be here in time to take you to your appointment," he said hoarsely. "But the plane was grounded due to ice. I'm sorry. I tried to get here as quickly as I could."

"You *know*?" she asked in a shocked voice.

Confusion glimmered in his dark eyes. "Angel, I've known since the day you found out," he said gently. "Do you not remember the day we rescued you from your abductor and how worried we were that something had happened to the baby?"

She shook her head. "I don't remember much about that day," she whispered. She lifted her gaze to meet his, her heart heavy. "Is that why you're here, then? Because of the baby?"

He swore softly and then crossed the room as if to pull her into his arms, but he hesitated when he drew abreast of her, almost as if afraid of her rejection.

"I'm worried about the baby, yes. But I'm more worried about you. I'm here because I can't live without you. I'm here because there is so much I need to say to you, Angel."

Before she could respond to his raw declaration, he slowly and painfully lowered himself to his knees in front of her, gathering her hands in his as he looked beseechingly up at her.

"I'm begging you to listen to what I have to say. Hear me out. Please."

Evangeline stared in shocked bewilderment at Drake's haggard features and the aching vulnerability reflected so clearly in his eyes. He was assuming a position of submission and humility. Tears choked her, clogging her throat as so much of the pain and devastation she'd tried so hard to make peace with bubbled up and threatened to burst free, much like a dam breaking.

"You refused to listen to me," she said thickly. "I was on my knees begging and you wouldn't even hear me out. You refused to give me a chance. Why should I give you the same? I gave you everything, Drake. Everything. I held nothing back. I gave you my submission. My love. My trust. My loyalty. And you threw everything back in my face. It was like you were just waiting for me to fail. You wanted me to fail. And when it appeared I had, you couldn't wait to throw me out. Do you have any idea how that made me feel?"

She was heaving for breath, the tears she'd tried so hard not to let him see sliding down her cheeks. She wiped hastily with the backs of her hands, dashing them away before she looked away, refusing to meet his imploring gaze a minute longer.

"You're right," he said in a subdued, defeated tone she'd never heard in him.

Her gaze swung wildly back to him at his admission, unable to believe he was admitting that she was right and he had been so very wrong. His grip tightened on her hands as though he feared she'd slip away and he'd never get her back. Well, he'd already lost her and not because he let her go. He'd shoved her violently out of his life in the cruelest manner possible.

"Why did you come for me, Drake?" she asked, ignoring his admission. "Why did you even bother rescuing me from that horrible man? I would have thought you would have been happy to be rid of me."

His face lost its pallor, going gray with answering grief and regret. So much regret and sorrow that it made her uncomfortable to look at. But when he spoke, he went back to his admission, to her earlier accusation.

"I know I don't deserve anything from you, Angel. Not the time of day, not even a look, certainly not your love. But I'm begging you as you once begged me to listen. If after this is done you never want to see me again, then I'll go. But you and our child will be taken care of. Always."

She swallowed but didn't answer, but neither did she tell him no. She didn't say anything at all. Just continued to stare at him, hurting with every part of her soul.

"You were right in that I was waiting for you to fail," he said, wincing at his admission. "I once told you that if my own parents didn't love me, how could I expect anyone else to? You may have thought it was bull-shit, but it's true. No one has ever loved me and then you . . ."

He broke off and swallowed heavily, and she was flabbergasted to see a sheen of moisture collect in his eyes.

"Then I met you and you didn't tell me as much as you showed me that you loved me. Every single day. In every action, every gesture, every look. You *showed* me what love is. And I showed you what love wasn't," he said painfully. "I couldn't believe that you loved me. Not my money. Not my power. You loved *me*, the man, and you only wanted the same from me. Not the things I could buy you or the lifestyle I could provide you. If anything you *tolerated* those things because it meant a life with me."

A glimmer of amusement curved his lips as he said the last.

"You scared the hell out of me, Angel. I had no answer for you. No idea what to do with you. When it was all so simple. All you wanted was my love, and that was the one thing I couldn't give you."

She sucked her breath in, her chest squeezing painfully.

"I thought I couldn't give you love," he said softly. "But I was wrong. I loved you from the start. I didn't know it. Didn't recognize it. How could I? I'd never seen or felt love in my life. All I knew was that when I was with you my entire world lit up. I was happy. I only felt content when I was with you. I wanted to do everything in my power to make you happy. I . . . loved you."

She looked sadly at him, shaking her head even before he finished his statement. He squeezed her hands, a request for her to let him finish.

"I was so convinced that no one could ever love me that I didn't rec-ognize it until it was too late. When I thought you had betrayed me, I was devastated. I was completely undone and so grief-stricken that I lashed out and said and did despicable, horrible things. I said terrible things. I reacted like a wounded animal and I only wanted to be alone to brood and to grieve the loss of the most beautiful thing in my life."

He broke off a minute and heaved a deep breath.

"And as the days went by, I started to think, did it really matter if you betrayed me? Was it such an unforgivable crime, given all I'd kept from you? I expected blind faith and trust from you while giving you nothing of that part of my life. What were you supposed to think? I'm sure you thought the worst. And you being you, so good and innocent, wouldn't have been able to live with that kind of man. So why wouldn't you do the right thing and set me up?"

"But, Drake, I didn't!"

He squeezed her hands again. "I know, Angel, I know. What I'm saying is that I missed you so damn much, I loved you so damn much, that I was willing to forgive you even if you had. And then . . . then I started to think back over everything. And I wondered. I doubted. I found it hard to believe you could do something so contrary to your loving, loyal nature. I was so fucked up, questioning everything in my life. When the real traitor was ferreted out, I had already made the decision to go after you, beg your forgiveness and do whatever was necessary to win you back."

He closed his eyes, tears sliding wetly down his cheeks.

"Because I realized I loved you. I love you with everything I am. Everything I have. Everything that is within me and everything that I'll ever be. Whatever I'll be is because of you. I told your mother on the phone, the day you disappeared, that I loved you and that no matter what I would find you and keep you safe. That I'd never let you go again."

Evangeline just stared, too confused and off balance to make sense of all he was saying.

"You were out of it when we got you to the clinic," Drake said painfully. "Barely aware of your surroundings. I begged you then. Told you I loved you and our child. I wanted nothing more than to bring you back to our apartment and spend the rest of my life making up for my mistakes. But the only thing you said was that you wanted to go home. To your parents. And you were so fragile, on the verge of shattering, that I would have done anything to make you happy again. So I let you go."

He stopped, choking out the last words and turning his face away but not before she saw the raw agony and utter despair. Pain and so much desolation. Everything she'd felt for the last month was mirrored in his eyes.

"But I kept in touch with your parents daily. Seeking any crumb of information about you. The slightest detail, no matter how insignificant, I devoured like a man starving. I couldn't stay away a day longer, Angel. I'm miserable without you and I think you're miserable without me. We're only whole when we're together. I know I have a lot of making up to do. I'll spend the rest of my life trying to catch up and atone for all I've done. But please, just give me the chance to make you happy. I know I can make you happy again, Evangeline. If you only give me the chance. The chance I denied you."

Evangeline's knees were perilously close to giving out. Her hands were still firmly in the grasp of Drake's, so she slid unsteadily to her knees in front of him. Alarm flared in his eyes and he was up immediately, sweeping her into his arms. He strode to the couch and set her down like she was the most precious thing in the world. Then he sat next to her, angled so they could face one another.

She felt light-headed and faint, her heart beating so fast that her surroundings were a blur. All she could see was Drake's beautiful face ravaged with every single emotion she felt. Could she believe him? Could she trust him?

"Just tell me one thing, Angel," he implored.

He waited a beat and then brushed his fingers over her cheek, and she was shocked to see it come back wet with yet more tears. She hadn't realized tears were streaming freely down her face now.

"Do you still love me or have I killed any chance of you ever loving me again?" he asked painfully.

She bowed her head, tears splashing onto her tightly clenched hands on her lap. When the silence between them became prolonged, Drake's tone grew more desperate and hopeless.

"Angel?"

His voice cracked and she peeked from underneath her lashes to see savage torment etched in every line and groove on his face, and he suddenly looked older than his thirty-six years.

"I'm afraid," she admitted in a husky voice. "I'm afraid to love you, Drake. You have so much power over me. You have the power to make me the happiest I've ever been in my life, but you also have the power to destroy me. That scares me."

"Oh, darling," he said, every word spoken in an aching, grief-stricken tone. "Don't you know? You have the same power over me. I've never been so miserable in my life as I have the last month and before you say it, I know it's my fault. I *know*. But I've learned something important from you. You taught me that it's okay to be vulnerable. That it's okay to love and be loved. That being loved is the single most beautiful thing in the world. I can't live without your love. I don't want to. And I swear you will never live without mine."

"You really love me?" she asked hesitantly, afraid to believe. Afraid to trust after so much hurt and pain.

"It breaks my heart that I've done this to you. That you doubt such a precious thing—that you are so very precious to me. But do I love you? I adore you. I love you more than I've ever loved anyone in my life. You are the *only* person I've ever loved," he amended. "I trust my brothers. I have an unbreakable bond with them. I'd give my life for them. But, Angel, you *are* my life. My entire world. My reason for getting up in the morning. My reason for living."

He placed his hand on her flat belly, rubbing his thumb tenderly over her womb.

"You and our child," he said huskily. "Please come home with me.

You and our baby. Let me love you, cherish you, protect you both. Or if you can't bear to live in the city, we'll move here. I don't care where we live as long as I have you."

Her head reared back in shock, her eyes wide as she stared incredulously at him.

"You'd live *here,* close to my parents?"

His expression was utterly serious, his eyes grave as he nodded.

Her mouth went dry and she licked her lips. She was trembling. Reaction setting in. This wasn't happening. It was all a dream. The result of wishful thinking and her dearest fantasy. She closed her eyes.

This isn't real.

"Open your eyes, Angel. Look at me. See me. See my love for you. I assure you it's very real. I'm real."

She hadn't realized she'd whispered her denial aloud.

"All you have to do is reach out and take what it is you want. It's yours. I'm yours."

Tentatively she reached out, her hand shaking so badly that it bobbed in midair. She slid her fingers over the stubble of his beard and lightly caressed his cheek in wonder. Could it be that simple? Did he truly love her and could they have the life together she'd so desperately wanted? The life she'd cried herself to sleep over for so many nights? A life she'd thought lost to her forever?

"Just say yes," he whispered. "Kiss me and say yes."

She stared at him for a long moment, her eyes searching his. All she saw was truth and sincerity. No secrets, lies or deception. It took every ounce of her courage. She gathered it tightly around her like a blanket and held on tight. It took several attempts but finally, she was able to say it.

"Yes," she said so softly that at first she thought he didn't hear.

But the savage spark that ignited in his eyes told her he had. And then she leaned up, pressing her lips to his, like the brush of a butterfly's wings.

He groaned low in his throat and then framed her face in his hands, tenderly, so gently that it was a caress, and he kissed her back every bit as sweetly.

She tasted the salt of tears and realized they came from both of them. Drake leaned his forehead against hers and closed his eyes.

"I love you, Angel. Yesterday, today, forever."

"I love you too," she said around the knot in her throat.

He reached into his pocket, jostling them both momentarily, and then he pulled out the ring she'd given Silas to return to him. With shaking hands, he slid it back onto her finger, expelling a sigh of relief when it was in place.

"I carried this in my pocket ever since Silas gave it back to me," he admitted. "I was gutted when he handed it to me, and I never once stopped hoping and praying for the day that I'd put it back on your finger. Swear to me you'll never take it off again."

For the first time, she smiled, and he looked awestruck. His hands went to her face, tracing the lines, thumbing her lip and stroking her jaw.

"I won't," she vowed.

"Ahem," came the clearing of a throat from the doorway.

They both whirled around to see Evangeline's mother standing behind her husband's wheelchair, tears glittering brightly in her eyes.

"Does this mean we have a wedding to plan?" Evangeline's father asked gruffly.

"It does, although I plan to marry her as fast as possible so she doesn't change her mind," Drake said in a voice that suggested he wasn't joking.

Brenda Hawthorn smiled. "I believe that can be arranged. Congratulations, my darling," she said to Evangeline. "I'm so very glad you've worked things out with Drake. It's been killing me and your father to see you so unhappy." Then she looked gravely at Drake. "Make her happy, young man. God has given you another chance to make things right. Make the most of it."

Drake's eyes were wet as he looked between Evangeline and her mother and he squeezed Evangeline to him, holding her as if he'd never let her go.

"I'm well aware that I am the luckiest of men and that I don't deserve Evangeline, but you can be sure that now that I have her back I'm *never* letting her go again and I'll spend every day of the rest of my life doing whatever it takes to always keep her happy. You—and she—have my word on it."

Then he grinned down at Evangeline, and she was shocked at the joy and relief brimming in his eyes. So much of the grimness and reserve that seemed ever present in his gaze had vanished. The shadows were gone. He looked . . . happy. Every bit as happy as she felt as she witnessed the truth and sincerity in his words and actions.

"Annndd," he said, drawing out the word as he glanced meaningfully back at her parents, "giving you as many grandchildren as possible."

EPILOGUE

The old whitewashed church in Evangeline's small hometown had been transformed into something straight out of a fairy tale. No expense had been spared in Drake's determination to give her the wedding of her dreams. The insides were draped from one end to the other in a cascade of elegantly arranged flowers, some of which had been flown in from all over the country. There were thousands of twinkling white lights, an homage to her love of Christmas, even if the holiday had already passed, and they were twined around a mountain of greenery and strategically placed to show the flowers to their best advantage.

Ironically, it hadn't been Evangeline who oversaw or even planned any of the decorating, arrangements or anything at all to do with her ceremony. Drake had firmly told her that he and her mother would take care of everything and all he wanted her to do was rest and take care of herself and their child.

To her further amusement, Drake's men—all of them—had each taken an active part in the plans. Silas had personally overseen the floral arrangements. Drake's enforcer was a man of hidden depths. He obviously had an eye for art and decorating. After all, it had been he who had taken Evangeline to have her hair and makeup done, and it had been he who'd given the makeup artist instructions on the look Silas wanted for her.

For the wedding, it was no different. Silas had flown the same artist from New York City to the rural area of Mississippi to personally arrange Evangeline's hair and makeup for the big day.

Evangeline sat in the bridal room of the church, which was no more than a tiny cubicle off the foyer on the opposite side of the church's nursery, eyeing her appearance critically in the mirror. Oh, she hadn't gotten dressed here, nor had her hair and makeup been arranged at the church. The artist had spent the better part of two hours at Evangeline's parents' home getting her made up, and after he was satisfied that she was, in his words, absolute perfection, she'd been driven to the church accompanied by Silas and Maddox. She was hurriedly escorted into the bridal room to rest—Silas's firm dictate—and to do any touch-ups she may require before she was summoned for the ceremony.

When it was time, a soft knock sounded at her door, and butterflies immediately took wing, scuttling around her belly in a nervous cacophony. Her mother reached over and squeezed Evangeline's hand, tears shining in her loving eyes.

"That will be Silas, darling. Your father is waiting in the foyer. Are you ready?"

Evangeline swallowed nervously but excitement and so much joy invaded her chest that the smile curving her lips felt bright enough to overshadow the sun. She nodded as her mouth went suddenly dry and her entire body jittered with excitement as she gracefully—or as gracefully as she could manage—rose to her feet with her mother's assistance.

"Evangeline," Silas said, warm approval in his eyes when she opened the door. "You look beautiful, sweetheart."

She blinked back the sudden sting of tears, and his voice turned chiding as he carefully wiped at the corner of her eye with his thumb.

"None of that on your wedding day. Your stylist took two hours. I assure you that Drake will have all our heads if I have to tell him that there has been a delay in the ceremony because you have to start all over again on your makeup."

Evangeline laughed and then impulsively she threw her arms around Silas and hugged him fiercely.

"You truly are my dearest friend," she whispered against his chest.

Silas squeezed gently and pressed a kiss to her forehead. Then he turned her and helped her into the foyer where her dad sat waiting in his wheelchair.

Drake checked his watch, frowning his impatience. His right foot was tapping, the sound muted by the carpeted aisles of the church.

Church.

He inwardly winced at what had to be sheer blasphemy. Him—and his men—in a church? They were lucky the entire building hadn't gone up the moment they stepped through the doors or that none of them had been struck by lightning.

What a sight it was to see his brothers in a church. All wearing expensive suits. Even the more rebellious I-don't-give-a-fuck-what-you-think Zander and Jax had dressed formally for the occasion. None of them dared risk hurting Evangeline's feelings, not because of any threat by Drake or Silas, but because they all adored her and it would kill them to ever be the source of her distress or unhappiness.

The attendance was small. In fact, the only people there other than Drake's men were Evangeline's parents, one or two distant relatives who still lived in the same town and two older ladies who were close friends of Brenda's, each of whom Evangeline called "aunt." Although, one thing that Drake had quickly learned about life in a small Southern town was that close friends were addressed and treated as family. But then Evangeline had adopted that same policy when it came to Drake and all his men.

She counted them as family. Her family. And pity the fool who ever fucked with her family.

The sides hadn't been divided into bride's and groom's. His men were the only attendants and so they lined both sides of the elaborately decorated arch, a show of support for both him and Evangeline. Evangeline was equally represented, a fact Drake would have ensured if his men hadn't stepped forward to do exactly the same of their own accord.

Maddox took a step forward now so he stood directly behind Drake. Where Silas would stand once he was finished helping Evangeline and her father down the aisle.

"Any second thoughts?" Maddox murmured.

"Hell no!"

Drake winced at the sudden explosive denial and glanced apologetically at the minister, who looked faintly amused.

Maddox chuckled. "Didn't think so."

Drake scowled. Then why the hell ask? But he didn't dignify his man's teasing with a response. He checked his watch again. What could be taking so long? Evangeline had been ready before she'd arrived at the church. That was half an hour ago.

A cold sweat broke out on his forehead and panic gripped his insides. What if she was the one having second thoughts? He turned, his intention to go find Evangeline and hustle her down the aisle—proprieties and ceremony be damned, when music suddenly swelled over the interior and the door at the end opened, bearing Evangeline's mom, escorted by Silas.

Wait a minute. Silas was going to walk behind Evangeline's father and push his wheelchair so Evangeline would be on her father's arm. If he was escorting Brenda, then who would make sure Evangeline and her father got down the aisle with no issue?

Hell, he'd go down and get Evangeline himself if it came to it. There was no way he was taking any risk that she had too much time to reconsider. The mere idea of coming this close and her not marrying him? It didn't bear thinking about.

Silas seated Brenda and brushed a perfunctory kiss over her cheek. Brenda smiled up at the big man and the two exchanged words, which had Drake frowning. If there was anything to be said regarding Evangeline, then it needed to be said to *Drake*. Not Silas. Not any of his men.

Then Silas turned, his gaze finding Drake's and with a lazy grin, he hurried back down the aisle, disappearing behind the closed door. Not even thirty seconds later, the music changed, not to the traditional wedding march, but to "Ode to Joy," a song Evangeline loved and one she had said was the most representative of their union.

Drake agreed.

The double doors swung wide and remained open, and then Drake saw her.

All the breath left his body and he swayed, adjusting his footing so he didn't humiliate himself by going to his knees. But Jesus. Never had he seen a more beautiful sight than his angel draped in the most elegant white dress. She shimmered from head to toe, adorned in his jewels. Her blond hair fell in waves down her back, unbound, not a single strand upswept. No veil obscured his vision of her face, a fact for which he was extremely grateful.

Her soft smile was radiant, lighting up the entire church. It was as though the roof had been peeled away and the sun's rays shone down on them all. Her vibrant blue eyes sparkled with so much love and happiness that Drake had to swallow back the knot of emotion threatening to choke him.

She stepped forward on her father's arm, Silas carefully pushing the wheelchair so Evangeline set the pace. Her father's face shone with pride, his chest puffed out, head held high but in his eyes was a clear warning to Drake.

I'm giving you my dearest blessing. Make her happy or I'll make you suffer.

Well, her father had nothing to worry about on that account because if Evangeline wasn't happy then Drake suffered. Period. Her happiness was his happiness. Her misery was his misery. And, God willing, neither would ever know a day of sorrow again. As long as Drake had Evangeline, he couldn't imagine ever feeling the barren emptiness that had been his entire life before her.

The closer they got to where Drake was standing, the more powerful the urge was for Drake to go to her, to sweep her into his arms and haul her before the waiting minister so they could get on with making her his. Legally, that is. Because she was already his and nothing, no legalities or anything else, would ever change that fact.

Marriage, or rather the official act of marriage, had never meant anything to Drake. Until now. In his mind, a piece of paper and a man of God's words meant nothing to him nor to anything he claimed as his. But he'd found himself surprisingly adamant about the matter of marriage.

Evangeline had softly told him that if marriage wasn't what he wanted, if it made him uncomfortable, they didn't have to do it. Him loving her was enough.

Fuck that.

He'd damn near exploded, his insides turning to ice when she'd made her statement. His first reaction had been to tell her that they were getting married and that it was not just important, it was everything to him. His second thought had made him sweat and he'd demanded to know if she was having regrets. And did she not want to get married?

He shook off those moments of despair and refocused on the vision before him. God, she was so beautiful. And his. She was completely and utterly his.

Silas slowly pulled the wheelchair to a stop and Evangeline turned, momentarily only having eyes for her father. Tears glistened in the older man's eyes and Drake suddenly had a glimpse of the future. Him in

Grant Hawthorn's place. Drake giving away his and Evangeline's daughter in marriage. It was a humbling and terrifying sensation all in one.

Giving their daughter away in marriage? Like hell. Their daughter would never marry—or ever have boyfriends—if Drake had anything to say about it. He was perfectly okay with his men being the only males in his daughter's—or, perhaps someday, his daughters'—lives. And even they would only be there to protect their lives. He shuddered at the very idea of daughters in the plural sense. As in more than one. Just as quickly, he suddenly pictured a half dozen daughters, all miniature replicas of Evangeline. He could feel the blood leaving his face and his knees growing weak. Six mini angels? He would be so fucked . . . and completely delirious with joy.

Evangeline kissed her father and he squeezed her hand before once more looking in Drake's direction. The men exchanged nods that spoke volumes. They had an understanding. Drake could well understand the other man's position.

Silas pushed the wheelchair to the pew so it would sit on the outside just beside where Brenda Hawthorn sat and then he took Evangeline's hand and brought her slowly to Drake, connecting her hand to Drake's.

"Take good care of her," Silas said gravely.

"Always," Drake vowed.

Then Silas melted away and it was only Drake and Evangeline. Evangeline's tiny hand in his. The others melted away. There was only Evangeline for him. No one else mattered. He stared hungrily at her, so relieved that this day had finally arrived, never mind that it had been only two weeks since his angel had forgiven him and had taken him back. Those two weeks—and the four before them—had seemed like an eternity.

Now the only eternity he contemplated was the eternity he planned to spend with his wife.

"Drake," she whispered, tugging gently at his hand.

He frowned, sure this wasn't part of the ceremony. She smiled up at him, taking his breath completely away.

"The minister is waiting," she continued whispering.

Ah fuck. He'd been so immersed in staring at her, taking in what belonged to him and thanking God for it that he'd just stood there like some gawking fool instead of proceeding with the ceremony. Oh well. Who could blame him? He was marrying the sweetest, most beautiful woman—inside and out—in the world. If that didn't warrant a few moments of staring while flabbergasted, what did?

"Can't have that," he murmured, tightening his hold on her hand. Then he lifted her hand and pressed a kiss to her palm, knowing that this too wasn't part of the planned ceremony. "I love you, Angel. I love you so damn much. Thank you for loving me."

Evangeline's smile warmed him to his toes. She didn't look terribly upset over his breach in etiquette, or that the minister stood waiting, amused exasperation in his eyes.

"I love you too, Drake. Now don't you think we've waited long enough? It's time for us to get married."

Hell yes it was. The longer he held things up, the longer it would be before he had her in their honeymoon suite making love to her until they both went blind.

As if sensing the direction of his thoughts, she grinned, mischief flashing in her eyes. Dear God, he suddenly had no clue or remembrance of anything having to do with the actual details of the ceremony and they'd even gone through a fucking rehearsal the night before, of all things. As if he needed coaching on how to make the woman he loved his! Only now his mind was consumed with only images of Evangeline—his wife—in his arms, in his bed, wrapped sweetly around him while he made love to her as many times as humanly possible. And even after he'd exhausted them both, he'd still be *thinking* about making love to her and plotting the next moment when he slid into her welcoming body. Hell, he just might spend the rest of his life with his dick as far inside her sweetness as he could go. He could certainly think of worse ways to spend what years he had left on this earth.

He'd never believed in heaven and hell but in short order Evangeline had made him keenly aware of both. Because when he was with her? Heaven. Absolute heaven. And without her . . . the very worst sort of hell. And well, if he had heaven to look forward to with Evangeline after their last day on earth? He suddenly didn't mind the idea at all.

Heaven was where angels came from and Evangeline was the sweetest of all angels. He wasn't a worthy man nor had he done anything to deserve redemption or even a glimpse of heaven and yet in Evangeline's arms, he'd been closer than any man could ever hope to get to such goodness.

Once more Evangeline tugged at his hand and he shook himself from his silent perusal of his angel, blinking in confusion. Laughter glittered in her eyes as though she were enjoying a joke at his expense.

"I think this is where you kiss me," she whispered.

Kiss her? They'd already gotten to the best part of the whole damn thing? Oh *hell* yeah. Kissing her he could definitely do. Something he planned to do a lot of. Next to the part where the minister declared them man and wife, kissing her was the best part of the ceremony.

With infinite reverence, he ran his fingers and palms down her face, caressing her pink cheeks, touching the fullness of her lips until he cupped her chin in his hand and then he leaned down to capture her mouth, shivering when she gave a breathy sigh of contentment.

No matter how often he kissed her—and he'd done little else since having her back—it was still like the first time all over again. Never would he get enough of her touch. Her warmth and her love.

His kiss deepened until he felt her lean fully into him, completely surrendering to his need to be as close to her as possible. Around him, seemingly a great distance away, he heard sounds of amusement, laughter, even teasing but he didn't give a damn. Not when he had what he loved most in his arms.

And if he wasn't mistaken and he had indeed paid correct attention to the trial run from the night before, kissing his bride came *after* the minister declared them man and wife. Which meant he was kissing his *wife*. His angel. The mother of his child and of the many children he'd promised to give her in the future.

"Mine," he murmured before plunging his tongue deeply into her mouth, uncaring of who witnessed his passionate declaration.

"Yours," she whispered back. "Always and forever, Drake. I will always love you and I will always be yours."

He closed his eyes as the betraying sting of tears burned his eyes. God but he loved this woman. More than he ever imagined loving another living person. For that matter, he'd never imagined anyone loving him. And yet the woman in his arms, the woman he'd just married loved him—had loved him—without conditions, strings. She'd never doubted him and she'd forgiven the unthinkable not once, but twice.

He gave up trying to suppress the wash of emotion that had flooded his very soul and he buried his face in her beautiful hair. He inhaled, taking her scent deeply so that it became a permanent part of him.

"I love you too, Angel," he said hoarsely. "I'll always love you. There will never be another woman for me."

She pulled away, concern in her eyes as she reached to cup his cheek. "Drake, darling, what's wrong?"

She looked alarmed as she studied his expression, no doubt seeing the evidence of tears in his eyes. Before he would have killed himself before ever allowing another person to see any perceived weakness in him. But with Evangeline? He knew he would always be safe with her.

"Not a damn thing," he said, smiling down at her. "If I'm not mistaken, the ceremony is over and you're my wife, Mrs. Donovan."

He was absurdly delighted by hearing his last name associated with her, but then judging by the sudden joy that lit up her eyes, he wasn't the only one gripped by that savage satisfaction.

"Which means," he said, reaching for her hand in preparation of hauling her down the aisle—now his wife—"that it's time to take my wife on her honeymoon."

Laughter rang out over the church and he marveled at how beautiful the carefree sound was. They'd made it roughly three steps when Drake's own joy took over and reality set in that this loving, generous woman was his! He swung her into his arms and carried her down the aisle, but he didn't stop at the door, took no time to visit with well-wishers nor did he wait for his men to catch up. He simply carried her to the waiting car, and he made love to Mrs. Evangeline Donovan on their way to the airport.